# Kathleen
# Of Sweetwater, Texas

*Linda Sealy Knowles*

Linda Sealy Knowles

ISBN-13: 9781092819138

**In Memory**
*My Love, Pete Knowles Sr.*

I would like to dedicate this book in memory of a sweet boy who once loved me and together our hearts became as one.

This sweet boy grew into manhood and asked me to become his wife and the mother of his children. After thirty-nine years together, God called this wonderful man "home."

Over the years, I became very determined to move my life forward. I began writing which put life back into my soul. I miss the love of my life every day as my heart is still over flowing with love for the young man that once loved me.

# ACKNOWLEDGMENTS

My warm and grateful appreciation goes to *Andy Kroha,* a very professional and gifted editor. She has been a joy to work with these past three years. Together we have published four books and I look forward to many more in the future.

# Prelude

**Kathleen Parker felt** her glorious mood had to be contagious. She was happier than she had ever been in her entire life. Finally, her papa had come home and she could share her exciting news with him. At the age of eighteen, she was in love! Tyler Chambers had come to work for her papa on their ranch several months ago and they had fallen head over heels in love with each other. Tyler was the most handsome young man she had ever seen with sandy blond hair and crystal blue eyes. She enjoyed being with him because he treated her like a goddess.

As she waltzed across the chicken yard with her basket almost overflowing with fresh eggs, she heard loud voices coming from inside the barn. The voices were not only loud but from the words they sounded angry. She recognized her papa's voice.

As she neared the entrance of the big barn doors, she heard her papa shouting at Tyler Chambers, the love of her life. She leaned back against the barn wall, watched and listened.

"It's your choice," her papa was saying. "You can get on your horse now and leave with five hundred dollars or you can help pack up Kathleen's things and leave with her before the sun sets." Papa was holding the paper money in his hand and waved it under Tyler's handsome nose.

"You'll not live here in my house married, to my daughter, and one-day hope to get your soft white hands on my ranch. You have just one minute to decide—five hundred dollars or Kathleen?"

Kathleen stood frozen at the entrance of the barn and watched her life change before her very eyes. Tyler never voiced an argument. He quickly grabbed the money out of her papa's fist and saddled up his brown mustang. He kicked his horse in the flanks and rode out of the big barn, not even giving Kathleen a

1

second glance. She watched him ride away as she swallowed back her tears of frustration and confusion.

Her papa turned and looked straight into her eyes. With no knowledge of what she had witnessed, he swept by her marching toward the ranch house where her ma waited to hear the outcome of his offer.

Kathleen hung her head and walked slowly to the house. How could she have ever believed that Tyler loved her? However, she did, and she was ready to give her young body, heart, and soul over to him. How did her papa know that he would choose the money over her hand in marriage? Well, none of that mattered now, she thought. *He is gone.*

Not a person to feel sorry for herself, Kathleen was determined to go forth from that day forward holding up her head. An enormous black barrier formed around her heart that would shield her from ever being taken in by another man's preposterous undying love.

Time passed as her mama had predicted with the days growing shorter and the nights longer. For years as she went to sleep, the dreams of romance with a handsome young cowboy faded away. Silly dreams; that is all they were.

# Chapter 1

Sweetwater, Texas, 1885

**The day started out** just like every day had for several weeks. Matt Moore stretched his tall frame and attempted to sit up on the side of his dirty, rumpled bed.

"Lord, I need coffee," he murmured to himself. Thunder sounded in the distance, and sheets of rainwater pelted on the windowpanes. As he stood, he looked down at himself. At least he had remembered to take off his muddy boots and trousers. He ran his hand over the long dark unkempt stubble on his face and smelled his own breath.

"Man, I must have eaten cow shit!" Before he completed his thought aloud, he heard a commotion on the front porch. Reaching to the floor for his britches, he rocked back and forth, as he placed one leg into the pants and then the other one. He swayed over to the front door while holding his head with one hand, and steadying himself with the other one. He felt like an Indian was beating a war-drum inside his brain. After making it to the front door without falling flat on his face, he jerked it open.

"Mercy," he murmured. On the porch was his big black, bay horse stomping around under the eaves for shelter from the fall storm. "Just a minute, Buck," he said to his horse. "I really had to be drunk to let you roam around outside all night. Sorry old boy. Let me get my boots on and I'll take care of you."

"Damnit!" Matt said to no one. He staggered over to the bed and sat down. He reached for his muddy boots and pulled them on his bare feet. He walked out the door, grabbed his horse's reins, and walked them both out in the cold drizzling rain heading to the barn. Matt lifted his face toward the sky and allowed the cold rainwater to wash the grime off his skin. He untied his red handkerchief from around his neck and held it out to catch rainwater. He tossed the cold, wet cloth over his face. It felt good and helped to clear his head a little. He still needed coffee.

Once the horse had a bucket of oats and a few pitchforks of hay, Matt went into the house to take care of himself. He put on a pot of coffee and placed a pan of water on the stove to warm. He needed to make himself presentable so he could take care of business at the bank. As he drank his first cup of morning coffee, he looked at the letter he had received from his fiancée, Lillian Larson. After four years of courting and planning to marry, she changed her mind. Who would have ever thought that the lovely Lillian would have betrayed him? She was so pretty with her long blond hair twisted high on her head like a crown. At the age of thirty-six, she still had an hourglass figure. Every man in town envied him walking out with her.

During a late night card game, one of the two Powell brothers offered to sell him their ranch. He had already decided to look around and purchase a piece of land so he would have something to offer Lillian. The land had a ranch house, one hundred acres of good grazing land, a few chickens, and a corral of working horses. The boys had already sold off all the cattle. After a change of money for a signed deed to the property, he decided to go ahead and make sure the place was livable like the young men had said. He had only been on the ranch two weeks when he received Lillian's rejection letter. She had left him for another man. So much for good Christian loyalty, he thought. That was three weeks ago, and he had not been sober a day since.

After a quick shave and a spit bath over the rest of his body, he changed into some clean clothes. He felt like the old Matt Moore that he knew before he hit the liquor bottle. As he started out the door, his stomach rumbled from hunger. Glancing around at his dirty house, he thought that he might check around in town for an old Mexican woman to hire as a cook and housekeeper. He liked things to be in order and he had neglected his place something fierce. Whiskey bottles, half-open cans of food and dirty plates and cups were scattered all over. He had been eating most of his meals in town at the one and only café. He could hardly stomach the food, but it was better than what he could throw together. Reaching for his dirty, brown Stetson, he sighed as he stretched his six-foot frame and headed for the door. He needed to pull himself together and forget about that sorry two-timing, unfaithful fiancée. Damn, he had hardly been out of her sight before she took up with another man. Women! He thought; who needs them.

As he rode into town, he felt like the top of his head was going to blow off. He needed to eat and go home and sleep the rest of the day. He would feel better after a long rest.

Once he completed his business at the bank, he felt better knowing that his money was safety in the Sweetwater Bank. He had transferred his funds from the bank in Abilene, Texas. For years, he had made Abilene his home base. He had driven numerous cattle drives all across Texas and always brought them to Abilene to sell, loaded them on the train in stock cars, and shipped them up north. He had saved his money and when the opportunity presented itself, he purchased the ranch in Sweetwater. He had asked Lillian to marry him and live happily ever after on his new ranch and after waiting four years, she readily agreed.

As he stepped out onto the weather-beaten boardwalk in front of the bank, a tall skinny youngster about twelve raced up to him. "Hey mister, are you Mr. Moore from the Powell's ranch?"

"Yep, that's me."

"Here's a telegram for you. Mr. Wagner at the telegraph office saw you ride into town and told me to hurry and give you this important message."

Matt reached into his pocket and tossed the young man a nickel. "Thank you!" The young man smiled as he caught the shiny new coin. A nickel! He could hardly wait to give the money to his ma.

Placing the message into his vest pocket, he walked to the Heavenly Hash Café. He looked around at the unkempt floors and dirty tablecloths. A big barrel of a man came from the kitchen wearing a stained white apron. "We ain't open yet for food," he bellowed. "Got fresh coffee if you want some."

"Coffee's fine." With his coffee sitting in front of him, he ripped open the telegram. Once he skimmed over the words, he said, "Well, ain't that a shame."

Slowly re-reading the words again, he felt his temper blaze up inside his gut. Lillian, his fiancée, wanted to come back to him.

She wrote that she had made a big mistake by running off with her young lover boy. *Well, well,* he thought with a sarcastic grin on his face, as he tapped the message on the table several times. She can wait until hell freezes over before I send for her.

He drained his coffee while stuffing the telegram into his vest pocket and left the café. Hell, he needed something stronger than that stinking, burnt coffee. He headed to the Red Garter Saloon.

# Chapter 2

"Senorita! Come quick! I have the stranger and he is hurt. He's lying in the back of the wagon."

"Coming Carlos!" Kathleen was in the kitchen putting a big pan of shelled peas on the stove to cook. She dashed to the door, but did an about-face and lowered the flame under the boiling pot. "Can't afford to burn supper," she said aloud to herself. As she leaped off the front porch, she walked over to Carlos, her old Mexican foreman, who had been on the ranch longer than her thirty years.

As Kathleen stood looking down at the man who Carlos had called the stranger, Kathleen asked, "Where in the world did you find him?"

"He was out beside the road lying near the ditch. I guess his horse had thrown him, and in the fall, he busted his leg. I could see the bone when I dragged him up on the wagon."

"You're sure this is our new neighbor? I haven't seen him up close, only from afar." Kathleen stood looking down at the poor dirty creature who looked to be a much older man than she thought he might be.

Kathleen Parker had lived on her parents' cattle ranch all of her thirty years. The ranch next door with one hundred acres of prime grazing land had been vacant for several months. The Powell brothers who owned it had left without telling anyone. No one knew where he or she could contact the brothers if they wanted too. Now, after many months, a stranger appears and claims to be the new owner.

"Yep, it's him. I have seen him several times riding close to our fences and I saw him once at the feed store. Thank goodness he is drunk, or else he would be squealing like a pig. That leg is bad." Carlos pointed to the man's left leg.

"You're right about him being drunk." Kathleen pulled the blanket back and looked down at the man's broken leg. She waved her hand under her nose. "Man, he stinks to high heaven. He smells as if he has not had a bath in a month of Sundays. Well, let's get him in the house and set that leg while he is still under the influence of all that whiskey. He will not have that silly grin on his face when he starts waking up. Call Juan and Pedro to come and help us."

Once Carlos's two grown sons came from the corral and barn to help carry the stranger into the house, Kathleen instructed them to place him in the spare bedroom. Rosa, Carlos's wife and the ranch's housekeeper, came out of the garden and immediately placed a big bucket of water on the stove to heat. "I can smell him all the way into the kitchen. He stinks like a skunk," she said as she wrinkled up her nose and started getting the box down with all kinds of bandages and rags.

The two boys, Juan and Pedro, removed the stranger's gun belt and boots. Kathleen said that she and Rosa would take care of removing the rest. "Rosa, bring that box of medical supplies and the big scissors. We'll have to cut his pants off."

Carlos came into the bedroom with two pieces of straight boards to be used to set the man's leg. By binding it tight, it would mend back together in time. Before setting the leg, Rosa gave his legs and private parts a good scrubbing. Once Carlos and Kathleen finished setting his leg, Carlos held him up in a sitting position while Rosa bathed the top half of his back. He was beginning to stir a little while trying to wake up.

"He's going to be in some pain but I'm afraid to give him any laudanum until some of that whiskey gets out of his body. Old Dr. Squires taught me how to minister that stuff when Pa was so sick and hurting."

An hour later Kathleen decided to chance giving the stranger some pain medicine. With all his thrashing and moving around on the bed, he was going to hurt his leg some more. Once he was resting peacefully, Kathleen washed his face with a warm washcloth, but did not attempt to shave him. Surprisingly, he was a handsome man that looked to be about forty or so. There were deep lines in his face that showed signs of working outside in the hot sun. He was over six-feet-tall with a muscular build and brown curly hair that was overdue for a haircut. She was guessing he might have big brown eyes but she had not seen them open yet.

Carlos came into the kitchen that had yellow-checked curtains on the windows and an oilcloth on the table to match. Rosa and Kathleen were preparing food for lunch. Carlos told the girls that he had made a trip over to the stranger's ranch and discovered his horse had made it back to his barn. He searched the place for a ranch hand or two, but did not find a soul on the place. He fed the man's two horses, and milked a cow that needed attention. He gathered a dozen or so chickens wandering loose around in the yard, and put them back in the chicken pen. Since things outside had not been in order, he decided he might need to go in the house and check things over. The place was messy but he had seen worse. The kitchen had many empty cans of beans and several empty whiskey bottles on the counter. Lying on the table was an opened letter. An unopened bottle of whiskey was sitting on the table next to the opened mail. Carlos picked up the letter, but not being able to read long hand writing decided to take it home and show it to Kathleen. Maybe it was of some importance to the stranger.

"You mean to tell me that there is no one working at his place. He has been over there for several weeks. Wonder if his help just up and left." Kathleen was confused.

"Si, it's in pretty bad shape, but I guess it could be worse. Look, I found this on his kitchen table along with several empty bottles of liquor scattered all around. Maybe it will tell us who he is."

Kathleen stirred the beans on the stove and then sat down at the kitchen table while Rosa was kneading a big bowl of dough for fresh bread. Kathleen took the letter from Carlos and said, "This looks like a personal letter from a lady." She fanned the letter under her nose recognizing a whiff of perfume. "Maybe it's from his wife, sister or someone."

"Read it," Rosa said very forcefully. She was a very straightforward person. "Don't guess. We could be here all day."

"Of course, you're right, but I feel funny—you know, reading his personal mail." Kathleen smelled the paper as she laid it back down on the table and smoothed it out with her hands.

"He'd read your mail quick enough. Now read." Rosa was a short, round Mexican woman who brooked no arguments from anyone. When she gave an order, her man and boys jumped.

Kathleen looked down at the lovely handwriting on the wrinkled parchment paper and said immediately. "Oh my, his lady friend is going to marry someone else." She laid the letter down on the table and stared off into space. She could almost feel her own pain all over again as she watched the love of her life ride away from the ranch. She had been eighteen; so happy and full of life. Her pa offered her fiancé five hundred dollars. "Kathleen or the money?" her papa demanded. Without hesitation, the love of her life had chosen the money and ridden out of her life, never even looking back. Hearing Rosa's voice snapped her back to the present.

"Does that paper tell the stranger's name?" Rosa asked.

"Well, let's see. The envelope was addressed to a Matt Moore, Post Office Sweetwater, Texas. So, I guess we'll have Matt Moore for a houseguest for a few days."

"I best get this bread ready to rise if we are to have it for lunch. I will cook a potpie with a little chicken in it for the evening meal. The pantry is nearly empty," sighed Rosa.

Kathleen looked at the big wooden rectangle clock that sat on the mantle of the fireplace. It was not nine o'clock yet. She still had time to make it into town and speak with Wilbur Crocker about the open position that he had at his establishment. The Heavenly Hash Café was a rundown building that housed the only place for the locals, stagecoach passengers, and strangers to get a hot meal. Hiring out as the help or cook was the last thing Kathleen wanted to do, but she needed money to support the ranch and the only way to get money was to go to work. The only other alternative was to sell some of her cattle for the low price of two dollars a pound on the hoof. The ranch had over five hundred head that needed to be driven to Abilene to sell. The going price in Abilene was eight dollars a pound. The only problem was she needed an honest trail boss to help her drive them there. Carlos was too old to head up a big cattle drive and his two boys had never been more than twenty miles from the ranch. She needed an experienced man that knew the trail and could be trusted. There had been many stories circulating about cattle drives that were ambushed and had all their cattle stolen. Many of the drovers were hurt and a few killed. Once Kathleen's cattle made it to Abilene and sold, she would not have any money problems for years. She could pay her ranch's taxes and settle her overdue accounts at the feed store, dry goods store and the veterinarian bill.

As the tall stranger lay asleep in the guest room, Kathleen changed out of her dirty jeans and muddy boots and put on a calico blue dress, trimmed with a soft white collar, her blue and white bonnet, and her good boots. She stood in the hall adjusting her bonnet before the slim mirror on the wall. She looked down at her dress, smoothed her hand down the front, did a quarter turn, and smoothed the back. Lifting her face, she looked closer into the mirror as she gave the underside of her jaw a few pats. At her age it was still firm. The weather was still too warm for her gloves or a shawl. Sighing, she guessed she looked fine.

Matt peeked through his blurry brown eyes and watched the trim figure standing in front of the tall mirror admiring herself. *Who in the blue blazes is that,* he thought to himself. Searching the room with his eyes, he realized that he was not at his own ranch house. There were pretty curtains on the clean window. A nice colorful patchwork quilt lay across his body. As he raised his head up a few inches off the clean smelling pillow, a pain like a fiery hot poker raced through his lower body. His breathing felt harsh as he tried to lie still. With each breath, he was sure a knife was stabbing him in his ribcage. *Damn, what happened to me*, he thought as he tried to be calm and relax so the pain would ease off.

"Oh!" he moaned aloud. He tried to get comfortable but he was in too much pain.

Kathleen heard a sound coming from the stranger's bedroom. She stood in the doorway watching her houseguest as he covered his face with his two large palms.

Walking close to his bed, she commented to him. "Well, I see you're awake. How do you feel?"

"That's a stupid question that needs no answer. If you've got any sense at all you know damn well that I feel like I've tangled with a grizzly and lost the fight." With every breath labored, he looked up at the slender woman all dressed for church. "Now I'll ask you. What's happened to me and where in the hell am I?"

"You, Mr. Moore, are in my ranch house which is located next

11

to yours. My man, Carlos, found you in a ditch, drunk and hurt. He brought you here."

"You got any whiskey in this establishment?"

"I sure do, but I got something better for you. I will get Rosa to fix you a cup of hot tea with some medicine mixed in it. It will relieve some of your pain and help you rest." As she turned to go into the kitchen, he yelled. "Listen here woman! Do not walk away from me. I have more questions, so keep your scrawny little butt here until I have some answers."

Kathleen continued walking into the kitchen and asked Rosa to make tea and put some of the laudanum in it. "Our houseguest is in a lot of pain and he needs complete rest. Hurry now because I have to get into town if I want a chance at the position at the café." Kathleen walked back over to the mirror to get one more look at her bonnet and gathered her drawstring purse.

"Just where do you think you're waltzing off to woman! I'm dying and you think that you're going to up and leave me here!" Matt bellowed, and then moaned as if he was in mortal pain.

"I have important business in town. Oh good, here comes Rosa with your tea. Thank you, Rosa. I will give it to him."

"Here, Mr. Moore, sip this tea and it won't be long before you'll be resting a lot better."

Matt raised his head, took a sip of the hot bitter tea, and spit it out of his mouth on the front of Kathleen's calico dress. "Now, look what you've done, you ornery old mule!"

"Nobody can drink that piss! Get out! I'll just suffer through the pain rather than drink that stuff."

"Carlos!" screamed Kathleen. "Get the boys in here, now!" Kathleen never raised her voice or lost her temper. She was a sweet tempered woman who did not get upset over small details. However, this morning, this stranger lying in her bed in her home, had made her loose her composure. Kathleen was going to see that he took the pain medicine even if it had to be forced down his throat by two strapping young men.

In a few minutes, Carlos stood with his hat in his hands watching his two sons stand beside the bed of the stranger. "Now, Mr. Moore, you will open your mouth and take this spoonful of medicine nicely by yourself or my two friends, Pedro and Juan here, will open your mouth for you," said Kathleen.

Matt shifted his eyes from one young man to the other. Both boys looked to be about twenty years old and very strong. They were prepared to follow the boss woman's orders. One of the boys softly laid his big hand on the two boards that held his broken leg together while the other looked like he was ready to harm his bruised, beaten up body.

The pain was almost unbearable. He was not drunk any longer. After looking the two big strapping boys over, he knew this was a fight he could not win. Without a word, Matt opened his mouth and Kathleen shoved the spoon down his throat, clacking the spoon on his teeth as she pulled it out of his mouth. One of the boys grabbed his chin and clamped his mouth shut. His body shuttered all over as he laid his head back down on the pillow. As the boys left the room with their Pa, they heard the stranger say to Kathleen, "You may have won round one, but you better prepare yourself for round two."

After Kathleen changed into the only other nice dress she had with a matching bonnet, she went outside and got in her small carriage. Carlos's son, Pedro, had it all ready for her. "I'll be home in a few hours," she said as she turned the horse and carriage toward the road that would take her the two miles to town.

Matt watched out the window as the young woman drove out the gate toward town. He laid his head back on the clean, soft pillow and soon drifted off into a painless sleep.

As Kathleen drove into town, she went straight to the livery. Albert Thornbees, the owner of Sweetwater Livery and Horse Stable, was thrilled to see her. He was a tall, bearded young man who wore large blue overalls without a shirt. His bare chest was hairy and his arm muscles were big and firm. Everybody called him Big Al because of his size. Ever since her parents had passed on, he had been trying to court her. He knew Kathleen needed help financially with her large spread. He had plenty of money and she was a nice looking woman. He really wanted her ranch. What better way of getting it than marrying up with her. Heck, he could do worse!

"Good day to you, Miss Kathleen. What's brings you to town all by yourself this fine morning?"

"Now Mr. Thornbees. You don't need to be asking me my personal business." Kathleen had heard the rumor that Mr.

Thornbees had offered to buy her ranch before her papa had passed away. Now he thought his sweet words would help him to obtain his dream of the nicest spread in Sweetwater.

"Oh, my goodness! I did not mean to pry into your affairs. I only meant that Rosa or Carlos always rides into town with you."

"You're forgiven. I got a few things to take care of and then I will be leaving town. Do you know if Doctor Squires is still in town this morning?"

"Well, his horse and buggy are still parked here in the livery."

"That's fine. I'll stop in at his office."

"You ain't sick are you Miss Kathleen?"

"There you go again, Mr. Thornbees, probing into my personal life."

He stood with his dirty hat in his hand, tapping it on his leg and looked down at the ground. "Sorry again, but I couldn't bear to learn that you had fallen ill. I had hoped that you would allow me to come out to your ranch Sunday morning and escort you to church. I'd be mighty proud if you would consent."

Kathleen gave him no response as she walked down the street toward her destination, the Heavenly Hash Café. She wished he would stop asking her to step out with him. It was embarrassing having to refuse him all the time, but she was not interested in him or receiving any kind of proposal in the future. He wanted her ranch—not her.

As she made her way into the café, she could smell cabbage cooking. The sign outside the door said that beef stew was on the dinner menu, but there was no aroma of beef cooking. The smell of burnt beans lingered in the air. Turning her nose up, she continued to the kitchen as she looked the place over. It was really worse than she remembered. The plank walls were rough and painted white at one time. The floor was part red brick and part painted narrow strips of wood. There were green checked curtains pulled back on the dirty glass windowpanes. Many tables and chairs were scattered around the room in no particular order. The floor needed a good sweeping before the place was open for the noon business.

"Mr. Crocker," Kathleen called. As she stood waiting, she adjusted her bonnet and smoothed her dress down the front. She used her hankie to wipe the moisture from her face.

"I knew it was you, Miss Parker. No one else calls me Mister," laughed Mr. Crocker as he pushed the kitchen's bat-winged doors wide open. He stepped in the dining room with a cigar dangling out the side of his mouth and a dirty white apron over his plaid shirt and workpants. His face was clean-shaven and his curly gray hair was covered with smelly hair tonic.

"To what do I owe this visit from you? I can't remember the last time you stepped through my door."

"I could offer a lot of excuses for not eating here, Mr. Crocker, but that's not the reason I have come. I noticed the sign in your window advertising for help. Has that position been filled?"

Mr. Crocker's mouth fell completely open as he reached for his cigar and pulled out a chair to sit down. He remembered his manners and motioned for Kathleen to sit first. "You want to work here, for me, in this here café?" He shifted his worn unlit cigar from side to side in his nasty stained mouth. He could not believe that this high and mighty woman wanted to lower herself to work in his smelly hole of a café.

"If you're still in need of help, I am in need of work." She watched Mr. Crocker as he looked at her in disbelief. "Is there something wrong with me?"

"Hell no! Oh, excuse my language. There most certainly ain't nothing wrong with you. I just cannot believe it that is all. A nice respectable woman working here sure can't hurt the reputation of this place. When do you want to start? Today, now, I hope!" Mr. Crocker was thrilled to have this fine woman working for him and he was going to do everything he could to make her happy. His business needed someone like her working for him.

"I guess I could work the lunch crowd for you and then start working all day tomorrow. How does that sound?"

"Can you cook?" Before she could answer, he led her to the kitchen and tossed her an apron. "This is what's on the menu for lunch. If you come early enough tomorrow, I could get back to serving breakfast. I had to stop because I didn't have any help."

As she was tying the apron around her small waist, she said, "Mr. Crocker, we need to talk about my salary. I want two dollars a day."

"Shoot fire woman, drovers don't make but a dollar a day. Two dollars is highway robbery!" She was a fine looking woman and he would be lucky to have her, but he could not afford what she was asking, he thought.

Kathleen started removing her apron when Mr. Crocker said, "Now wait just a darn minute." He stood looking down at Kathleen and rubbed his smooth face as he pondered the situation. "How about a dollar a day? That seems fair."

"A dollar a day and not a cent less and I don't have to share my tips, if I get any, and I want to be paid every Friday."

"You drive a hard bargain woman. You better be worth every penny of your pay!" He said as he chomped down on his cigar and stormed out of the kitchen.

Kathleen smiled until she turned around in the dirty kitchen and realized what a big undertaking she had just accepted. "A dollar a day will buy food items that are needed for my own pantry," she said aloud to no one in particular.

*First things first,* thought Kathleen, as she walked over to the big worktable. After she cleaned the table and the utensils, she sliced the big chunk of beef that was lying out on the worktable into thin slices to cook for an hour. Once the meat was simmering, she peeled potatoes and carrots to cook separately. Once the meat and vegetables were cooked, she would mix them together and make gravy. She mixed up several big pans of cornbread and placed them in the oven. A pan of fresh butter beans and peas had already been cooking on the back of the stove. After discovering a dozen cans of peaches, she quickly made several pans of peach cobbler. Since she still had a little while before the café opened, she quickly grabbed the broom, went into the dining room, and swept the floor. Rearranging the tables in an orderly fashion, she wiped the chairs and removed some of the dirty tablecloths, giving the tables a good swipe. They looked better without the stained cloths.

Kathleen was in the kitchen finishing the final touches on the food when Mr. Crocker came into the room. "Gaud almighty woman! It is hotter than blazes in this kitchen. Why don't you have the back door open?"

"I know it's hot but I was afraid the flies would come in and carry off the food. We have to be careful and try to keep this place as clean as possible."

"Of course, you are right but I do not want you fainting dead away from heat on your first day. The dining room looks mighty fine. I do not know how you did all this by yourself in such a short time. I came to help you."

"Speaking of help, do you have someone to help with cleaning and washing the dishes?"

"No, not now. I did have a little Chinese man, but he up and quit. He went to work at the laundry."

"I can't cook, wait on customers and serve them all by myself and clean up. I'm sure you can find someone to help me out for a very small salary."

"Woman, you're gonna put me in the poor house before your first day is even over." Mr. Crocker sat down, picked up a newspaper, and started fanning himself.

"You can help me today with the customers. I know I must look a sight." Kathleen's hair was wet on the back of her neck and her long curls hung down the side of her face. Her lovely dress was damp on her back and under her arms. The hem of her skirt was dirty from dragging on the nasty floor. "If you take their food orders, I'll dish it up for you."

"Wait a darn minute. You look just fine. Those burly men would much rather have you out there sashaying around. I will dish up the plates while you wait on them. Besides you can't get tips back here in the kitchen."

"You know," said Mr. Crocker, "I have been planning on putting in a door with some screen on it. I'll get busy and have a door made to help make this room a lot cooler." He looked at Kathleen and gave her a big smile. He had found a jewel in Miss Parker and he wanted to make her happy.

Having a few minutes before the lunch crowd, Kathleen stepped out on the back porch for a breath of fresh cool air. As she was fanning herself, she saw a dirty little boy, about five or six years old, hiding behind a large trash barrel. He peeked out at her and quickly hid his face again.

"Well, hello there." Kathleen spoke softly to the youngster. "Why are you hiding?" Instead of receiving an answer, the little tyke darted out from behind the barrel and raced out of the alleyway. Kathleen gave a big sigh and returned inside to welcome her first customers.

The first day was a big success. Mr. Crocker stood at the cash register counting his money. He shifted his unlit stub of a cigar from side to side in his mouth. He was thrilled with all the customers and boasted that there was not a morsel of cooked food left in the whole place. He was going to have to get busy and cook some dry beans and sausage for the evening crowd because Miss Parker was getting ready to leave for the day. When word got around that the lovely Miss Kathleen Parker was working at his café, he would have some curious people stop in to eat that did not normally patronize his establishment. The smell of fresh coffee and the delicious aroma of peach cobbler had everyone ordering lunch and bragging about how good everything tasted.

# Chapter 3

Matt Moore had slept most of the day. His leg hurt him something awful. He was trying to be a good patient and not ask for any more pain medicine. He would take a little bit before he went to sleep for the night. Rosa, the old Mexican woman, had treated him very well. She had come into his room several times to check on him and once returned with a nice tray of soup and cornbread. She had gotten one of the boys to help him with his personal needs. As he lay on the nice clean sheets that smelled of sunshine, he felt fortunate that some caring folks had discovered him. After dozing off again for about an hour or two he woke to the jingle of horse's bridles and the clip-clop of a couple of mules or horses in the front of the house. The boss woman must have arrived home, he thought.

Kathleen got down out of the carriage with the help of Pedro. She was excited about her new job, but she was very tired. She was used to hard physical work on her ranch but cooking, cleaning and smiling most of the morning was enough to wear a person down in the shimmering waves of heat. She felt good about working and earning some cash for the ranch. As she made her way into the house, she felt the weight of coins in her dress pocket. She had received many tips, but she had not taken the time to count her money before she left for the day. She was eager to get home and check on her houseguest. Dr. Squires was going to come out later this evening and check him over. She was worried about his ribs.

Entering the front door, she stopped in the front hall and looked into the wall mirror as she removed her bonnet and hung it on the coat rack. She gave her face a glance and wiped at some flour that was on the side of her neck. "Lord have mercy, how long has that been there? That fool Crocker could have at least told me that I had something on my neck," she murmured aloud to herself.

"Do you have another fool that you are caring for in town, Katy?" Matt asked Kathleen as she started walking down the hall toward the kitchen.

Kathleen stopped, turned, and looked into the spare room at her houseguest. "My name is Kathleen. To you Sir-- it is Miss Kathleen!" *The nerve of some people and a perfect stranger at that,* thought Kathleen.

"You look more like a Katy to me, so it's Katy as far as I'm concerned. Now, answer my question. Are you taking care of someone else while I'm laid up in your home?"

"It is no business of yours what I do or where I go. In addition, *No* I am not caring for anyone else. Rosa and I have our hands full taking care of you."

Matt chuckled as he watched her turn and walk away from his doorway. He could hear her speaking to Rosa but he could not make out their conversation. A little while later, the mistress of the house appeared at his doorway again. She had removed her dress, unpinned her lovely midnight hair, allowing it to fall in a long plait down her back. Wearing a brown split-tail skirt and an oversized man's shirt tied at the waist with old scuffed up riding boots, she looked very young.

"How are you feeling this evening?" Kathleen asked as she held her riding hat in her hand.

"Where are you off to dressed in that get up?"

Kathleen flushed with embarrassment as he took in her appearance. "Never you mind how I look you old drunken fool. I got some business to take care out in the pasture and I do not have time to stand here and mince words with you. Do you need anything before I leave? I'll be back before Dr. Squires gets out here to see you this evening."

"I don't need a doctor. Your woman has taken excellent care of me and I will be out of your hair real soon."

"I'm glad to hear you at least appreciate Rosa's help. Carlos and I want the doctor to check you over, especially your ribs."

"Where have you been all day? Why did you leave here as fresh as a daisy and come back looking like a tired old washwoman? What did you do in town?"

Kathleen was sick and tired of men trying to get involved in her personal and private business. She turned and walked out the front door. She could hear her houseguest bellowing obscenities and demanding that she come back in his room.

"I'm not through talking to you, you little tight as--!" His words faded away as she walked into the barn and let Juan help her onto her saddled horse. "Ready?" Kathleen asked him as they rode toward the east pasture.

As Juan and Kathleen rode out in the pasture, they stopped near a small stream that ran across the open field. At the edge of the stream, in the soft muddy grass were two new calves. They were dead. "Coyotes, my guess," Juan stated plainly.

"I think you are right. Look at the poor animals. They have big chucks of meat torn off their flanks and hindquarters. Their tails are nearly chewed off at the top. The rectangular tracks with the toes all close together are the marking of coyotes for sure. Now that they have had a taste of fresh meat, they will be back. We will have to stand guard until we can kill them or they will kill all of our new born and young calves. Do you think you and Carlos can take the first watch tonight?" Kathleen asked.

"We will do it and I bet we get them tonight, too." Juan grinned as he turned his horse to leave and head back to the ranch.

"I hope so. If not, I will stand watch with Pedro tomorrow night."

Kathleen watched Carlos and Juan ride out after dark toward the pasture to get set up and wait on the coyotes to show. She really hoped that the coyotes did make an appearance so she would not lose anymore of her valuable herd. Every head would count when it came time to take them to Abilene to sell. Turning, she went back in the house and removed her dirty boots at the door. She was exhausted from the long day. All she wanted to do was fill the tub with hot water and soak her tired body in it.

As she walked toward the kitchen, her houseguest demanded that she come into his room. "You know you aren't a very good hostess. I've been lying in this bed all day without any company but sweet Rosa and that stupid doctor that you had come to see me."

"Mr. Moore, if you remember you aren't an invited houseguest. You *Sir* are someone Carlos found dead drunk in the ditch close to my ranch. You need to lie there and thank your lucky stars that he had the decency to bring you here. He could have just left you for the buzzards to pick your intoxicated bones!"

"Woman, if you call me *sir* one more time, you're going to be sorry when I get up off this bed."

"Stop sprouting threats and tell me what the doctor said about your condition," Kathleen said as she walked over to the foot of his bed and straightened the quilt that was hanging down to the floor.

"The fool complimented Carlos for doing a good job setting my leg."

"That's good and what else did he say. What about your ribs?"

"My damn ribs are just fine. He thinks that I may have a concussion because he found a big knot on the back of my head. He gave me the creeps--touching me all over, like he *liked doing* it."

Kathleen tossed her head back and chuckled with laughter. "You are too funny, if I may say so. You know that he's a doctor and that's what doctors do—feel you I mean."

"He won't lay his paws on me again I can assure you." Matt gave her a hard look. "You look like you're about to drop. Why are you so tired?"

"I worked at the town's café today and then rode out to check on part of the herd. Coyotes are attacking my new calves. They killed two last night. Juan and Carlos are heading out there now. Hopefully, they will get rid of the problem."

Kathleen turned to walk out of the room when he told her to stop. "Get your tail back in here. What did you mean you *worked* at the café in town today? Are you referring to that establishment the town calls Heavenly Hash?"

"Yep, the one and only."

"What in the devil are you doing working in that hell hole?"

"Listen, I'm too tired to discuss my personal business with you tonight or for that matter any time. Now excuse me. I am going to take a hot bath and go to bed. Pedro will be in to help you settle in for the night. Do you need more medicine to help you sleep?"

"No, I'm fine. Don't want to get too dependent on that stuff."

As Kathleen walked out of the room, he yelled. "You don't need to work in that pigsty. If you need money, I can help you! I got plenty of it," he said as he leaned off the bed and yelled to an empty doorway.

Kathleen could not help but smile at Mr. Matt Moore. He was a take-charge-kind of guy. Well, he had another thing coming if he thought for one minute he was going to start giving her orders and telling her what she could or could not do. She grinned as she sat down on her big four-poster bed. She pulled her knees up, laid her head down on her soft pillow, and went off into dreamland. Rosa came into to help Kathleen with her bath, but seeing her lying on the bed fast asleep, she shook her head and covered her fully clothed body with a quilt.

Kathleen was having a sweet dream of riding her golden mustang through the wide-open meadows covered in prairie wheat and wild flowers. Her long black hair was hanging loose down her back blowing in the warm breeze. She was young and so in love. Her horse was practically flying as she giggled and thought of her love working in the south pasture. She was going to sneak a visit with him while all the others were working closer to the house. As she approached the handsome young man, shirtless and tan all over, she stopped her horse. *What in the blazes is that sound* she thought as she tossed and turned while floating in her dream world. Suddenly Kathleen was instantly awake to sounds of moaning and cussing. In a daze, she sat up on her bed. Glancing down at herself, she realized that she had never put on her nightclothes as she stood, trying hard to wake up. *There it was again,* she thought. Moaning sounds coming from the room across the hall.

As she shook her head to gain her balance, she eased her door opened and listened. In the guest room, was the noise of someone moving around and using some of the worst foul language she had ever heard. She opened the door and witnessed Mr. Moore standing at the foot of the bed, trying to reach the chamber pot. He had pulled it close to the bed but he could not seem to get it near his body so he could relieve himself.

"Mr. Moore, you cannot stand on your leg. For gosh sakes why didn't you use the bell beside the bed to ring for help. That is why Rosa placed it there," explained Kathleen.

"Have mercy woman and shut your mouth. Help me with that pot before I piss all over myself and this floor," said Matt. Just as Kathleen walked over to him, Carlos entered the bedroom.

"Here Missy, I'll take over now. I will help the mister. Go, go, I will get him back in bed." For the first time, Kathleen noticed that Mr. Moore was out of the bed shirtless and dressed in his knee-length white cotton underpants. Black chest hair disappeared down to his waist and into his white underwear. She could not seem to take her eyes off him.

"Now that you have your eyes full of my body, get your butt out of here so I can get some relief."

Kathleen felt her face flame with embarrassment as Carlos placed his hand on her back guiding her to the door before she realized that she had been staring at her houseguest. "Call me when you have him back in bed Carlos, and I will give him medicine to ease his pain."

As Carlos shut the door, she leaned her body back against it and held her face in her long slender hands. She was not fully awake. That had to be the reason she was staring at Mr. Moore. She had already seen most of his body when she helped Rosa bathe him and assisted Carlos with setting his leg.

She finally got a grip on herself, walked back into her room, and picked up a brush. She looked in her wall mirror and could not believe the way she looked. Her long hair had come loose from around her face and it was sticking out in all directions. Golly, I could have scared the man to death if he had not already been awake, she thought. "I look like a wild haired witch!" she said aloud to herself with a chuckle.

Carlos knocked on her door and said that the mister was back in his bed and Rosa was awake making some tea. "Thank you Carlos. Please go back to bed. I will get myself a cup of Rosa's tea and stay with Mr. Moore until he settles down."

"Si Missy. Until morning," he said as he went down the hall to his bedroom.

After thanking Rosa for the tea and herding her back to bed, she entered the guest room and saw Mr. Moore lying in the bed with his right arm thrown over his eyes and forehead. Carlos had left the lantern burning on the table across the room.

"You going to just stand there or you going to come over here to get a better look at me?"

"Don't you think that you have embarrassed me enough for one night?" asked Kathleen.

She heard a little chuckle coming from down deep in his throat. "If you say so."

"Would you care for a cup of tea to help relax you? I think you should take another dose of pain medicine tonight. I know your leg has been hurting since you placed your weight on it."

"Yep, it's throbbing like a horse in heat."

"Mr. Moore," Kathleen sighed as she spoke to him, "would you please try to remember that I'm a lady and I can't permit such foul language in my home."

"Sorry. I will try if you will stop calling me *Mr. Moore*. Please. Please call me Matt."

"Good night Matt." Kathleen gave him a half grin, walked over, turned the lantern down, and left the room.

Matt lay in the bed watching Kathleen retreat from his room. She was a very intriguing woman. She reflected pride in the way she held herself and kept her private thoughts to herself. He grinned to himself thinking that he might even get to liking her when his body healed and he was not in so much damn pain. He had not been around too many women because of his line of work, but there was definitely something different about Miss Kathleen, he thought. He flipped and turned as he tried to get comfortable and go to sleep.

Kathleen was up earlier than normal so she could help with some of the morning chores before she had to head to town and begin a long day at the restaurant. She was to prepare three meals a day and she needed to get an early start at making coffee and biscuits. After she spoke with Rosa about the care of their houseguest, she changed into her blue floral day dress and sturdy brown leather shoes. Since the restaurant's kitchen was so hot, she left off one of her crimson under slips.

Mr. Crocker was already there in the kitchen speaking to someone when Kathleen arrived. Mr. Miller, a local man who did carpentry work, was putting in a new screen back door. "Just like I promised you Miss Kathleen, a new door, so the kitchen won't be so blasted hot. What'd you think?"

"My goodness, this is a surprise and a very welcome one, I must say."

"Well, well! Now get the coffee started because we'll have some early birds wanting some in just a bit," ordered Mr. Crocker.

Kathleen could not help but grin as she hurried to do as he instructed. Once several big pots of coffee were heating on the stove, she grabbed up a clean white apron and began making biscuits. As the biscuits were baking, Kathleen walked into the dining room and made sure the tables and chairs were in order. There were plenty of coffee cups and saucers clean and ready to use.

Mr. Crocker was placing some money and change in his cash register as Kathleen brought up the subject of some help in the kitchen. "What kinda' help are you talking about now, woman? I just got you a new door and you haven't worked a full day yet!"

"Mr. Crocker, we need someone to help wash dishes. You and I cannot do it all; cook, take orders, serve the customers and wash dishes. We need a young woman or a man, I do not care which, but someone who can help me in the kitchen once the food is prepared and ready to serve. When breakfast is over, I have to have a clean kitchen to prepare lunch. Get my meaning?"

"Damn woman, you're going to break me. All right, all right, I will try to find someone or if you know someone that will be great. However, I am not paying them a fortune! Twenty-five cents and three square meals a day—not a red cent more!"

Kathleen walked back into the kitchen and took out a big slice of bacon. She heard thunder rumbling outside so she walked over to the new back screen door and looked out. Seeing that the sky had turned black, she stepped out on the small porch and felt the cool breeze. She saw a big wooden barrel turned over on its side and a small barefoot sticking out the end of it. Realizing that a small child was hiding inside the barrel, she quietly walked over to it. Lying inside the barrel was the youngster that she had seen yesterday. Once he saw Kathleen, he tried to scamper away from her.

"Oh no you don't, you little bugger. You ran from me yesterday, but not today." She reached for his small arm and held tight as he fought her to get loose. "Let me go, you mean old witch. I am not yours. Leave me be!" He screamed and kicked.

"Settle down little one and let me get a good look at you. Come on in the kitchen before the sky opens up and we get drowned out here in the rain."

"I can't go in there! That big mean man will kick me and toss me out on my butt."

"No one is going to do anything to you but maybe give you a

big buttered biscuit."

"Really?" The youngster stopped squirming and let Kathleen pull him up the steps into the kitchen that smelled like heaven. He was so hungry that his stomach growled loudly. It had been at least two days since he had eaten any real food. The oats that the horses ate in the livery stable did not taste too bad, but he only ate that when there was not anything in the trash barrels in the alleyways of the businesses or homes.

"Here." Kathleen tossed him a wet cloth and told him to wipe his face and hands with it and to sit down at the side table next to the open door. After she was sure he was clean, she sat a hot biscuit with a warm cup of coffee with a lot of sugar and cream in it for him. "Now you enjoy that while I slice this here bacon and get eggs mixed up to scramble for our customers. You and I will talk in a minute."

Once the morning customers begin to arrive, Kathleen took their orders and rushed back to the kitchen for coffee. After serving them coffee, she hurried into the back and cooked their order. Mr. Crocker had left the restaurant and had not returned for several hours. When he came back, Kathleen was more than furious with him. All morning she had taken the customer's orders, cooked and cleaned up the tables and stacked the dirty dishes beside the tubs of hot soapy water. When she needed a clean dish, she washed and dried it. She had a good mind to just close up the place and go home. She could not continue to do everything all by herself.

Mr. Crocker was grinning as he made his way to the kitchen. An old Indian woman trailed behind him. She had come to town looking for a job. She was dirty and exhausted from walking miles from heaven knows where. Mr. Crocker had hired the small Indian woman and brought her to the restaurant to work with Kathleen.

"This is Prairie Flower and she speaks English. I found her over at the general store looking for work. She can cook and clean for you in the kitchen. She can start right now." As Mr. Crocker was speaking to Kathleen, he noticed the little boy that had been trying to raid his trash barrels hiding under the kitchen table.

"What's that nasty brat doing in my kitchen?"

"You don't concern yourself over that child. I will care for him." Kathleen walked over to the table and sat down a plate of scrambled eggs and another biscuit for the little fellow. Kathleen noticed that the little bugger was hiding from Mr. Crocker under the table.

"I want to know if you are going to help me with your customers or not. I am exhausted from running back and forth from the dining room to the kitchen, caring for the breakfast crowd by myself!" Kathleen glared at Mr. Crocker, as she demanded an answer from him.

"Keep your voice down, woman." He held his hands out in front of himself trying to quiet Kathleen down. "I'm back to help. I went to try to find you some help and here she is."

"Fine," Kathleen said as she turned to the Indian woman. "Please come over to the sink and I will give you a pan of water so you can wash up a little. You look worn out already. I will give you some breakfast as I tell you what I need you to do for me. What do I call you?"

Kathleen looked at the little woman who was barely five feet tall. She had dark hair sprinkled with gray streaks plaited into two long pigtails down her back. Her eyes were dark as molasses and her tan skin was smooth with deep lines at the corners of her eyes. When she spoke, her teeth were straight and white as snow. A thought raced through Kathleen's mind that at one time this little woman surely had been an Indian warrior's beautiful princess.

"Please madam, call me white man's name, Lucy. If I work here with white people, I want to be called Lucy." Lucy was thrilled to be led to this kitchen where there seemed to be plenty of wonderful smelling food. The boss woman appeared to be nice and did not seem to care that she was an old stinking squaw. That is what most white people called her. She needed to work and support herself because her old Indian man had died and there were no men left in her village that could take care of her. With no man, she had to leave her people, go off, and die.

"Lucy, it is then. My name is Kathleen and this little fellow's name is?" Kathleen looked at the youngster as he crawled out from under the table. "Tell us your name son."

"Sammy," he replied. Sammy was so thankful that Kathleen did not let that mean old man toss him out of the kitchen. Once, while he was digging in his barrels for food, he had come out and said for him to get away from his door and to stay away. He was really a scary man.

"All right, Lucy and Sammy, we have our work cut out for us today. Lucy will eat her breakfast and start washing this stack of dirty dishes and Sammy you can help her by drying some of the plates. We all have to work to earn our pay and the food that you eat."

Once the day ended, Kathleen's pockets jiggled with her tips. She was so tired, but with Lucy's help, everything went very smoothly and they had some food leftover to help with tomorrow's lunch menu. Lucy helped clean and peel the vegetables for beef stew and roll out and cut dumplings. Sammy carried out the trash and kept the floors swept when he was not eating. Overall, it was another successful day and Kathleen was ready to turn out the lights and head home. As she prepared to leave, she looked at Lucy and Sammy. *Oh my goodness, what am I going to do with those two?* she thought. Walking over to the kitchen table, she eased herself into a chair.

"Lucy and Sammy, please come and sit with me for a minute." She knew that Sammy was an orphan, but she had no idea where or how he came to be in Sweetwater. Lucy had just come in to town and did not know anyone. She had been carrying a small bag with all her possessions in it.

The two stood before Kathleen as if they were criminals and she was their judge. Both of them hung their heads down as they stood waiting for her to sentence them back to the streets with no shelter or food.

"I live on a ranch that is not too far from town. I do not have a spare room because we have a houseguest who has been hurt, and the couple that lives with me are helping to care for him. I can make a pallet for you and give you a safe place to stay until we can make better arrangements. Would you both like to go home with me tonight? We will be coming back to the café tomorrow to work."

"Oh, I would be happy to go home with you. I can sleep in your barn," said Lucy.

"I can't leave from here," said Sammy sadly. "My mama might come looking for me." Sammy wiped away the mist in his eyes. "Besides, I've got a dry barrel to sleep in."

"How long have you been in town without your folk's sweetheart?" Kathleen asked as she pulled him into her side.

"Oh, I don't know, but I know my mama didn't want to leave me," Sammy said as his bottom lip began to quiver and a tear slipped down his dirty cheek. Kathleen hugged him and wrapped her arms around his young body. "Tell me, darling. What did you hear your mama say?"

"She told her new friend that I wouldn't be no trouble but he said I would too. He gave me a penny and told me to go in the store and get a piece of candy and I did. I could not find them when I came out. I ran down the road yelling to the top of my lungs for them. I ran and ran but I could not find them. I know my mama will come back for me." He hid his face in Kathleen's chest and tried so hard to hold back his tears.

"Well, its' settled. Both of you will come home with me tonight. After a good bath and clean clothes, you will feel better. Me too!" Kathleen said as she stood and started walking to the front door. "I need a hot tub of warm water to soak my weary bones in for sure."

# Chapter 4

Carlos and Rosa met Kathleen in the front yard. She was late and they were both concerned for her. "We were worried Senorita!" Carlos said in a very deep voice. "It's much later than we expected you to be. Who do you have with you?"

"I'm sorry that you were worried. We had a full day and many customers even with the bad storm we had in town. Is everything all right here?"

"Si, but the Mister has been a wild man ever since supper. He's worried much about you," explained Rosa as she looked at the old Indian woman and the young boy.

"Help them down Carlos. Here comes Juan now. He will care for the carriage and horse."

"Rosa and Carlos, we have a couple more houseguests for tonight. This is Lucy, my new helper at the restaurant, and this young man, is my new sidekick until his mama returns for him. His name is Sammy. We have had our supper, but we are all in need of a hot bath," Kathleen said with a smile. "You can help me with that, right Rosa?"

"Yes, but please go in the house and shut that *Mister* up. He has squawked for the last hour—demanding to know when you're coming home."

As the trio followed Rosa into the house, Matt attempted to sit up in his bed. "It's about time you got your sassy behind home woman. Git in here now!"

Lucy and Sammy stopped in their tracks and looked at Kathleen. "Go into the kitchen with Rosa and help her put water on the stove to heat. Sammy, I bet Rosa has a piece of pie and some cold milk just for you."

Kathleen watched the homeless pair trail behind Rosa into the kitchen as she gave a big sigh and entered Matt's bedroom. "Good evening," she said as she gave him a smile.

"Don't you *good evening* me," Matt said as he attempted to run his hand through his long mass of hair, giving it a much neater appearance. "I want to know why in this world you have to leave your home every day, and go work at that stinking Heavenly Hash Café. You have more work than you can manage right here on this ranch."

"Mr. Moore, it is no concern of yours what I do every day."

"Maybe it is not my business, but I'm lying up in your house almost like a damn prisoner." Holding up his hands, he said quickly, "I know I'm not really in jail but I feel trapped because I can't move around or get up on my own. My guard dog is pleasant enough but she doesn't visit with me or give me any information about what's going on around here."

"I'm sorry that you are bored. On that shelf above your head are plenty of books that you could read while healing. I know it has been lonely for you shut up in this room, but this is a working ranch and Rosa and the men are too busy to come in and chat with you."

Kathleen reached above his head and placed the book *"Moby Dick"* on the side of his bed. "I think you will enjoy this adventure."

"I'm not going to enjoy any damn thing until you answer my questions!"

"All right," Kathleen sighed and shook her head, "if you must know I will tell you so you will stop pestering me about my private business." Kathleen was tired so she pulled up a straight chair to make herself comfortable. She reached up at the crown of her head and pulled a few pins out of her hair to allow the long plaited rope to hang loose down her back. "Oh," she said, "that feels so good," as she rubbed the top of her head. She looked at Matt as he waited patiently for her to spill her guts to him. She thought that in order to have peace in the house she might as well tell him why she was working as a cook for someone else.

"My ranch has plenty of everything it needs but cash. I do not want to have to start selling my cattle to make ends meets, so therefore, I took this job to help with daily expenses. I don't intend to work there very long."

"My Lord woman, the money can't be that good for you to be working yourself into an early grave. You left here right after sunup and now it is dark as pitch out there. What did you make today? Fifty cents?"

Kathleen laughed as she leaned back in her chair and reached into her apron pocket and counted her tips for today. Smiling, she looked over at his grim face and said, "I made two dollars and fifteen cents plus the dollar that Mr. Crocker is paying me. That is enough for a weeks' worth of supplies for the house."

"Listen to me." Matt attempted to pull himself up into a sitting position on the bed. "Damn it! I'm so sick of hurting." Kathleen stood while adjusting a pillow behind his back. "Why don't you just lie still?"

"Quiet woman, sit back down and hear me out. You do not have to work. You're caring for me and I'm going to pay for your services, which I can assure you will add up to a lot more than two lousy bucks!"

"Mr. Moore, neighbors and hopefully friends, don't charge for helping one another. Please don't worry about me."

Realizing that he was not getting anywhere discussing money with her, he quickly changed the subject. "Who are those people you brought home with you? More mouths to feed."

"Please Matt, I don't want my other two guests to feel like they are a burden to us. The old Indian woman started working with me today. She is homeless and has no family that will help her. The little tyke is Sammy. His mama ran off and left him all alone in town. He is only five or six."

"How in the world did you end up as their caretaker, too?"

"Mr. Crocker found Prairie Flower, who wants to be called Lucy, at the general store looking for a job. He needed someone to help me at the café, so he hired her. I discovered Sammy sleeping in a wooden barrel in the back alleyway. His mama left town with a *new friend* who did not want him tagging along. Bless his heart. He was starving when I took him in the kitchen and fed him."

"I would like to get my hands on that so-called *mother*. So, what are you going to do with the boy? Turn him over to the sheriff to be placed in an orphanage?"

"No, I could never do that." Kathleen shook her head and placed her hands over her face. "He's only been with me one day and I already feel responsible. He's so independent and brave to be so small and all alone." Kathleen bit her bottom lip trying hard not to shed a tear as she thought about finding the little boy asleep in that nasty barrel. "He can stay here, of course, but I'll have to discuss his care with Rosa and Carlos."

Matt could see how she felt about the child's living conditions and how dangerous it was for him to have been left in a strange town all alone. Damn the whores of the world who had kids and cared more about themselves than they did about their babies, he thought.

"How's the old woman working out for you? Is she a good worker, and can she speak English?"

"Yes, she's a hard worker for someone her age. Whatever that is?" Kathleen smiled as she looked at him. "She is from the Arapaho tribe that is traveling to Oklahoma City. I am worried that the job is really too much for her. She has to stand on her feet all day washing dishes in hot water. She peels and chops vegetables, sweeps and mops the floor, too. She's strong and willing to help me no matter what I ask her to do."

"When I get back over to my place, I plan to get myself a housekeeper and cook. I want someone to live in. Not some jaw-yapping woman that tells all my business when she makes a trip to town. Maybe, this Lucy would consider working for me. She can do her work and rest a lot. She would have her own room and a horse and carriage to go to town for supplies."

"That's sounds like a wonderful job for her but of course, she needs to *like* you. So, you had better stop all of your yelling while she's here," laughed Kathleen.

"Listen, I'm serious about that job of yours in town. Quit tomorrow and stay home where you belong. I will pay you tonight for services rendered and in advance for Rosa's continued help."

"I've got to go check on my houseguests and talk with the boys about today's activities on the ranch. I will say goodnight after I have finished with some of my last minute chores." Kathleen stood and walked out of the room without giving him an answer about the café job.

Kathleen hurried in the kitchen and made sure that Lucy and Sammy were having their baths and preparing for bed. Rosa was a wonderful, loving woman who enjoyed caring for people. She was doting on Sammy already. Once Kathleen was sure that her little houseguests were ready to bed down for the evening, she walked out to the barn and spoke with Pedro and Juan about the coyote situation in the far pasture. Both young men were happy to report that the problem had been taken care of last night. They had rounded up the newest calves and their mamas and placed them in the pasture closest to the ranch house. She was pleased with the young boys' plan of action.

Every day for the rest of the week, the trio, Kathleen, Lucy and Sammy, all worked at the Heavenly Hash Café and returned home each evening exhausted. Mr. Crocker's establishment was building a reputation as a nice, clean place to eat. All the local towns' people were dropping by in-between meals to have coffee or coffee and a small dessert. At meal times, the place was generally crowded with the stagecoach passengers or people coming to town to do business. Kathleen encouraged Mr. Crocker to hire more help. She knew that after a few weeks, she would be resigning and she wanted him to have help with the restaurant. At first, he complained, but he soon agreed to place another sign asking for help in his front window. He felt very fortunate to have had Kathleen see the sign, come in, and ask for a job. Maybe his good luck would continue. He would ask Kathleen to do the interviewing and hiring of the new people.

Saturday morning arrived and Kathleen left Sammy at the ranch house to run and play. She and Lucy would only work through the breakfast and lunchtime. Mr. Crocker was on his own for Saturday night suppers and Sunday dinners if he decided to remain open. After returning home around 2:00 p.m., Kathleen saw Matt sitting in a rocker on the front porch. He had his broken leg propped on a box and was playing checkers with Sammy.

Carlos ran out, met Kathleen and Lucy in front of the barn, and held the horse's head while the women debarked from the carriage. "Thanks Carlos," said Kathleen as she and Lucy each removed a package from the back of the carriage. They strolled over to the front porch.

"This is a pleasant surprise I must say. You, Mr. Moore, look downright human sitting there in that chair. I see you have made friends with my sidekick."

"Yep, I shore have. He is a big help running errands and

helping Rosa pick and carry things. You are certainly lucky to have such a good helper on your ranch. I might just try to steal him away from you when I leave here—soon." Matt reached across the checkerboard and rubbed his big callous hand across Sammy's clean hair.

"Soon, you say?" Kathleen asked with uncertainty in her voice.

"Yep, Dr. Squires came by earlier and said that I can start using the crutches that he brought me so I can start moving around by myself. They work really well. That's how I got here," he said as he motioned to the comfortable rocker.

"Well, that's mighty fine." Kathleen said trying to hide the disappointment in her voice. She had begun to like having the ornery old goat around. She was certainly going to miss their nightly conversations. At least she felt that they had become friends; now, he would be her neighbor instead of a houseguest.

"Well, soon, I will have to give that mop of yours a fresh haircut. You'll want to look your best when you travel into town and get fresh supplies for your house," Kathleen said as she continued into the house.

Lucy followed close behind and went directly into the kitchen to seek out Rosa. She would offer to help prepare dinner for the men. She could not remain in the house without working for her room and board, she thought.

Kathleen changed into her tight fitting denims and put on her old western boots. She needed to ride out to the far pasture and make sure all the cattle that remained out there were doing all right. Carlos said all was well but she needed to see for herself. Kathleen pushed open the screen door and stepped out on the porch wearing a long sleeve fringed western jacket.

"I do declare, Miss Annie. Just where do you think you're heading in your western finery?" Matt asked with a smirk on his face.

"Annie? Why are you calling me that?" Kathleen did not know what he meant by his remark to her.

"Well, you're dressed like Miss Annie Oakley, a lady in a western side show that I saw in Houston a few years back. All you need to do is tote a .22 rifle on your shoulder and you could pass for her."

"You are full of you know what, Mr. Moore! Leave me alone and go back to your checkers." Kathleen headed as fast as she could toward the barn.

"Hey, wait up!" Matt yelled to her prissy butt as she practically ran away from him.

Kathleen stopped and turned, giving him a hard stare that said to go to Hades but she did not say it. "What now?"

"Can't you take the carriage and allow me to be your chaperone as you look over your ranch. I'm begging you to take me away from this porch and house."

Kathleen felt the angry wave in her body melt away as she took in his features as he pleaded with her. She slowly thumbed her western hat off her head and allowed it to hang down her back. She walked back to the porch and placed one foot on the edge as she looked at him.

"What about your leg? Don't you think the buggy ride will be too much?"

"We'll never know 'til we try," he commented with a sassy grin.

Kathleen shook her head, walked back to the barn, and told Pedro that she was taking the carriage. "Our houseguest wants to go sightseeing," she said laughing softly. "I know he's going to be sorry come nightfall but he's a stubborn ass."

Pedro and Kathleen walked the horse and carriage as close to the front porch as possible and Juan helped Pedro lift Matt into the carriage seat. Sweat had broken out on his upper lip by the time they got him perched onto the seat with his leg propped up on the front railing.

Kathleen drove down the road and was just settling back to enjoy the scenery when he demanded to drive. "You're deliberately hitting every rut and hole in this road," he said as he reached for the reins and began to leisurely drive.

"With the pace you are driving this carriage; we will be next week getting out to the north pasture." Kathleen laughed but decided to just sit back and enjoy the afternoon ride. She sighed very big and leaned back against the bench seat. She was tired from the long day she had already put in at the café. Nearly twenty cowpunchers had ridden into town to get an early start on their first free day from the trail drive. A bath, whiskey, and a woman was all they had on their minds until they passed the Heavenly Hash Café. The aroma of bacon and hot biscuits brought them to a halt. It was all she and Lucy could do to feed the hungry bunch of men. At the end of the morning, her apron pockets jiggled with silver coins. The men were very appreciative and showed her how generous they could be with their cautious grins, shy winks and money. As Matt continued his slow pace, Kathleen glazed at Matt and smiled.

"What're you thinking about that's giving you a silly grin on that sunburned, turned-up nose of yours? You got a secret that you're hiding?" Matt asked as he pulled back on the reins a little.

As he was looking at Kathleen while waiting on her answer, he pondered his feeling toward this young unmarried woman. He had been her houseguest for nearly two weeks and whenever she was near, he had a queer feeling that he had never felt for any other female. Being around this cantankerous bossy woman had brought on a warm feeling inside the pit of his stomach. Could this little woman have already woven a place in his heart? How was he going to continue to be indifferent to her if she brought him so much happiness just being in her presence? All his life he had been drifting from one cattle town to the next without a thought of another soul until he met Lillian. He had been searching for the kind of love that gave him happiness and contentment. Looking back, he knew that his feelings for Lillian were shallow in comparison to what his heart was doing when he was near the lovely creature that sat next to him now.

"No, Mr. Moore, I don't have a secret that I'm hiding from you." Kathleen laughed as she looked out over the last of the wild flowers before the cold snap came and killed their blooms.

Matt sat silently beside her while driving the young frisky horse. Kathleen noticed his aged, weathered face, as he seemed to be making the trip just fine. His dark brown hair had streaks of gray under his ragged old Stetson hat that had seen many years of wear. The afternoon sun was setting in the west as they entered the north pasture where the cattle were grazing on the last of the summer grass. Kathleen pointed to Matt to guide the carriage over to the stream so the horse could get a drink of cool water. She stood in the carriage and looked over her herd that she was so proud of owning. As she held her hand over the top of her eyes to block out the setting sun, she was happy that she did not see any more signs of the varmints that haunted the cattle. She started to take her seat when she glanced down at Matt. He had lowered his head down to his chest and he appeared to be dozing. She gave him a big grin and then smiled with satisfaction.

By the time Matt and Kathleen had made it back to the ranch, the sun had finally set behind the horizon. Juan's dog came out of the barn yapping and woke Matt up out of a sound sleep. "We're home old man," whispered Kathleen as she placed her hand behind his shoulders. "Careful, place your leg down into the wagon. Here come Juan and Pedro. They will help you down and give you the crutches. Can you walk by yourself?"

Matt could not believe that he had fallen asleep on the way home. The rocking of the carriage and the fresh air must have caused him to drift off for a minute.

"I got out here, didn't I?" Matt snapped while Juan and Pedro placed his good leg down on the smooth ground. Carlos handed Matt his crutches and he placed them under his armpits. He hobbled off with jerky movements but made it to the house. Sammy held the door wide open for him once he made it up the porch steps. Everyone stood still and watched him make his way inside the house. Rosa stood in the hall and assisted him to his room.

After a hardy supper of chicken and dumplings with several homemade biscuits, Matt could hardly keep his eyes open. Between the fresh air and the bouncing around of his hurt leg during the wagon ride out to the far pasture, he was ready for bed. He rubbed Sammy's hair while the boy laid his head on his chest for a good night hug. After watching Sammy leave the room, Kathleen smoothed Matt's bed covers, walked over and turned the lantern down low. Matt was asleep before she left his room.

# Chapter 5

Matt was awakened from a restless sleep. Someone was stabbing him repeatedly in the lower part of his body. He was trying to open his eyes but they seemed to be waxed or plastered shut. He could hear whimpering sounds and the pain felt worse than ever. The lantern that Rosa had left burning low on the table was making a sizzling noise. He tried hard to see in the pitch-black room. Finally, he heard something like footsteps approaching. *Please stop the pain;* he tried to say to whoever was coming near.

As Kathleen entered Matt's room, his face was sweating as he hung over the edge of the bed while attempting to get up.

"Lie still before you hurt yourself," said a voice so sweet it sounded like an angel whispering to him as he felt her breath brush over his cheeks and strong hands pushed him back on the bed. He smelled an unidentifiable scent as he tried to see whose hand wiped his face with a cool cloth. As the coolness of the cloth swept across his forehead and eyes, he instantly shot awake like a flash of thunder. He sat straight up in bed and tried to reach the scent that floated around him.

"Matt, you must lie back down. Rosa is getting you some medicine. You did too much today and it is my fault. I should have never let you hang your leg over that railing on the carriage. You must lie still and let me check your leg," demanded Kathleen. Slowly, Matt's eyes opened just a peep and he saw that some vicious crazy person was not attacking him. He had a nightmare. He flung an arm across his forehead and eyes as he sighed. Thank goodness, he was in Kathleen's guest room just like before. He was safe.

Kathleen bathed his face, neck and arms as she stood over him in her long flimsy white gown.  She had not even taken the time to put on a robe.  Her long midnight black hair flowed loose down over her shoulders and trailed down to her hips.  She looked like a goddess.  He was so thankful that this lovely woman was caring for him.

Matt lay back down on the bed and lifted the covers to his armpits. Rosa entered the room with a cup of hot tea and the bottle of pain medicine.  The pain medicine was the foulest, nastiest stuff he had ever put in his mouth but it did the job. Sleep, wonderful sleep overtook him.

For days, while Matt was recovering he sat by the window or on the front porch slouched down in a chair and watched everyone go about his or her chores.  He was moody and mean-spirited. The nightmare that he had awhile back was still vivid in his mind. After thinking about it, he was sure that the stabbing pains in the dream came from Lillian.  It was her way of trying to tell him that she never really cared for him. *What a crazy dream,* he thought.

He was ready to go home and get back to work.  Once he had purchased the ranch, he had started making plans to make something special out of his one hundred acre spread.  He had ordered lumber and new water closet items for the ranch house when he first arrived.  While still in Abilene, he had purchased fifty head of cattle that should be arriving soon.  He was retiring from the cattle driving business. After fifteen years of herding all types of cattle from Texas, Colorado, Montana, and Kansas City, he was ready to settle down and become a full time rancher. He had felt that he had a new life cut out for him; home, wife, maybe a few tow-headed youngsters, and then came the damn letter from Lillian.

Sammy had been drawing a circle in the dirt out in the front yard when he noticed Mr. Matt sitting in a chair by the window. He tossed his stick down, raced into the house and went directly over to his new friend.

"Hi Mr. Matt, what have you been doing this morning?  Have you had your breakfast? Miss Kathleen told me to make sure you ate when you got up. Have you eaten some of Rosa flapjacks?"

"Yep, I ate.  Why aren't you in school?"

"Shoot fire, Mr. Matt.  I ain't big enough yet.  Miss Kathleen has been teaching me my letters before we turn in each night.  She teaches me good!"

"You sleep on a pallet in your teacher's room?"

"Suppose' to but when she starts snoring, I scoot up off the floor and slide under the covers beside her. She never knows I'm there."

"So, she snores does she?" Matt could not help but chuckle. He could only image Katy lying on her side with the covers pulled up to her ears while humming a soft snore.

Kathleen had her routine all planned out each day. She was up before sunrise. She dressed in her work clothes, rushed out to the chicken yard, and disturbed her sleeping fat hens. Once the eggs were gathered, she placed them in a pan of water to soak clean. She opened the back of the barn and let the workhorses out to exercise in the corral. Then she would sit down on the low milking stool and milk Betsy, her pet cow that she had raised since she was a young girl. She carried the warm milk in the house and strained it at the kitchen counter. Rosa and Lucy would be in the kitchen with the blue granite coffee pot brewing. After a fresh cup of coffee, she would redress for work. She gave Sammy a small list of chores that she expected him to complete while she was gone; she headed out for a full day's work in town.

The Heavenly Hash Café was a busy place ever since Kathleen had practically taken it over. With Lucy and Mr. Crocker's help, they served a nice hardy breakfast, lunch and dinner meal. Kathleen had instructed Mr. Crocker to place a sign in the window for more help. In a day's time, Kathleen hired Mrs. Lorraine Porter, a widow woman, who had three mouths to feed at home. Her husband had died last year while working on a cattle drive. She had been working at Mrs. Washington's Rooming House making ten dollars a month. Kathleen told her she would make that kind of wages in tips if she were pleasant and kind to the customers. Mr. Crocker suspected that Kathleen made sure that Mrs. Porter took food home to her children but he did not object, too much.

Lucy did more of the cooking since she had gotten used to the ways of the white people's food. She helped wash dishes in between preparing food and helping to keep the floors clean. Kathleen prepared most of the main dishes and helped take orders and served the food to the customers. Mrs. Porter proved to be a good worker and a very pleasant woman. Both women's pockets jiggled with tips at the end of the day.

Kathleen had stocked her pantry at home and her bills at the general store and livery were paid. She wanted to stay home and work like she used to, but until she could get her cattle to market in Abilene; she would have to continue working at the café. She was tired every evening, but she had gotten used to the long days. Coming home to a warm house filled with the wonderful aroma of good food and the knowledge that the bill collectors were not at her door, made all the work worthwhile.

After a long day at work, Kathleen arrived home to find Matt standing on the front porch with the aid of his crutches. He had been waiting on Kathleen to return home. He watched her as she descended from the carriage. She was a beautiful woman with long slender legs. She walked with the grace of a queen toward him. He slowly stepped down off the porch and hopped out on the uneven ground to greet her.

"Welcome home, Katy," he said with a sheepish smile.

"Well, if this isn't a surprise," she said as she stopped and looked him over. There standing in front of her was a very handsome, lean but well-muscled, cowboy in brand new duds. He had a new cowboy boot on his good leg and a moccasin slipper on the injured one. Kathleen felt herself blush because she realized that she was staring at him like a lovesick calf.

"How long have you been walking around on that leg without me knowing anything about it?"

He stood towering over her wearing a lazy smile. "I wanted to surprise you and it looks like I did. Dr. Squires was out a few days ago and he said that I could start putting weight on my leg so here I am. All ready to move back to my ranch in the morning."

Kathleen breathed deeply as she wrapped one arm around her waist while she placed the other up close to her long slender neck. "You sure you're ready for such a big move." Kathleen was not ready for him to leave. She did not really understand why she suddenly felt so sad.

"As ready as I can be, I guess. I need to hire at least two or three men to help me around the ranch. I wanted to talk with Lucy tonight, too." He looked over his shoulder at the small Indian woman standing behind Kathleen. "Let's continue this

43

conversation over supper. I'm starved and I know you're ready to get in the house and settle down after your long day."

Kathleen felt the pressure of Matt's hand on the center of her back as he guided her up the porch into the house. Sammy came running and threw his arms around her legs and buried his face into her skirt. Kathleen stooped down, gave him a tight hug, and kissed him on the cheek. "How's my little man doing today? Looks like you took good care of Matt. He's going to be leaving us soon."

"No, no, not Mr. Matt, don't let him leave us, please!" Sammy's voice broke as he fought back tears. Sammy was attached to Matt and to discover that he would be leaving was almost too much to bear. Everyone that claimed to love him had gone away and left him behind.

"Hey, little buddy. I told you that I only live a mile or so from here. Shoot fire, boy, you can walk through the pasture to my ranch and see me anytime. Now, come on and let us go sit down and eat. I got a hollow leg that needs to be filled."

After a wonderful supper of venison roast with vegetables followed by a delicious apple pie with thick cream poured over the top, Matt pushed back his chair and looked over at Lucy.

"Lucy, do you enjoy cooking, washing dishes and slinging hash for that bunch of rowdy cowboys in town?" Matt cut his eyes over to Kathleen, waiting for her to answer for Lucy, but to his surprise, she made no reply.

"I like work with Miss Kathleen."

"How would you like to come and live on my ranch with me? You see, I need someone to keep my house clean, cook and wash my clothes. You will have your own room and I will let you drive the horse and carriage to town or even over here to see Rosa and Kathleen whenever." Matt noticed that Lucy never took her eyes off Kathleen as he spoke about the job. "So, what do you think? Of course, I will pay you a monthly wage."

Kathleen had been around Lucy long enough to know that she liked Matt and she liked what he said about her new working conditions. She would have a home with Matt.

"Lucy, I think that you should take Matt's offer. If you do not like it over there, you can always move back and be with us, right Rosa?"

"Si, Mr. Matt's a good man. Take the job and clean for him. I will come help you to get things in order. Carlos said it was a mess but the two of us can clean it good."

Matt glanced over at the sheepish look on Carlos' face and laughed. "So, Carlos, my place is a pigsty?"

"Don't put words in my mouth, Mr. Matt, but what I seen was plenty bad."

"Carlos and boys," said Matt, "I need to hire several good men to come and work full-time for me. I want to get my ranch in good working order before winter hits hard. I have fifty head of cattle arriving soon and my barn and corral need repairing. Do you know any men that would be good workers and trustworthy?"

Juan looked at his pa and said that the two brothers, who worked at the Sawyer farm, were losing their jobs because the Sawyer's were selling their farm to a family that had several big sons. "They are good boys and need to work to support their family in Mexico. I can ride over tomorrow and have them come and talk with you."

"That's fine. I would sure appreciate the help. I could use a couple hands to help me repair my barn and fence. Whatever time you have to spare would be appreciated and I will pay a decent wage."

Juan and Pedro looked at their pa and he nodded and said, "Saturday, after your chores are finished here."

"Rosa, how would you like to leave this old man you been married to for years and come and be my woman? You're a mighty fine cook!" Matt said as he rubbed his full stomach.

Rosa blushed from the top of her head to her toes and grinned big as she hit Matt with her dishcloth. "Now, Mr. Matt, Lucy is a good cook. You won't be sorry you hired her," said Rosa.

After the table was clear and all the dishes washed, Kathleen went in the pantry to put away some preserves and canned peaches that she had purchased at the General Store. She felt a strong warm body pressing up against the back of her shoulders and all the way down to her buttocks and long legs. Matt's large hands circled her arms and held them tight. Kathleen froze as she glanced down on the hands that held her captured. *Oh, Jesus, please do not let me react like a love-starved old unmarried woman!* She thought.

Kathleen gasped as she arched her backbone straight. "Mr.

Moore, what do you think you're doing?" When she felt his cool lips brush against the side of her neck, all of her senses seem to come alive. She tried to turn toward him but he only laughed as he kissed her again. Relaxing his hold on her, she flipped around, nearly causing him to tumble backwards. He realized from the blush on her face that he had frightened her. For days, he had wanted to capture her slim body; taste and smell her, hear her whisper his name while she leaned into his body.

Kathleen had wanted Matt to show some sign that he wanted her, but she was not as prepared for his surprise love attack in the pantry as she thought she would be. It had been years since a young man had touched her, made her heart pound in her chest, and the blood rush through her veins. She swallowed so hard it hurt her throat as Matt looped an arm around her waist and led her back to the kitchen table. "I've got to sit down before I fall flat on my face," he said.

"That's what you get for trying to steal kisses like a young, randy cowboy," said Kathleen trying to make light of the situation that just took place between them.

"I just came to the kitchen for another cup of coffee before I turned in. I could not resist after finding you all alone in the small dark room. Don't try and tell me that you didn't like my kisses," he said challenging her. As if to prove his point, he leaned in closer to her lovely face and placed a kiss over her rosy pink lips. Surprised, she kissed him back and instantly stood.

"Good night, *Mr. Moore.*" Kathleen leaped up from the table and headed toward her room. "Katy, my name is Matt. Remember that in the future—or else."

Since the next day was Saturday, Kathleen instructed Lucy to stay home. She and Mr. Crocker could handle the breakfast and lunch crowd. Mrs. Porter did not work on Saturdays since she had to care for her children. Mr. Crocker would have to get busy and re-hire the old Chinese man who had been coming around the café since it had gotten busier. He was sorry that he had left and gone to work in the dirty, hot laundry.

"Darn it Kathleen, is every one leaving me now that I have a successful business? Are you going to leave me, too?" Mr. Crocker complained. He had finally taken a liking to Lucy, the old Indian woman, who was a hard worker and did not yak all the time like most women. "Alright, I'll mosey down to the laundry and speak with the old wiry Chinese man. If he gives me any sass, I'll threaten to cut that long pig tail of his off!"

Kathleen laughed as he rushed out the door while she put two big pots of coffee on the stove to brew. Today's menu was going to be simple; vegetable soup and ham sandwiches. Apple pie would be the only choice for dessert. While the coffee was brewing, Kathleen placed several onions in the beef that was simmering in a large cast iron pot. Mr. Crocker would slice the fresh cooked ham into thin slices to go between the large pieces of fresh baked bread from the local bakery. Kathleen had convinced Mr. Crocker that it was cheaper and easier to buy the bread. The jingle of the cowbell over the door announced the arrival of the first breakfast customer.

With the little Chinese man working again in the kitchen, Kathleen had cooked, cleaned and left the café in good order for Monday morning. She walked to the livery to get her horse and carriage. Mr. Thornbees was watching and waiting for Kathleen to return to go home.

"Good afternoon, Miss Parker. Did you have a good day at the café?"

"Actually, I did. Thank you for inquiring. How was your day—so far?"

"It would be a great day if you would consent to go on a ride after church tomorrow and have a picnic with me. I'll supply the lunch."

"Now Big Al," Kathleen sighed.

"That's a first at least. You've never called me by my first name before."

"Well, Al, we've known each other since we were children. I believe I can call you by your first name. Anyway, thank you for the kind invitation but I do not have the time to go on picnics or any other activity that does not involve work on my ranch. Since I started to work, I have many chores that are left unattended."

"What's that lazy bunch of Mexicans doing while you're slaving away here in town?" He said in a nasty tone of voice.

Kathleen felt the hair on the back of her neck rise. She could not believe that fool of a man would try to charm her one minute and then speak ugly about the people who were practically her family.

"Please do your job, Sir and bring me my horse and carriage out front." Kathleen gave him a nasty glare, turned, and walked out of the stable. *Oh, how I would like to take a crop to him*, she thought.

Mr. Thornbees immediately knew that he had put his big foot in his mouth. If he got his hands on the lovely Kathleen and her ranch, there would be time enough to rid the place of that high-handed Mexican family. He had no use for sorry Mexicans who came across the border and acted as if they were better than white folks were. One day that old man, Carlos and his two sons would be sorry, he was thinking, when he heard Kathleen call to him.

"Do I need to come and get my own carriage, Mr. Thornbees?"

# Chapter 6

"Well," Matt said, "it looks like I'm at yours and Lucy's mercy today. I want to move back over to my house as soon as you two can help me get it livable again. Do you think that you will have some time today to spare?" Matt asked Rosa, hoping they would be able to help him.

"Si, Mr. Matt. Right after the kitchen is clean; we will carry our cleaning supplies over there and get it all ready for you, right Lucy?"

Lucy got up from the table. She looked down at her feet and spoke softly to Matt. "I am pleased to work for you Mr. Matt. I will work hard, clean and cook for you," Lucy said and rushed out of the kitchen to pack her few belongings that Kathleen had given her.

Kathleen had slept late and was walking into the kitchen when she heard her name. "Do you think that Kathleen will help us today, too?" Matt asked Rosa.

"Of course, I will help. What am I volunteering to help with?" she said as she poured herself a cup of fresh brewed coffee while glancing around the room at the Matt and Rosa.

"Today is cleaning day at my house and Rosa and Lucy are going to go over and make my house livable. I am going over and I was hoping you would tag along and lend a hand in decorating the place. I have a lot of furniture there but it needs a woman's touch."

Kathleen looked to Rosa and said that she had already decided not to go into town for church service. "I can go for a while but later I need to ride over my ranch and check on my herd. I know the boys do it every day, but I like doing it, too."

In less than two hours, the flat bed wagon was loaded with Matt, Sammy and all the brooms, buckets and mops that Rosa could find around their place. Rosa had prepared a big picnic lunch for everyone to share at lunchtime. Kathleen, dressed in her denim pants, rode her horse while Rosa and Lucy drove her small carriage over.

In no time at all, the three women had Matt's house looking very presentable. Rosa had instructed Matt to sit and watch in his big comfortable chair with a footstool. He had a wicked grin on his face as he peeked at Kathleen bending over while she swept and mopped all around him while he pretended to be reading his mail. Usually, he did not like her wearing those men's tight fitting pants away from the house, but today he did not mind at all.

After lunch, Matt's house was cleaner than he ever believed it could be. Lucy had used beeswax on the cleaned wooden floors and all around the dark mahogany window seals and doors. Kathleen and Rosa rearranged the furniture and placed clean linens on the big double bed. Kathleen donated one of her mother's quilts, which gave the bedroom a homey touch. Several colorful braided rugs were taken outside, hung over the clothesline and beaten to remove the dust. The house took on a homey feel and Matt could not have been more pleased with the results. Now all he needed to do was to fill his pantry with staples and canned food until the spring garden produced fresh items to be canned. Tomorrow he and Sammy would drive into town, get supplies for his kitchen, and feed for the farm animals.

Once back at Kathleen's ranch, Matt hobbled to the guest room, stretched his long legs out on the clean bed, leaned back, and relaxed for the last time. He was grateful for the treatment and care that he had received from Kathleen and Rosa the past several weeks. Kathleen had been a gracious host but it was time for him to move his carcass back to his own ranch. He grinned crookedly at the memory of the first time he had seen her. He was still in a fog like dream as he watched her place her bonnet over a crown of midnight dark hair. He smiled when he thought of how feisty she became when he spewed medicine all over her. His eyelids grew heavy while he felt a cool breeze flowing through the window. His last thoughts of Kathleen were that she was a very sad, hardworking young woman. She needed a friend, not a lover. She needed someone to talk to and to share her deep dark secrets. He wanted to be that person.

Monday morning, when Matt had awakened, the sun was already high in the sky. The house was quiet as he dressed and gathered his clothes and personal mail that had collected. He limped into the kitchen to find it empty but he heard voices coming from outside. He hobbled over to the screen door and saw Sammy poking sticks in Rosa's fire that she had built to wash clothes.

"Good morning, Mr. Matt," Rosa called from the well. "I will be inside in just one minute to get your breakfast. Miss Kathleen left several hours ago for the café."

"Take your time," he mumbled as he headed back to his room to get ready to move back to his ranch after a trip to town.

When Kathleen arrived home, Rosa had supper on the back of the stove ready to serve as soon as she cleaned up. With cooking and preparing food all day, she did not have the appetite she normally had, but Carlos and the boys would not sit at the table to enjoy their evening meal until she sat down with them. Rosa and her family never ate their meals in the dining room when her parents were alive, but once her parents had passed away, Kathleen insisted that the loving Mexican family eat with her. She never understood as a child why they could not eat at the table with her folks.

During dinner, Kathleen asked about Matt's move back to his ranch. Sammy was full of information and he told of their trip into town for supplies. "Mr. Matt gave me a nickel and I got a sack of peppermint sticks."

"Sammy, I don't like you taking money from anyone. I have money to get you whatever you need."

"But Miss Katy, I earned it by carrying his supplies into the house and feeding his chickens and the milk cow!"

"My name is not Katy. Please call me Miss Kathleen, Sammy."

"Mr. Matt calls you Katy," he said as he hung his chin down to his chest, embarrassed that she had scolded him in front of the others.

"So, he's all settled?" Kathleen inquired looking at Carlos and the boys.

"Si, Miss Lucy is taking excellent care of him. She is not timid Indian woman like the way she acted over here. She practically demanded that he go to bed after his trip to town. He didn't argue." Laughing Carlos got up and poured everyone more coffee. Rosa gave him a sweet smile.

Later that evening, as Kathleen prepared for bed, the house seemed so quiet. She was glad that Matt was able to move back to his ranch and start living his life. However, she never would have guessed that she would have developed an attraction for the big blockhead. She hoped by moving Sammy into the guest room she would not be missing the sound of Matt's breathing, the bedsprings squeaking as he twisted and turned or his continuous demands for companionship. She wanted him gone and now he was. She grabbed the pillow off his bed and smothered her face into the middle of it, drawing a deep breath. Rosa had washed the bed covers. His scent was gone—he was gone. She cried.

Why did he have to come into her life? She wanted things—her feelings—to get back to the way they used to be. She did not need to care about another man who did not feel the same way about her. Kathleen realized that she was overly tired from working all day. She slumped on the guest bed, grabbed the pillow he had used, and pulled it into her stomach hugging it tight against her middle. She went into a deep sleep with tears on her face. Rosa and Sammy found their Mistress sound asleep.

Rosa whispered to Sammy that tonight he could sleep in Kathleen's big bed all by himself. He smiled as Rosa tucked him in and made the sign of the cross as she whispered a prayer.

Matt was happy to be back at his ranch and he was grateful for the little old Indian woman, Lucy, who was working for him. He relaxed in the long tub of hot water and allowed the water to seep into the pores of his skin. His ribs were not broken but they were bruised and still hurt when he took a deep breath or tried to pick up something heavy. He still did not know exactly how he had fallen off his horse and landed in that damn muddy ditch. He knew he had been drinking, but in all his years, he had never been that drunk before. He was very thankful that Carlos had found him and brought him to Kathleen's ranch. As he leaned back and allowed the hot water to soothe his body, he thought about her. That hardheaded woman was working herself to death when it was not necessary. He had plenty of money and he had offered to loan her some until she could sell her herd. She was not having any loan.

She needed a ramrod and a few good men to drive her cattle to Abilene where they could be sold. He knew once word got around that he drove cattle herds all over the western states, that she would be asking him to help her. How in the world was he going to refuse her since she and Rosa saved his life?

As Matt was hobbling out of his barn, carrying a pail of fresh milk, Juan rode up to the corral. Two young Mexican men who looked to be in their early twenties and a white youngster about seventeen accompanied him.

"Morning Mr. Matt!" Juan jumped down off his young pinto pony and pointed at his young friends. "I bring over my friends who want to work. They are good riders, shoot straight, and track really well, too."

"Do they speak English?" Matt was looking the young men over and they were dressed nice and appeared clean.

"Si!" The young Mexicans said simultaneously. Matt laughed as he looked at the youngsters and Juan.

"Tie your horses and water them. Come into the house. We'll talk."

Lucy looked at the young men and motioned for them to take a seat at the table. She served each one a cup of fresh coffee and placed a platter of fresh baked sugar cookies in the center of the table. The young men stared at Lucy and the cookies.

"Help yourself, boys," Matt said as he pulled out a chair. "Lucy, this is Joseph and Gabe Garcia and Timmy Waller. You fellows will do whatever Lucy asks you to do. She will be cooking you three hearty meals every day.

In less than thirty minutes, Matt had learned enough about the young men to hire them. He told them that he wanted them to live on the premises, out in the bunkhouse and they could take their meals in the house with him unless he was having company. The boys were surprised that they would be eating three square meals a day and have a nice clean place to live. At the last ranch where they worked, they rode back and forth to their parents' farm or stayed over and slept in the smelly old barn. Matt told them that they could work out their days off between themselves since they were kin to each other. He needed two of them to work the weekends, but the chores would be only the necessary ones. His cattle out in the pasture would need to be checked on twice a day.

Matt quizzed the younger man about his age. He wondered if his folks cared that he worked away from home. Timmy said he was seventeen and that he did not have any family that would miss him. Once the young men rode back home to gather their personal belongings and Juan had gone back to Kathleen's, Matt and Lucy sat on the front porch. She was peeling a pan of apples while he sat with his bad leg propped up on the railing.

"Well, Lucy, we have the ranch all ready for my new herd to arrive. I look for them to arrive most anytime now. What did you think of the three young men who will be working for me?"

"You need a litter of piglets and big mama sow. Young boys eat plenty."

Matt laughed and shook his head while he reached into her pan and stole a piece of apple. "I guess you're right. I will get the boys to build a pen tomorrow out behind the barn. Don't want it too close to the house. Do we need anything else?"

"Dog. Maybe a young pup to train. Bark at strangers, guard barn animals and kills snakes."

"Did you have a dog of your own?"

"No, but wanted one." Lucy had completed her task of apple peeling and just sat and looked out at the evening sky.

"Someone's coming, Mr. Matt." Lucy got up and went into the kitchen to prepare a couple of apple pies for tomorrow's dessert.

Matt watched as the young man from the telegraph office rode over to the corral and jumped down off his horse. He led it over to the water trough. He brushed his hat off his head and spoke with excitement in his voice.

"Got a telegram for you, Mr. Moore. Brought it right out since you were laid up with a busted leg."

"Appreciate it sonny." Matt nodded as he reached into his vest pocket and tossed the young man a half dollar. "Gee! Thanks. Do you want me to wait while you read it? You might want to send some words back."

"No, if I have to send a return message I will do it tomorrow." As the young man turned to retrieve his horse, Matt called to him. "You wouldn't know by chance, if someone has a litter of puppies they're trying to find homes for?"

"Sure do. Mrs. Martha, who owns the boarding house, her big blond dog had a passel of puppies about two weeks ago. I want one

54

but Ma says no; I can't have another animal on the place."

Matt watched the young man ride down the road out of sight before he opened his telegram. He read the words but could not believe what he was reading.

*Darling, I arrive Sweetwater 17 of November. Meet me. Your beloved fiancée.*

"Damn, damn, double damn!" Matt said from the top of his lungs. Lucy raced to the screen door and looked out. She saw Matt holding a piece of paper swearing to the high heavens. "Shoot fire! The seventeenth is tomorrow."

Lucy was not sure what had upset Matt because he stormed off the front porch, hobbling faster than she could have believed possible. He went into the barn and in a few minutes she heard him calling her name.

"Lucy, I'll be back in a while. I'm going to visit with Kathleen."

Kathleen had worked all day at the café and then rode out to the north pasture to look over her herd. As she rode into the yard, she saw Matt propped up on the porch talking to Carlos. Pedro hurried and helped her down off her horse and then took the animal and went into the barn to give it a good rub down and a bucket of oats.

"Good evening, Matt. Missed your second home already?" Kathleen smiled at her own jest.

"I wanted to talk to you, if you can spare an old man a few minutes of your time."

"Let me get us both a cup of hot coffee, and we will sit out here on the porch."

A few minutes later, Matt was sitting in the porch swing. He patted the empty seat next to him. He took his coffee while Kathleen sat down with one foot tucked under her bottom as she faced him.

"You have a very serious expression in your eyes tonight. Has something bad happened over at your place already?"

"No, nothing like that. I did hire three young men today that Juan brought over. I am sure fortunate to have Lucy. She's a jewel."

"Come out with it then. Tell me what's going on now."

"I got a telegram. You read all my personal mail while I was laid up. You already know that my fiancée betrayed me with another man while I was busting my ass trying to get my place ready for her. We had an understanding for several years and I finally had a home and land. She readily agreed to marry me and well, I don't have to tell you about my *rejection* letter and what it said."

"I'm really sorry about reading your personal mail. Carlos and Rosa felt we would learn who you were if we read the letter."

"Never mind that now. I had already gotten myself pulled together when she wrote me that she was sorry and things did not work out between her and her lover. She wanted me back. She was sorry. Well—horse hockey!"

Kathleen sat while using one foot to push the swing very slowly back and forth. She did not know why he was telling her all of this now. He was very angry so she waited for him to continue with his story.

"I didn't answer her letter. I never intended to answer it because I did not want her in my life ever again. Liar, cheater are a few of the nicer words that I would use to describe her. Now, this evening, I get another telegram telling me that she is arriving here tomorrow. She signed it *Your Fiancée.*"

"Oh my," Kathleen said very softly as she covered her mouth with her hand. She could feel a knot forming in the pit of her stomach. She could not believe that the only man who had come into her life since she had sworn off love would be having this type of trouble. He claimed to detest this Lillian woman a little too much to suit her. What would he do when he saw her again? She knew that she should not have released the bond from around her heart. He could never learn how she felt about him. She did not want anyone's pity.

Matt looked over at Kathleen as she wrapped her arms across her stomach. "What am I going to do with her—when she arrives? I am not bringing her out to my ranch. No sir. By the time the stage arrives everyone in town will know that she is coming to marry me."

Kathleen could not help but laugh. Matt looked so forlorn and lost. He really didn't know what he was going to do.

"I don't see anything funny!" He stared at Kathleen as if he would have liked to choke her.

"Hey, don't give me that darn mean look of yours. I haven't done one thing to you and I wasn't really laughing at you." Kathleen took a deep breath and attempted to offer him a solution.

"Matt, you are a big boy. This woman *cannot* make you marry her. Just put her up in the boarding house until she can return to wherever she came from."

Matt felt better once Kathleen had offered him a solution to his woman troubles. He liked sitting on this porch as the swing continued to sway back and forth. The crickets and katydids were beginning to sing. The night air was cool enough to keep away the mosquitoes. Every so often, a bullfrog would croak; an owl would hoot from a distance. He had only been away from Kathleen's ranch one day but he missed it—or was he missing this stubborn, beautiful woman sitting next to him?

"You know since I am sitting here beside you, spilling my guts about my love life, why don't you tell me why a lovely young woman with beautiful midnight hair is living all alone with no husband and little ones underfoot." He reached across her face and placed a lose strand of hair behind her ear.

"Now who's digging their spurs into my personal business?" Fidgeting with the long black rope of hair, she avoided his question. She was not ready to bare her soul and tell him about her long lost love of years ago.

"Well, I guess I best head on back to my place. I got a busy day tomorrow." The swing stopped and he pushed himself up by using his good leg while giving Kathleen a small grin. "Wish me luck?"

"You'll do just fine. I'm sure you can handle one little bitsy woman."

# Chapter 7

The stagecoach arrived on time and a crowd had gathered. Matt hoped that they were not on the platform waiting to witness the arrival of his so-called fiancée. There were no secrets in this town if a message came across the telegraph wire. Once the stage stopped at the depot and the rocking of the carriage stilled, the door flew open. In the entrance was a lovely woman with golden hair, wearing a green velvet bonnet with a bird's nest perched on top of it. Lillian was the first one to try to exit the door. One of the men on the boardwalk reached for her hand to assist her down onto the platform. Lillian smiled and thanked him. She had seen Matt in the crowd. She rushed passed the nice man and hurried to greet Matt.

"Oh Matt, darling, I knew you would be here waiting anxiously for me to arrive." She threw both of her arms around his neck and hugged him tight.

Matt reached for her arms and slowly removed them from his blushing red neck. "Why are you here?"

"Oh, sweetheart, I had to come after the way I was mistreated by Andrew. He carried me away and just left me in a god-forsaken ghost town. I never really wanted to go away with him and leave you."

Matt realized that they had drawn an audience who were eagerly listening to their conversation. "Let's get your luggage. This is no place to talk."

A young man about thirteen rushed over to Matt and asked if he could help carry the woman's parcels. "Yep," replied Matt. The stagecoach driver was placing several large pieces of luggage on the boardwalk. "That's all for now," he said to Matt. "The lady has more luggage coming on the next stage in three days."

Matt thanked the driver and turned to Lillian. "What did you do? Bring everything you own?"

"Well, of course, darling. I need all my things with me since this will be my new home."

Matt started walking down the boardwalk with the youngster trailing behind him, dragging several pieces of luggage. Lillian was standing alone so she hurried up beside Matt and asked where he was taking her.

"I have you a room reserved for several days at the boarding house. In three days, the stage will be arriving and you can get right back on it and go back wherever you came from."

Lillian knew that she had better wait until she and Matt were alone before she tried to change his mind. She was here in Sweetwater with Matt and here she was going to stay, she thought to herself.

Once the trio arrived at the boarding house, Matt introduced Lillian Larson to Mrs. Martha Washington. "Welcome, Miss Larson. Of course, you won't be a Larson long now will you," laughed Mrs. Washington.

"I hope I will be changing my name soon," Lillian said as she attempted to snuggle up against Matt's free arm.

"Mrs. Washington, Miss Larson will be here until the next stage arrives and then she will be returning home. Which room have you assigned to her? I want to deposit this baggage."

Mrs. Washington gave the young couple a strange look as she guided them up the stairs into the third room on the right.

"I hope you'll be comfortable here Miss Larson." As she turned to leave the room, she instructed them to leave the door open while visiting. "House rules do not allow men upstairs but this once. I'll give you a few minutes of privacy."

Lillian walked over to the dresser next to the window and removed her new hat. She had purchased it for the trip along with her two-piece green suit with a white ruffled blouse. The dark green matched her emerald eyes. She wanted to be beautiful so Matt would not remember that she had betrayed him. She planned to rush into his waiting arms and thought he would forgive her.

"Why did you come here, Lillian?"

"Darling, you have always called me Lil. Why so formal now? Aren't you glad that I came to my senses and came to be with you?"

"It sounded to me like you had no other choice. Running off with a cowpoke and having him desert you in a ghost town—isn't that what you said earlier?"

"But, Matt, I didn't have to come here, to be with you."

"Why did you?" Matt stood in the center of the room with both hands on his hips as he allowed his anger to show in his words. He had not even removed his Stetson.

"Please Matt," Lillian purred. "You're making me feel quite unwanted." She swayed over to him with a pout on her rosy lips. "You know that you're glad to see me. We had many good years together." Placing her hand on his chest and wiggling her long fingernail inside his shirt, she tried to snuggle up against him. "We've shared many wonderful evenings together after you returned from a cattle drive. I was always there for you, remember?" Matt stood as still as a stone statue.

"Oh, Matt, you aren't even trying to understand what happened to me after you left to come to this place. I was alone again for weeks waiting for you to send for me." Lillian turned her back to Matt, placing her face down into her soft smooth hands pretending to cry.

Her tears had no effect on him, as he looked her over. Lillian was a dressmaker by trade and he knew that she had not done a hard day's work in her entire life. Her body had not been exposed to the hot sun of summer and not a strand of her golden hair was ever out of place.

"I have no interest in trying to understand what you did with that *younger version of me* or why. We are all washed up, finished, a lost cause. Got that? I want you away from me and my new hometown as soon as the next stage arrives."

"But Matt, you can't mean that. You are being so hard and cruel! *Besides,* I have no money to purchase a return ticket. I cannot just leave. I have no place to return too. I gave up my little shop and house in Abilene." Lillian hung her head down in her hands and peeked through her fingertips at him, hoping to see a glimpse of pity and a possible change of heart.

Matt had been heading out the door of her room while she was pleading her case to stay. He stood staring at the ceiling as he calmed his anger.

"Well, my dear, you have gotten yourself in a pickle. You are a big girl; one that can certainly take care of herself." Matt reached into his vest pocket, unfolded some money, and placed it on the side table next to the window. "This will help while you are waiting on the next stage. Your ticket home will be waiting for you at the Stage Depot. Use it."

Matt saw Mrs. Washington standing guard near the staircase but he did not even acknowledge her presence as he stormed down the stairs and out the front door. All he wanted was to get away from that betraying hussy and return to his ranch. He was trying to prepare for his small herd and he did not have time to mess around with a fool of a woman who thought she could just show up and reclaim his love.

As he rode home, his thoughts kept drifting from Lillian to Kathleen. Those two women were different as daylight and dark. Kathleen was a strong, fearless, young woman who had to stand on her own two feet from an early age. She had taken on the responsibility of caring for her parents until their death and for running her big five hundred acre spread with nearly one thousand cattle. She worked from sunup to sundown without complaint. Her face and neck were tan and her hands had calluses. She was slim as a reed and when she walked, she appeared to be floating straight and tall. He enjoyed watching her as she plaited her coal black hair in a rope that hung nearly to her waist and when she smiled; her emerald green eyes sparkled with mischief.

Lillian was a lovely mature woman of thirty-six with golden blonde hair that she wore twisted on top of her head. She was very petite with dark brown eyes. Her complexion was pale as flour because she worked inside all day. She did not care for any outside work or activities unless it was a long buggy ride away from the city. She was a very talented seamstress who had a small shop on Main Street in Abilene. She had several women that worked for her. Matt was trying to remember but she never talked much about what she did while he was gone out on cattle drives for weeks at a time. They had an understanding. When he was in between jobs, he stayed at her little house at night and left early in the morning so her nosey neighbors did not see him.

As the sun peeked over the barn, Kathleen stood on the porch thinking about her life. She had had a lifetime of loneliness. In just a few short days, Matt had given her a dream that there might possibly be some hope that there could be happier days in her future. Now he was gone out of her house, out of her life as his heart belonged to another. As she collected eggs this morning, she overheard Pedro talking to Juan about Matt and his new woman in town. From the greeting, the couple gave each other at the stage depot, everyone was speculating about a quick wedding celebration.

Someone was knocking softly on the front screen door as Rosa made her way to answer it. Kathleen's heart gave a flutter as she recognized the man in her thoughts. She ran a hand over the rope of her hair as she made her way to the parlor. With one hand, she touched the buttons on her blouse, smoothed her waistband with the other and quickly gave her cheeks a pinch for color.

Matt was standing in the parlor with his brown Stetson in his hand. When he saw Kathleen, he motioned to her to come and sit. She walked in the room with a ramrod stiff back and dropped down onto the green velvet sofa without bending. With no greeting to him, Matt was suddenly puzzled why she was acting shy and nervous in his presence. Just last night, she had been a good listener and offered him great advice. She had shown him a softer side of her personality and appeared to have a sharp wit and good humor.

A light blush had come over Kathleen's face as Matt gave her a hard stare without a comment. Kathleen positioned herself on the end of the sofa and asked what she could do for him. Matt's response was not what she had expected. He knew something had happened for her to change the way she was behaving in his presence.

"First, I want to know what has gotten your rear end jacked up on your shoulders tonight."

"Mr. Moore! I will not be spoken to in that manner. I'm not one of your ranch hands that you can speak to with such vulgar language."

"Right there-- is what I'm talking about. Last night you were almost human; listening and offering advice to me about my problem. What's happened to cause you to change your feelings and turn back into that stiff-necked, bossy old prude that I first met?"

"Well, I never! Please leave my house immediately!" Kathleen stood and pointed to the door.

"Sit down, before I stand and force you to sit, Miss high and mighty." Kathleen slowly lowered her slim frame back down on the sofa while listening for Rosa or Carlos to come. She knew they had to hear all the commotion coming from the parlor.

"Can't we stop this bantering? Dang it woman. I thought maybe, just maybe, you would be anxious to hear that I took your suggestion and put Lillian up at Mrs. Washington's boarding house until the stage returns."

"Why would you want to do that when I heard that there is going to be a big wedding celebration very soon?"

"What?" Matt shook his head side to side and swore under his breath. "Whoever started that damn rumor is a fool for sure. You don't believe that, do you?"

Kathleen didn't respond but looked out the window and saw that stars were beginning to come out and it was going to be a cool, lovely evening.

"Look, I can tell that you don't believe anything I've told you about my dealings with Lillian. I am not going to repeat myself. I came tonight to thank you for your suggestion about settling her at the rooming house. I am not going to marry her or any woman in the near future. This is my last conversation about all of this. I apologize if I have offended you in any way tonight."

Matt adjusted his good leg as he pulled himself up and began hobbling toward the entranceway. Kathleen jumped up off the sofa and called to him.

"Matt, I'm sorry, too. I am glad that you took care of your problem. I'm glad that I was able to help you." She gave him a sweet, shy smile. "Listen, I like you and I want us to be good friends."

Matt looked at Kathleen and wanted to pull her into his arms and extinguish the burning desire he had for her. He was afraid that he was losing his heart to this spitfire of a woman.

"You have to *trust* a person before you can be really good friends Katy." He placed his Stetson low down on his eyes and marched out the front door.

# Chapter 8

Matt was a hardworking man who treated everyone fair and straight. As the trail boss of many cattle drives, he learned quickly the ways of an honest, trustworthy man. He could spot a rover that spelled trouble right away and he would always send him packing. Matt believed in preparing for the future; therefore, he never gambled and squandered his hard-earned money. With his job, a man never knew when he might be hurt and laid up for days. He felt secure knowing that he had a sizeable bank account to fall back on for when he decided to settle down in one place. Now he was set, but he felt lonelier than he had ever been. His hopes of a nice home, land, wife and children had fallen by the wayside because of one lying, cheating woman who could not keep her drawers in check. *Well*, he thought, *things have to start looking up because they have gotten as low as low can be.*

Matt had been sitting in his kitchen having a cup of coffee as he listened to Lucy hum an old Indian song as she sat rocking on the front porch. He had noticed that she enjoyed sitting outside every evening enjoying the cool night air. He could hear the boards creaking on the porch as she moved the rocker back and forth. Matt left the kitchen and went outside to join her. "Mind some company?" he asked as he eased himself into his new porch swing. He enjoyed Kathleen's swing so much that he had installed one on his porch. Lucy had made several pillows to toss in the swing to make it more comfortable.

"Hey, I know that you have heard rumors that I might be getting hitched." Matt watched Lucy as she continued to darn a pair of his socks in the dim light of the lantern sitting next to her rocker.

"I heard."

"Well that's a bunch of lies!" Matt said as he watched one of his ranch hands pumping a pail of fresh water to take back into the bunkhouse.

"Even if it were true, I want you to know that you have nothing to fear about having a new mistress coming to live here with us. This is your home as long as you want it to be. Understand?"

"I understand, but what if white woman don't want old Indian woman living under her roof."

"Lucy, believe me. I would never marry someone who didn't like you," he gave her a shy grin, waiting for her reaction to his statement.

Lucy placed her mending down in her lap and shook her head. "Mr. Matt, you are too kind to me, but you can't see what the future may bring." Both Matt and Lucy laughed together for the first time, enjoying the cool of the evening.

Early the next morning, Matt and two of his new ranch hands rode into town to get some supplies to make a few repairs. Juan had dropped by last night and told him that his new herd would be passing through town and headed his way tomorrow. Matt's plan was to lead the rovers out to his ranch with the help of his new men and guide the cattle to his ranch. He wanted to put them in the pasture that had plentiful legumes, clover, and tall wheat remaining from the summer. Next spring, he would have several fields of corn and many acres planted with wheat and hay.

Kathleen was serving Al Thornbees, the livery owner, when Matt and his two men entered into the Heavenly Hash Café. She looked at him and nodded her head toward an empty table next to the wall. Matt took off his Stetson and hung it on the hat rack, as he looked her over from head to toe. Kathleen blushed as he brushed by her walking to the table.

"Now, Mr. Thornbees, have you decided what you're having? As you can see, I have many customers."

"For now, just bring me some more coffee and then I will give you my order," he said slowly giving her a shy grin. As she turned to walk away, he grabbed her by the elbow.

"I didn't see you this morning when you drove in. I hate it when I'm not there to take care of you."

"That's all right. Little Jeffrey took care of me just fine," she replied as she shook his strong hold loose from her arm.

"Can't we get any service here?" Matt was watching the scene between the big chap from the livery and Kathleen. He wanted to get up and smash that flirtatious look off his face.

Kathleen glared at Matt as she hurried to the kitchen to get a fresh pot of coffee. When she whirled around from retrieving the coffee off the stove, Matt was standing directly behind her. "Gosh," she said out of breath. "You almost made me scald you with this coffee. What are you doing back here?"

"How long has that big ape out there being grabbing at you?"

"Oh, you mean Big Al?" She sat the coffee pot back down onto the stove. "Al has been trying to get me to step-out with him for years. He does not want me. He only wants my ranch."

"Don't talk like that Katy. I'm sure he wants you—and you do have a nice ranch," he said grinning. "If he keeps bothering you, let me know. I'll take care of him."

"So, now you have become my protector. Isn't taking care of one woman at a time enough to keep you busy?"

Matt turned to walk back to his table when he stopped and glanced back at Kathleen. "Don't keep jabbing at me with your smart remarks. I'm on a short fuse as it is," he smirked.

******

Later that afternoon, Matt and the new ranch hands had ridden to the outskirts of town to meet the men who were bringing his new herd to him. Matt left one of his ranch hands behind at the ranch. The young hand, Timmy, greeted Carlos as he rode in to Matt's front yard. He got down from his old bay horse and wrapped the reins across the hitching post.

"Morning Lucy," said Carlos as he walked up on the porch removing his big sombrero.

"Mr. Matt is not here." Lucy said.

"That's fine," he said as he eased himself into the empty rocker next to hers. He noticed that Lucy was shelling peas. "I just stopped by to talk to you for a minute."

"Can I get you a cup of coffee or some water?"

"No, thanks, I'm up to here with that black liquid," he said as he pointed to his eyes with his left hand. "I stopped by this morning to tell you that I saw a tribe of Arapaho Indians walking on the back side of Kathleen's north pasture. I was scouting the new calves when I saw them; a very poor bunch of people with many women and small children."

Lucy stopped shelling the peas and sat very still in the rocker. She could not believe that her old tribe was coming this close to ranches and farmhouses. She had longed to see her older sister one more time. Her sister had begged and pleaded for her two sons to volunteer to care for Lucy since she had no one else in the tribe. Her nephews did not want to lose face with the old chief so they ignored their mama's pleads. A few days later, the old chief told her that she was banished from the tribe. She would never forget his words.

"You old woman and have no man to care for you. We go now. You stay." She watched her sister walk slowly away until she was out of sight. Lucy shook her head, trying to keep tears from forming in her eyes.

"How far is this place that you last seen them? Can I travel there with a horse and wagon?" Lucy asked with hope in her heart.

"It's about ten miles due north and yes, a horse and wagon could travel over the land. Why?" Carlos asked.

"I want to see my sister one last time. I want her to know that I am safe and live in a warm wigwam. This will make her last days happy. We both shed many tears the last days we were together."

"I'm sure you can get there, but you need to take someone with you. It will not be safe out there all alone. You might wait until Mr. Matt gets home later today. I am sure your people will be camping out that way for a few days. Kathleen will probably lose a head or two of cattle, but I'm sure she will turn her head, knowing they have children to feed."

"Yes, I will wait for the return of Mr. Matt. I need to go in to town and buy supplies for my people; corn meal, sugar, coffee, flour, and peppermint sticks for the little ones." She smiled as she looked at Carlos.

"Why do you want to help them after the way they treated you? They forced you to live alone in the middle of nowhere." Carlos shook his head still not understanding how a tribe of men could mistreat their old women folks.

"I help my sister and the little ones. You would do the same if you were me."

Carlos smiled and gave a big sigh as he stood. "I had better get on home. I will tell Rosa. She'll want to hear about your visit with your sister."

Lucy got up and went into the house to prepare for her trip to the north pasture. She had so many nice things that Miss Kathleen and Mr. Matt had bought her since she had been living with them. She wanted her older sister to have something warm to wear while sitting near the fire. As she was placing things by the front door, Matt came in.

"You aren't leaving me already?" He looked concerned as he looked at her things stacked near the front door.

"Mr. Matt, Carlos told me that my tribe, my people, are camped near the back pasture of Miss Kathleen's land. I need to use the horse and buggy, if you do not care."

Matt stood very still and listened to Lucy tell why she wanted to go and see her sister. "I want to go in town and get some supplies to take to them."

"You can have anything you need Lucy, but you cannot go alone. I will tell one of the boys to go with you. They can stay away from your people but I do not want you to travel to see your people by yourself. While in town, get anything you want to take them and have it charged to my account."

"I use my money," she said very proudly.

********

In Mrs. Washington's boarding house, Lillian was fuming. She had been pacing up and down in the room that Matt had rented for her until the stage returned. *Mr. Moore has another thing coming if he thinks for one minute that I am going to sit in this room while waiting on a stagecoach,* she thought. She was not going to return to Abilene. She wanted to make Matt change his mind about their engagement and she had to be near him to do that. She had come to Sweetwater to marry him and that was what she was going to do. Matt acted as if he did not want her but she could feel his desire for her when she rubbed up against him. He still wanted her and she wasn't going to let one of the wealthiest men in Texas get away.

After having a weak moment and running away with that young buck, Andrew, and writing Matt a note, she soon discovered that she had made the biggest mistake of her life. Her young lover had taken her money and deserted her in a ghost town about fifty miles from Abilene. Once settled back at home, in Abilene's rooming house, the local banker had a little too much to drink. He had leaned across the dining table and scolded her for being so foolish. He had divulged that Matt was one of the richest men in Texas and she had tossed him aside for a younger man. Lillian could not believe her ears. She knew that Matt had always worked hard, did not drink or gamble away his money like so many of his trail hands did. "Over the years, that Moore fellow made great investments," whispered the banker.

Matt had courted her for nearly five years and she had been faithful to him all that time. *Well, as far as he knows*, she thought. She was not going to sit on her tuff and allow another woman to win his heart and his bank account when she knew that he still had feelings for her. She was going to repack her belongings, and go back to the stage line. Once she cashed in her return ticket to Abilene, she would head straight to Matt's new ranch. She was going to settle in and make him change his mind about her.

Once Lillian had completed her packing, she went down to the parlor to thank Mrs. Washington for the room and return her key. Mrs. Washington was speechless as Lillian slapped the room key in her hand. Lillian said she would be back shortly with a carriage to pick up her luggage.

Lillian paraded down to the stage depot and told the little man that she was cashing in her ticket that Mr. Moore had left there for her.

"But Miss, Mr. Moore said that you would be picking up the ticket and using it to go back to Abilene."

"My plans have changed. Give me the ticket," she demanded. The clerk handed over the ticket and she immediately gave it back to him. "Now my good man, cash in this ticket."

After counting out the refund for the ticket, she placed the money into her small drawstring purse and marched away toward the livery stable. The little old man leaned out the ticket window and watched her go into the office that connected the barn and livery.

Al Thornbees was writing some figures in his account book when he heard a sound at the front of his office. As he glanced up, he was very surprised to see a lovely woman with golden blond hair marching toward him like an army sergeant on a mission. He jumped up from his chair sending it rolling backward about three feet from where he was sitting.

"Good day, madam," he said while removing his dirty, stained black hat. "Names Albert Thornbees, but you can call me Big Al. What can I do for you this fine morning?"

"I need to rent a horse and carriage and I need someone to drive me. I have some luggage that I will need to pick-up and take with me. It is at the boarding house. Do you think that you can help me?"

"May I ask where you're headed with my equipment?"

"I am going to Matt Moore's ranch. I am his fiancée and I will be residing at his place while we are preparing for the wedding."

"Well, well, well. This is good news. I had heard that you had arrived but I was also told that you were leaving—soon."

"Now, Big Al," said Lillian as she laid her soft hand on his chest, touching some of his black chest hairs. "Don't believe everything that you hear?"

"I guess you have proven that statement to be true, that's for sure." Al was thrilled to hear that this flirtation, sassy, blonde-haired woman was going to be hitched to that Moore fellow. He was worried that Kathleen might have an interest in him. With Moore out of the picture, he could continue with his own pursuit. He was going to win Kathleen's hand in marriage or die trying. He did not need someone getting in his way. He wanted her ranch and he intended to turn it into an empire.

"Jeffrey!" Al bellowed for the youngster who worked part-time for him.

"Yes sir, Mr. Thornbees. What can I do for you?"

"Nothing for me, but I want you to drive this lady out to Matt Moore's ranch. Stop at the boarding house and get her luggage. Now, don't be late getting back here."

Once Jeffrey loaded her luggage into the carriage, he drove Lillian out to Mr. Matt Moore's ranch. As they got near, Jeffrey pulled the horse to a stop. "Yonder it is, right over that hillside. We'll be there in just a few minutes."

Lillian reached into her small purse that she had wrapped around her wrist and pulled out a comb and small mirror. Jeffrey watched as she patted her hat and smoothed a few strands of hair. She pushed out her lips and pinched her cheeks until they turned red. He was in awe of her as she looked into that small mirror at herself.

"Now, I feel a little bit more presentable. What do you think?" She turned her face toward Jeffrey and smiled.

"Gosh, madam," Jeffrey stuttered as he felt the blood rushing to his face. "I can't rightly say about you being pres-er-able, but you shore are nice to look at."

Lillian laughed and thanked the young man. She guessed he was about thirteen. He was a very handsome young man with soft brown hair and big round cinnamon eyes. Soon, the young girls would be giggling every time he got close to them, thought Lillian.

Jeffrey drove the carriage as close as he could to the front door. He jumped down, walked quickly over to the door, and knocked loudly several times. He called to the inside of the house but received no answer,

"Sorry, madam, but no one is at home."

"Most folks in the country never lock their doors. Turn the door knob and see if it will open."

Jeffery turned back to the door and gave the doorknob a good twist and sure enough, it opened. "You were right; the door is unlocked but do you think you should go in without anyone being here?"

"Young man, this is going to be my home in a couple weeks. I believe that I am welcome to enter. Now, get my luggage and be quick about it. I want to go in and get settled while Mr. Moore is away."

Lillian reached into her purse and brought out her small hand mirror again. She looked at herself and patted her hair. The young man shook his head as he thought that he had never been around anyone who spruced up as much as this pretty woman did. Of course, he was inexperienced when it came to girls and pretty women-folk.

Lillian gave Jeffrey fifty cents, told him good-bye, and quickly shut the front door behind him. She was relieved to have the house to herself. Quickly inspecting the house from room to room, she was pleasantly surprised to find the house in good order. All the furniture was dusted and clean and the kitchen was spotless. She opened a door to a large bedroom and discovered it had to be Matt's room. A very large bed with a pretty quilt was in the center of the room between two tall windows. There were not any curtains decorating the windows. Of course, she would soon make this a more suitable room for a new married couple. She walked across the hall and looked into another bedroom. It appeared to be a guest room except for a bedroll lying up against a wall. Why is that old bedroll in this room when there is a perfectly nice double bed, thought Lillian?

She retrieved her luggage from the foyer and settled into the guest room. She wanted to be unpacked and prepared for Matt's temper before he returned. After making herself a light supper, she was exhausted. She decided that she would go to bed and rest. Once Matt returned, she would get up and surprise him. She smiled to herself as she pulled the covers up around her chin and went fast asleep.

# Chapter 9

After Lucy had gathered all the supplies that she was going to take to her sister, she could not locate Matt's ranch hand anywhere. She asked the dry goods store clerk if he knew the whereabouts of Joseph Garcia and he said that he had walked across the street to the Red Garter Saloon with a couple of other guys. With the help of the clerk, she had packed everything in her wagon and climbed upon the high bench. After waiting patiently for Joseph's return, she took the reins in hand and drove herself out of town. While Lucy was driving near Kathleen's ranch, Sammy waved to her as he rode his horse along the corral fence. Once she got closer to the fence, he yelled to Lucy, "Where you going Miss Lucy?"

"My old tribe is camped near the back end of Kathleen's land. I want to go and see my older sister."

"Golly, I ain't never seen real Indians before, except for you I mean. Can I ride out there with you? I promise to be no trouble."

Lucy smiled as she thought about Sammy's comment that he had never seen an Indian before. She understood his curiosity. She had never been away from her tribe. It was after having to live among the white man that she learned their ways.

"Come. You must stay close to me. Tie your horse to the back of the wagon. I might let you drive."

Lucy and Sammy drove the wagon as fast as they could over the rough terrain and trails through the woods and out in the open pastures. After what seemed like hours, they finally reached the area of woods where the tribe had camped. Lucy ordered Sammy to stay with the wagon and horses. She would come back for the supplies in a few minutes. He nodded as she got down and started walking slowly toward the campsite. She was afraid because she was not sure if she would be welcomed, but she was determined to see her sister. Once several dogs and children had spotted her, the dogs barked and the children watched. A small boy raced away yelling for his mama to come quickly. A group of Indian braves formed a line on the hillside and watched as she approached. With her insides trembling, she saw her two nephews. She did not flinch. She would die before she showed her true feelings—fear. The young and old members of the tribe appeared to be surprised to see that the old squaw had survived alone in the wilderness. Many moons had passed and she should have been dead by now. One of her nephews who she recognized as White Feather, stepped forward, but did not say anything.

Lucy spoke first. "I came bearing gifts," she said pointing to the wagon. Lucy looked at her young nephew, as he made no sign that she had even spoken to him. He looked toward the wagon and at Sammy. Finally, he signaled with his right hand. A young Indian boy raced toward the teepees. She was sure the child was going to get her sister. Lucy looked past the men and saw many teepees and small children milling around barefooted and shirtless. She was pleased that she had purchased peppermint sticks, big bags of sugar, cornmeal, coffee, and several cans of molasses syrup. She remembered to bring tobacco and flint. Everything she brought was useful and needed.

It was not long before she heard a commotion coming through the crowd that had gathered. Her sister, Wise Mother, was walking slowly with the aid of her two daughters-in-law. Her oldest son, White Feather, stepped in front of his mama and said something that no one else could hear. He made several hand gestures that told Lucy he was trying to prevent the visit between the two sisters.

At first, Lucy thought her sister might turn around and leave without seeing her, but to her surprise she said something to her son in their native tongue. Her words were loud and harsh. White Feather stepped away from his mama and allowed her to pass. Lucy stepped forward with a big smile and embraced her older sister. She was surprised to see that her sister's health had gotten worse.

"I prayed you would survive this cruel world, Prairie Flower," said her sister in little more than a whisper.

"It was hard at first, but the Spirits have been good and provided for me. I keep white man's house who is a good man. I need nothing. I heard that you were near, so I brought some gifts." As Lucy was speaking softly to her sister, Sammy had eased down off the wagon and walked to her side. He was watching the Indian braves and all the smaller children. "Sister, this is my protector today, Sammy. He came with me to help. He has never seen real Indians before. He is very brave."

"Bless you, child. May the Spirits protect and guide you on this earth." Sammy quickly hung his head and said thank you.

"Sammy, will you help the young braves get the supplies that we brought my sister and pass out the peppermint sticks to the younger children." Lucy reached into the back of the wagon and pulled out a big heavy fur coat. She wrapped it around her sister's shoulders and hugged her for the last time. Lucy knew in her heart that she would never see her sister again.

Sammy took Lucy's hand and attempted to help her to their wagon. He was sure that the Indians Spirits' were surrounding them. As they drove away, he turned to see the younger children waving their peppermint sticks in the air. Most of their lips were covered with the sticky candy.

Lucy drove away from the light of the campfires into the darkness. She pulled to a stop, reached behind the seat, and got a big lantern. After lighting the lantern, she tied it to the front side of the wagon where it would cast light out for her to see the trail. The horse had a great sense of direction in the dark, but the light made her feel better. The moon was hiding behind some evening clouds, which made for a very dark night.

Back at the ranch house, Rosa was beside herself. She had sent Juan and Pedro out to look for Sammy. When he didn't come in for supper, they thought he was down by the lake fishing and had lost track of time.

Kathleen arrived home from a long day at the café and heard Carlos talking to his sons about going after Sammy. "What's going on? Where's Sammy?" Kathleen's heart was racing with fear that something had happened to the child who had won her heart.

As the small group was huddled together in the front yard, Matt rode up and slowly got off his horse. "Good evening," he said. He looked from Kathleen to Carlos and knew instantly that something was wrong. "What's going on?"

"Oh, Matt," Kathleen answered as she hurried to his side and took his arm. "Sammy is missing." Matt wrapped his reins across the hitching post and took Kathleen's hands into his big rough hands.

"Kathleen, I'm sure Sammy is with Lucy. After I told her that her people were camped on your land, she wanted to go to them." Carlos said very quickly as he looked at Matt.

"Lucy was headed out to the north pasture to take supplies to her old tribe members. She was desperate to see her sister. I told her she could not go alone so one of my ranch hands was going to go with her. She should be home by now." Matt stood with his hands on his hips looking toward the dark road.

"No sir, she's not home. We just came from your place. Joseph, one of your new hands, said that he was to go with her, but when he finished with his business in town, he could not find her anywhere. The other fellows had not seen anything of her today. They were grumbling that they had to cook their own supper," said Juan.

"The Indians are camped on the north end of your pasture, Kathleen. They are passing by on your land heading to Oklahoma. I am sure they will help themselves to a couple of your cows. They're a scruffy looking bunch." Carlos said as he looked at Kathleen.

"I don't care what they do with my cattle as long as they don't harm Sammy." Kathleen replied.

"Kathleen, I'm sure Lucy will protect the boy with her life if needed." Matt said very firmly. "Carlos, can your boys ride with me to go after Lucy and Sammy?"

"Si," Carlos said as he looked toward the open road. A light was waving side to side as a signal and the jingle of harnesses could be heard in the wind.

"Look, I see a wagon. It's Lucy and Sammy," Carlos said as he started walking to the corner of the corral.

Kathleen walked around Matt and stood next to Carlos as Rosa made the sign of the cross, praying silently. Lucy drove the wagon as close to the group as possible.

"Oh Lucy, we were so worried about you and Sammy,"

Kathleen cried.

"Sammy, climb down from that wagon right this minute. You have had us worried to death. I've a good mine not to give you any supper." Rosa was so happy to see Sammy but she could not control her anger. She wanted him to know that he could not disappear like that ever again.

"I'm sorry Rosa," he said. "I had to go with Lucy to see her sister. We were never in any danger since the Spirits were surrounding us with their protection."

"Spirits! Heaven help me," said Rosa.

"Please don't make me go to bed hungry." Big tears formed in his big blue eyes as he rubbed them. He wasn't only hungry, he was exhausted, too. He had missed his lunch and mid-day siesta.

Rosa scooped the child up in her arms and cradled him as if he was a small infant. "Oh, my little be'be. I feed you good. But, you can't go off without telling someone, you understand?"

Matt walked over to the wagon and helped Lucy down. "Did you get to see your sister and give her the supplies?" Matt was very concerned about his little Indian housekeeper.

"Yes, Mr. Matt. She is well. They needed the supplies," she said as she remembered the small children. "I want to go home." Lucy turned to Kathleen and said that she should have taken a minute to tell someone that Sammy was going with her. Kathleen reached for her and hugged her tight. Lucy liked the hug because it was rare for her people to embrace each other in a loving way.

With a lump in her throat, she bid Kathleen and the others goodbye. "Tell Rosa I come tomorrow." Lucy turned to get back in the wagon when Matt took her by the elbow and stopped her. "Lucy, where is my ranch hand that I ordered to go with you?"

"After I get supplies, he was nowhere to be found. I waited for a while and then left without him. Sammy was riding his horse in the corral when I passed by here. He begged to go with me so I let him. I should not let him go with me."

"He should have asked Rosa first before he left with you. Both of you are home now and that is good. I will drive you to the ranch. Let me tie my horse to the back of your wagon."

Matt bid Kathleen goodnight and said, "I wanted to talk to you tonight but we'll do it another time."

Matt knew that Lucy was sad after visiting with her sister so they drove home in silence. He stopped in front of the house to let Lucy get down. He didn't share with her the news about Lillian. He was pleased that she would be gone in three days and things could get back to normal. He had a lot of work to do with his new herd. He had to place his brand on each cow. This wasn't a job that he liked, but a very necessary one. He didn't have time to worry about a scheming, lying woman.

Lucy entered the dark house and lit the lantern that sat on a table in the foyer. A luminous glow lit the room, casting shadows all around. Lucy went straight to the kitchen and lit another lantern. She went into the pantry and sliced herself a piece of pie. She noticed crumbs on the counter where the fresh baked apple pie sat earlier. After drinking a big dipper of cold water, she went into her bedroom and entered the water closet. Her eyes had adjusted to the dark so she didn't bother to light another lantern. After dressing in a long cotton gown, she unbraided her hair and combed it out with her fingers. As she started moving toward her bed, she saw movement coming from under her covers. Tiptoeing back to the table, she lit the lantern and carried it over to the bed. Bending down close to the pillow, she saw a golden haired woman sleeping soundly. Holding the lantern above her head, she leaned closer to get a better look. Sensing someone in the room with her, the woman sat up in the bed and screamed. Immediately, Lucy stepped back away from the scared woman.

"Who are you?" Lillian screamed at Lucy. "Get away from me you dirty Indian. I have a gun. I will shoot!" Lillian was up on her knees holding the quilt under her chin like a shield. Her eyes were wild with fright and she could not stop screaming nasty words at the petite Indian woman.

Matt had placed his horse and Lucy's in the stable. He had given Lucy's horse an extra rub down and fed both animals a bucket of oats. He walked by the bunkhouse and signaled good night to his men as he blew out the lantern. Hanging it on a side door of the barn, he walked toward the house. Matt stepped up on the front porch when he heard a blood-curdling scream coming from inside the house.

"What the hell!" Matt scrambled for his rifle that he kept by the front door and charged into Lucy's room. He yelled Lucy's name as he took in the scene before him.

Lucy was standing beside the bed holding a lantern above her head while Lillian was screaming like someone was attempting to murder her. She cowered down behind her bed covers.

Lillian was here in his house—in Lucy's bed. *Gosh Almighty, what next,* thought Matt.

"Oh Matt, darling! Thank goodness, you're here! This filthy squaw was fixing to scalp me. Make her go away, please!" Lillian was sitting on her knees as she pointed to the door. "I won't stay a minute in this house with that Indian."

"Shut the hell up, Lillian, before I have to gag you," Matt said. "You don't have to worry about anyone bothering you because as soon as it's daylight you're going back to the boarding house."

Lillian settled down on her backside on the bed and lowered her face as she pretended to cry. Watching her pitiful performance, Matt turned to Lucy. "I'm sorry about this. Do you mind sleeping in the other guest room tonight?" With his arm across her shoulders he whispered, "Please don't worry about this woman and I apologize for her ugly words toward you."

Lucy turned and sat the lantern down on the table as she left the room. She made no reply to Matt. She knew she would be up early to pack and go to Kathleen's ranch. The crazy blond woman was here to stay, even if Mr. Matt didn't know it yet.

Matt whirled around and faced Lillian again after he watched Lucy close the door to the guest bedroom.

"Now that we are alone, I want to know what the hell you think you are doing by coming out here where you know you aren't welcome. I made myself perfectly clear that we are finished as a couple. We are not getting married—ever!"

"Oh Matt, you know that I have told you over and over how sorry I am. I will never betray you again. I love you and only you. Come, let me show you how much I care," she said as she reached her arms out to him, allowing her gown to slide off one shoulder and show her soft white breast.

As Matt stood looking at her, he wondered what in the world had ever made him think that he loved this woman enough to ask for her hand in marriage. Matt walked slowly over to the bed. He reached his hand out and touched Lillian soft gown jerking it back up on her shoulder.

"I want you packed and ready to leave at first light. I am

taking you back to town and don't even think about coming here again."

"I'm not leaving here, and you can't make me. Please, let me stay here," she pouted with real tears in her eyes. "I won't be any trouble."

Matt sighed and turned as he left the room without answering her pleads. "Hell, I don't know what I'm going to do," he said under his breath.

# Chapter 10

With the rooster announcing the beginning of a new day, Matt walked out to the bunkhouse to give his men a piece of his mind for not going with Lucy to the Indian camp. Instead, she had a six-year-old boy with her. He told them that if they could not obey his orders and directions, they needed to pack up and leave. His orders were to be obeyed to the letter.

Matt went back into the house to get his first cup of coffee and some good hot biscuits. Instead, he found a cold coffee pot and no biscuits. More important, Lucy was not there. He searched the guest room and found it empty. The bed looked like no one had slept there. It was very neat and clean. "Damn," he said aloud.

He walked to Lucy's room and pushed opened the door. Lillian was sleeping soundly. A soft snore came from under Lucy's quilt that Lillian had pulled over her body.

Matt went back out to the bunkhouse and helped himself to a cup of the boy's coffee. He told the men that they had to cook for themselves today. He didn't want to go into details about Lucy's departure. He was really hoping he could go and talk to her about returning.

He laid out the chores for the day that included branding of the cattle. Each ranch hand had a task to complete. He told them that he had an errand to do and he would be back in two hours.

Matt rode over to Kathleen's ranch to check on Lucy. He was sure that she had walked over there earlier that morning because the horse and carriage that she used was still in the barn. He really wanted her to return because she had only been gone one morning and his house felt cold and empty without her.

When he arrived at Kathleen's house, she was already dressed and ready to head to town to work at the cafe. Everyone was awake having a hot delicious breakfast. The aroma of fresh coffee was coming out onto the porch as he stood and knocked on the door.

"Good morning, Matt," said Carlos. "Come in. Lucy is getting ready to go into town with Kathleen this morning. She's in the kitchen." Carlos stepped aside and allowed Matt to enter the house as he placed his sombrero on his head and walked toward the barn.

"Morning, Mr. Matt," Rosa said. "Come, sit. I will pour you some coffee and you can join Sammy for some flapjacks and bacon."

"That sounds good, Rosa but I don't want to put you to any trouble. I had a good cook until last night. Sure was hoping I could get her to return home with me."

"Sit. Eat. Maybe she will listen to reason in a little while."

Kathleen rushed into the kitchen and was surprised to see Matt sitting at the breakfast table. "Well, this is a surprise. Why are you here so early?"

"I know you've talked to Lucy. Don't act like you don't know who's over at my place."

"Yes, she told us earlier. Lucy feels that she is not wanted and she is not going to return to your ranch as long as that woman is there."

Matt placed his hands over his face and shook his head. "Damn it, I don't deserve any of this. You know that fool woman says she isn't leaving until it's time for the stage and now Lucy is up in arms and has left me." Matt pushed back his chair from the table and looked at Sammy. His eyes were as big as saucers as he listened. Matt knew he should not be having this conversation in front of the child.

"Walk out with me, Kathleen." As he moved to go outside he thanked Rosa for the breakfast and he noticed Lucy hiding behind the bedroom door.

"Lucy, please come out here. Please."

"I'm here, Mr. Matt. I not go back to your place while crazy white woman there. I didn't try to scalp her, but maybe I should have cut out her tongue."

Matt tossed back his head and laughed. "Yes, that might have solved all of our problems. Well, Lucy, I don't blame you for being upset with her. She wasn't very nice and I am sorry for the way she treated you last night. You do know that she was afraid of you, because she has never been around Indians. She has only heard bad stories of Indians raiding wagon trains and killing people."

"She don't want me there. I not go where I not wanted. I stay here until she goes away. Then, I come back home."

Matt sighed and shook his head side to side. "Is that a promise? You will come back to my ranch in a few days?"

Lucy smiled at Matt for the first time while nodding her head. She turned and went back into the bedroom to finish getting ready to go to the café with Kathleen.

As Matt retrieved the reins from the hitching post, he noticed Kathleen was still waiting outside for him. He noticed that her shoulders were shaking with laughter as she held her hand over her mouth. His uneasiness vanished quickly as he joined her laughter. The guilty feeling disappeared as he told her he didn't really see one damn thing funny about his situation.

"Oh, Matt," Kathleen said as she wiped her eyes, "you really have a problem. I was so happy you had everything under control and she would be leaving. Now it seems matters are worse."

Kathleen circled Matt and sashayed back into the house to get her things for work. She grinned and said to him, "I was sure you could handle one little gal from Abilene."

Matt shook his head and cussed under his breath as he limped to his horse and mounted it. He rode straight to town and stopped at Dr. Squires' office. He wanted the doc to examine his leg and make sure it had mended properly. For the past week, he had managed to walk on it without the aid of a cane. It did not ache or pain him any longer, but if he was going to sit in a saddle for days, he wanted to be sure the leg was well enough for riding long and hard.

He had planned to talk with Kathleen last night about driving her herd to Abilene before the weather turned too cold. Carlos had spoken to him privately about the taxes that were due soon. Kathleen's job at the café had been paying the ranch's daily expenses, but there was no extra for the taxes due at the end of the year. Matt knew that Kathleen wanted to ask him to take her herd to Abilene to sell, but she would not consider asking until his leg was well.

Matt needed to hire six or eight men and get prepared to make the one-hundred-mile trip. If they left within the next two weeks, they could be back before Christmas and Kathleen could quit her job. She would have enough money to last several years without worrying about her taxes and other expenses needed to run her big spread. Once he was sure that his unwanted houseguest had left town, he was going to make his final plans. With enough men, he could charge some of the local ranchers to take part of their herd along with Kathleen's herd. This arrangement would give her some extra money for her ranch, too.

Kathleen had left Matt on the front porch as she and Lucy finished getting ready for another big day at the café. Kathleen was angry that Matt's old girlfriend had shown up and talked ugly to Lucy, but she was happy to have her old friend working with her again, even for a little while. As they prepared everything in the kitchen for the big breakfast crowd, which had grown to a sizeable number every morning, Al Thornbees entered. He walked over to a table by the window and took his seat. Lucy walked softly over to him with the big coffee pot in her hands. Before Lucy could pour him a cup of the hot brew, he said under his breath, "Git old woman. Send Kathleen over to my table."

Lucy turned away from him and eased over to Kathleen. With a nod, she spoke and said, "The stable man wants you to come to his table."

"You take care of him. I'm busy here at the moment."

"No." Lucy walked through the bat-winged doors leading into the kitchen.

Kathleen watched Lucy walk away. It was not like Lucy to be rude to a customer or short tempered with her. Big Al had to have said something to make her act that way. Kathleen took her orders into the kitchen to begin preparing them. Al came to the swinging doors and pushed one side open. "Can't a man get service around here or do I have to come in here and whip up my own eggs."

Lucy turned her back and grabbed a bag of trash to take outside. She wanted nothing to do with that big man who wore big britches and thought he could get Kathleen's attention.

Lucy's disappearing act didn't go unnoticed by Kathleen or Mrs. Porter. "Go back into the dining room Al. I will be there in a moment. There were customers ahead of you this morning."

"You can't make an exception for an admirer of yours?" He said as he leaned up against the wall grinning like a fool in love.

Kathleen reached under the counter and pulled out a big yellow bowl containing clean fresh eggs. "You can stand there all morning if you like, but there are still three stacks of hot cakes and scrambled eggs to be cooked before I get to you."

Lucy came back inside and grabbed the coffee pot on the back of the stove as she walked pass the owner of the livery. "You better get out of the doorway. I'd hate for Lucy to scald you with coffee." Al gave Lucy a grin and returned to his table. Lucy served everyone coffee, but the man she now referred to in her thoughts as *big blue britches.*

As Al sat reading the *Sweetwater News*, the local newspaper put out every Friday by Charles W. Doolittle, a lovely blond haired woman came through the door. Al recognized her as Matt Moore's fiancée. He wondered why she had returned to town so soon. Al stood and motioned for her to sit at his table. "Please Madam; you may join me at my table since all the others are occupied."

"Well, that's mighty gracious of you. Aren't you the owner of the livery?"

"Names Al Thornbees and you're Miss Lillian Larson."

"You have a good memory." Glancing around at the busy little café, she said. "How does anyone get service around here?"

Mrs. Porter walked over to the table and said good morning. "What can I get you to eat?"

"Finally," she said very sternly. "Coffee first, with cream and sugar. Hurry, I have been awake for hours."

Kathleen came through the kitchen doors carrying a large platter of hot flapjacks, scrambled eggs and a pile of crisp bacon. She stopped suddenly when she saw the new customer. She stood out because she was dressed in fancy city clothes. She knew immediately that this had to be Matt's old flame from Abilene. Al grinned when he made eye contact with Kathleen. He beamed because he thought her actions were because she was jealous of the lovely woman sitting with him. After Kathleen served her customers, she re-entered the kitchen and asked Mrs. Porter if she knew the woman sitting at Al's table.

"You mean the 'Queen', Miss High and Mighty?" she replied sarcastically. "She demanded that I hurry with her coffee. You can see that's just what I'm doing." She was sitting at the worktable sipping a fresh cup of coffee. Kathleen could not help but laugh, "You and Lucy have shown me a side of yourselves that I didn't know existed."

"Well, the Queen is sitting with Al and both have demanded special treatment." All three women laughed as Kathleen started preparing more food. Mrs. Porter slipped out of her chair and went out to take Lillian and Al's orders.

"Lucy, please go and refresh the royal couple's coffee cups please," said Mrs. Porter, "while I help Kathleen."

"I don't think they want me to serve them."

"Go now, don't worry. They want coffee." Mrs. Porter had her hands full of dirty dishes.

Lucy hesitated at the stove and finally picked up the blue granite pot and walked out into the café. She walked around pouring everyone a refill and ended up standing beside the table where Lillian and Al sat. As Lucy began pouring coffee into Lillian's cup, Lillian jerked back away from her causing the tablecloth to shift on the table. Lucy stopped pouring as Lillian screamed at her. "Look what you're doing? You are trying to scald me. Get away from me before I call the sheriff and have you put in jail." Lucy backed away from the table still holding the coffee pot.

Kathleen came out of the kitchen and saw Lucy backing away from the blond woman. Al was smiling like a big baboon.

"What's going on in here? I could hear screaming all the way down the street," yelled Mr. Crocker as he came charging into the front door of his café like a big roaring bull. He was late coming to the café because he had banking business.

"I told this old squaw to stay away from me last night and now this morning she is trying to scald me with coffee." Lillian was pointing at Lucy while Mr. Crocker looked all around at everyone. As Lillian continued to shout at Mr. Crocker, Kathleen eased around to stand beside Lucy.

"I'm not eating in a place that allows Indians to serve people," Lillian screeched. As she attempted to get out of her chair, she bumped into Kathleen's platter of food that she was holding. Losing control of the platter, all the breakfast food slipped onto Lillian's chest and in her lap. The food splashed on her face and in her lovely hair.

Kathleen was as surprised as Lillian was. The women customers snickered and the men howled with laughter at the scene-taking place in front of them. Kathleen mumbled, "Oh, my" and tried her best not to laugh.

"You did that on purpose you filthy Indian!" Lillian screamed as many of the customers looked from one woman to the next. Kathleen did not know what to do at first. She grabbed a dishtowel and attempted to wipe some of the food off Lillian's soiled dress.

"Keep your hands off me— you *Indian lover!*"

"Al!" bellowed Mr. Crocker. "You better take your lady friend out of my place before I grab her by that blond hair and toss her fanny out onto the street. No one comes in my place and insults my women folk." He looked at Lillian and told her she was not welcome in his establishment again. Several of the regular customers clapped their hands and nodded in agreement with Mr. Crocker.

Al stammered and tried to say that Lillian was not his woman. He had just given her a place to sit. No one wanted to listen to his excuses as Mr. Crocker practically pushed him out the front door with Lillian.

Once out on the boardwalk, Lillian stomped her dainty foot and screamed, "Just look at me!" Lillian was trying to shake food off her skirt and off her bosom. "I've got to get this sticky mess off me. Do you have a place that I can get clean? I can't ride home with food all over me."

Al was so embarrassed that all he wanted to do was get away from this crazy, mean-spirited woman. She really had messed things up for him today with Kathleen. He had planned to ask Kathleen if he could take her to church this Sunday. He knew he would have to wait a few days to get back in her good graces because of this ill-mannered woman. He sighed and looked up and down the street. He knew customers in the café were watching him and Lillian, but he had to help her. He gave her a hard look but he did feel sorry for her. She pleaded with him for help as she fought back tears.

"Follow me; I have a house next door to my livery where you can get cleaned. I sure was wanting some of that good breakfast. Damn, if I ain't hungry."

"Listen to me, you pee-brain! You make it sound like I asked her to pour that hot food on me. I would not have ridden all the way into town if I had not been starving myself. I haven't had anything to eat since yesterday."

"Hey, lady! No more name-calling if you want my help. Because of you, I might not be able to eat at the Heavenly Hash Café anymore myself."

"Heavenly Hash! What a name. Lord help me. I have to get myself back out to Matt's ranch as soon as I get this oatmeal off my body. It is sticky and it feels like glue."

As they entered Al's small house, he went into the bedroom, got a washcloth and towel, and laid them on the bed. "I'll bring in some hot water as soon as it's ready. You can undress in the bedroom."

Lillian looked around the small structure and was surprised to find it very neat and clean. The table and hutch were of solid oak. In the bedroom, a large four-poster bed had big fluffy pillows and a wedding ring pattern quilt. *Of course, he would have a big bed,* she thought. *He is a very big man.* She walked over to the single window and pulled the curtains together. She removed her dress and using the dry towel, she wiped the food off her face and neck. She looked in the mirror and tried to pick dried oatmeal out of her hair.

Al had gone outside to the well and pulled up a bucket of fresh water. After placing it on the stove to get hot, he walked over to the partially closed bedroom door and watched Lillian as she stood in front of the mirror in only her camisole and crinoline half-slip. He watched her run her hand over the top of her breasts after she wiped food off her chest. She looked in the mirror at Al as he walked into the bedroom as she was preparing to remove her camisole.

Al pushed the bedroom door opened all the way, as he walked in unannounced. He poured the warm water into a floral pitcher as she continued watching him in the mirror. "You need any help?" He asked as he sat the empty bucket on the floor, never taking his eyes off her body.

"Help? What kind of help can you offer me?" she purred. He eased over to her and reached for the silk ribbon on her camisole. As he began to untie it, his husky voice said, "Why don't you let me surprise you?"

# Chapter 11

Later in the evening, Matt returned to his ranch to find Lillian sitting on his front porch. As he rode his big bay gelding into the yard, he glanced at her and continued to the barn as she stood to watch him. His three young ranch hands followed closely behind him.

"Mr. Matt, do you think your new woman has cooked supper for us like Lucy? I'm so hungry I can feel my backbone all the way through my stomach," said Tim, the youngest of the men.

"Let's get this damn straight. She ain't my woman. She's leaving as soon as the stage arrives. And, no she has not cooked any supper. You boys will have to cook your own supper, for a while anyways. That woman, on the porch, don't cook."

As the men unsaddled their horses, Matt heard grumbling about which one of them was going to cook tonight. "I feel like going to get Lucy and bringing her home," Joseph said.

Matt walked slowly to the house. He was tired and he did not intend to listen to his uninvited houseguest's whining and complaints. She had best stay out of his way. After branding the fifty head of cattle and repairing fences, all he wanted was a hot bath and his clean bed.

As Matt strolled over to the front porch, he removed his wide-brimmed Stetson and patted it on the side of his good leg. "Lillian," he said as he gave her a nod.

"Oh, Matt, I didn't think you would ever return today. This has been such an awful day for me. I went into town to get something to eat and I was mistreated by those women who work at the café."

"Lillian, I don't want to hear about your day. If you do not like it here or in town, you can leave. You will be leaving my ranch in two days, if not sooner. Now, I am going in to take a bath, and hit the hay. Step aside," he said as he opened the screen door and went in to the kitchen to heat some bathwater.

"But Matt, you don't understand," she said as she trailed behind him. "There's no one here to cook or clean. I had to go to town to get something to eat. You need to hire a housekeeper."

Ignoring Lillian, Matt walked into the pantry and gathered some food. He tossed a loaf of day old bread on the table beside the bowl of butter. He reached in the cabinet and set a jar of blackberry jam beside his plate. "Supper," he said as he lifted a bucket of cold water on to the stove.

"Why can't you hire a housekeeper? I cannot eat bread and butter. That awful man at the café said I couldn't eat at his place anymore, like I care."

"I can tell you really made a good impression on our local citizens."

"It was all that stinking Indian's fault!" said Lillian, as she made an ugly face.

Matt jerked his head up from spreading butter on his bread. "You mean Lucy?"

"Yes! She tried to scald me with coffee while I was in the café waiting on my breakfast. A tall skinny woman came over and dumped a whole platter of food all over me."

Matt could not help but laugh. He knew the tall skinny girl had to be Kathleen. He could see her defending Lucy by retaliating in some way.

"You think the way they treated me was funny, don't you? Thank goodness Al was there to help me."

"Big Al? That big ox from the livery?"

"Yes, he was a perfect gentleman and took me to his place so I could get clean. I had oatmeal in my hair and all down my dress."

"I'm sure you compensated him for his services." Matt went out the back door leaving Lillian staring after him with her mouth open.

Matt came back in the kitchen carrying a galvanized tub and went straight to his bedroom. Lillian trailed behind him demanding to know what he meant by that nasty remark.

"Woman, get out of my way and go finish your supper. I do not have to explain my words to you. You know what I meant. You showed me what kind of woman you are while I was away on cattle drives." Matt stopped and turned facing her. "You know what is funny. I always pictured you working in your dress shop sewing and waiting patiently for my return. What a fool you played me for."

After Matt had completed his bath, he went to bed. He laid thinking about this awful situation. He hoped that after Lillian left on the stagecoach, he could have a long talk with Kathleen. She was on his mind constantly. He pictured her sitting on her porch swing tossing her head back laughing as he drifted into a deep sleep.

Matt was so tired he was drifting in and out of sleep. He felt Katy's soft hands rubbing his back and kissing his chest. He nuzzled her neck while listening to her sweet cooing words in his ear. While rubbing his callous hands over her back, as he placed his face in her hair, something did not feel right. He shook his head and lifted his face to look down on his love that he cradled in his arms.

"Heaven help me!" he said, and gave Lillian a big push off his bed. She landed on her backside on the hard wooden floor. Matt sat up and looked down on the uninvited intruder. "Get yourself out of my room. I pick and choose my whore whenever I want one."

"Oh Matt," she cried as she pulled herself up on the edge of his bed. "You know you want me. Please—let me love you. We shared many great times together. We were going to be married for goodness sakes." Lillian stood before Matt pleading to him to change his mind while holding a very thin cotton shift over her naked body.

Wearing only his white knee length cotton underwear, he got out of bed, grabbed Lillian's arm, and led her across his room to the door. He opened it and pushed her out into the hall, locked the door and returned to his bed. "Lord, help me," he said as he covered his head with his pillow. Lillian was screaming every ugly, obscene word she could as she banged on his door.

********

The sun was peeking over the top of the tall pine trees as Kathleen, Lucy and Sammy were driving the small carriage into town. Kathleen had enrolled Sammy in the public school and today was his first day. It was too early for school to begin so he would eat breakfast and sweep the dining room floor at the café to earn a nickel. He could hardly wait to show Mrs. Porter and Mr. Crocker his new cowboy boots and new denim pants. He was wearing the nicest clothes that he had ever owned and he was so proud. He was excited about going to school because Carlos had told him that he would make friends with other children. Lucy had said that he would learn to read and he could teach her, because she wanted to read white man's words.

In her white shirtwaist and blue skirt, Kathleen got down off her carriage in the livery. Lucy and Sammy got down and walked on ahead toward the café. Al Thornbees came hurrying out of his small office wearing his blue overalls with no shirt. He was using his big red bandana to wipe his breakfast off his chin.

"Morning, Miss Kathleen. How are you this fine morning?" he said while stuffing the bandana in his back pocket.

"Fine Al, just fine."

"Listen," he said as Kathleen turned to walk away without any conversation. He could tell she had something up her craw.

"I'm sorry about what happened in the café yesterday. I didn't even know that *woman.*" He reached out and took Kathleen's arm in a strong grip so she could not continue to walk away.

"Really? Rumor has it you both were well acquainted after leaving the café. However, you are grown people and can do whatever you please. If you don't mine—remove your hand."

He quickly removed his hand and tried to voice words to convince her of his innocence. "Lies, they're all lies! You know how people like to start rumors."

Kathleen never looked back at him. She knew that he was standing in the livery door watching her every step. *Oh, how that man disgusts me*, she thought.

After everyone had arrived to work, Mr. Crocker filled the cash register. Lucy, Mrs. Porter and Kathleen along with Sammy were in the kitchen making biscuits, slicing ham, frying bacon and stirring the mixture for flapjacks. It was too early for customers when a soft knock came at the back door. Kathleen wiped her hands on her apron and went to see who was there. Matt was standing on the stoop with his big Stetson in his hand.

"Well, this is a surprise. What brings you to this back door so early, Matt?" Kathleen leaned on the door looking at him with a silly grin on her face.

He noticed how fresh and pretty she looked. "I woke up early and I'm starving. I knew if I came to the backdoor, you might take pity on a poor cowboy and let me in. I see others are outside waiting for you to open but I wanted to be your first customer."

Kathleen stepped aside and allowed Matt to enter. He gave her a cock-eyed grin and walked over to the table by the backdoor. "Good morning, Lucy." Matt called to his little housekeeper. "How about a big cup of black coffee?"

Lucy smiled and walked over to Matt and poured him a cup. "I guess you want eggs, too."

"What I want is for you to return home. The men and I both miss you. They are already fighting among themselves as to who is going to cook. Joseph is threatening to return home."

"White woman still there?"

"Only for another day," Matt replied with a smile on his face.

"I come home after she gone—not sooner. I bring boys supper when I leave here tonight. Tell them." Lucy turned away and began cooking scrambled eggs.

Kathleen walked over to Matt with a big plate of crisp bacon and flapjacks. "I have wanted to talk to you. What did the doctor say about your leg?"

"It's fine. He gave you and Carlos all the credit for it being set properly in the first place."

"Can you come over for supper tonight?" Kathleen asked. "I have something I need to discuss with you."

"I will be happy to sit my feet under Rosa's table, especially since I don't have anyone to cook for me." Matt spoke the last part loud enough for Lucy to hear.

Lucy did not respond, but with her back turned, she smiled and continued to fry a skillet of ham.

Sammy raced over to Matt's table and pulled out a chair and sat down. "Mr. Matt, guess who's going to school today?"

"Well, let me think on this for a moment," he said as he sliced his flapjack and pushed a big piece in his mouth. "It wouldn't be a little squirt like you, now would it?"

"It sure is! I am going to learn my let-tars. What's letters, Mr. Matt?"

Matt tossed his head back and gave a hearty laugh. Gracious, how he had missed this youngster. "Well, now let's see. Letters are your ABC's. ABC's are letters. Wait that did not make sense. Letters are what you will learn and then you will put letters together to form a word. Words are what you will learn so you can read. Now, does that explain things better for you?"

"I better just wait and be surprised. I have a pretty teacher but she ain't prettier than Miss Katy."

Matt raised his eyebrows after hearing Sammy call Kathleen, Katy. He knew that the little ears had overheard him calling her his pet name. He could not help but smile across the table at Sammy.

"You know, bud, you ain't going to be able to say ain't anymore. Teachers don't allow their students to say that word."

"But Mr. Matt, you just said it."

"Well, I know but I ain'—am not in school." Both of them laughed.

The cowbell on the front door of the café announced their first customers. It was time to get busy and serve the hungry men who came in every morning. Matt finished his breakfast and said good-bye. He gave Kathleen a salute with two fingers, touching the brim of his Stetson and smiled. He was already looking forward to supper at Kathleen's home. As he walked past Sammy, he said to be a good boy as he rubbed his clean hair.

Matt stopped in the Red Garter Saloon to talk to Bull, the bartender. "Kinda early for even you, Mr. Moore, to be coming in for a drink," Bull said as he was taking chairs down off the tables and putting them onto the floor.

"Morning Bull, nothing for me. I just filled up on flapjacks and hot coffee at the café," he said as he rubbed his stomach. "I wanted to ask if you know any good men that might be in need of a few weeks of work. I got a herd that I want to drive to Abilene."

"So, Miss Parker is ready to sell her cattle." Bull walked around his big shiny oak bar and rung out a stinking rag and started wiping it down.

"Is there anything that you don't know that goes on in this town?" Matt laughed as he leaned against the bar. He looked around the dark, dingy room where smoke still clouded the ceiling. A pretty soiled dove came through the door behind the bar with a fresh brewed cup of coffee. She walked past him as if he was not there.

"There ain't much that goes on that I don't see or hear, that's for sure," he grinned as he watched the petite girl drag herself up the staircase. "I heard that fiancée of yours ran your housekeeper off your place. What'd she want? To have you out there all alone," he laughed showing a big gap between his teeth. "Everyone is speculating about a big wedding to be very soon."

"You can spread the word that if there's a wedding in town, I won't be the groom. My so called fiancée is leaving on the stage to Abilene tomorrow."

"That's so? Maybe if she stayed, she could take up with Big Al at the livery," said Bull. "I heard tell that he took really good care of her yesterday."

Matt did not give a response to that comment. "Do you know any men who might help me on my trail drive?" Bull knew immediately that he was not going to get a reaction out of his customer. *Shoot fire*, he thought. *I was hoping to have a good story to tell the men later.*

"Yep, I do." Bull thought for a minute, "but they're sleeping off a big hangover. I'll tell them to look you up when they come down."

"Appreciate it." Matt turned and walked out of the saloon thinking about Lillian and Mr. Thornbees. In the five years that he had courted her, he did not realize that she was so promiscuous. Everyone seemed to like her and her shop was very successful. She sewed for the most prosperous women of the city. For days, he was miserable after he received the farewell letter from her. Thinking back on all the events that had occurred since then, he was relieved that she had shown her true colors. What a fool she had made of him while he was away working for their future. He looked up into the heavens and said a silent prayer, thanking God, for showing him the true Lillian.

As if on cue, thunder roared in the distance. He needed to get home and make sure the boys were busy riding his fences and checking on his new cattle. Some of the cows were ready to drop their calves and he wanted to make sure the newborns were all right.

After several hours of working with his men on the range, he came back to the house. Once he entered the front room, he saw that Lillian was packed and ready to return to town. He was surprised, but well pleased that she was finally getting out of his life.

"Well, I see you're ready to go in to town. That is good. It looks like rain this afternoon so if you are ready, I will go hitch up the carriage to haul your luggage. Matt turned to go out of the door.

"Matt, I'm not returning to Abilene," she blurted out the words quickly. "I'm staying here in Sweetwater. I got a job as a seamstress at Dolly's Dress Shop. She has a small space in the back that I can rent. Since she got married, the place is vacant." Lillian stepped back a few paces after she laid out her new plans for her future.

Matt pushed himself away from the doorway and stood starring at her. His eyes narrowed as he looked at her as if he did not quite understand the words that she had spoken. With his dirty, stained Stetson still on his head, he crossed his big arms across his chest. His expression was as fierce as any mad cowboy she had ever encountered. However, to her surprise, he whirled around, walked out the screen door, and left her standing alone.

He had to get away from Lillian. He had never thought that he was a violent man, but he wanted to place his big rough hands around her skinny white neck and give her a good shaking. The last thing he wanted was for Lillian to remain in Sweetwater. He wanted her gone. There wasn't anything that he could do to make her leave town. She had a right to live and work there. Getting a grip on his anger, he went to the barn and got the black carriage. In a few minutes, he pulled up in front of the house and loaded her luggage.

Matt looked at Lillian while she stared back at him. Their eyes met like two opposing opponents ready to do battle. Lillian prepared for Matt to roar like a lion and tell her she could not stay but not a comment came forth from his tight lips. She would have rather him yell at her than give her the silent treatment. She wished she knew what he was thinking. When they were courting, he could be so kind and sweet to her. Now, Matt was not showing any emotions and Lillian did not know what to think. He offered her his hand and helped her onto the carriage without any expression on his handsome face.

As the sky darkened and the thunder continued to rumble in the distance, the carriage pulled up in front of Dolly's Dress Shop on Main Street. Matt jumped down and offered his hand to assist Lillian down on the boardwalk. She was reluctant to accept his help and get down. She wanted to try one last time to plead her case and hope that he would change his mind about her. After a minute, she knew that Matt was not going to change his mind and she was not going to be a part of his future. As Matt sat Lillian's luggage on the boardwalk, Dolly came outside and spoke to the couple. He removed his hat and gave her a polite nod. Placing his hat back on his head, he hurried back to the carriage and drove away. He did not stay long enough for Lillian to thank him for the ride or say good-bye.

On the way to Kathleen's ranch, Matt began to feel relieved. He was not happy one darn bit that Lillian was staying in Sweetwater. However, this was a free country and he could not make her leave. He hoped that she finally understood that he wanted nothing more to do with her.

After stopping by his ranch, he swapped the carriage for his bay horse and headed to Kathleen's. Just as he was beginning to feel good, Mother Nature opened her arms and dumped the dark sky on him. He looked into the black sky and feeling the rain on his face, he shouted toward heaven, "That two-timing woman-- is out of my hair. Thank you Jesus!" He gave his bay horse a kick in the sides and rode faster to get to Katy.

As Kathleen drove her horse and carriage into the yard of her home, a loud crack of thunder interrupted her thoughts. She was glad that Matt was coming over tonight to talk with her. Her horse had stopped when another streak of lighting flashed across the sky. The horse reared and sidestepped. Kathleen was fighting the frightened animal by pulling on the reins when a strong pair of hands pulled him to a complete stop. Matt had raced out of the barn and got the horse under control. A strong wind had come up and the rain was pouring down upon Kathleen and Lucy. Before Matt could help both of them down from the carriage, they were soaked to the skin.

"Where's Sammy?" shouted Matt.

"Carlos came into town earlier and brought him home. He's

inside warm and dry, that's more than I can say about us," laughed Kathleen as she took in their appearance. All three looked like drowned rats.

"Hurry inside and I will take care of your horse."

Kathleen and Lucy rushed to the front porch where Rosa was waiting with big bath towels. "Come and let me fix you both something hot to drink while you get out of those wet things."

"Matt is in the barn. He will need something dry to put on, too."

"You and Lucy take care of yourselves and Carlos will help Mr. Matt."

In less than thirty minutes, the family was sitting down to a hot supper of beef stew, cornbread, and stuffed peppers with rice and fiery pieces of beef. Kathleen looked at Matt as he ate. She tried not to smile as he sat across from her covered with one of Carlos's multi-colored ponchos. Carlos' baggy drawstring pants hit Matt up over his ankles. His blackish, gray hair had dried and curled on his neck and around his ears. Matt had not cared one bit about his appearance until he noticed Kathleen watching him as he shoved in Rosa's good food.

"Listen sister, I see you looking me over," Matt commented while Carlos and Rosa were enjoying a goblet of red wine. "You like this big, robust Mexican man?"

Kathleen could not contain her laughter. "So," she said smiling, "you think the clothes make you a real big tough Mexican?" Before he could answer, she continued with another jest. "You better get some clothes that fit your tall frame before you try to cross over the border." Carlos and Rosa joined in the playfulness and laughter.

"Mr. Matt, your clothes will dry in a little while. I hung them in front of the fire. You and Kathleen go into the warm parlor while Lucy and I clean the kitchen. Besides, Lucy and I want to do— what you say Kathleen? Oh, I know. Woman-to-woman talk, yes that is it."

"Come on Matt. Rosa is pushing you away from her table before you eat her tablecloth," said Kathleen as Rosa and Lucy chuckled.

The couple entered the parlor to find Sammy stretched out asleep on the braided rug. His face was lying on a wrinkled piece of paper. The letter "a" was written on it about ten times. Kathleen stooped down beside Sammy and prepared to lift him off the floor, when Matt moved her aside and picked up the child. "Go and turn his covers back and I will carry him to his room. This young man is getting too heavy for you to be picking up."

Matt laid Sammy on his bed and smiled down at the sleeping child. He couldn't understand how a mother could abandon her child for any reason. He hoped that one day he would be able to have a son as sweet and kind as this little one. Kathleen interrupted his thoughts as she moved him out of the way with her hips. She removed Sammy's boots and socks and pulled off his shirt and pants. She slipped a fresh nightshirt over his head and the little fellow never stirred. Kathleen leaned down, kissed him on the forehead, and whispered goodnight, sweet dreams.

As Kathleen walked back into the parlor, Matt had already made himself comfortable on the sofa in front of the blazing fire. He had one barefoot relaxed on top of his knee and his arm was lying over the back of the sofa.

"Come and join me," he said as he patted the cushion. Kathleen sat down but his arm was so near to the back of her neck and shoulders, she didn't dare relax. She held her hands underneath the folds of her skirt to keep from reaching out and touching him. She wanted to run her palm over his muscular thigh. She had a trembling feeling in the pit of her stomach as she stared into the dancing sparks in the fireplace. She desperately wanted to lay her head over on his shoulder and feel his strength and warmth.

"Now this is the good life," whispered Matt. "I have a nice fire, soft cozy sofa, full belly and a pretty gal sitting next to me. What else could a fellow want on a rainy, cold night?" He said as he twisted a strand of her hair around his finger.

Kathleen shifted her body sideways to face Matt. "Before you get too cozy and warm, and possibly fall asleep, I have some business I want to talk to you about."

Sitting up straight, Matt gave Katy his full attention. "My ranch is going to be in serious trouble soon if I can't come up with money to pay my taxes. The bank gave me a one-year extension last January. At the end of this December, they want the two years' taxes paid in full. I need to get my cattle to the stockyards in Abilene. Can you or should I say, will you drive my cattle the one hundred mile to Abilene, Texas?"

"I wondered how long it would be before you asked for my help." He held up his hand to signal for her silence while he finished talking. "If I drive your cattle to market, it's going to have to be in the next two weeks, if not sooner. If we wait much longer, the weather will be too cold and the grass that the cattle need to graze will be dried up on the trail."

"I can be ready to go in a day or two at the most. I have to arrange things in town at the mercantile, notify Mr. Crocker that I have to quit my job, and get Sammy more school clothes and a warmer jacket. Other than that, I will be ready whenever you say."

"Let me get this straight. You're planning to go on this cattle drive?" Matt quizzed Kathleen to make sure he understood her correctly.

"Of course, they're my cattle and I want to help get them to market."

Matt sat looking into the fire. The wood had burned down to hot coals, but the room was still toasty warm. He had never had a woman on any of his cattle drives and he sure as hell was not fixing to start. Women were trouble from the get-go with having to have special treatment such as privacy, sleeping arrangements, bathing and whatever else they felt that they might need. He had learned earlier from other trail bosses that women spelled *trouble*. No way was he going to take a woman on this trip. *Never have and never will*, he thought.

"Katy," he said, using her pet name, "I know you feel responsible for your cattle. You want to make sure that they get to Abilene. I do understand your situation, but this is the way it's going to be. If you want me to take your herd to Abilene I will do that for you, but alone. I will have about six to eight men to help me. You're not going."

Kathleen jumped off the sofa and began pacing back and forth in front of the fireplace. "There's no reason I can't go. I can ride, rope and shoot as good as any man. I will be a big help."

"No," he responded calmly.

"I knew you were going to say I couldn't go."

"If you knew I was going to say no, why are you so upset?"

"Well, I was hoping that just maybe you would want me to go, but no, you have to be stubborn and bull headed because I am a woman. Well, mister, I am going. I will get someone else to help me drive my cattle to Abilene. You aren't the only trail boss that I can hire."

Matt slowly stood and began removing the big Mexican poncho. He reached for his shirt that had been drying in front of the fire." Go ahead; I can't stop you from doing what you want to do." As he buttoned his shirt, he did not say another word to try to convince her to change her mind.

Kathleen watched him dress and prepare to leave without having her problem solved. She needed a trustworthy man who was good at his job. After Matt pulled on his boots and reached for his wet Stetson, Kathleen mumbled, "Wait Matt. I'm sorry." She hung her head down as tears glistened in her eyes. "I need your help, but I still don't understand why I can't go." She really wanted to hit the big, overbearing ignoramus over the head and make him change his mind.

Matt's anger disappeared as fast as it had come, when he saw how sad and downhearted she looked. He was not used to explaining his decisions to anyone but he didn't enjoy witnessing her disappointment. He would love to grab her and kiss those feisty lips of her senseless.

"Katy, women are trouble on a trail drive. We are not going on a Sunday afternoon picnic. It's being in a saddle eighteen hours a day, breathing in a fog of dust, always on the lookout for wolves and other dangerous critters that attack the herd, unpredictable weather and unexpected, dangerous stampedes. You would be in the presence of filthy talking men who swear every other breath. I don't need or want the burden of a woman on my trail drive. I will be responsible for everyone and everything that happens on the drive. Therefore, I make the rules and everyone will abide by them. If you want me to take on this job, I'll be happy to do it. I will be helping a good friend and neighbor—just like I was helped in my time of need." Matt looked into Kathleen's eyes and said, "I'm too tired to fight with you anymore tonight," he sighed as he laid his head back on the sofa and closed his eyes.

Kathleen's elbow rubbed against his side as she gazed into the coals in the fireplace. They cracked and sparkled with enough warmth to make the room very cozy. She was so disappointed that Matt refused to let her go on the drive. She took a deep breath and turned to face him. As she started to speak, the soft humming of a snore was coming from him. He was asleep.

Carlos came into the parlor to tell Matt good night. Kathleen stood and looked at him. Immediately, he recognized the disappointment on her face. He had been on the ranch all of Kathleen's life and he had witnessed the expression on her face many times.

"Matt will not let me go on the trail drive to Abilene."

Carlos was not surprised and tried to assure her that Mr. Matt knew what was best.

"Well, he's going to be our houseguest one more night. He fell asleep while we were discussing the trail drive. Let us turn his long legs around and cover him with a blanket. I'll toss another log on the fire."

"I'll check on his horse before I turn in," said Carlos as he went out the door.

# Chapter 12

The sun was already climbing to its mid-morning position by the time Matt had hired an old greaser to be the cook on the trail drive. The old fuzzy faced, bow-legged character came with good recommendations from several men who had used him on their drives. His nickname was Cookie and he knew the trail to Abilene. It was important to have an experienced chuck wagon driver and good cook. He would drive ahead of the herd and find a place to stop for the noon meal and a resting place to settle the cattle down for the night.

Matt, with the help of Cookie, selected an army wagon that Al Thornbees had stored behind his livery. The wagon had a strong canvas cover that tied together at the front and back. The wagon came strengthened with extra hard wooden axles and had a big sturdy box mounted on the rear.

Matt purchased strong mules to pull the chuck wagon. He purchased a small string of good cattle ponies for the men. Each cowhand would have four mounts to ride. On some days, the riders would change their horse three or four times a day. A very tall young man, named Slim Johnson, hired on as the wrangler. His responsibility was to care for all the extra horses.

Matt instructed Cookie to drive the wagon over to the mercantile and purchase all the staple goods like flour, lard, coffee, sugar, and cornmeal for the trip. He would get fresh food like fruit, butter, eggs, and bacon for a week. On the trail, there were several outposts where Matt could refuel their supplies. Most of the meals would consist of beans, bacon, hot biscuits and coffee. Matt like good meals for his men so he requested heavy stews with fresh game; potatoes, carrots, and onions for dinner and scrambled eggs, hot fluffy biscuits, bacon, flapjacks, and fresh fruit when possible.

He liked the men to have beef jerky, dried fruits and hard candy in their saddlebags to help ward off hunger between meals.

Three days passed and Matt had hired eight men to help with the trail drive. Juan, Carlos and Rosa's oldest son, had pleaded with his father to allow him to go along. Matt agreed that he could make the trip. The men had new chaps that covered the front of their denim jeans and new spurs for the heels of their boots. Each man had a rain poncho and a fur lined heavy jacket. Matt had purchased all of these items without Kathleen's knowledge. He knew the men did not have the funds to purchase the equipment that would keep them dry and warm. Every man would have a new bedroll that would be stored during the day in the back end of the chuck wagon to stay as dust free as possible. Matt knew if his men had full bellies, clean bedrolls and were warm and dry, he wouldn't have disgruntled trail hands that might sneak off in the middle of the night.

Every man on the drive had a very important job. Several jobs rotated each day, but the same experienced person always held a few. Matt was an easygoing trail boss as long as each man pulled his weight. He did not put up with a slacker who did not do his job. Boredom and unpredictable weather were enough to cause tempers to flare, but a lazy trail hand could set the men to fist fighting. Once they got to an outpost, Matt would fire the misfit and try to replace him, if needed.

Matt, Carlos and the boys led the new trail hands out to Kathleen's herd. He had the men check the cattle who looked like they would be dropping their calves soon. They rounded them up and corralled them together in another pasture. If they had their calf on the drive, the mama cow could die of milk fever if she got separated from her calf. Matt always had one rider watching the cows for newborns on the drive, but it was hard to catch all of them. If a mama cow lost her baby, a cowhand would have to milk her. Before the men moved the cattle, there had to be a head count and the rumps checked for the Parker brand. This was no easy task, as the cows did not like to walk through the narrow chute. By doing this, they found many of the younger cows still needed a brand. After several days of working from sunup to sundown, pushing, shoving and roping the cattle, the job was completed. Matt instructed the men to take two days to spend with their families and gather their personal items. He paid each man a week's salary. They would be able to purchase personal items and leave their families some money while they were gone. They would meet in the north pasture at sunup.

When Matt rode home, Lucy greeted him. She had moved her things back to his place the day he had taken Lillian to town. It was nice to arrive home and have a good hot meal and plenty of warm bath water heating on the stove. His ranch hands were happy to have Lucy back home too. He had not heard any more grumbling about leaving. Lucy had started washing their clothes, too. Life was good but after the trail drive, Matt hoped to make it even better.

With the help of his three ranch hands, he felt that he was leaving his place in fair condition. The young men would watch after Lucy and help with the fall garden. They would keep a close eye on his fifty head of cattle and watch for newborn calves. He had over thirty big sitting hens and many little chicks running around in the chicken yard. Lucy collected, washed and cleaned the eggs each morning. Kathleen would stop by and pick them up. Mr. Crocker paid fifteen cents a dozen. Matt had purchased two large sows and one of them would be delivering a passel of piglets soon. He felt confident that his men would take care of his place while he was gone. Carlos would stop by every day and be a silent protector of his ranch and Lucy.

During the next two days, Matt rode in to town and had lunch at the Heavenly Hash Café. He looked for any excuse to see Kathleen. She took a few minutes and sat down with him at a table.

"Word is going around that you tossed your fiancée out of your home into the street. Now, she has to work her little fingers to the bone after she traveled miles to be with you. Shame on you." Kathleen grinned at Matt as he looked to the ceiling.

"Lord have mercy," he commented quietly.

"Yes, I agree." She chuckled loudly. "Are you coming over tonight for a farewell supper?"

Smiling very big, he asked, "Is this an invitation? If so, I accept."

"Good. Bring Lucy too. Sammy has missed you both. He asks about you every day."

********

The morning air was crisp and cooler than the day before as he rode to the Heavenly Hash Café to say good-bye to Kathleen one last time. They had talked for hours last night about the trail drive and all he had done to prepare for it. She was surprised to see him this morning, but very pleased.

"I wanted to tell you good-bye, again. Have you thought of anything you need to ask or want me to bring you from the big city?"

When she didn't answer him, he continued. "Well," he cleared his throat. He wanted to give her a kiss, but after looking around at the gawking customers, he thought better of it. "I'll send you a wire once we arrive in Abilene." He reached for her hand and gave it a firm squeeze, causing her to look up at him. Kathleen smiled, but never spoke a word as she walked with him to the front door of the café and stepped out on the crowded boardwalk.

He held her hand tightly before turning it loose. They stood like two statues, frozen in time, as they locked their eyes upon each other. A good-bye hovered on her lips. She tried not to let the stinging tears under her eyelids run down on her cheeks as she lowered her face. He ran his fingers over her quivering bottom lip and lifted her chin. Deep dimples appeared in his ruddy cheeks as he smiled.

His thoughts ran to kissing her again, but he did not dare. It was one thing to steal a kiss in the twilight but quite another in broad daylight on the boardwalk. "Take care," he murmured as he stepped onto the road and untied his big bay horse from the hitching post. She watched as he mounted and reached in his vest pocket for a small brown cigar. He smiled and said something to an old man sitting in a chair on the boardwalk. The old man nodded enthusiastically as he caught the coin that Matt flipped to him. Turning around, she rushed back into the café and hurried over to the window. She rested her head against the windowpane and closed her eyes as she said a silent prayer. *Please God, keep him safe and bring him back home to me.*

Matt shifted in his saddle as he headed to the edge of town where the men and herd were moving slowly for the first leg of their trip. He looked back for one more glance at Kathleen, but she had already gone back inside. He pictured her waiting for him to return. *One thing about her,* he thought, *I would bet my life that she is not anything like Lillian.*

Once Matt was out of sight, she heard a customer requesting more coffee. She got a grip on her emotions and walked back into the kitchen. The day had just begun and she had hungry men to feed.

The sheriff came in for supper and ordered a cup of coffee and one of everything on the menu. He made the remark to Mrs. Porter that he had not eaten all day.

When Kathleen came out of the kitchen, the sheriff waved her over to his table. "Miss Parker, a young woman came by my office earlier today asking if I had seen a little boy about so high. She pretty much described little Sammy. She said that she was the boy's mama and that he had run away a few weeks back. I told her that a youngster was staying out your place. I did mention to her that she should come over here and speak to you. Has she come around today?"

Kathleen stood still with the pitcher of tea in her hand. She was suddenly very afraid, instead of feeling relieved or happy for Sammy.

"Sammy told me that his mama had a new man friend and he didn't want him to go away with them. He heard this man and his mama fighting whether to take him or not. They left him all alone for gosh sakes!" Anger flared up inside her and it was all she could do to contain her feelings in front of the sheriff. She wasn't going to hand Sammy over to his mama who had mistreated him in such a manner.

"It seems like his mama has had a change of heart and is looking for him," said the sheriff, matter-of-factly.

"Surely, she can't just take him away from my ranch. He has a nice home and people who love him." Kathleen was very frustrated that the sheriff didn't seem to be concerned at all about Sammy's welfare.

"Miss Parker, you ain't the boy's ma. His mama has the right to her son. If she deserts him again in my town, I will place the boy in an orphanage. That is it. Now, can I have the food that I ordered? I'm starved."

Kathleen could not control her anger any longer. She turned and rushed into the kitchen. Mrs. Porter watched her as she shoved a large piece of meatloaf on a plate. She added a glob of mashed potatoes, drowning them with rich gravy that nearly floated off the plate. She grabbed a smaller plate, filled it with green snap beans, and topped them with a hunk of golden cornbread. She hurried back to the sheriff, slammed the two plates in front of him, and said in a firm tone of voice, "Enjoy your meal!"

When she returned to the kitchen, Mrs. Porter wanted to laugh at Kathleen's actions but she knew something was very wrong. Kathleen was a mild mannered person who was kind to all of their customers. "What in the world did the sheriff do to ruffle your feathers?"

"Listen, I need to go home. Can you stay a little longer this evening and help Mr. Crocker clean up? I am worried about Sammy and I need to get to the ranch. I want to make sure he is safe." Kathleen was already gathering her bag and wrapper.

"Sure, go ahead. You can tell me tomorrow what is going on. My kids will be fine. We have meatloaf left over and that is one of their favorite things to eat." She gave Kathleen a smile and a little push toward the backdoor.

Kathleen hurried to the stable and instructed Jeffrey, Al's young helper, to get her horse and buggy. She was relieved that Al was not anywhere around. She did not have time to deal with his questions as to why she was leaving the café early.

Kathleen was anxious to get home so she drove her horse faster than usual. She was hoping that Sammy was inside having his supper and getting ready for bed. Rosa always heated a tub of hot water and made sure he scrubbed his hair and neck each night.

As she approached the house, she stopped her horse, leaped down from the buggy and raced into the house. Carlos looked surprised to see her as she stood looking at him and Sammy. They were playing a game of checkers.

"My goodness, Kathleen, what's wrong? Why are you home so early?" Rosa noticed that Kathleen was breathing hard and fast. "Tell us, what's wrong?"

Kathleen felt a little foolish but very relieved after seeing that Sammy was safe. She walked over to the table and pulled out a chair next to Carlos as she patted his rough hand.

Still not answering Rosa's questions of concern, she commented to Carlos that he had a very tough opponent as she smiled at Sammy.

"Si, this rascal has already beat me dos." Carlos gave Kathleen a wink as he looked at her flushed face. Rosa walked over, sat a cup of hot tea in front of her, and said, "Drink."

"Sammy, please go to the barn and tell the boys to wash up for supper. It will be on the table in a few minutes."

"Yes, madam," Sammy said as he slid out of the chair and darted to the front door, slamming it as he went out.

"Now little ears are gone, what's happened?" Rosa stood next to Kathleen while Carlos sat waiting patiently.

"I think Sammy's mama has come back to Sweetwater to find him. The sheriff said that a woman came in his office inquiring about a boy like Sammy. He told the woman that a boy that fit the description was out here with us." Kathleen walked toward the front door and pushed open the screen looking toward the barn. "Have you noticed a woman lurking about today?" Carlos shook his head no.

"If Sammy is her son, the sheriff said that she can take him away from us and we can't do anything about it. I got so mad I wanted to hit that fat old fool. All he could think about was his stomach."

"This can't happen to our little Sammy. He's so happy here. She can't just drag him all over the country side with someone who doesn't want him to begin with. I wonder why his mama's boyfriend changed his mind about Sammy." Rosa looked at Kathleen as she wiped tears from her eyes using the tail of her apron.

"I don't know, but I'm scared for him and all of us. We'll keep him home from school for a few days." Kathleen knew in her heart that she should ask Sammy what he wanted to do. Go with his mama or stay here. However, for now, she would wait and pray about this situation.

Kathleen walked out on the porch and stood looking toward the sunset. Her thoughts went straight to Matt, who had been gone for only one day. She missed him already. If he were here, she would have him check the woman out that was looking for Sammy. Matt seemed to have all kinds of connections. She knew that he would be upset, too. He could not understand how any woman could have abandoned their child. While Matt was recovering and staying with them, Sammy had been his shadow. It was hard for Matt to leave the boy once he moved back to his ranch.

Kathleen waited for the boys to come out of the barn. The two older boys were laughing and swinging Sammy high in the air between them as they walked to the house. Juan dropped Sammy's hand, took her horse's reins, and led him and the buggy into the barn.

# Chapter 13

Trail drive

Matt awakened early and laid for several minutes glancing up into the morning sky. The gray clouds stretched over the tall Cedar trees with the rust colored leaves showing that fall was quickly turning into the beginning of winter. He forced his eyes open and rubbed his hand across his rough whiskers. The first day and night on the trail drive had been successful. The lay of the land and the lovely landscape was easy travel for the cattle, and the men he had hired appeared to know how to handle the herd and themselves. Cookie was an excellent cook and knew how to choose a place to stop for lunch and for the cattle to rest at night.

As Matt stood and prepared his bedroll to go in the chuck wagon, his thoughts went back to Sweetwater. He was wondering how Kathleen was this morning. He could picture her getting dressed for a full day's work at the café. Soon, she would be able to quit that job, stay home, and do what she loved to do— work on her ranch.

When Cookie saw Matt placing his bedroll in the chuck wagon he called to him. "You want a cup of dark brew this morning, boss man?"

"It smells too good to pass up," he replied. Matt saw some of the other men wondering toward the chuck wagon for coffee and breakfast. The men worked in shifts and after their hot meal, he would give them their daily instructions and assigned partner. After today, most of the men would have the same job and partner for the duration of the drive. That way, Matt would know where each man was located.

With the weather conditions good, Matt hoped to cover a

distance of fifteen miles. Abilene was only one hundred miles from Sweetwater, Texas so he hoped to be there in less than two weeks. It was not possible to travel a great distance each day. When the grass was green and plentiful, they would stop and let the herd graze to replace the weight that they would lose traveling long miles on the other days. The days that they stopped, the men who did not stay with the herd, had to round up the calves and their mamas and check the horses' hooves for rocks and pebbles and their hides for scratches and sores. It was very important to keep the animals safe and in good health. All the tack had to be cleaned, oiled, and repaired.

Once the herd moved forward, the chuck wagon drove ahead of the cattle to find a place to stop for the noon meal. Cookie and his helper would start cooking the beans. Matt had been leading cattle drives since he was in his early twenties and he believed in having everything organized.

After a few days on the trail, they came upon the Hard Rock River. The river got its name from the Indians because the bed of the river had many rocks and it was hard for horses and other animals to cross. Matt instructed the men to move the cattle across very slowly. "Let them drink their fill and get the feel of the bottom of the river. They will get their footing and move through the water at their own pace safely," he said.

Later in the evening as the men gathered around the campfire watching the herd moving in and out of the water, two riders rode up from over the hillside. They stopped short of coming into the camp. Matt figured one man to be in his early thirties. His Stetson was shading his eyes. The other man appeared older. He had gray streaks in his dark hair, and stubby gray facial hair that was in need of a razor. He was a very big man and his hat hung on a cord down his back.

The men watched the strangers. Cookie walked to the rear of the chuck wagon and reached for this double barrel shotgun. He cocked it and stood ready for the first sign of trouble.

"Howdy," called the younger rider. "Care to share a cup of coffee with two riders headed toward Sweetwater?"

"Sure, get down but leave your hostlers on your saddle horn," said Matt.

The men did as asked and walked slowly over to the campfire.

Matt pointed at some clean cups sitting on a makeshift table next to the chuck wagon.

"Looks like you two have traveled a good piece." Matt looked the men over as he walked over and sat on a boulder near the fire.

"Yep, came from Abilene heading to Sweetwater."

"Not much in Sweetwater. What takes you there, if you don't mind me asking?"

"Woman trouble; my wife ran home to her folks and I'm going after her." Several of the men snickered. Matt gave them a hard look and joking said, "Hey, you guys. You ain't never had woman trouble, so don't be laughing at this young man."

"Sure appreciate the coffee mister," said the young man. Matt noticed that under his Stetson hat he once had a pretty head of blond hair, which now with age, had a few streaks of dirty gray. He also had a scar under his left eye that looked like he had might have gotten it in a fight. Matt's guess was that this young man looked to have lived a rough life.

"Where are you taking this big herd?" The cowboy asked.

"Abilene." Matt answered as he watched the old man as he stood looking over the men and the campsite.

"We still got daylight to burn so we best be moving on. Thanks again for your hospitality." The young rider moved to his horse, strapped on his gun belt and mounted his big black horse. His partner followed him and both rode away headed toward Sweetwater.

"Joe," Matt said to Joe Powell, a short, dark haired man. "Follow those two a little ways and make sure they don't circle back toward us. I didn't like the way the big man was looking us over."

# Chapter 14

**Lillian came awake** suddenly with the morning sunlight in her eyes. For a moment, her mind was a blank. She had finally had a good night's rest because she had refused to allow Al to stay over in her little apartment. He had been sneaking in the black door of the dress shop for several weeks. She was going to have to stop allowing him so much freedom. The big man was beginning to think of her as his property, even though she knew he secretly wanted that Parker woman.

Outside of Lillian's window, she could hear the sound of approaching horses trotting by the little dress shop. She glanced at the clock and saw it was a quarter to eight. She had to hurry if she wanted to have breakfast at the Heavenly Hash Café and get back to open the dress shop on time. Now that she lived in the back of the shop, it was her responsibility to open it for business.

Lillian was still fuming that she had to humble herself and apologize to Mr. Crocker for her ugly behavior toward his employees when she first arrived. He forgave her and said since Lucy, the old Indian squaw, was not working at the café any longer, that she could eat there. She hurried down the street, passing the dry goods store and the Red Garter Saloon before entering the café. Al was still lingering at his regular table when she entered. He jumped up and pulled out a chair inviting her to sit at his table. He raised his hand signaling Mrs. Porter for coffee.

She sat quietly at the table as she waited for the coffee to arrive. Al looked hard at her, wondering what she was thinking. At age thirty-six, she still looked very young and trim. After spending long nights in her bed, she did not look worn and used like the soiled doves at the Red Garter Saloon. He knew that there had been many men entertaining her in the past but he didn't care.

114

Each morning she looked fresh as a daisy with her mass of golden curls plaited into a crown on top of her head. She could cast a bright smile and her emerald eyes sparkled with mischief. Under all that fancy garb she wore, her skin was silky and white. He wanted to take her back to his place for a morning tumble.

Laying his napkin across his lap to hide his desire for her, he asked nicely, "What you say after you finish your breakfast, we mosey over to my place for a little while. We won't be disturbed."

"Now, Al." Lillian said softly as she removed her hand from his tight grip. "You know I have to open the shop this morning." She paused before she continued. "We need to stop seeing each other so much. People are beginning to whisper about us. Besides, how can you court Miss Parker if people are gossiping about us? You know she will hear."

Al glanced around the room at the other customers as he felt his face flare red from anger. He leaned close to her face and said, "People ain't talking about us. I would be the first to know if they were." He whispered through clenched teeth as he continued. "I have people that owe me big time, and they would tell me if they heard anything negative about us."

He sat back in his chair glaring at the beauty queen. "You're trying to play games with me and I won't have it. I'll be at your back door tonight and you best not keep me waiting, you hear." Al stood and shoved his chair up to the table. He gave her a nod and said loud enough for other customers to hear "Have a good day, Miss Lillian."

While waiting on her breakfast, Lillian pondered what would he do if she didn't let him in. His tone was threatening and he sounded like he might hurt her in some way. She never thought he was a violent man. *Do not tell me that I have picked another loser,* she thought to herself. She still wanted Matt to take her back but it never hurt to have another man on the hook. She hoped that while Matt was on the lonesome trail drive he might reconsider how he felt.

Kathleen came from the kitchen carrying Lillian's breakfast. She knew that this woman still wanted Matt to change his mind and renew their engagement. She had said as much to some of Kathleen's oldest friends. Of course, her friends couldn't wait to tell her since they knew that Mr. Moore was a frequent visitor at her ranch and always spent time in the kitchen of the café. They giggled as they whispered to her that Mr. Moore had a crush on her.

Kathleen could not help but feel a little sorry for the woman. She had really messed up her life by two timing Matt with a younger man while he was away on a trail drive. However, in truth, none of this was Kathleen's business and this woman was a stranger in town with no friends. Lillian had taken a job at Dolly's Dress Shop and had a nice place to stay. It appeared she was here to stay in Sweetwater—married to Matt or not.

"Good morning, Miss," said Kathleen as she placed the food before Lillian. "Would you like more coffee?"

"Please call me Lillian and you're Kath—?"

"Kathleen Parker. Please call me Kathleen. Do you like working at Dolly's?"

"Yes, so far. You know in Abilene I had my own dress shop and had women working for me. It's strange having to take orders from someone else."

"The way Sweetwater is growing, maybe you can have your own shop again. There's enough business for two dress makers, I'm sure."

"You're kind to say so." As Kathleen started to walk away, Lillian spoke. "May I ask why you're working in this place, slaving over a hot stove, when you have a big fine ranch a few miles from here?"

Kathleen thought for a second before she answered the strange woman. Giving the woman a grin she said, "The same reason most people work; for the money. I am only working here temporarily. Once my herd is sold, I will be able to retire from my duties here and work on my ranch."

"So, it's your cattle that Matt is driving to Abilene."

"Yes. I am very fortunate to have such an experienced, honest man helping me get my herd to market."

"I would say you are since Matt retired from the business a while back. When he left Abilene, he said that he would never ramrod another cattle drive again. However did you convince him to do it for you?" Lillian remarked while raising one eyebrow.

Before Kathleen made a nasty reply to the woman, whom minutes before she was feeling down right sorry for, she excused herself and returned to the kitchen. Sammy was peeking from under the bat-winged doors while waiting for Kathleen's return.

Lillian watched Kathleen stop at the door and speak with the little boy. She brushed his hair back away from his forehead and gave him a loving pat on the shoulder. Lillian could not hear what she said to the child, but she wondered who the little fellow's mother was.

After finishing her platter of bacon, eggs and hot biscuits, Lillian hurried to the dress shop to open up for the day. Dolly had arrived a few minutes earlier and had already turned the closed sign to open and pushed back the drapes.

"Good morning, Miss Lillian," said Dolly.

"Good morning to you, too." Lillian returned the smile but wanted to slap Dolly silly. She had asked her several times not to call her *Miss* Lillian. She was older than Dolly but not enough to be addressed like an old maiden aunt.

"We have several dresses to complete for Mrs. Barnes, the banker's wife. She is traveling the first of the week for Houston and she will need her new wardrobe. So, please make her dresses your first priority this morning." Dolly laid out the three dresses in front of Lillian and said she could begin with the hemming. All the dresses had been pinned and were ready for sewing.

Lillian was fuming inside as she sat down in a comfortable chair near the big picture window. As she was hemming the first dress, the doorbell jingled and a frail young woman entered. Lillian had not worked in the shop long enough to know if this was a regular customer or someone new. Where was Dolly, thought Lillian? How in the world will I finish these dresses if I have to stop and help everyone who comes through that door?

Just as Lillian had put everything down off her lap, Dolly came from the back. "Oh good morning," said Dolly to the new arrival. "How may I help you today?" Dolly asked very cheerfully.

Lillian noticed that the young woman was not looking for an expensive dress. The young customer wore a plain calico blouse with faded flowers tucked into a long navy skirt that had been washed many times. Her brown shoes had seen better days, too.

When the young woman did not answer right away, Dolly said, "You must be new to our town. I haven't seen you in my shop before."

"Yes," she said as she began coughing. Lillian noticed that she held a white handkerchief to her mouth and quickly folded it out of sight when she wiped her lips.

"I only arrived late yesterday and I'm in need of a few ready-made dresses if you have something in my size; something simple and not too expensive."

Dolly had taken in the young girl's attire. She was in need of some of her simple everyday dresses that she sold to the dry goods store for the farmers' wives.

"Come in the back with me. I know I have dresses in your size. You will be easy to fit." Dolly went through the rack of dresses and selected a printed green floral that had a small white collar trimmed with a cotton lace. "Is this something you would like or do you want something with a little more flare? This dress is exactly one dollar and I have several more like it, but in different colors. Dolly had a feeling that the young woman's pocketbook wasn't overflowing with money, like so many of her customers.

"This is perfect. May I try it on?"

After the young woman had purchased three dresses and a few pieces of new under garments, she waited for Dolly to wrap her purchases in brown paper tied with thin brown cord. As she turned to leave the shop, she stopped and faced Dolly again. "May I ask if you have seen a little boy about so big? His name is Sammy and he ran away from home and I'm searching everywhere for him. He was here in Sweetwater about a month ago. I am about crazy with worry."

"Oh my, I guess you are!" Dolly said as she held her hand over her mouth. "I'm sorry to say that I haven't seen a little boy like that. A month is a long time to be all alone without his parents and no home."

"Why did he run away?" Lillian spoke for the first time since the girl came into the shop.

"I hate to say," said the young girl but before she could say anything more, a coughing fit took over her small body. Dolly ran into the back and returned with a glass of cold well water.

"Thank you, Miss. You're too kind."

"Where are you staying?"

"I am staying at Mrs. Washington's rooming house," she said as she left the shop.

Dolly watched from the window as the young woman left her shop and walked slowly to the rooming house with her bundle. "That girl is so sad. I can't imagine having a lost child out there somewhere," commented Dolly to Lillian.

"She never did say why the child ran away and how old he was. I bet the little tyke was mistreated by someone close to her," remarked Lillian without raising her eyes up from her stitching.

# Chapter 15

After all the cattle had successfully made it across the river, the men were preparing to settle down for the night. The line of cattle had stretched out nearly two miles long, but once across, the riders had bunched them as close together as possible. This had been one of the hardest days on the trail drive. The men took turns coming to the chuck wagon and eating their fill of biscuits, beans and fresh fried deer steak. One of the young men had shot and cleaned a small doe. Cookie had cut the meat into long narrow strips. He pounded the fresh meat and covered it with flour. He dropped each piece into the hot lard. It was a treat for the men to have fresh meat so soon. The men were fed and with the night music of crickets and bullfrogs sounding off, everyone stretched out around their assigned campsites. In the far distant, a harmonica played the tune *In the Sweet By and By*. Repeatedly, the tune played until it lulled the cattle and most of the trail hands asleep.

The sun came up the next morning with bright gold and purple streaks in the dim sky. Cookie did not ring the triangle bell like he normally did to announce breakfast on the trail. He didn't want to spook the cattle so he walked over and nudged a trail hand with his boot to wake him. Each man would take a turn in waking another until everyone was up and preparing for the new day.

Matt told Cookie and his lead rider that he was going to take a packhorse and ride over to the outpost that was about five miles ahead of them. He would get fresh items, like readymade bread, eggs, butter and dried fruit. He would meet them as soon as he could.

Sherman's General Store was a sturdy two-room cabin built

from tall pine trees. Handmade wooden shingles covered the slanted roof. The front room was long with two cast iron potbelly stoves positioned at opposite ends. Matt rode up to the side of the building that was shaded and spotted two tow-headed little boys sitting up against the building out of the sun. They were watching a little girl who sat in a wooden wagon. They looked like they hadn't seen a good meal in days and their clothes were all but rags. Figuring their folks were in the store, Matt asked the older boy if he wanted to earn a few pennies.

"Yes sir," he replied while nodding his head so fast up and down Matt couldn't contain his smile. "Just watch my horses," he said as he wrapped the reins around the hitching post. "Can you do that for me while I get some supplies?"

"Yes sir," the boy said with a smile.

Matt entered the cabin and after he adjusted his eyes from the sunlight, he saw a petite, frail young woman. She was in the corner of the store counting her coins. She wasn't dressed any better than the three children sitting outside. He was sure she was their mother or older sister.

When Matt was a small child, he could remember his mama working from daylight to dark to feed him and little sister, Julie. He could see her counting her few pennies that she had earned by selling eggs to the storeowner. Before he thought better of it, he approached the young woman. She quickly stepped back away from the rugged, dusty stranger who was unshaved, wearing pointed boots and brown leather chaps. His hostler hung low on his hips.

"I'm sorry, madam. Your young'uns are watching my horses and I promised them payment for their help. I would like to give you the money that they have earned so you can purchase your supplies."

The young woman moved further away from him as she shook her head side to side while looking at the floor. "I'm sure they were happy to help you. We don't take charity, Sir. Please go away," she said as she turned her frail body away from the stranger.

Matt leaned his tall body closer to the woman and whispered. "Madam, I know you need money and your children are hungry. Please take the money that your little ones earned. Pride don't put food in children's stomachs."

The young woman looked up at Matt and her eyes filled with tears. "Thank you. You are the answer to my prayers. My man went away looking for work, but it's been so long," she murmured.

Matt slipped a twenty-dollar coin in to her small rough palm. "Take care," he whispered, as he walked over to the counter.

"Well, hello stranger!" Boomed the voice of John Sherman; owner of the general store. "I heard that you married and settled in Sweetwater."

Matt reached over the counter and offered his hand to the owner. "Good to see you, too," chuckling about the marriage.

"I have settled in Sweetwater. You got that part right. Got me a nice spread with a small herd of cattle, but no wife; I am not married. *She* had a change of heart which suited me just fine."

"Well damn. So, you settled in on your new ranch. Is it as nice as you hoped?"

"Even better," he replied. "I'm on one last trip to Abilene with a large herd. This will be my last trip, unless it is my own cattle that I will be moving. I need to get some fresh supplies for my chuck wagon."

Matt noticed the young woman standing behind him with her arms full. He stepped aside and motioned to the store clerk to go ahead and wait on her.

"You have a paying customer," Matt said as he touched his hat while looking at the young woman.

"She can wait." The storeowner sounded very nasty as he glared at the little woman.

"I have money," she responded softly holding out her hand.

"You can't pay for all that stuff with the sixteen cents that I gave you earlier."

Matt watched and listened to the exchange between the storeowner and the young mother. "John, I'm disappointed in you. I've never known you to be a rude man to such a lovely lady." Matt gave his friend a hard stare as he walked away from the counter.

After paying for her supplies, she told Mr. Sherman she would be right back with her wagon. Matt stepped up to the counter and picked up a handful of her supplies. "John, give me twenty-five cents worth of that hard candy." Matt walked out of the door following the young woman around to the side of the cabin.

The boys were wearing big smiles and helping their mama. Matt went back in the store and retrieved the bag of candy. John shook his head as Matt walked back out to the children.

"Here's your payment for watching my horses," he said as he placed the bag of candy in the little girl's lap. The boys looked at the bag of candy with enormous eyes. Matt smiled as he passed out two shiny copper pennies to each boy.

"Madam, I hope your man will return home soon," Matt said speaking very softly.

"He went to Abilene to look for a job. He should be back soon. God Bless you, Mr.--?"

"Just Matt. You take care of these sweet young'uns," he said as he rubbed the tallest boy's hair and smiled down at them.

Matt watched the little family walk away from the general store with the little wooden wagon. All of them were wearing a smile as their mama passed out a piece of hard candy to each of them. As Matt watched them walk toward the field of tall pine trees, he saw several wooden coffins stacked behind the store. He shook his head as he thought that the storeowner had a little of everything for sale.

Once back in the store, he noticed a barrel of soda crackers, apples and coffee beans. The shelves were lined with cans of molasses, boxes of cigars and drawstring tobacco bags. On the counter was a coffee grinder, a basket containing chunks of fresh cheese and a cash register. From the rafter, a large scale, that weighed items hung down. Under the counter were jars of hard candy and peppermint sticks. Behind the counter were boxes of ammunition, several rifles, a few pistols, soap and men's toiletries. Sitting on a table near the front of the counter were baskets of fresh eggs, bunches of carrots, turnip greens, long stems of green onions and jars of canned tomatoes.

"John, I see you have a good supply of perishable items."

"Yep, I have a peddler who passes by here regularly. He barters with local farmers and keeps me supplied with the goods. Good arrangement for both of us."

"Let me see how much of these items I can take off your hands," said Matt as he ate a piece of cheese and a cracker.

The setting sun cast a reddish glow over the horizon. Matt breathed in fresh clean air as he stretched out on his bedroll. A deep sense of relief settled over his body. It was a big job moving five hundred head of cattle over a hundred miles, but he was doing it for someone special. His thoughts strayed to Kathleen and little Sammy. Seeing that mother of three this morning made him miss the little fellow. He also missed Kathleen very much. He knew that he was falling in love with her. He smiled to himself as he thought about her. On one hand, he wished he had stuck to his original plan and stayed away from women. Lillian had left a bad taste in his mouth when it came to trusting another woman. On the other hand, he could not stop thinking about Kathleen's midnight black hair hanging down on her white shoulders as she stood in her long cotton nightgown. Her beautiful spirited eyes could look right through him. She could aggravate the devil out of him one minute and the next he wanted to grab her and kiss her senseless. He really admired her spunk and ability to work as hard as any man.

Matt tried to rest but he flipped and flopped over on his bedroll. He watched puffs of smoke rise from the campfire into the quiet night air. The sounds of a man's laughter and soft music from a harmonica sounded in the distance. Today had been a very hard day. He had ridden mostly in the river, pushed, and shoved many of the cattle out of the water. The outpost had been a good ten-mile ride, which put a strain on his bad leg. Not being able to rest, he sat up and faced the campfire. His thoughts strayed to the little family that he had met at the store. He was pleased that he had helped them get some supplies. The woman had thanked him several times for his generosity. Shaking his head, he really hoped her man had not abandoned her and those little children.

"Hey Boss, can't you sleep?" Cookie walked over to the fire and squatted down beside it. He tossed another log on the fire and sparks of wood chips went flying high into the night air. He spit a stream of tobacco juice into the fire and listened to it sizzle. "You want some grub?"

"No thanks. I guess I'm just too tired." Matt rubbed his face with his rough palms and sighed. "While my leg was busted, I had to lie around for weeks. I guess I got a little soft and I'm not a hundred percent myself yet, but for gosh sakes, don't tell the fellows I said that."

"Shucks Boss Man. I ain't no old woman who runs off at the mouth."

"Good, I'll be fine after a night's rest." Matt tried once again to rest. His thoughts were of Kathleen as he finally drifted off to sleep.

The next morning Cookie nudged him awake with the toe of his boot. "Morning, Boss Man; I know it is a little early but we're in for a bad storm today. I thought you would want to know. The sky is rolling with dark heavy clouds and there is thunder rumbling in the distance. The cattle are already getting a little restless."

Matt sat up and went in the bushes for a moment of privacy. When he returned, he poured himself a cup of black coffee and asked if all the men were moving about.

"Yep, and I got bacon and flapjacks cooking. I have been awake for hours preparing a good hot meal. The men are going to need it because we're in for a long, rough day." Cookie started passing out plates of flapjacks to the men who were ready to eat.

Within the next half hour, all the men had grabbed some grub and were preparing to prevent a stampede. It was not long before the rain started drizzling and the men slipped on their rain slickers. Matt looked into the dark clouds and saw streaks of lightning flash followed by the roar of thunder in the distance. Tumbleweeds blew across the campfire and swept on out into the open prairie.

"Sure hope there's not any hail in them thar clouds," commented Cookie as he handed Matt another cup of hot brew. "You know I heard tell that hail can be as large as baseballs and knock a fellow right out of his saddle."

Matt grunted at Cookie's comments and told him to hurry and tie the back and sides down on the chunk wagon. "Keep everything as dry as possible," Matt yelled into the wind as he went to get his horse.

The men rode around the herd while circling them into a tight bundle. Some of the cattle that were standing, moaned as they pushed over other cattle that were lying down. Calves bawled when they got separated from their mamas. The big herd was hard to contain but as long as the animals stayed close together, the men had a chance to prevent a stampede.

It wasn't long before the rain came down in full force. Sheets of rains swept over the men and the poor critters. This was no kind of weather for man or beast to be out in. The riders laid low over their saddles with their yellow slickers covering their bodies. The harsh winds made it difficult to keep their hats on their heads. In between the thunder and lightning, Matt was sure he heard gunfire. The cattle heard it, too, and they began to moan and move around in small circles. Matt rode quickly to where he thought the gunshots were coming from. Perry Raines, a tall skinny young man from Abilene, was waving his hat and riding fast toward Matt.

He reined his horse to a stop near a small ditch, and water splashed up on his horse and onto Matt's chaps. "Two men drove off about a dozen head!" he yelled into the wind. "I chased after them but one of the men turned and fired at me. Sorry boss, I didn't stop them but I got a good gander at one of them. He was that big wrangler who stopped for coffee. I'm sure of it." He took out a big dirty hankie and wiped the rain from his eyes.

"You did good, boy. I'm glad that you didn't get hurt. We'll catch up with those bushwhackers, you can count on that. Nobody takes what's mine and gets away with it." Matt turned his horse around and went back to the rear of the herd.

More of the cattle began to rise to their feet with each strike of lightning. It was hard to restrain them. The herd trailed out over two miles but as far as he knew, none of the cattle had been hurt or lost. Only the dozen or so head that those no good cattle thieves stole were missing. Matt was proud of the men he had hired because each one worked hard and long, keeping a tight rein on the herd.

It wasn't long before the noon hour, when the storm dissipated as fast as it came up. Everything as far as the eye could see was wet. Moving the herd was slow as the animals sloshed through deep puddles of water and mud. The chuck wagon moved alongside the herd. Occasionally, the wheels would sink into the dark deep mud. Cookie and the horse wrangler, Jimmy, kept the wagon moving as best as they could with the crack of a whip over the mule's heads. During the storm, Cookie had prepared sandwiches for the riders. When the sun peeked out from the light grey clouds, the men stopped and ate their lunch. After a few hours of moving the herd forward to drier ground, Matt signaled for everyone to settle down for the night. The men filed by the chuck wagon to retrieve their bedrolls and a handout of supper much like lunch. There was no grumbling from the tired men. A cup of hot brew warmed their insides as they stretched out their tired bodies for a goodnight's rest.

Before Matt could retire for the evening, he had to ride the length of the cattle drive and back. He stopped and talked with each trail hand and made sure they were doing all right after the long day. He thanked each man for a job well done. He promised that they would see his appreciation at the end of the drive in their pay.

Matt returned to the campfire and handed his horse over to Jimmy, the young horse wrangler, to take care of for him. This had been the longest and worse day of the journey so far. With today's set back, they should arrive in Abilene in about four days. Matt was pleased that this had been an uneventful trip until today. If those no account gringos had caused a stampede it would have really set them back several days or maybe even a week. The gunfire could have scattered the herd all over the countryside. He was thankful that he had hired experienced, hardworking young men.

# Chapter 16

**After Glory Richardson**, Sammy's mama, had left
Dolly's Dress Shop, she walked slowly down the boardwalk until
she arrived at Mrs. Washington's Rooming House. While staying
in a shack near Abilene with her good for nothing boyfriend, she
had taken money out of his pants' pocket while he slept off a night
of drinking. She needed money to travel back to Sweetwater to get
her son. She had begged and pleaded with Ty to turn around and
go and get her little boy. She could not believe that they had ridden
away and left her son while he was in the dry goods store. She
cried continually once she realized that they were not going to go
back for her child. Ty lost his temper, slapped her hard across the
face, and warned her that she would get more of the same
treatment if she did not shut that squalling. Later he said he was
sorry and as soon as they settled in Abilene, he would go back and
get Sammy for her. She realized after a few days that he had lied to
her when he made that promise.

Once she had walked a little ways down the boardwalk, she
found a bench outside of the dry good's store and eased down on
it.  She tired very easily and had a bad cough. The doctor in
Abilene had said she had the beginning of consumption.  He called
it a lung disease and suggested she should move out of the city into
the wide open spaces of the country. He told her she needed fresh
air. After revealing to the doctor that she had cared for her mama
while she was sick, he was sure of his diagnosis.

Glory knew that she was not in good health and that her days
on this good earth were numbered. All she wanted to do was lie
down and rest. She knew that something was bad wrong because
she coughed up blood, had bad chills at times along with fever, and
no appetite. The doctor had given her cough medicine, which made

her rest better and sleep. She desperately needed to find her son, Sammy.

After resting for only a few minutes, Glory continued on to the boarding house. She had a room that was on the second floor facing down on Main Street. Mrs. Washington watched as her new boarder climbed the flight of stairs as if she was going to the gallows. She could tell that the young woman was breathing hard while trying to stifle a cough.

Once Mrs. Washington was sure her boarder had enough time to settle in her room, she carried up a tray with cookies and fresh brewed tea. "I thought you might like to have some nice tea while you are resting," said Mrs. Washington as she sat the tray down on the table near the window. She could not help but notice several bloody white rags on the bedside table.

"Child," said Mrs. Washington with much concern in her voice, "are you sick?"

Glory slowly rose up from the bed and placed her stocking feet on the floor. "I'd had a bad cold and have been coughing a good bit, but I have medicine and I am recovering nicely. Please, there is no reason to be concerned over me. Thank you for the tea and cookies."

"Gracious. Seeing those bloody rags did give me a fright, but you know how you feel. Please do not hesitate to ask me for anything you might need. Supper is at six sharp."

Glory watched as Mrs. Washington walked to the door and let herself out. After she was alone, she took a spoonful of medicine and laid down for a long rest. She would start her search for her son when she woke up this afternoon.

While Glory was resting, her ex-boyfriend Ty Chambers and his sidekick, Moose Whitman pushed through the bat-winged doors of the Red Garter Saloon. They dragged their boots as they walked over to the bar and settled the top half of their bodies over on it.

"Well, well," grunted the bartender and owner. "Never thought I'd see the likes of you again. You had such big plans in Abilene. What'd you do with that pretty little gal you left here with?"

"You shore ask a lot of questions," replied Ty. "Give us a beer and shut your trap."

"Listen, you little turd," said Bull, the owner, as he grabbed the front of Ty's vest and pulled him practically on top of the oak bar. "This here is my establishment and I will ask as many questions as I like. If you don't want to listen to my chatter, you best get your dirty boots out of here."

Ty tossed two bits on the bar and turned to walk out. The bartender called to him and he stopped and turned around. "That was a pretty rotten thing you did to that little gal leaving her kid all alone to care for himself. Not even school age either. Well, from the looks of you, the kid made out a whole lot better. He has a nice wealthy family looking out for him. Ain't that something? A kid can manage better than the likes of you. Now get out and don't darken my doors again!"

Ty turned away from the bartender and said under his breath to Moose. "Let's get some grub before I decide to kill that big mouth piece of trash."

The lunch crowd at the café had thinned out and Kathleen was in the kitchen preparing deer steak for the dinner meal. She was busy cutting up onions while Mrs. Porter was peeling potatoes and cleaning the last of the summer carrots. Mr. Crocker had gone to the butcher to get fresh bacon and sausages for tomorrow's breakfast and Sammy was attempting to sweep the dining room floor around the few remaining customers. The doorbell jingled and he looked up to see two men entering the door. He immediately recognized the smaller of the two men. He dropped the broom as he rushed into the kitchen and peeked under the wing-bat doors. The broom handle, hitting the floor, sounded like gun fire and everyone jumped from the noise.

"What on earth?" Mrs. Porter asked as she jumped from the noise that came from the front room. She saw Sammy pressing his small frame up against the wall as he peeked under the doors. Kathleen noticed Sammy and asked him why was he running and hiding?

Sammy rushed over to Kathleen and with his bottom lip quivering and tears in his eyes; he wrapped his little arms around her waist and hid his face in her apron. Placing her knife down on the counter, she stooped to his level and asked again, what was wrong.

"It's him," he whispered as he attempted to wipe his nose. "He's out there—the mean man who wouldn't let me go with my

Mama."

Ty had spotted Glory's brat the minute he came through the door of the café. He looked different but only because of the clothes he was sporting. He knew that the kid remembered him, too. That was the reason he dropped the broom and raced into the kitchen.

Mrs. Porter walked out to the dining room where the two strangers had chosen a table near the front window. She told them that the café was all out of the hot meal that they served at lunchtime, but she would be happy to make them a ham sandwich with a large slice of apple pie. "If you're still in town at suppertime we will have deer steak with mashed potatoes and peach cobbler," she commented.

"Sandwiches sound good with hot coffee for me and a big glass of milk for this little fellow here," said Ty, making fun of Moose because he did not really like coffee.

Mrs. Porter gave Ty a smile as she turned toward the kitchen to go and prepare their late lunch.

"Now Sammy, are you sure it's the same man. Did you see your mama with him?"

"No, Mama's not out there. Another big man with white hair on his face is with him. I ain't never seen him before."

Kathleen led Sammy over to a chair while she walked to the kitchen door and looked into the dining room. The two men were the only customers in the place and they seemed to be relaxed and enjoying their coffee and milk. The younger man appeared to be nice looking while the big man looked like the very devil himself. Kathleen had never seen either one of the men around town.

Kathleen walked over to a big chest in the corner and got a large quilt and pillow out of it. She spread it out on the floor and told Sammy to lie down and try to take a nap. "After you get up, I will give you a piece of your favorite pear pie and a cold glass of milk."

In a few minutes, Kathleen walked out of the kitchen into the dining room pretending to check the salt and peppershakers. She wanted to get a good look at the man who would leave a child to survive alone in a strange town. She was surprised to see a young, handsome man with dirty blond hair and a bad scar under his eye, instead of a cruel monster.

Later in the afternoon, Glory Richardson woke up from her nap. She was starving which was very rare for her. Since she had been sick, her appetite had disappeared. As she untied her parcel, she shook out one of her new dresses and slipped it on and prepared to go over to the café to get coffee and pie. It would be another hour before the evening meal was ready at the rooming house. She eased down the staircase and walked out on to the boardwalk. The cool, crisp air felt good to her flushed face. As she entered the café, the aroma of deer steak simmering and fresh bread filled the air. Taking a seat, she waited for someone to take her order. Finally, an attractive tall woman with coal black hair pulled back away from her face walked over to her table.

"Well, hello," Kathleen spoke to Glory while holding a pencil and pad. "Aren't you new to our town?"

"Kinda. You see. I did come this way weeks ago, but we camped on the outskirts and just came into town to get some supplies," Glory answered.

"It's always nice to have new families settling," said Kathleen.

"I'm not staying—," Glory began to cough until she was out of breath. Kathleen hurried over to the counter and grabbed a fresh glass of water. When Glory removed the handkerchief from her mouth, Kathleen noticed blood on her bottom lip and in the corner of her mouth. She drank half of the water and thanked Kathleen for her kindness.

Kathleen sat down across the table from the young, attractive girl and asked if she was sick. "Yes, I am but please don't concern yourself. I would like some coffee and a piece of pie. I'm so hungry today." Glory smiled as she saw Mrs. Porter coming with her order. She had overheard Glory tell Kathleen what she wanted.

After a bite of pie and sip of coffee, Glory asked Kathleen if she could ask her a question. "Of course," said Kathleen, "ask away."

"I'm looking for my son. He is a little fellow—only six. His name is Sammy. Samuel Richardson, but I call him Sammy. The sheriff said that I was to come here and ask about him."

Kathleen could not breathe. She felt the blood draining out of her face. She felt sure she might faint. First, the monster who had abandoned Sammy showed up today, and now his mama. His mama was sitting across the table from her. This was the woman who allowed her boyfriend to leave her son in a strange town, to fend for himself, only a small child. She had to stop herself from reaching across the table and slapping the woman silly. She could easily scratch her eyes out and call her every filthy name that she had ever heard. Anger was pounding in every pore of her body. If she lived to be a hundred, she would never understand how a mother could have abandoned her child and gone off with a piece of trash. Getting herself together, she sat back in the chair and sighed.

With cold, direct words, Kathleen asked Glory when she had last seen her son.

The young woman fell silent and appeared to be very nervous. She could feel tension coming from the nice friendly woman. She did not have time to play cat and mouse games with anyone much less this nice person. The fastest way to find her son would be with the truth.

"I was forced to leave my son here in Sweetwater all alone. My new man would not allow me to take him with us. He would not let me stay, but he promised to come back for him as soon as we found a place in Abilene. It wasn't long before I knew that he had lied to me." Glory's cough continued to get worse as she tried to talk. Kathleen encouraged her to take her time.

"After I knew for sure that he wasn't going to bring me back here to get my son, I waited for him to go into town. I walked out of the woods to the open road, hitched a ride on a freight wagon, and worked as a cook's helper to pay my way. I was luckier than most women. The old man was good to me and appreciated my help without demanding anything else in return."

Glory hung her head and did not meet Kathleen's eyes. Without too many words, she had told Kathleen what type of life she had lived. "Please, I am sick but I've got to find my son. I love him so much and I do not want him to remember me as a terrible person. I want to find him a home with people that will love him as I do. I ain't placing him in an orphanage or on a farm where he will be worked to death." Glory's coughing began racking her body while tears flowed down her face and blood formed on her lips again.

Kathleen gave her a wet cloth to wipe her tears away and to clean her mouth. She wanted to share the news that Sammy was in the kitchen safe. He already had a family that loved him as if he was their own. Words would not come forth from her. She was afraid. She needed time to think. She excused herself and went back into the kitchen and cried on Mrs. Porter' shoulder.

"You heard her, didn't you? I know I have to let her see Sammy, but he's not going to go away with her, not as long as I live."

"She does not look like she could travel very far, if at all. The way she is coughing up all that blood, she needs to be in a bed with someone taking care of her. She ain't for this world very long, if you ask me." Mrs. Porter shook her head as she went out to the dining room to see if the young woman wanted more coffee.

Kathleen stood looking down at the little boy whom she had grown to love these past weeks as her own. She knew that he cried himself to sleep many nights wanting his mama. He missed her and wanted her to come back for him. She must have been a good mama to him or else since he had a nice place to stay, he would not care if she ever came back or not.

Once Mrs. Porter came back into the kitchen, Kathleen told her that she was going to talk with Sammy's mama. "I am going to tell her that Sammy is living with me at my ranch. I will invite her to come and see for herself how nice my home is and that everyone living there already loves him."

"Go in there and tell her now before the boy wakes up. You are right. She will be happy to know that her son is well and happy."

As Kathleen entered the dining room, Glory had disappeared. Kathleen stepped out onto the boardwalk and looked both ways, hoping to get a glimpse of her. She did not see anyone that looked like Glory, but she did see her man friend and his big sidekick walking toward the saloon. *I wonder if Glory knows he is back in town*, thought Kathleen.

After the café closed for the evening, Kathleen and Sammy drove home. Sammy was afraid that he was going to see that man again so he sat as close to her as possible. Once they arrived home, Kathleen spoke privately with Carlos and Rosa about seeing Glory, Sammy's mama and her old boyfriend. She explained to them about how frail and sick Glory was. "All she wants is to find Sammy and get him settled into a nice home with someone who will love him like she does."

Rosa immediately spoke in Spanish to Carlos and both of them nodded their heads. "Kathleen, you are a wonderful person. God has put you on this earth to look out for helpless people and people who are in need. You go into town tomorrow with the boy and tell that poor woman her son lives with you—us. She needs to be here, too. I will help care for her. Poor child, she is very sick from what you have told us tonight. She needs to be with her son, but she needs care."

"Mrs. Porter said that her life is short now that she is coughing up so much blood. I feel she is right and she should be with her son as much as possible. Sammy needs to know that his mama loves him now and when the time comes for her to depart this world, she won't have a choice, but she will be in a better place."

"Here, Sammy will have a nice home and many people who love him. This will give her comfort while she is spending her last days with him. I will go in my room now and pray extra hard that God will bless this reunion and the hard days that we will have in the future," said Rosa as she wiped her eyes and then made the sign of the cross as she walked into her bedroom.

Kathleen walked into the guest room to make sure it was ready for Glory. She was going to invite her to the ranch tomorrow. She would move Sammy back into her room and he could sleep with her. The nights were too cold for him to sleep on a pallet. Glory needed to have her room to herself where she could have privacy and not be disturbed while resting.

Kathleen got ready for bed and her last thoughts were of Matt. She knew he would be pleased to know that Sammy's mama had come back to Sweetwater, but would be sad under the circumstances. He would be mad as hell to know that Glory's old boyfriend was hanging around town. *Oh, Matt, I wish you were here with me.* She sighed as she laid her head on her pillow and went fast asleep.

# Chapter 17

Once the breakfast crowd thinned out, Kathleen told Mrs. Porter and Mr. Crocker that she was going to see Sammy's mama. She placed her bonnet on her head, wrapped her shawl across her shoulders, and walked to Mrs. Washington's Boarding House. Mrs. Washington greeted her and immediately took her to the second floor to Glory's room. She knocked on the door and after a long few minutes the door opened. Mrs. Washington took in Glory's frail appearance. There were dark circles surrounding her eyes and bloody rags covered the nightstand. Dried blood was spattered on her neck and old gown. She was unsteady on her feet as she stood holding onto the door.

"Morning, Glory. Sorry to disturb you but Miss Parker wants to visit with you this morning," said Mrs. Washington. "I'll tell her to come back later in the day."

Kathleen stepped around Mrs. Washington into the room. "I'm sorry Mrs. Washington. I must speak with Glory this morning—now preferably, if you don't mind?" Kathleen looked at Glory as she walked slowly back to the bed.

"Of course not, I remember you from the café. Please, excuse me, but I must sit," Glory said as she gave a small cough, looked up into Kathleen's eyes and sat on the bed.

"Mrs. Washington, please leave Glory and I alone. We have some private business to discuss." Kathleen walked over to the door and stood while Mrs. Washington made her exit with a big frown on her face. The proprietor did not like it at all that she had been dismissed and asked to leave the room.

"Now that we are alone for a few minutes, I want to talk to you about your son."

"You know where my boy is?" Glory had gotten so excited that she went into a coughing fit. It took her several minutes to calm down and breathe easier.

"Sammy is living with me on my ranch. Please lay back on your bed and I will tell you how and why I have your son." Kathleen smoothed the covers on the bed and fluffed the pillows. After Glory was comfortable, she pulled up a cane chair and sat down beside her.

"Sammy was sleeping in an empty trash barrel in the alley behind the café. He had been digging in barrels for scrapes of food. One morning, I found him asleep and I brought him into the café and he has been with me ever since."

Tears formed in Glory's eyes as Kathleen talked about her son. Hearing that her son had been eating out of garbage barrels to survive, nearly broke her heart. "I am so thankful that you found my baby and took him under your wing. I prayed and prayed that he would be safe."

"At first, I brought him to work with me and then later I left him at my ranch with my housekeeper and her family. Since then, I have enrolled him in the first grade of school and he is a star pupil. He loves school and *I love him*." Kathleen said the last part very quickly.

A lump had formed in Kathleen's throat. She was fighting back tears. Glory needed to know how much she loved her little boy. "Sammy seems very happy with us. Please do not give him away to someone else. I want him to continue to be with me and my family."

"Are you a married woman?" Glory wondered how her husband felt about Sammy.

"No, I'm not, but I have a five hundred acre spread and at this very moment half of my herd is on a cattle drive to Abilene. Money will not be an issue in caring for Sammy. I will give him everything that he needs, while making sure he does not become a spoiled brat. I can promise you that he will have plenty of love and guidance from others on the ranch, too."

"You are so beautiful. I can't believe some man hasn't snapped you up already." Glory said as Kathleen's face blushed a bright pink. "Thank you," murmured Kathleen.

"I have been busy taking care of my parents, who have passed on, and my ranch. Maybe one day, I will meet someone and marry in the future. Now Glory, I came here today, to ask if you would like to come to my ranch and stay in our guest bedroom while you are recovering from this sickness."

Kathleen looked down at the young woman as she wiggled her finger for her to lean in a little closer. "You and I both know that I am not going to get better. Let's be honest with each other for Sammy's sake, please."

Kathleen did not know how to respond so she did not say anything. Finally, she asked Glory again if she wanted to go and live on her ranch to be near her son.

"If you're sure I won't be too much trouble, I will be happy to go with you. I can't wait to see my boy."

"Well, that's settled then. After I am finished at the café this evening, I will bring my horse and carriage here and we will head to your new home. Sammy is at the café and I will bring him in to see you before we leave. He will be one happy little fellow. He never gave up the idea that you would come back for him."

# Chapter 18

The morning sun had been up for several hours and Matt's herd was only a few miles away from Abilene. He had instructed the men to gather the herd as close together as possible while he rode into Abilene's stockyard to arrange for the sale of the cattle. This was always an exciting day but a very long one. His cattle would stretch out for two miles and it would take many hours to drive them through town out to the stockyard. As the cattle arrived, each steer had to be shoved through the cattle chute and recounted. This was no easy task as some of the animals could be very stubborn. After the deal with the buyer was completed, the cattle would be loaded in the train's stock cars headed to the northern states to be re-sold.

Matt was satisfied with the arrangements he had made with the boss man of the stockyard, so he rode back to his men and the herd. With instruction on how to drive the herd into town and to the stockyard, he told Cookie to go on ahead and prepare plenty of food for the men.

"Men, listen up! It will be a couple of days before you will be able to go into town and kick up your heels," he said. "I know it will be tempting to want to ride on in and have a good cold beer, but the job is not over until I tell you. Stay close to the cattle and let us get this job completed. After I pay you your money, you're on your own, do as you please, and you do not have to answer to me any longer." Matt heard some chuckles and saw many nod their head in agreement. "Let's get the cattle rolling!"

The first thing Matt did once he had gotten the first bunch of cattle into the stockyard and running through the cattle chutes, was to head to the telegraph office. He wanted to send a telegram to Kathleen and let her know that her cattle had arrived in Abilene safe and sound. He was not going to tell her about the stolen dozen head because he planned to find them and possibly, the men who raided the herd.

He wanted to say a few personal things to her, but he knew that many would read the telegram. Therefore, he wrote that he would be selling the herd and heading home in three or four days. He signed it "With regards, Matthew Moore." Matt joined Cookie at the chuck wagon and ate a big plate of beef stew and hot biscuits. He sure was going to miss this old man's cooking.

After eating his fill, he walked around the stockyard. There were several men dressed in their Sunday suits and wearing shiny boots. Matt recognized the men to be the *buyers* of the cattle. City slickers who thought they knew everything about cattle. Over the years, Matt had learned to let them run off at the mouth all about cattle—their size, the horns, how they were built, how poor they looked. He did not care about their stupid comments. As long as they paid his price, they could say what they wanted.

The three men went into a small office away from the busy stockyard and cut a deal on the price of the cattle by weight and the number of head. Matt was pleased with the arrangement for Kathleen's cattle. He would receive a bank draft and a large amount of cash once the men had completed the head count of the cattle.

After Matt left the two buyers, he continued walking around the stockyard and he noticed a fenced area that had a small amount of cattle eating big bales of hay. As he got closer to the cattle, he recognized Kathleen's brand on the rump of several of them. Plain as day—a long straight line with a horseshoe design turned sideways forming a large P for Parker. He was surprised to see the dozen cattle here in Abilene. He figured the men would have sold the cattle to the Mexicans that lived on the outskirts of town. As he stood pondering about the animals, a young strapping boy walked over to him.

"Need some help, sir? You want to buy a cow to have dressed out?"

"No thanks son. I would like to know who owns these cattle." Matt asked the young man as he slipped a half dollar into the boy's palm.

"Mr. Sawyer! Mr. Sawyer, the butcher. His shop is closed

tonight but he will be opening bright and early in the morning." The young boy pocketed his new fortune and disappeared into the darkness.

Later in the evening after checking in with Cookie and some of the men, Matt needed to report the theft of his cattle to his friend Walt Williams, the Sheriff of Abilene. The light was on in the sheriff's office as Matt opened the door. His old friend was standing at the coffee pot pouring coffee that resembled thick mud.

Walt looked up at the man entering his office and roared, "Well, hot damn! I never thought to see the likes of you again." He stretched his large hand out and gave Matt a firm handshake. Matt was a big man, but standing beside Walt he was small in comparison. Walt stood six foot five and weighed approximately two hundred fifty pounds. He had a handlebar mustache that was streaked with gray. He had the deepest dimples a person could have in their cheeks. His eyes were green and his complexion was a bright red from being outside in all types of weather.

"Good to see you again, too. I am surprised a little myself. I heard tell that you were retiring and moving down to Mexico."

"That was a dream I once had. But, I guess someone will turn my boots up here and I'll be laid out in that old grown up cemetery at the edge of town."

"That's not likely to happen any time soon, I hope," Matt said chuckling a little.

"How's the little gal that followed you to Sweetwater after she dumped you and ran off with that good for nothing cowboy. Did you make an honest woman out of her?"

"I thought you knew me better than that. She made a big enough fool out of me while I was away on cattle drives. I didn't know that I was the butt of all the men's jokes until later, but I wasn't about to give her another chance."

"She sure is a fine looking woman, but she never looked my way," commented the sheriff.

"She's still in Sweetwater. I hope she will get homesick and head back here. Hey, enough fool talk about women. I came in to report a rustling. On my cattle drive one-day last week, we had a terrible rainstorm. Two men tried to stampede my herd and steal part of it. Fortunately, they only got away with about a dozen of my cows."

"Did you actually see the two men?"

"My young wrangler recognized one of the men. The two had stopped at our campsite one evening and we shared our coffee with them."

"Great, give me a description of the man, and I will post a warrant for his arrest."

"I was looking around the stockyard this evening and I discovered my cattle. They are in a corral at the far end of the yard, and a kid told me that the butcher, Mr. Sawyer, owned the cows. The cattle have my employer's brand on their rump, a large P for Parker."

"Well, all right then. You come by in the morning and have breakfast with me. Then, we will pay a visit to Mr. Sawyer and ask for his bill of sale. I am sorry to say that he is going to be one mad son of a gun. I bet he won't have a thing showing his rightful ownership of those cows," laughed the sheriff.

The next morning was cold with dark gray clouds and a soft drizzle of rain. Matt would have liked to stay tucked in bed with a sweet smelling woman. It sure was not a day to go to the stockyard and have an argument with a big burly man who butchered cattle for a living, thought Matt.

After getting dressed, he met the sheriff at Mary's Cafe across the street. The sheriff was waiting on him and from the looks of the place; it looked to be a good place to eat. Some of his men were there having a big breakfast. Jason Costa, one of his young rovers, walked over and said that the men were taking turns having their morning meal. Matthew gave him a nod and he walked out the door heading toward the stockyard.

A young woman, who looked to be about fifteen hurried over and took their breakfast order. "That there is Mary's oldest daughter. She is going to be a beauty one of these days and Mary is going to lose her best helper." The sheriff grinned at Mary as she took another customer's money. Matt could not help but notice the sparks between the sheriff and Mary. He laughed and shook his head, thinking that love was certainly in the air.

It was still a little early for the butcher shop to be open but the sheriff banged on the front door anyway. "Come back later. I'm not open yet!" A loud booming voice came from inside the shop.

"It's me, Sawyer! Walt. Open up and let me in. I've got some business to talk to you about." Walt hit the door with his fist one more time as the door jerked opened.

"What do you want this early, Walt? You know I am too busy first thing in the morning. The *old hens* will be coming in for fresh meat and I must have it cut and ready. I don't want to hear any squawking from them." He walked back behind his meat case as he wiped his palms on his clean white apron.

"Put that meat cleaver down and come out here where we can have a discussion. Sawyer, this here is Matt Moore from Sweetwater and he just brought up that five-hundred head of cattle that is in the stockyard. While on his drive here, a couple of cattle rustlers stole about a dozen of his cattle. Well, sir, those fine beef cows are in your corral. They still have the Parker brand on their hind quarters."

"The hell you say! I bought a dozen head of beef from a big cowhand almost a week ago. I got a bill of sale for them too."

"That's mighty fine. Just show me the bill of sale and we will have us a discussion for sure," said the sheriff with a big grin on his face.

"Well, I got it locked up and I'm too busy to stop and go get it. Come back later!" He wiped his sweaty palm down across his apron. He turned to walk behind the meat case again.

"Sorry to inconvenience you this morning, but if you don't produce that bill of sale or some other kind of proof that you paid for those critters, I'm going to have to lock you up."

"Well, you can't do that. What have I done?"

"Why, you have in your possession stolen goods and if we had been much later, the people of Abilene would be eating stolen beef." Sheriff Walt looked at Matt and howled with laughter.

"Shut that laughter up you old fool and get out of my shop. I've got work to do." Sawyer did not realize that he had just made his first big mistake of the day. Sheriff Walt grabbed Sawyer's shirt collar and gave it a little shake. He leaned down at the little round fat butcher and growled, "Show me proof that you paid for those cows, now."

"Well, I can't, actually. I paid a big man named Moose a hundred dollars for all of them. He grabbed my money and rode off. I called to him to give me a bill of sale but he only laughed and fired his pistol at my feet. I watched him ride away. That is the god-awful truth. He scared me—and I don't scare easily."

Matt looked at the butcher and spoke for the first time. "Was this Moose a big fellow, white hair and bushy facial hair?"

"Yep, that's him. Do you know him?"

"My young wrangler on the cattle drive got a good look at one of the men who rode off with my cattle and it seems to be the same man who sold you my steers." Matt answered the butcher.

"I never buy stolen animals and you know that Walt."

"Well, Matt, what do you want Mr. Sawyer here to do with your cattle? They're still your cattle even if he did give that other guy money for them."

"I believe I could live with a sixty dollar payment and a dozen thick steaks for my men tonight. Cookie, my cook, sure knows how to cook and we could have a celebration dinner. You could join us Walt."

"You mean I've got to buy those cows again—from you?"

"Well, if you don't want them, we'll just run them in with the others and my buyer will be glad to get more steers to ship up north," said Matt.

"Sawyer," said Walt, "either pay Matt or give up the cows, now! We ain't got all day either. You got customers lining up outside."

"Well, I want a bill of sale this time!" Matt and the Sheriff both laughed as they watched the butcher open his cash register. "I'll be back later to get my steaks," said Matt walking down the boardwalk toward the stockyard.

# Chapter 19

**After the Heavenly Hash Café** closed for the evening, Kathleen and Sammy drove the horse and carriage down to the front of Mrs. Washington's Rooming House. Once they arrived, Kathleen turned to Sammy to give him the good news about his mama.

"Sammy, we're going inside to get a young woman and take her to the ranch to live with us. This woman is very sick and we are all going to take care of her. But, there is something very special about this person that I think you are going to like."

Sammy sat very quietly as he listened to Kathleen. "What is special? Do you mean she can do some kind of trick?" Kathleen laughed and said that she didn't mean that at all.

"The person we are going to take home with us is your mama. She is upstairs waiting for you, right this minute."

Sammy stood straight up as he slid off the bench and leaped down off the carriage. He looked at Kathleen with a big smile on his face, turned, and raced up the steps of the boarding house porch. He pushed the big wooden door opened and stood in the foyer looking up the staircase. Mrs. Washington had heard the door open, but when she walked into the foyer, Sammy raced around her and headed up the stairs. He starting calling "Mama, Mama, where are you?"

Kathleen came into the house and apologized for the intrusion. Kathleen hurried to the top of the stairs and took Sammy by the hand. "Please Sammy, I know you are excited but when we go into her room you must be gentle with her. Remember, she is not well."

The little fellow had tears in his big eyes, and he stood looking from door to door. Kathleen knocked softy on a door and it opened slowly. Standing beside the door was Glory, Sammy's mama. She was wearing one of her new dresses and her long auburn hair was pulled back with two large clips. Her lips were pink and her complexion was white as snow. To Sammy she was an angel standing before him. "Oh Mama, I knew you would come back for me," he cried as he pressed his face into her skirt and hugged her slim legs.

"I'm so sorry, baby. I will never leave you alone again, I promise." She patted him on his back as she ran a hand through his soft clean hair. "Please, please forgive me. I love you so much," Glory said, as she held her son close and tried to wipe away her tears.

After a few more minutes of loving and kissing each other, Kathleen picked up Glory's small bag with all of her belongings and said it was time to go home.

"Oh Mama, you are going to be so happy at Katy's ranch." Sammy said using Matt's pet name for Kathleen. "She took me and Lucy there and we ain't never hungry no more. I love Katy, Rosa, Carlos, Juan, and Pedro. Mr. Matt too, but he is not home now. He's off getting us some money!"

"Lord help us Sammy. You are wearing your mama out with all of your chatter. Let's get her in the carriage and you can tell her more about the ranch on the way home," said Kathleen.

"Please, Miss Parker. I love the sound of his voice," said Glory, with almost a breathless voice. "I have missed him so much."

Once the trio arrived home, Carlos, and Pedro came from the barn and helped carry Glory and her belongings into the house. Rosa was in the kitchen preparing the evening meal. She hurried to the door to help make Glory feel welcome and assisted her into the guest room.

"This will be your room. It has a nice rocker in front of the window and you can sit here and watch all the men work from the barn to the corrals. A nice breeze comes through here too, but if you are cold, we will shut the window."

"You are too kind. Sammy says he is happy here and talks about someone else by the name of Lucy?"

"Si," Rosa laughed. "Lucy is a small Indian woman who came to live here for a little while, but now she works for Mr. Matt who lives on the next ranch. You will meet her soon," said Rosa.

"Supper will be ready in a few minutes. Do you feel like sitting at the table with the family or would you rather have a tray in this room? I can prepare it for you," said Rosa.

"I don't want to be a burden to you my first night, but I am really tired. Maybe I should stay in my room. Something light with a cup of tea would be plenty, thank you."

Kathleen came into the room and assisted Glory with her gown and robe. She walked over, turned back her bedcovers, and fluffed up her two pillows. "I hope you will be comfortable in this room."

Glory walked over to the bed and sat down. She coughed and wiped her mouth. "I know that I will be, thanks to you. I am so happy to see my son so well taken care of and happy. He does love it here. I can see that already."

After Kathleen helped Glory to lie down and get settled in the bed, she pulled the rocker to the side of the bed and sat down.

"Glory, tomorrow evening, I would like to talk to you about your old boyfriend. I am worried about him. Do you know that he is here in Sweetwater?"

"No, I didn't know that," she said as she started coughing. "I don't want him near me or my son. Tyler is not a nice person," she said as she coughed and wiped blood off her lips. "I found out too late."

"Please lay back and rest. You are exhausted tonight. We will talk again tomorrow evening. Rosa will help you with your medicine and bring you something to eat. Sammy will be in shortly for just a few minutes. He is going to stay home from school tomorrow so he can help you settle in. That's how he put it."

"Good night Miss Parker," said Glory with a sweet smile.

"Kathleen. My name is Kathleen," she said with a sweet smile.

Kathleen went in the kitchen and sat down next to Sammy. She spooned a small portion of field peas over a soft piece of cornbread. "Well, little man," said Kathleen to Sammy. "Are you happy that your mama has come to live with us?"

"Shore am! I am so glad we are a long way away from Mr. Chamber Pot. That man scares me and I heard him say bad words to my mama."

Carlos laughed at Sammy. "Why'd you call the man chamber pot?" Carlos glanced around the table at Pedro as he snickered.

"Well—cause that his name. Chambers—Tyler Chambers. I

just figured he acted like—poop- I call him that behind his back."

"Sammy!" gasped Rosa. "Young man, I don't allow that kind of talk in this house. Now you apologize immediately."

If Sammy could have hung his head to the floor, he would have done so. "I'm sorry, everybody," mumbled Sammy, "but he did ask why I call him that name."

Kathleen was sitting very still in her chair. She could not believe that Sammy had said that Glory's old boyfriend was Tyler Chambers, her Tyler; the one and only love of her life. She had walked into the dining room of the café today and she did not recognize him sitting at the window having a late lunch. How could she have not realized the only man she ever loved was in the same room with her after twelve long years? Rosa had spoken to her and when she did not answer, she asked Kathleen again.

"Are you all right, honey? Did you have a long tiring day?"

Kathleen looked up at Rosa and gave her a nod. Her throat felt closed and her eyes filled with unshed tears. "Please, child, come with me," said Rosa as Sammy and the rest of the men watched Kathleen leave the table.

"Pedro touched his papa's hand and whispered, "What's wrong?" He gestured with his head toward Kathleen as she left the room with his mama.

"I believe she knows Mr. Chambers from the past."

*******

Early the next morning, Matt had completed the sale of Kathleen's herd and paid off his men. They had a celebration dinner last night with Sheriff Williams as their guest. Cookie had outdone himself cooking the big, thick beefsteaks that were part of the deal with the butcher for the payment of the dozen stolen beef.

After Matt gave the men their pay for the trail drive, they all disbanded and went in different directions. Juan stood beside Matt as they said good-bye to the men and watched as they rode away. Several of the men headed to the Last Chance Saloon for a cold beer and a warm body to cuddle. A couple of the men headed to the men's bathhouse for a steaming hot bath, shave and a fresh haircut. The cold beer and woman would be next on their list. Matt laughed as he told Juan that wranglers and rovers never change. "They get cleaned-up, eat a good meal, and head straight for the saloons to spend their hard-earned money on whiskey, cards and women."

"You ever do that, Mr. Matt?" Juan asked.

"Sure. When I was young and full of myself, but it did not take me many times to realize how dumb I was being. I figured that if I was ever going to have anything, I needed to give up those bad habits and start saving my money. I found an honest banker and he helped me invest some of my hard-earned cash." Matt looked at Juan. "Do you want to go with me or spread your wild oats while we are still in town? You got money. I'll never tell, whatever you decide to do."

"No sir." Juan shook his head real hard and fast. "I'll party back home with my own kind a few miles east of Sweetwater. I got the prettiest little senorita waiting for my return. I do want to go to the mercantile store and get a trinket to take to her and few Christmas presents while we are still here. Do you mind?"

"After I send Kathleen a telegram, I will be over there myself. See you there." Matt smiled at Juan as he pulled himself onto his big, bay horse and rode over to the telegraph office. He nodded to a few women walking on the section of newly built boardwalk as he passed by. With so many cattle drives coming straight down Main Street, the Cattlemen's Association constantly had to repair the boardwalk because of the stray cattle that jumped onto the walkway and damaged the boards. This was a busy town in the spring and summer. It was rare to have a herd driven into town this late in the fall.

Matt's telegram told Kathleen that he and Juan should be home in less than three days if the weather held. They both had two horses and a pack mule for their supplies that they were bringing home.

Juan had stopped in the leather shop before heading to the mercantile store. He had seen a nice rope that would be perfect for Pedro as he trained the horses. He selected a long fancy riding crop to use to tap the horses on the rump without getting too close to them. Pedro would be very pleased with his choice of gifts for him. As he looked around, he saw gloves that were hand-made out of the soft, smooth leather. They would be nice for his papa to wear to church during the winter. Mama had made them all mittens. *That is fine for a boy—not a man,* Juan thought.

As Matt got off his horse, he saw Juan walking out of the leather shop. He had several packages and was wearing a grin you could see from a mile way. "Well, son, I see you have made a few selections already. I best get busy if we are going to hit the trail for home in a while."

"Si, Mr. Matt. I like that leather shop. Nice things but I could not afford too many items in there. My pockets would be empty before I left town," he laughed.

"I think I will have a peek in there while you are in the dry goods store. See you in a bit."

Matt walked into the store and saw a younger version of the storeowner. "You must be old man's Knapp son?"

"Yes, sir, I shore am. Homer Knapp is my name. Pa is getting some lunch at the house and most likely taking a short snooze. What can I do for you?"

"I was hoping to find a small saddle for a youngster about so big," Matt said as he held his hand up a little past his waist. I want it to be fancy. You got anything like that."

"Come back here with me to my storeroom. This is a one of a kind saddle specially made for a rich kid, but the little fellow would not even get on the horse. His pa pleaded and begged for several months and finally he gave up and brought it back. Pa felt sorry for the dude, so he gave him some trade back for it. Here it is!"

Matt looked at the soft brown leather seat on the saddle. He ran his hand over the smooth surface. He could not believe his luck in finding such a nice piece of workmanship carved into the leather. The saddle horn and stir-ups were strong and well built. Sammy would love this saddle.

Matt cleared his throat and finally asked, "How much you want for this saddle?"

Before Homer Knapp could answer, Mr. Knapp, the owner of the leather shop walked in. "I can't believe my eyes. Matt, how are you old man?"

"Fine, you old buzzard bait. You are looking none the worse since I saw you last. Life treating you good?"

"Hell no! However, the missy is still feeding me right handsome and that is all I need to keep going. Got my son back from California working for me and he's a great help." He nodded at Homer, his tall, lanky son that had been waiting on Matt.

"Who do you want to get a small saddle for? You done got a youngster big enough to ride?"

"No, but I got a little sidekick that trails after me, and I want to give it to him for Christmas. I was asking your son how much this fine piece of workmanship was worth."

"I don't look to ever have any grandchildren, while I am alive anyways, so you can have this special made saddle for thirty dollars. I made this for a rich fellow and I got good money for it then. You take it and let that little friend of yours enjoy it."

"You know I can buy a man's saddle for twenty," Matt said as he closed one eye.

"Go ahead, get one, and let the little fellow fall off of it," replied Mr. Knapp while holding his hands out.

"I'll take the special made saddle for thirty. You are right of course. I wouldn't want my little friend to get hurt." Both of the men smiled as they shook hands.

After settling with his old friend for the saddle, Matt made his way down the boardwalk to the dry goods store. Juan was busy selecting Christmas gifts. "Mr. Matt, thank you for letting me come along on the drive. I never had so much money at one time. I have gotten some nice gifts for my folks and several other special people. Most of the time, I make my gifts by hand."

"Well, son, there's nothing wrong with hand-made items. However, you earned every penny of the money I paid you. You did a good job for a first timer. I'll be sure to tell Carlos how proud I am of you."

Juan blushed and gave Mr. Matt a nod as he scooped up a bag of hard candy for his girlfriend's brother and sisters. Matt circled the store looking for the perfect gift to get Kathleen. He knew he wanted something nice, but not too personal. He saw a heavy poncho with several bright colors and fringe on the bottom. This would be just the thing for her to wear while riding over her property this winter. It would protect her from the freezing wind.

After having their packages wrapped in brown paper, they tied their bundles onto the pack mule. "Are you ready to head home?" Matt asked Juan as he checked his saddle and adjusted the stirrups.

"Si! I'm ready for some of my mama's tortillas and her hot

chili with fresh baked cornbread," he said laughing as he headed out of town with the packhorse trailing behind him.

# Chapter 20

Kathleen allowed Rosa to lead her to the bedroom and ready her for bed. "Kathleen, child, you're going to be just fine in a little while. You have just had a shock, but you will be fine once you realize your old boyfriend is nothing but trash. He was a no good, young man! He rode off without even telling you good-bye when you deserved an explanation. He didn't care about your feelings then and he don't care about that sick girl in the other room." Rosa sighed and made the sign of the cross as she looked down at Kathleen. Her eyes had a glazed looked and she did not act as if she had heard a word that Rosa spoke. Rosa pulled the covers back on the bed and Kathleen lay down and curled into a ball as she pulled the quilt over her head. Rosa turned off the lantern and left the young girl heart-broken and all alone in the dark room.

After a few hours of lying in the bed, thinking about what she had learned tonight, Kathleen got up and walked into Glory's room. She stood over Glory as tears threatened to spill as she watched the young woman sleep. The love of her life, at the age of eighteen, was now Glory's boyfriend. She remembered watching as Tyler grabbed the five hundred dollars out of her papa's hand and rode away without even looking back. He abandoned Sammy in Sweetwater without giving a care or thought to his well-being, she thought. How could she have loved a person who would do an awful thing like that?

She walked over to the window in Glory's room. She looked out over the lovely landscape of her ranch; the ranch that men desired more than her. She could feel the shame and grief again that she had felt as she watched the love of her life ride away. After he left, each day presented many challenges. She had no self-confidence, and it was not easy leaving her home to go to church or into town to shop. She knew the whole county was talking behind her back. She dreaded the uncertainty of her future so she vowed never to allow another man to enter her heart and have the ability to break it again.

She wiped tears from her eyes as she turned to face Glory with a new strength forming inside her. She had so many questions to ask about Tyler, but as she looked at the sweet, sick girl, she saw that she was finally sleeping soundly. Kathleen noticed the sticky spoon lying next to the dark bottle of cough syrup. This girl looked too young to have dark circles under her eyes and her skin was so pasty white; she looked too young to be the mother of a six-year-old. It was a shame that her life was going to end soon from an incurable disease. She should be at home in the arms of her mother; not lying here dying in a stranger's guest room. Kathleen and Rosa would assure her every day that her baby boy would be well taken care of and loved. Glory would never have to worry about Tyler Chambers coming near her or Sammy ever again. She would die before she allowed that low-life to hurt either one of them.

Kathleen adjusted the covers over Glory's frail body and said a prayer over her. "Lord, please have mercy on this mama. Help her rest and receive comfort as she struggles to be here for her son. Please, let her see that I love Sammy as if he were mine. Amen." She dried her eyes, walked softly out of the bedroom, and went into the kitchen for something to nibble on. She had not finished her supper and she was hungry.

Carlos was in the kitchen eating a piece of apple pie when Kathleen walked in. She walked over to the old man, placed her hand on his shoulder, and spoke softly to him. "I'm fine—now. Please do not worry about me. I do not have any feelings in my heart for Tyler, only anger for his actions toward Glory and Sammy. I cannot believe that when he saw me today at the café that he did not say something. I can't believe he actually came back, but I pray that he leaves Sweetwater soon."

"It is possible that he was surprised to see you. He's the one that left here with no good-byes."

"I have a lot of questions to ask Glory about him. I want to know how she met up with him—things like that," she said to

Carlos.

"Si, I am wondering the same thing."

Tyler Chambers and his big, old burly companion, Moose Whitmore, were lying low in their room above the Last Chance Saloon. Tyler had pretended to be asleep as he lay in the bed plotting his strategy for getting his hands on some easy money.

As he sat up on the bed, he looked at Moose who was sitting by the window looking down on the street. "What are you gawking at old man?" asked Tyler.

"Hey, partner, it's good to see you awake. I'm hungry. Let's go eat."

"Listen, you're an endless pit of a cow. I am not made of money. Anyways, I have been making plans to get our hands on some real money. We will be able to move on down to Mexico and live like kings. Every night, we'll have a different gal," he laughed as he hit Moose on top of his head.

"Sounds good, but how we gonna get that kind of money, rob a bank?" Moose asked as he rubbed his head.

"Not quite. You remember me telling you about Glory's kid. The one I made her leave here when we went off to Abilene."

Moose shook his head as he remembered the night Tyler told him about sneaking away from the kid. Moose thought that Tyler had done a bad thing, but he did not voice his opinion. He had deserted the boy's mama miles from Abilene in a rundown shack because she cried and whined for her son.

"The brat is living with Glory at Kathleen Parker's ranch and that Parker gal has got a lot of money. She just sold part of her herd, five hundred head, in Abilene this past week. The herd that we stole the dozen cattle from back on the trail were part of the Parker woman's. We are already spending some of her money," he said laughing like a fool. Moose watched Ty walked around the room grinning like he had a trick card up his sleeve.

Her ramrod is bringing her a bank draft home as we sit here." Tyler jerked back the raggedy curtain hanging on the dirty window and looked down on the street.

"What're we going to do with a bank draft? That's only a piece of paper, ain't it?"

"The bank draft will be turned into cash you idiot, and placed in the bank, here in Sweetwater. That Parker gal will have plenty of money to hand over to us as ransom money."

Moose sat staring at Tyler. He did not understand who was going to get kidnapped. He waited until Tyler finished telling him his big money making scheme.

"We kidnap Glory's boy because the Parker woman loves the little boy. She will pay any amount of money for his return. Right?" Moose asked, finally understanding the scheme of things.

"Moose, my man, you got it right. Yes, we take the boy; hide him out, and have a ransom note delivered to her. Once she pays us, she gets the boy back; simple as one, two, three."

"What about the law? You'll have the sheriff and a posse on our trail and everybody in the county will be looking for us."

"We put in the ransom note that if they tell anyone about the kidnapping, we will kill the youngster. If we have to prove that we have the boy, we can cut one of his fingers off and send it to them. Man! We will get that money in a flash. No questions asked."

Moose stood up and walked around the room. "Listen to me, you young whippersnapper. I don't hurt women or babies." Moose's voice quivered as he spoke to Tyler. "You might take the boy, but he ain't going to be hurt. I don't like people hurting children."

"Of course we won't harm the boy, but we have to make them think that we will or they won't give us the money. See?"

"Yep, I got you now. When do we grab the boy and where do we hide him afterward?" Moose felt better knowing that Tyler was only kidding about hurting the child. He sure would like to get his hands on some big money. He really would like to have the means to put a good distance between himself and Tyler. He was tired of him and his mean-spirited ways.

"You're going to grab the youngster and take him to the shack that Glory stayed in outside of Abilene. I am going to stay here and when I'm sure that Kathleen Parker's money is in the bank, I will send them the ransom note. I will be here for a little while to see what they are going to do about trying to get the boy back without having to give us the money. Then I will join you at the shack and be there for the exchange. Afterward, we can head to the boarder and start living the good life."

"When and where do I kidnap the boy?"

"You'll go out to the Parker ranch and watch for the boy to be outside alone. You know boys. They are always outside playing. When he is alone, you grab him and ride away. I'm sure it will be awhile before the boy is missed."

"How am I going to feed him?"

"I'll go over to the dry goods store and get some beans, link sausages and a few other things. You will be just fine for a couple of days. You ain't gonna starve for gosh sakes!"

**********

Matt and Juan awakened to the sound of howling winds and dark gray clouds overhead as they hurriedly got their gear on their packhorse and saddled their horses for riding the last miles home. The rain began peppering down and the wind blew harder. The two men decided that they had better find an old cabin or a cave to hold up in until the bad weather ended. After moving slowly through an open field of dead wildflowers, Juan spotted the top of an old brick chimney about a hundred yards off the road in a thicket of tall pine trees. The rain was pouring down and the horses were soaking wet with mud caked on their underbellies. The cabin came into sight and they hurried into a leaning barn that would protect the animals from the bad weather. After removing their saddles and draping their saddle blankets across a crumbled stall, they used an old rag and wiped the horses as dry as they could.

"I'll check out the well when the rain lets up and then I'll water and feed them," said Juan.

Once the two men were inside the cabin, Juan checked out the fireplace. "Looks like this place has been used by others not too long ago; there's still wood stacked on the floor."

"There are two bunks here but only one mattress. You can take it and I'll sleep on the floor," said Matt.

"No thanks," laughed Juan. "Mama would kill me if I slept on that nasty thing and brought home bed bugs. I'll sleep on the floor beside you in front of the fire."

The storm slammed tree limbs upon the roof and rain spattered the windowpanes. "We got here just in time," said Matt, as he opened two cans of beans. The coffee was brewing and the two men were thankful that they were able to find the small haven— even if it did leak like a sieve.

Early the next morning the rain was still coming down in a fine drizzle. Matt and Juan drank hot coffee and ate a hard biscuit.

Food was the last thing on their minds. They wanted to get home as soon as possible. They saddled their horses and rode as fast as they could in the foul weather toward Sweetwater.

Wiping her hands on her apron, Kathleen heard a noise at the back door of the café. She walked over and opened the door. "Oh, my goodness! Oh, my," she said as her hand went to her hair as she smoothed her long black braid. "Come in," Kathleen said to Matt as he stood looking weather beaten from traveling the last miles' home in the storm. "Where's Juan?" she asked as she closed the door to keep the rain from coming in.

"I sent him home. I know his folks are anxious to see him."

"Of course. Oh, Matt, it's so good to see you. I was worried when you did not make it home yesterday. The storm was bad here," she said as her words trailed off. She could not take her eyes off his face, his hair. *His hair—oh my, he is all wet*, she thought suddenly. "Oh Matt, come over here to the sink and let me get you a dry towel. I do not know what I was thinking. I'll cause you to catch your death while standing there in the doorway."

"I'm fine, Katy, stop fluttering around like a hummingbird and come here. I've missed you." His voice was rough and husky sounding as he pulled her close.

Matt was going to kiss her. Right here, right now. Kathleen moved her body closer allowing his breath to rush over her lips. People were coming from all different directions calling his name. Everyone was excited to have him home.

He leaned away from Kathleen, but he ached to kiss her. They needed privacy, but none was to be found. She lowered her eyes and placed her hands in her apron as he turned to speak to Mr. Crocker and Mrs. Porter. Matt shook Mr. Crocker's hand as he asked for a big cup of strong coffee.

"Give me your slicker and let me hang it up for you. I bet you're wet all the way down to your union suit," said Mrs. Porter as Kathleen's face turned a bright red.

Matt chuckled as he saw the shocked expression on Kathleen's face. "You're right, but after I drink my coffee I will head home to my ranch. If I know Lucy, she'll have me in dry clothes faster than a rattler can strike."

Kathleen sliced Matt a piece of apple pie and placed his coffee in front of him. "Sit with me for a minute while I enjoy this feast," he said as he scooped a piece of pie into his mouth. "I want you to make me a whole pie, just for me. No sharing with anybody." Matt grinned as he sipped the coffee.

"There's not much I can refuse you now that you carried my herd to market. So, you will have one apple pie in a few days, Sir."

"I have taken care of everything at the bank. You, Miss Parker, are now a very wealthy woman. I signed some papers as your agent but there are papers you need to sign to finalize everything."

"Thank you so much for everything. I'll never be able to repay you."

"Have you given Mr. Crocker your notice? You do not need to work here any longer. He'll manage without you."

"Yes and no. I told him that I was not going to work once you arrived home, but no, I have not told him when my last day was going to be. I think he has it figured out," she said smiling.

"I do see a couple of new faces working here." Matt turned in his chair and stood up. "I better get home and check on my place. I'm sure everything is fine, since Carlos was checking in on the boys every day."

As he was placing his slicker back on, Kathleen said that she wanted him to come to supper and bring Lucy if the weather permitted. "I have several important things to tell you."

"Has something happened that I should know about?"

She walked him to the back door and stepped out on the small porch with him. "Sammy's mama has come back to Sweetwater."

"What! When?" Before Kathleen could answer, he was showing anger for the woman who abandoned her child.

"Matt, listen to me. Glory, that is her name, is sick. Very sick and she is staying out at my ranch."

"Lord help us all." He slapped his Stetson on his wet hair and said that he would be over tonight, no matter the condition of the weather. He leaned into her quickly and placed a hard kiss on her rosy lips. "Damn, if I care who seen that!"

Kathleen hung her head as she entered back inside the café. She heard giggling coming from Mr. Crocker and Mrs. Porter as they stood huddled up against the tub of dirty dishes.

*They can laugh if they want, but I am not blind*, she thought, as she watched sweet loving sparks fly between them. She grinned as she glanced their way. She knew they saw Matt kiss her.

"Back to work, you two lovebirds. We got a few stragglers in the dining room that want to be fed," she said as she went through the bat-wing doors to take the latecomers order.

Mrs. Porter and Mr. Crocker looked at each other in surprise. They both thought that they had kept their feelings hidden from each other. "Lorraine, Mrs. Porter, I didn't know that my feelings for you showed. I hope you do not mind that I have loving feelings for you and your young'uns. If you had a pa, I would go and speak to him. I'd ask if I could step out with you, court you, oh for heavens sakes, this is so darn silly. We aren't children. I want to marry you—soon! That is, if you'll have me?"

Mrs. Porter stood with her hands over her mouth as she watched Mr. Crocker stumble through his much-unexpected proposal of marriage. His face had soap suds on his chin and his hands were dripping wet. The front of his apron had chicken grease stains with flour spotted all over, but he never looked so handsome.

"Oh my goodness, look at me. I'd had my hands up to my elbows in dish water and my hair coming down—."

"Shut your mouth woman. You never looked more beautiful." Mr. Crocker placed one of his wet hands over her mouth. He looked down into the eyes of the most beautiful forty-five year old woman he had ever seen.

She reached and removed his large, rough palm off her mouth as she said, "Yes, yes, and yes! I would be honored to be your wife."

Kathleen laughed and clapped her hands in joy as she had overheard the last part of Mr. Crocker's proposal. "Oh Kathleen, you heard! I can't believe this big bear of a man wants to marry me."

"Why not? You are the best thing that has ever happened to him and if I may say so, for this café too. Lucy and I will be glad to help with the wedding." Kathleen hugged Mrs. Porter and then Mr. Crocker.

"You know, Kathleen, I want to tell you that the day you came to work for me actually saved this place. I never told you but I was planning on selling out and moving on. Shore glad you came through that door," he said as he smiled at his bride-to-be.

"Let's feed those people so we can get out of here. You two

have a lot of planning to do and I have a bit of news to share with Matt. I wanted to tell you that I would continue to work the rest of the week. Maybe you can get another lady, *in need,* to come and work for you," she commented with a grin.

# Chapter 21

As the stars were beginning to come out, Matt rode into Kathleen's yard. He was tying his horse to the hitching rail when Sammy dashed out the front door, leaped off the porch and grabbed Matt around the leg. "Hold on partner. Careful with the bad leg," he said laughing as he picked the boy up into his arms.

Sammy hugged Matt around the neck and asked, "Ain't that leg ever going to get well?"

"I hope so son, I hope so. Have you been a good boy while I was away? You know old St. Nicholas will be heading this way in a couple weeks."

"Heck, I know that, but I've got a big surprise for you in the house. You will never guess! It's something I wanted so badly and now I have it."

"I thought you just said you had a surprise for me?" Matt tickled Sammy as he sat him back down on the ground and took his hand.

"Well, it's kinda for you but mostly for me. You want to guess?"

"You just lead me to this big surprise," said Matt as he opened the door and entered the foyer.

"Good evening, Matt," said Kathleen.

Matt looked up and saw the most beautiful young woman in the world standing in front of him. He let out a whistle as he took off his Stetson and placed it and his gun belt on the coat rack in the foyer.

"I do declare Miss Kathleen; if you ain't the prettiest gal I have ever laid eyes upon. If I had known you were getting all gussied up, I would have put on my Sunday duds." Matt looked at Kathleen with her long black hair flowing down her back. She was wearing a new green dress with tiny buttons down the front with soft lace trim on the collar. The sleeves were puffed on the shoulders and tight at the cuffs. She was wearing soft black slippers.

"Come on, Mr. Matt. I wanna show you my surprise." Sammy started pulling on Matt's arm toward the bedroom.

"Sammy, let's take Mr. Matt into the parlor and tell him about your surprise first. We want to prepare him so he will not be too shocked. All right? First, you go and tell Rosa that Mr. Matt is here. She will want to say hello before dinner."

"Shucks," he mumbled under his breath and sighed, "All right, but you won't tell him my surprise while I am gone, will you."

"I promise," she said as she held up two fingers as she had seen him doing with Pedro.

After Sammy left the room, Matt asked if the surprise was his mama in the guest room.

"Yes, he wants you to meet her, but Matt; she's so sick and frail. She has consumption and she bleeds from the mouth all the time. She is so weak I do not know how much longer she will be with us. Really, God is the only one that knows that."

"Mr. Matt, it's so good to have you home. We are thankful for your help and now Kathleen can stay home, work her ranch, and not worry about keeping a roof over our heads. I hope you are hungry because I got a big dinner ready to go on the table," said Rosa excited and happy as she reached to give Matt a big hug.

"Give us a few minutes Rosa. Sammy has a surprise for Matt."

"Si! We'll eat when you are ready." Rosa turned and went back into the dining room.

Sammy took Matt's hand and led him to his mama's bedroom. He stopped and knocked on her door.

"Come in," a weak voice called.

"That's my surprise, Mr. Matt." Sammy pointed his small fingers at the small frail girl lying in the bed. "My mama came back to town to find me and she did, too. Come in and meet her."

As Matt walked into the room with Sammy pulling him and Kathleen following close behind, he nodded his head at Glory.

Sammy climbed up on the bed next to his mama and said, "Mama, this here is my new sidekick, Mr. Matt. He has been gone for a while but now he's home for good."

Glory tried to sit up a little taller but she was so weak that she had no strength in her upper arms. "Please madam, stay like you are. No need to sit up to talk to me," said Matt.

"To tell the truth, I feel as if I know you all ready. Sammy talks about you all the time. Thank you so much for taking care of my little man. He cares for you very much."

"I love him, mama just like he was my real papa." Sammy beamed up at Matt.

"You have a fine boy, Miss Glory," said Matt with a lump in his throat. He had no idea that Sammy's feelings for him were so strong.

Kathleen walked over to the bed and took Sammy's hand. "Come on gentlemen and let's go feast on the wonderful dinner that Rosa has put together as a welcome home party for Matt and Juan. Glory, I will bring you a tray in a few minutes."

"So nice meeting you, Mr. Matt," said Glory, trying hard not to cough. "Miss Kathleen, please only bring me a little bit to eat. I'm not very hungry tonight."

After the trio went to the dining table, Matt was still emotional about Sammy's remark about his true feelings for him. He shook hands with Carlos, Juan and Pedro before he sat down to the table. After a short grace, everyone enjoyed the platters of food. Once the kitchen was cleaned, everyone went into the parlor to hear about the adventures that Juan and Matt had on the trail drive. Juan had many exciting things to tell, since he had never been on a trail drive before.

Matt told about the two cowboys rustling their cattle, but how the beef had been discovered in the corral at the stockyard. He explained how his friend, the sheriff, had helped him get the money for the dozen cows back from the butcher.

Juan shared about the long, hard days of pushing the cattle and herding them together during a bad thunderstorm. He talked about the long nights laying in his bedroll listening to the sound of the harmonica. It was soothing and peaceful. Overall, he was glad he made the trip, but did not think he wanted to go on another one anytime soon. Everyone laughed.

Kathleen said that she had some exciting and unexpected good news. "Mr. Crocker and Mrs. Porter are going to get married soon; maybe before Christmas. They have had feelings for each other for a while."

"Who would have ever thought that big bear of a man could get a nice lady like Mrs. Porter to marry him," said Carlos.

"Carlos, shame on you," said Rosa. "That man gave Kathleen a job when we needed the money. He is a good catch for Mrs. Porter. She has three hungry mouths to feed and care for until they are grown. That is a big responsibility for a man to take into his house. I'd say she is pretty darn lucky to have, what you say, oh, to reel him in." Every one busted into laughter again.

After dinner Matthew said he better head home because Lucy was feeling a little under the weather. He had not talked with his ranch hands about the ranch since he left. Kathleen watched Matt strap his gun belt on his lean hips. He opened the door for her to walk out with him.

As Kathleen pulled her shawl tighter over her shoulders, she looked at Matt. "All right, I know you have something to tell me. I have noticed the way you kept looking toward Glory's room. What's going on?" Matt said as he led her to the porch swing.

"You think you know me pretty well, don't you?"

"I think that I know when something is bothering you, yes," he replied.

"Matt, you aren't going to believe this—just like I couldn't at first. Glory's old boyfriend that made her leave Sammy here in Sweetwater is Tyler Chambers; my Tyler, the young boy, who chose money over me, when I was a young girl."

"You're joking. How can that be?"

"Be? Well, it just is. She met him in a small town while she was working as a barmaid in a saloon. She said that he charmed her into coming with him to Abilene, where he was supposed to have a job lined up. After traveling awhile together, he got tired of Sammy. Well, you know the rest."

"How did you find out that her boyfriend was this Tyler fellow?"

"That's the part that has me worried. He has followed Glory here. She hasn't seen him, but when he came in the café with his partner Sammy recognized him. He was so frightened that he ran into the kitchen and hid. He told me that his mama's mean boyfriend was in the dining room. I went out in the dining room to get a good look at him, but I didn't recognize Tyler."

"What does this man look like?" Matt asked because he was going to pay this fellow a visit.

"He's tall and very lean. His sandy blond hair is now a dirty, light brown and he has a bad scar under his left eye, like he had been in a knife fight with someone. Of course, he did not look like the young handsome boy I knew nearly thirteen years ago. He looked too thin and rugged," she said as if her mind was wandering back to the past.

"Why do you think he came back here?"

"Glory said that he had told her he would never let her go. She was his and she had better not try to leave him. Since he didn't want her child, she couldn't figure him out."

"I'm glad you told me about him. Please don't worry. I will have a talk with him and the sheriff. If he even thinks about coming near Glory or Sammy, I will have him locked under the jailhouse. Come walk me out to the barn to get my horse."

Matt removed his jacket and wrapped it around Kathleen's shoulders as he walked into the barn pulling her in behind him. He had missed this woman so much and he was not leaving tonight without a kiss.

Matt turned and faced Kathleen. He walked toward her as she stepped back. He leaned into her as she pressed back into the barn wall. He was holding her tight, too tight, and too close. Breathing was hard.

"Please Matt, you're hurting me," she said, barely above a whisper. Guilt floated through him as he heard her words. He was almost crazy for wanting her so badly. The moment he saw Katy, he knew she was like no other woman. Even with his body in great pain, he released her. She was genuine, a true woman.

Matt needed more of her soft, tender kisses. He loosened his hold but still held her close to deepen his kiss. His Katy was shy and hesitant, so she turned her face away.

Kathleen lowered her forehead and placed it in the middle of his chest while trying to get control of her emotions. She wanted Matt in every way a woman could want a man, but she was afraid, unsure, untrusting of his true feelings.

Matt knew she had never experienced a kiss by a man in her life, certainly not with true passion, so he lifted her chin so he could see into her eyes.

"Katy, I'm not going to apologize for stealing a few kisses. To tell you the truth, I want much more from you," he said with a soft chuckle. "I better let you go back in the house before we have to beat the newly engaged couple to the altar."

He pulled his horse close and got on him, and she watched him ride away. "Thank you Lord for allowing Matt into my life," she prayed as she shivered from the loss of the warmth of Matt's jacket. She hurried back into the house.

*******

As the weeks passed by, Kathleen had gotten into her daily routine of caring for her ranch. With the cold winter days nearing, bales of hay and bags of oats had to be carried out to the pastures to feed the remaining five hundred head of cattle that had not been sold with the others.

Matt was busy at his own ranch with his small herd of cattle. He had gathered his cows closer in to his ranch house and the men carried bales of hay and spread it out for the animals to eat. Some mornings, the top layer of the water troughs were covered with a sheet of ice and the men would bust the crusted layer. Matt had traveled to a small farm about twenty miles away and purchased himself a nice bull to help increase his herd. He hoped by spring, he might see some little white faced calves out in the pastures. He and Lucy had gotten into a nice routine. She cooked him three meals a day, kept his house clean and washed his clothes regularly. They would sit in the parlor at night like two old married people. She knitted and he read the newspaper. Several times a week he would visit Kathleen.

Glory and Sammy were always very pleased to see Matt. The doctor was surprised that Glory was still alive. He gave Kathleen all the credit for her improved health. Glory appeared at times to be stronger, and then other days, she could hardly lift her head. Sammy did not want to leave her and go to school, but thankfully, Glory insisted that he learn to read and write.

When Kathleen and Rosa drove into town, they stopped by Matt's ranch and asked Lucy if she would like to go with them. She readily agreed and Kathleen left a note for Mr. Matt telling him where Lucy had gone. Lucy asked as she got into the carriage, if they had seen the bad white woman, Lillian.

Kathleen and Rosa laughed and said no, but not to worry. She was working at the dress- makers shop so they should not run into her. "We are going to the café and talk to Mrs. Porter about her wedding plans. We want to offer to help with the refreshments," laughed Kathleen.

"I can do that, too," replied Lucy, "if old Indian squaw is allowed to be there."

When the three women entered the Heavenly Hash Café, a loud voice boomed from the kitchen. "Welcome ladies," said Mr. Crocker. "Lorraine is waiting for you. She saw you coming."

"It's Lorraine now," said Rosa, as she followed the other two ladies into the kitchen. "About time he called her by her given name since they are engaged," replied Kathleen.

"Oh, my goodness, I am so glad to see you all. I am a bundle of nerves with so many things to do before the wedding next week. I wanted to wait until spring, but that bull headed man in there said no way was he going through another winter without a woman to warm his sheets." All the women laughed at the way Lorraine spoke about a man and woman.

"Praise the good Lord!" said Lorraine and she looked to the ceiling. "Will you help me prepare and serve refreshments to our guests? I wanted to serve cake and coffee but no, you know who says, we are cooking enough food to feed everyone who attends. He has invited the whole town. There's a note pinned by the door with an announcement of our pending wedding inviting everyone who comes through that door. He even placed one at the post office!"

"Now Lorraine, you have to be proud. Mr. Crocker is happy and he wants everyone to know that he is getting married. Not everyone in town will attend, but you will have a big crowd for sure. Oh, what a celebration!" Kathleen was almost giddy as she talked about decorating the café with Christmas wreaths and holly branches.

"Oh, I can't thank you enough. I have to move all of our belongings over to Mr. Crocker's house and get Christmas gifts for my children. I have to bake cookies and get things ready to decorate the tree. That man says that he's getting the biggest tree he can find."

Rosa, Lucy and Kathleen could not help but smile. "Who would have ever thought Mr. Crocker was so romantic and loving toward children. You, Lorraine, are one lucky woman. Enjoy everything that he does for you," said Kathleen as she gave Lorraine a big hug.

"That's good advice. Enjoy, love and be loved. Make your man happy because when he's happy, the world is good," said Rosa.

"Don't be sad. We help you," said Lucy.

"Oh girls, I feel so much better. You have lifted a load off my shoulders. Thank you so much. We will supply the food if you will come here and cook some of it the day before and the morning of the wedding."

"No problem and we will decorate while the food is cooking. We'll close the café the day of the wedding," declared Kathleen.

Afterward, the three women went shopping at the dry good's store. The store had taken on a gala appearance since they had been in it last time. There were barrels of apples and oranges placed by the door with small containers of pecans and walnuts. Every kind of stick candy was sitting on a shelf, just waiting for a customer to purchase some to fill Christmas stockings. There were all types of baby dolls laying in homemade cradles and broomstick horses with different colored yarn manes. Carved wooden horses, wagons, corrals, and play guns were sitting on a table in the center of the room. Lovely homemade dresses hung on racks and new western wear for men was stacked in the back of the store with new soft slippers, sensible high-top shoes, and cowboy and work boots. All types of women's trinkets from bracelets and necklaces to ceramic birds, vases, and pretty dishes decorated the shelves of the store. The Christmas spirit had certainly arrived in Sweetwater.

Lucy eased close to Kathleen and said that she had never seen so much stuff. "Most of it useless," she added. Kathleen and Rosa laughed at her curt remark.

Kathleen went to the back of the store and chose several gifts for Juan, Pedro and Carlos. Looking at the women's things, she chose a new cotton gown and a robe to match for Glory.

Last year, she had made her Christmas gifts for everyone, but with no money worries, she wanted this year to be special. She decided she would have to make a trip to town very soon without Rosa. Sammy's big gift from St. Nicholas was going to be a new pony, but she did chose some new western boots, a new hat and a shiny belt bucket like the ones the men wore for him.

Rosa picked up a few wooden toys that he could play with inside the house.  She chose a new checkerboard set for Carlos, since he was like a big kid and enjoyed playing the game. She had decided that she would have to make another trip to town alone in order to complete her shopping.

Later that evening, Matt came calling on Kathleen after supper. He accepted a cup of coffee but refused pie or cake. "Lucy had a big stew cooked and I ate my fill," he said as he ran his hand across his stomach.

"Lucy tells me that you girls are going to help with the wedding refreshments at the café. Let me know if I can help in anyway.  You know, I am happy for those two, Wilbur and Lorraine. They are like two young lovebirds."

"That's for sure. I've seen them kissing and Mr. Crocker patted Mrs. Porter's fanny," said Sammy.

"Sammy!" screamed Rosa, before she realized her reaction.

"You, you, shouldn't repeat things like that," said Rosa, trying to calm down.

"I'm sorry," he said as he hung his head down, embarrassed that she scolded him in front of Matt.

"Sammy, why don't you go and check on your mama before it's your bedtime?" Kathleen rubbed his wet hair and patted his back as he passed by her.

Rosa went into the kitchen still mumbling under her breath about children repeating everything that they see and hear. Kathleen looked at Matt and shook her head. "Sammy doesn't miss much that goes on around him."

"I'll sure have to start looking over my shoulder when I steal a few kisses from you, like about now," he said, as he pulled her close and placed his lips over hers.

"Matt, what has come over you?" Kathleen's eyes moistened.

"You, you've come over me and I want you more than I can show you," he said as he nuzzled her neck and kissed her again behind the ear, taking in the sweet smell of her freshly washed hair.

Kathleen's heart was so full of love that she could only look up into his eyes. Before Matt released her hands, he led her over to the sofa. "Katy, we have many things to discuss."

She twisted her hands slowly while lowering her eyes.

He sat still while she adjusted herself close to him. "Are you afraid of me?"

"No!" she opened her eyes and looked into his. Her voice shook as she whispered, "I've never felt afraid of you, only afraid of my own feelings."

She lowered her face and wiped her hands across her lap as she felt herself blush.

"I love you, Katy." Matt whispered.

Her eyes closed tightly as she said softly, "Please say that again so I'll know that I am not dreaming."

"I love you," he said the cherished words to her again.

She opened her eyes and ran her fingers over his bottom lip as if to make sure the words came from him. "Oh my love, I've waited so long to hear those sweet words."

"I have had feelings for you almost from the beginning, after our first meeting, when I was laid up in your guest room. I want us to start planning a future together, that is if you say yes to my proposal".

Kathleen's eyes sparkled with tears as Matt lowered himself down on one knee in front of her. "Katy, my love, will you consent to becoming my wife?"

She threw her arms around his neck and sighed into his neck, "Yes, yes, and yes. I love you and I want to become your wife." They kissed and kissed again repeatedly. Finally, they pulled away.

"I have made a mess of this proposal," he growled more at himself than to her. "I don't have a ring for you. I should have waited until I could have placed a ring on your finger,"

"A ring doesn't matter," Kathleen said softly as she placed her finger under his chin and lifted his face to look into her eyes.

"How soon can I make you my woman?" Matt asked.

"If I had my way, we would run away now, tonight," she said laughing with joy. However, Matt, there is Glory lying in my guestroom practically on her deathbed. There is uncertainty about the whereabouts of Tyler, which is causing me to be afraid for Glory and Sammy. A wedding is coming up in a few days for Mr. Croaker and Lorraine. Let us not spoil their big moment by over shadowing their day with our wedding announcement. At their reception, Carlos can make an announcement about our wedding."

"Are we gonna have to have a big shindig like theirs?" Before

Kathleen could answer he said, "Why can't we ride off into the sunset and find a parson and then camp out under the stars for our first union together." He gave her a cocky grin and moved in to capture her sweet lips again. "It doesn't look like I have a say so in this matter, does it?" Matt sighed.

"I know Rosa is going to want to make a big fuss over our wedding. I am like a daughter to her. I will have to visit Dolly's Dress Shop and let her help me with a wedding dress. With Christmas almost here, I have so much to do."

"Alright, I should have realized that all of your close friends are going to make a fuss over the wedding, and rightly so. You are dear to them and this will be a very special occasion for you –and me," he said as he nibbled on her neck.

"Oh Matt, you are one of the sweetest and most understanding men that I know. I love you dearly."

*******

After a few days, the sun came out and the weather was cool and crisp; a perfect day for a fall wedding. Everyone had arrived at the church dressed in his or her Sunday best. Pedro had volunteered to stay home and care for Glory who was too weak to travel to town to join in the celebration. Once Kathleen, Matt and Sammy entered the church, she commented to Matt that she believed the whole town had turned out. He laughed and said that they had heard there was to be "free food" at the café afterward.

As the organ struck up the first note, everyone settled down in the church. Mrs. Wingate, the church organist for the past ten years, looked over her wire-rimmed glasses as she watched everyone sit up straighter and stop their chatter. The wedding march began softly and the two double doors of the vestibule opened. The minister walked out of the side door and took his place in front of the church. He was wearing a dark brown frock coat that came down to his thighs with a matching vest and solid brown bowtie. He carried his Bible tucked close to his body with one hand up to his chest. He had combed his thinning hair over the bald spot, as he did every Sunday.

Mr. Crocker and his best man, Frank Thomas, the local barber, trailed behind the minister dressed in brand new dark suits. He had purchased the suits and Mrs. Porter had the dressmaker, Dolly, tailor the suits to fit perfectly. The barbershop was directly beside the café and Frank Thomas had been cutting Mr. Crocker's hair and giving him a shave occasionally for years. He gave his friend the royal treatment earlier this morning. He had slicked down Mr. Crocker's hair with sweet smelling tonic water and Kathleen thought he never looked better.

As the music continued softly, Patricia Anne, Mrs. Porter's thirteen-year-old daughter, wearing a long pink dress with a collar that came up to her neck and covered both of her shoulders, walked proudly down the aisle. Mr. Crocker had been very generous with new clothes for all of his new family to be.

Patricia completed her walk down the aisle. She stopped on the opposite side of the minister and Mr. Crocker. She winked at her new step-father-to-be as she turned to face the wedding guests. Mrs. Wingate played the wedding march loudly and everyone quickly stood up.

Sammy sat on a pew between Kathleen and Matt near the front of the church. He fidgeted and climbed up on the pew placing his hand on Matt's shoulder. "What's everyone looking at?" he said loudly.

"Quiet." Matt responded and placed his hand over Sammy's mouth. Mrs. Porter walked down the aisle in a lovely blue dress that flowed down to the top of her new slippers. Her gown had long sleeves that had puffs on the shoulder and fit tightly at the wrists. The bodice fit perfectly at the waist and showed off Mrs. Porter's trim figure. She wore her hair pulled back with a bun tucked on the back of her head with a long string of pearls woven into the hair. Mr. Crocker thought she was the most beautiful bride he had ever seen. When Mrs. Porter stopped in front of the men, Mr. Crocker reached for her hand and looked down into her lovely face. Both turned to face the minister. He still could not believe that she had agreed to marry him.

The minister gave a nod to Mrs. Wingate, who was now in her glory as she continued to play as if she was performing a recital. He cleared his throat loudly, but to no avail. Finally, after exhausting his patience, he called her name. She stopped and placed her soft, old hands over her mouth with an embarrassing giggle. She whispered, sorry, removed herself from behind the organ, and took her reserved seat on the front pew.

"Today, it gives me great pleasure to marry this man—." he

hesitated and several of the men snickered. He continued and said, "And this lovely woman."

After glaring over his wire-rimmed glasses at some of the men in the congregation, the minister began the ceremony. First he asked , "Wilbur Crocker, do you take this woman, Marie Lorraine Porter, to be your lawfully wedded wife, to have and to hold from this day forward, for better, for worse, for richer, for poorer, in sickness and health, and forsaking all others till death, according to God's holy ordinance and there to I give thee my troth. Signify by saying I do."

Mr. Crocker sounded like a bullfrog as he said, "I do." Several of the children laughed. He blushed and pulled at his tight collar.

Matt watched as Kathleen took one of her lovely hankies that he had brought her back from Abilene, and wiped the corner of her eyes.

The minister repeated the vows to Mrs. Porter, and she said I do very softly.

"In the presence of these witnesses and with the power invested in me by God, I now pronounce you man and wife."

The newly married couple stood gazing into each other's eyes. "Kiss her!" a cry came from the back of the church and everyone laughed and clapped their hands in celebration of the marriage.

After the kiss in front of the congregation, Mr. Crocker locked fingers with his new bride and yelled that everyone was welcome to the Heavenly Hash Café for refreshments and wedding cake. Mrs. Crocker gave him a wifely glare and he said quickly. "Well, they are." Mrs. Crocker shook her head and several of the women folk laughed.

Sammy pulled on Matt's arm and motioned for him to lean down. "Why are those old ladies crying? Ain't they happy?"

"Don't say ain't and yes, everyone is very happy," replied Matt as he patted Sammy and gave him a shove to move out of the church. Matt reached for Mr. Crocker's hand and congratulated him. Kathleen was looking around for Sammy when she saw him race out the front door of the church with two of his school friends; but Matt was watching Kathleen. Her long midnight black hair was hanging loose down her back, and her eyes were red from the tears she fought to hold back as she had listened to the vows.

As he watched Kathleen give Lorraine a sweet hug, Matt's

heart was beating wildly as he realized that he couldn't wait to repeat the same wedding vows to Kathleen—his Katy.

Kathleen, Rosa and Lucy hurried to the café to help with the food for the reception. From their hotel room, Tyler Chambers and his friend Moose were watching the wedding guests as they made their way out of the church.

"Today will be a perfect time for you to grab the boy, Moose. Everyone will be busy with the celebration and will not have their attention on him. He most likely won't be missed until they get ready to head back to the ranch. After a day, I will get a ransom note out to Kathleen. We want her to be very worried about the boy. Once she knows that he has been kidnapped, she will do anything we ask to get him back. Once she has received the note, then I will head toward the cabin to meet up with you. I will hide out and watch for them to make the money drop. I will ride to the cabin and we will turn the little fellow loose. We will head to the boarder and live like kings."

"How am I supposed to get the child today? He will probably be with other boys playing." Moose said as he rubbed the back of his neck.

"Hang around close to the back of the café. Kathleen probably allows him to play in the alleyway behind the café and other businesses." Tyler noticed the uncertainly on his partner's face as he walked around the hotel room. "Don't start to chicken out on me now, you hear? This can be done without anyone getting hurt."

"I dun told you that I don't hurt women and children." Moose was checking his saddlebags to make sure he had everything needed to camp out for a few days. "I can't take no pack horse. That will slow me down too much."

"Now, you're talking like the old Moose I know. Hurry up and get your horse saddled. Remember, you have to stay out of sight. If you grab the boy in a little while, you will only have to camp out one night before you make it to the cabin." Tyler was looking down toward the café and was watching the people as they entered the reception laughing and joking with each other.

## Chapter 22

After a long evening of celebrating, visiting and laughter, the wedding guests filed out of the café door heading home. All the single girls had a piece of wrapped wedding cake to place under their pillows. This ritual was supposed to bring them luck, and they would dream of their true love.

Once the newly married couple had departed the Heavenly Hash Café to spend the night at Mrs. Washington's Boarding House for their honeymoon night, Kathleen and Rosa sat down for a cup of coffee. Lorraine's oldest daughter was going to watch the other two children in Mr. Crocker's house—their new home.

"What a wonderful wedding," said Kathleen. "Lorraine made a lovely bride."

"You know Kathleen, Carlos didn't make the announcement of your wedding to Matt."

Kathleen glanced toward the doorway of the kitchen and sighed very big. "I know. Matt and I decided this morning that we would wait to make the announcement in church tomorrow."

Matt and Carlos walked into the dining room with their cups of coffee and sat down. "What a day? Lucy has everything in the kitchen put away. Do you want me to round up Sammy?" Matt asked as he pulled out a chair and straddled it backward.

"I guess we better gather everything and get on back to the ranch. Pedro will be glad for the help with the nightly chores and I am sure Glory is ready for some company, too."

Everyone looked at each other but there was no movement from any of them. They were all very tired from cooking, decorating, and serving the guests. Lucy came into the dining room and said that she had called Sammy from the alleyway but he was not out there.

"Let me go outside and call him. He has been having a great

time today playing with all his school friends." Kathleen walked to the front of the café and went out onto the boardwalk. Matt joined her and took her hand.

"Come on, let's walk around back and see if he's playing down the alleyway."

"You just want to get me in the dark," giggled Kathleen as she skirted away from him.

"You just wait until I catch you!" he said laughing as he walked faster.

*******

"Sammy! Watch out!" screamed one of the boys. Sammy had been chasing a ball out in the open field behind the livery when he heard his school friend yell to him. As he retrieved the ball and looked up, he saw a rider on a horse headed straight toward him. Before he could move out of the way of the horse, he felt himself lifted up off the ground. His body was slammed face down across the lap of the rider. The breath was knocked out of him, and his right arm lay up behind his back. He was sure it was broken. He tried to scream but he didn't have any air in his lungs. Tears streamed down his cheeks and his nose stopped up. He tried to twist and wiggle his little body to get in a more comfortable position but the big monster pushed down on his back and snarled. "Stay down brat before I have to hurt you."

"Please," Sammy was able to squeak out, "my arm is hurting." The big man grabbed Sammy's right arm and pulled it out in front of him. He jerked his small frame up to sit in front of him. "Stop that squalling and sit still. I don't want to hurt you."

"Who are you? Where are you taking me?" Sammy asked softly.

"You are going to stay a few days with me while my friend takes care of some business with your folks. When the business is over, then you can go home—back to your mama and that Parker woman."

"You know my mama?" Sammy asked as he used the sleeve of his new dress shirt to wipe his runny nose.

"Just lean back against me and enjoy the ride. We will camp in a little while."

Sammy leaned back into the chest of the biggest man that had ever held him. He could feel the muscles in his big arms and his soft beard rubbed up against his neck. His breath smelled of stinky whiskey.

Sammy had played hard in the field with his friends and he had not eaten very much at the reception. He and his friends wanted to get outside and play ball in the open field. He was tired and before he realized it, his head was nodding and he was fast asleep. After what seemed like only minutes, he felt his feet touch the ground. The big man removed his saddlebags and tossed them on the grass. He unsaddled his horse, walked him to a small stream, and then hobbled him in a grassy area away from the camp. When he returned to where he left Sammy, he was carrying an armful of firewood and a fresh canteen of water. He squatted down on one knee, smoothed out a ring in the dirt and made a fire. Wiping his hands down the side of his britches, he went to his saddle bags and got several cans of beans, two forks, two cups, the coffeepot and a small bag of coffee beans. Sammy never took his sleepy eyes off the big man. The man took out his knife and opened the beans. He set them on the edge of the fire to get warm. He placed the coffeepot in the fire. The aroma of the coffee beans smelled so good to Sammy. "I bet you aren't allowed to drink coffee," said the big man. "I'll pour you a cup of water."

Once the meal was over, the large man laid out his bedroll next to his saddle. "I don't know about you, young fellow, but I'm beat. Lie down and keep your trap shut unless you hear a big bear or something."

Sammy looked around at the dark woods that cast all kinds of shadows. He watched the big man settle down on his bedroll. He slipped his feet out of his scruffy boots that had big spurs attached with a star twirling on the end and placed his black hat over his face.

"Hey mister. Where am I going to sleep?"

"I don't give a damn, but be quiet wherever you lay your head." Sammy stood still while glancing around the fire ring. Maybe he should try to escape when the man went to sleep. However, he was not sure which way was back to Sweetwater, he thought as an owl gave a loud hoot. Sammy immediately jumped right in the center of his captive's stomach. "What was that?" Sammy cried.

"Oh! You trying to kill me with those shiny black shoes?"

The monster looked into the eyes of the frightened little boy. "Come on, and lay here beside me. Now be still and quiet. There ain't nothing out there but the horse."

Sammy rolled off the big man's stomach and tucked himself as close to the man's stomach as was possible. He was feeling safe and warm. Right before he drifted off to sleep, he asked the big man, "Sir, what's your name?"

"Moose, just call me Moose."

After a long ride the next day, Moose and Sammy rode up to the cabin that was going to be their home for a couple of days. Both of them were tired from traveling and sleeping on the hard ground with very little to eat. Sammy looked at the building that Moose called a cabin. He thought it was more like a rundown shack that looked worse than an out building that Kathleen used to store her winter feed.

Sammy was stiff and tired from riding for hours. Once Moose stopped the horse and sat looking over the area and the shack, Sammy tried to get off the horse.

"Hold on, boy." Moose got down and lifted Sammy to the ground. He steadied him as he led his big black horse over to a stall attached to the cabin. He unsaddled the animal and placed his saddle on a rotten looking rail. He took his horse blanket off and rubbed the horse's back while picking up a bucket. He slung the blanket next to the saddle and walked over to the well. After pulling up a fresh bucket of cool water, he used his hand to cup himself a big palm of water to drink.

"Come over here and get yourself a scoop of water before I give it to the horse. I have to go to the bushes and pee. You need to go?"

Sammy scooped up several palms of cool water and drank. "Yep," he replied to the man and followed him into the dark bushes.

After their necessities were completed, Moose motioned for Sammy to follow him into the cabin. He lit an old lantern that sat in the middle of the table. Once the room had light, Sammy thought that he had rather sleep outside under the stars as they did last night. The room had a fireplace on the back wall. It had been used recently. It had two bunk beds but only one mattress. There was a nest of rats but they quickly scurried out a hole in the wall.

After a quick meal of beans and link sausage, they prepared for bed. Moose rolled his bedroll out over the top of the single, dirty mattress. After checking on his horse and banking the fire, he removed his boots and stretched out on the bunk. Sammy stood looking around the room wondering where he was supposed to sleep. Tears welled up in his eyes as he wiped his runny nose on his sleeve. He was cold, tired and scared. He wanted Kathleen. Finally, Moose noticed the child standing, looking all around with tears in his eyes. He lifted his thin blanket and gave it a little wave toward Sammy. He scooted in the bedroll next to the big man. The space was small but they were so tired that they did not notice.

# Chapter 23

**Kathleen and Matt** hurried out into the dark alley. Matt playfully pulled at Kathleen and stopped her at the back of the café. He tried to nuzzle her neck but she pushed him away giggling like a young sixteen-year-old girl.

"Stop Matt. I've got to find Sammy before it is too late. The temperature is dropping and we all need to head for home. I know that Lucy and Rosa are as tired as I am."

"Shucks, you're no fun." Sensing the urgency in Kathleen's voice, he took her hand and pulled her along behind him. "Sammy!" Matt yelled as he pulled Kathleen into the alley.

After walking to the end of the alley that opened up to a wide-open field, Matt saw Jimmy Walker running toward him. He had removed his suit jacket and his Sunday shoes. His clothes were dusty and he had streaks of tears running down his dirty face.

Jimmy ran straight into Matt's two tall legs and threw his small arms around them. Kathleen bent down to Jimmy's level and asked him what was wrong. "Why are you crying son? Are you hurt?"

He shook his head so hard that his straight blond hair flipped back and forth across his face. "No madam. I ain't hurt but I bet Sammy is," he replied while running his hand across his nose removing the snot that had formed.

"What do you mean son? Where is Sammy now?" Matt asked quietly.

"A man—a big man on a black horse rode right up to Sammy and grabbed him. He jerked Sammy off the ground and carried him away. I screamed for Sammy to watch out—but it was too late." Jimmy threw his arms around Kathleen's neck and shed tears onto her new dress.

"Jimmy, listen to me and stop crying—please. How long ago

was this? Did you know this big man? Did he hurt Sammy?"
Kathleen was so scared that she rattled off one question after
another.

"Kathleen, please. Let me have Jimmy." Matt took Jimmy out
of Kathleen's arms and he held him tight and patted him on his
back as he started walking back toward the café.

"Jimmy, had you ever seen this man and his horse before?"
Matt asked.

"No, sir I don't think so." Jimmy replied. He had stopped
crying and he felt safe now that he was in Matt arms.

"Do you think that Sammy may have known him?"

"I ain't sure, but I don't think so because the man jerked him
up onto his horse and I heard Sammy cry out. I called to the man
to bring Sammy back but he rode off that way and never even
looked back at me. I tell you something, Mr. Matt, that man scared
me."

"One more question before I take you to your folks? Did you
see anyone else besides this big man on the horse?"

"No sir. No body. Sammy and me was just fixing to come
back to the café when I saw the big horse riding fast right at
Sammy. I yelled for Sammy to watch out, but I guess he didn't
hear me."

Kathleen was walking beside Matt and Jimmy, listening to all
the questions and answers. She was so afraid. She knew that some
monster of a man who rode a big horse had kidnapped Sammy.
Why? She asked herself. *What did this person hope to gain by
taking a child away?*

After meeting Jimmy's parents in front of the café, Matt
explained quickly what had taken place in the field. Matt ushered
Kathleen back into the café and asked Juan if he would go get the
sheriff. There was precious little time before dark and Matt knew
he had to get on the kidnapper's trail as soon as possible. He
already had a good start.

In less than an hour, Matt had ridden to his ranch, changed out
of his Sunday clothes, and grabbed his bedroll and a few personal
items. Lucy had hurried into the kitchen and packed some food in
his saddlebags. Juan had volunteered to travel with Matt and he
agreed. He had enjoyed Juan's company on the trail drive and he
proved to be a good tracker too. Carlos watched his son leave with

Matt. He said a silent prayer while making the sign of the cross across his chest as they rode out of the yard.

Kathleen stood on the front porch as she watched Matt and Juan leave. Rosa hugged her and told her to come back inside before she caught her death. She slowly followed Rosa back inside the house. Kathleen was not looking forward to telling Glory, Sammy's mama, what had happened to him today. No mother wanted to hear that her son had been hurt, or even worse, kidnapped by a stranger. Nevertheless, she had no choice but to tell her.

Glory had stayed home because she was too weak to dress and ride into town and attend the wedding celebration. Pedro had stayed behind and watched over her and the ranch. Now that everyone was back from the wedding, Glory was eager to hear all about it, especially from Sammy. He had promised to bring her a piece of wedding cake.

Kathleen walked slowly into Glory's room. She was propped up with two pillows; most of the time she was lying down fast asleep. However, this evening, she had brushed her long pretty hair and was plaiting it as Kathleen stopped and watched. Glory glanced at Kathleen and smiled.

"Good evening Kathleen. How was the wedding?" she asked as she looked behind her to see if Sammy had followed.

"It was lovely. Everything was nice and Mrs. Porter, Lorraine, looked beautiful."

"That's nice," Glory said before she started coughing. Kathleen offered her a clean handkerchief. "Thank you," she said out of breath.

"Where's Sammy?" Glory whispered as she took a small sip of cool water.

"Glory, something has happened. Today, after the wedding, Sammy was playing with his friends in the open field behind the alley. A man on a horse rode up and grabbed Sammy and rode away with him."

"What?" cried Glory?

"Jimmy Walker said a big man on a large horse took Sammy."

Glory struggled to get out of the bed. She tried to swing her small feet off the bed and sit up straight. "I've got to go find him. I can't," she started to say as a coughing fit shook her body so hard she fell back over on her side. Kathleen rushed over to her and pulled on her small frame re-positioning her on the pillows.

"Please lay still, Glory. You can't go after Sammy. Matt and Juan have already left. Juan is a great tracker and Matt is sure they will pick up the man's trail pretty quick."

"Kath, I think it may be Ty. I know he's mad at me for leaving him and running back to Sweetwater to get my baby. He had said many times that he wouldn't let me go." The coughing racked her body again. After wiping the blood off her mouth, she continued.

"I don't know why he felt that I was his property, but ever since I took up with him, he was very possessive of me. He didn't like it when I cooked and fed Sammy and heaven help us if he saw me playing with him. He would scream at me to leave Sammy alone and come and sit in his lap and talk to him."

Glory lay back on the pillows as tears trailed down her cheeks as she tried to convey how her life was with Tyler Chambers. "I was happy at first with all his attention. I never had anyone to show any affection toward me. My mama was overworked and tired all the time because she had seven children to care for. I was the oldest so she screamed at me from the time she got up in the morning until every last child was in the bed at night." Glory's spoke so softly it was all Kathleen could do to hear her. "My pa would whip the younger babies for any reason he felt justified. I would stand over them and take the blunt of the punishment. I didn't have a dress or blouse that didn't have rips in the back." Glory wiped her eyes and drank a cup of water that Kathleen had given her. "When I was fifteen, a wagon train passed on the road that went directly in front of our home—our shack, I should say. After it got dark, I sneaked out my window with only the clothes on my back with my shoes tied around my neck. I had a fifty-cent piece in my pocket that I stole from my mama's underwear drawer. She had hidden it from my pa, but I felt that I had earned it. I ran and ran until I caught up with the wagon train. I begged the leader of the train to let me go with them. I had no idea where they were going but I did not care. I needed to get away and start living my own life. My folks would only miss the work that I did every day around their place. At the time, I didn't know that I was jumping out of the frying pan into the fire. I was forced to become the wagon master's woman. He wasn't a mean man, but he was demanding and very jealous. I had to stay away from the other wagons, especially the male family members. I couldn't attend the wagon train dances at night or sit out under the stars with the other ladies because their men would join us. I was pretty much a prisoner. After we traveled into Texas, I waited until Herbert left me alone while he took care of business. I sneaked away. I went into the livery and stole an old mule. The mule could hardly walk, but bless his heart; the poor soul carried me miles. I walked into the nearest town and begged for a job in all the stores. The only person who looked my way was Jon Williams, the owner of the Silver Slipper, the local saloon. He took me in and gave me my own room. It was clean and had a big bed. I was thrilled to have my own place. I soon learned that the only catch to the room was I had to share it several times a night with a paying customer. I wasn't a young innocent girl any more. I was forced to be with Herbert, the wagon master most every night and I didn't get nothing from him but hard work—and a baby in my belly. I was sad at first when I was sure I was going to have a child. Jon and the other women at the saloon were so good to me. The helped me with the delivery of Sammy. They seemed to feel that Sammy was their baby too. Jon, the saloon owner, was like a grandfather to him. I only worked after Sammy was asleep every night. An older woman who cleaned the rooms watched Sammy for me. Sammy was a good boy and he never got in anyone's way or into any trouble. Everyone loved him. Jon was good to me. It could have been worse, but he only took a small share of my money each night. Sammy and I had good meals, nice clothes, and shoes. I even had money in my pocket. The best part of the deal was Jon told me that I could leave anytime I wanted. I wasn't a prisoner being forced to work for him." Glory closed her eyes remembering her past before she met Tyler.

Kathleen's mind was a thousand miles away from Sammy's kidnapping. She sat and listened to Glory as she poured out her heart and soul to her. She had never told them about her life before she met up with Tyler. Kathleen had wondered, but with her being so sick, she felt that she should not quiz her about her past. Being with Tyler, the man who forced her to leave Sammy alone in town was enough to know that she had lived a rough life.

"Glory," Kathleen said softly, "How did you meet Tyler?"

"I came downstairs one evening. He was standing at the bar talking with a few other men. I noticed him right away, a tall handsome young cowboy. He looked like he had just come from the Cowboy's Rest because his blond hair was still damp. He turned and leaned with his side on the bar and his boot propped on the boot rest. He gave me a cocky grin and a small salute. His crystal blue eyes looked straight at me; like magic, drawing me to him. The next thing I knew I was upstairs with him. From that night, I was his girl. He wouldn't allow me to have other customers so he bought up all my time each night for several weeks. The only problem we had was when he learned that I had a little boy. He didn't take to Sammy and Sammy was afraid of him. I didn't know how to solve this problem but I felt if Tyler was around Sammy more often he would love him too. Sammy was so easy to love."

"Did he ever warm up to Sammy?"

"Not really. We went on carriage rides away from town, but he never let me take Sammy. We ate dinner at the local cafes', but Sammy had to eat in the saloon kitchen. I would beg Tyler to allow Sammy to spend time with us but he would say that it was late and he should be in bed."

"Did you ever feel that you should end your relationship with Tyler, because of Sammy?"

"Yes, but I knew Tyler wouldn't allow it. He said in many ways that he owned me. He nearly killed a man because he bumped into me in the saloon. It was an accident, but he made the man apologize to me and then he threw the man out into the street. The poor fellow had to be carried away to the doctor. Tyler was a mean man when he drank, but he could be so kind and sweet to me when he wasn't drunk." Glory sighed, "When it came to Sammy, I never understood why he treated him like he didn't exist."

"So, Glory, you feel that Tyler could have had some hand in Sammy's kidnapping?"

"Oh Kathleen, who else would want to take a child that they don't even know? If they did know him, surely they would know that he was a homeless child who was staying with your family. So why—unless they knew that you had just come into a large sum of money!" Glory's coughing increased so Rosa gave her medicine to help her to relax so she could breathe easier.

After Glory lay resting, Kathleen asked, "So Glory, you are thinking that Tyler knew about me selling my herd and that I have money in the bank. He knows that Sammy lives with me. So, you are thinking that he would do anything to get his hands on my money, even kidnapping Sammy?"

"Kathleen, Kathleen, come quickly!" Rosa was standing at the front door.

When Rosa saw Kathleen in the hallway, she grabbed her arm and pulled her in the parlor. "There is a young man on the porch and he said he had a very important message to give you and only to you. I am thinking it is something important about Sammy."

"Listen, go out the back door and get Carlos and Pedro. Tell them to come quickly."

Kathleen watched Rosa scoot toward the kitchen as she walked slowly to the front door. She opened the heavy wooden door and saw a young man standing on the porch looking all around. Kathleen was wondering who this young man could be. She had never seen him in town before. She spoke to the young man and asked if she could help him.

"I am Kathleen Parker. You have a message for me?"

"Yes, madam."

"Please step into the house where it is a lot warmer."

"Thank you. That would be nice," the messenger replied.

As Kathleen led the young man into the parlor, Pedro and Carlos entered the hallway and followed them into the room. The messenger looked at the two men and then back to Kathleen.

"Madam, the message I have is for your eyes only. I must meet with you in private." The young man was beginning to realize that the small fee he was to be paid was probably not enough for his trouble.

"You will give the message to Miss Kathleen now. We aren't leaving and if you want to leave here in one piece, you'll give her the note." Pedro's face was red and the veins in his neck were pulsing. The young man could feel the hostility coming from the Mexican.

"Hey, I don't want any trouble. I just want to take a reply to the man that gave me the message so I can collect my fee. I need the money so I can make my way to Abilene. Home."

"Pedro," Carlos spoke softly. "Let the young man do his job."

Carlos turned to the man and said very softly but firmly. "Give Miss Kathleen the note, now. We are family and she will tell us what the note has to say anyway."

Kathleen stretched her hand out to retrieve the note. The young man looked from Pedro, Carlos, and back to Kathleen. He reached into his soft leather vest and pulled out a crumbled looking piece of paper. He handed it over to Kathleen. "I must have a reply, please madam."

Kathleen glanced at the note quickly. She wasn't surprised to find a ransom note, but it still made her sink down onto the parlor couch. She handed the note to Pedro who read it aloud.

"If you want to see the boy alive, bring ten thousand dollars to a cabin near the road thirty miles outside of Abilene. There will be a cross next to the road that will show you where the cabin is located. Drop money near the well and ride away. You will find the boy tied to a tree two miles down on the Abilene road after one hour. No sheriff or posse. Boy will die if I see anyone besides you."

Pedro looked at the stranger with daggers in his eyes. Carlos and Kathleen both looked at him as they listened to Rosa crying. The young man's face had turned white as a sheet.

"Hey, I didn't know what was in that note. Honest! I ain't no part of a kidnapping going down. I just wanted to earn five dollars." The messenger walked over and sat down in a chair next to the fireplace. He felt sick to his stomach and his knees had gone weak under him.

Carlos motioned for Rosa to come to him. He gave her a big hug and patted her on the back. "Go in the kitchen and bring this fellow some coffee. We have questions for him and I don't want him passing out on us."

Carlos walked closer to the messenger. "Son," Carlos said in a gentler voice, "who gave you this note to bring out here to Kathleen?"

"Hey Mister, I'm a stranger in Sweetwater. I went into the saloon and asked the barkeep if he knew of anyone needing some help. I have been without money for a few days and I needed money for feed for my horse and a little for myself. This tall, blond fellow walked over to me and said to come over to his table, he might be able to give me a small job. Honest, mister! I am not in on a kidnapping." The youngster hung his head down and clapped his hands together between his knees.

"Son, for some reason I believe you. Here is Rosa with a sandwich and some hot coffee. Eat up while we discuss what you just told us." The man thanked Rosa and bit into the sandwich.

Kathleen patted a chair for Carlos to sit down beside her. She looked at him; neither had to say anything because they both knew who the mastermind was behind the kidnapping. "Kathleen, I have got to go and try to catch Matt and Juan. Glory has talked to Rosa about a shack where she stayed with Tyler before she came here. I would bet that it is the same isolated cabin. I believe we could locate it without having to exchange any money to get our boy back."

"Yes, I was just thinking that I wish Matt was here. Let Pedro ride ahead and find Matt and Juan. You and I will follow tomorrow after I get the money out of the bank. I want to take the money because I want Sammy home unharmed. I will send Tyler an answer. Let's let him believe that we will follow his instructions to the letter so he will think that his plan is a solid one. Let the messenger take him my note saying that I will leave in the morning with the money and hope to make the drop early the next morning. At 9:00 a.m. How does that sound?"

"Si," replied Carlos. "That will give Pedro time to find Matt and tell him our plan. Write your answer to Tyler and give it to this young man." As Carlos walked toward the door, he stopped and turned to Kathleen. "Give him a few dollars for his help. He just got caught in the middle of our trouble."

Pedro walked over to his mama giving her a kiss. "Mama, please pack me some food while I go and saddle my horse and prepare my bedroll. I want to head out as soon as I get my things together."

"Go Son. I will get the things I know you will need." Rosa went into the kitchen while Kathleen got up and walked over to her desk and got pen and paper. She wrote her note to Tyler agreeing with his demands. She opened a drawer and counted out ten dollars in her palm. She walked over to the young messenger. "What is your name?"

"I'm Johnny Johnston from Abilene. I left home to go join up with the Texas Rangers but they turned me away because they said

I was too young. After working on several different ranches and a couple of cattle drives, I'm ready to return to my folks in Abilene. They have a big ranch. I should have never left home, but I was too bullheaded to listen to my pa. I want to get home and work for my folks. Maybe I will settle down with a little gal that I left back in Abilene." He grinned and hung his head.

"Please take this note back to the man who gave it to you. If he asked if we questioned you about him, just shake your head and tell him that you didn't know anything to tell us. Here is some extra money for your trouble. After that fool pays you, please head on home. If he refuses to pay you the five dollars that he promised you, please, for your sake don't get into an argument with him. This man is dangerous and mean. I have given you ten dollars. Promise me you will just leave."

"Yes madam, I understand. I have run into men like him before. I will just turn and get on my horse and ride out of Sweetwater. I do not want to be shot over five dollars. I have met up with his kind before."

As the young man saddled up to leave, he thanked Kathleen and Carlos for the money. He rode toward town and Kathleen let out a big sigh. "I guess I should tell Glory that she was right about Tyler. At least she will know that we are doing something to get Sammy back."

"I am going to help Pedro. Why don't you go and tell Lucy to come and stay with Rosa and Glory while we are gone? Matt's men can fend for themselves or the girls can cook some soup and cornbread for them. Lucy can decide what to do."

Kathleen went into Glory's room and gave her the news about Tyler. She lay back on the bed and said she wasn't surprised. She didn't think that he would hurt Sammy, because he had never hurt him before with his fists; only with his cruel words. Glory hid her face in her hands and wept. "My poor, poor baby, this is my fault, I am sure of it."

Kathleen stood on the front lawn of her ranch and waved good-bye to Pedro. He would travel fast heading toward Abilene. He knew that Matt and Juan had traveled long into the night and wouldn't be very far behind the man that took Sammy. Since he was a big man carrying extra weight, his tracks would be easy to follow. The hoof prints would dig deep into the packed dirt road, and if he rode into the woods, there would be many signs; broken tree limbs and bushes pushed and turned over. Pedro was sure he would pick up Matt's trail by tomorrow evening if not sooner.

**********

Matt and Juan rode long into the night. They only stopped to cool down their horses and let them drink from a stream. They camped out the first night and got up before daylight the next morning. After another day and night of travel and following an easy trail, they arrived near the isolated shack where the big man held Sammy captive. They tied their mounts behind a big boulder close to the shack and waited. A lantern glowed from inside and smoke came from the chimney. Juan crawled near the big man's horse in the stall. He whispered to the animal to keep him calm and quiet. He continued over to the window of the shack and listened for any sounds coming from inside. He could hear a man's voice talking to Sammy about going outside to relieve himself.

Juan hurried back to Matt and said that Sammy seemed to be all right. "They are getting ready to come outside to go take a pee," said Juan.

"Might be a good time to take the big man down; did you see him?" Matt asked.

"No. I just heard his voice. We can move in closer and get a good look. There's a cluster of thick bushes near the stall where he has his horse."

"Lead the way and let's see who this monster is that carried Sammy away."

As the two men moved in closer, Moose and Sammy went into the bushes near the shack and came out laughing. One of them had said something funny. Matt and Juan looked at each other. "What do you think?" Juan asked.

"I have seen that man in the café with Tyler Chambers. I am sure now that Tyler is behind this kidnapping. I expect he has already delivered Glory or Kathleen a ransom note demanding money."

As Matt and Juan were making their plans to get Sammy away from Moose and capture him without either one of them getting hurt, a horse and rider rode up to the cabin. Both men hunched down close together and watched. The man swung down off his horse and hurried into the cabin. He didn't even bother to tie the poor animal that had been ridden hard and fast.

Loud voices came from inside the cabin. "What the hell do you mean letting that brat roam around free? Why haven't you got him tied up so he can't get away?"

"Why Ty, he ain't going to run anywhere. He's a good boy and he does what I tell him."

"You're a dumb ass! Don't you know he's worth ten thousand dollars? If he gets away, we won't be able to collect a penny. Now tie him to that chair. We need to ride into town and get some supplies before we head to Mexico tomorrow. We're going to be as rich as kings come this time in the morning."

"Please Moose; don't let him tie me up. You ain't gonna leave me here by myself, are you?" cried Sammy as he raced over to Moose.

"Shut your trap and sit down in that chair." Ty yelled at Sammy as he reached for a piece of rope.

"Now Ty. There is no reason to tie the child. I will stay here with him while you ride into Abilene. I don't need to go with you."

"You ain't got the brains God gave a billy goat. You will tie him up. I need your help with the supplies."

"Now look here Tyler. There ain't no need to be calling me names. I do not like it. You need to be nicer. I don't have to do anything I don't want to do."

Tyler threw the rope across the room with disgust. "Fine with me if you want to stay out here and baby-sit; I am tired, dirty and hungry. I'm going into town and have myself a good time with a certain young woman. I'll purchase us a pack mule to carry our supplies and you can just bet that I am going to take the price of the mule out of your share of the ransom. When I get back, we'll make our plans for the money drop tomorrow morning."

"Who is coming with the money?" Moose asked.

"Shut up fool! You are too dumb for words. I will tell you everything when we are alone."

Moose walked over and placed both of his hands under Tyler's armpits lifting him off the floor. Moose gave him a good shake before he lowered him to the floor. "I done told you to stop calling me names. Next time I might just really have to hurt you."

As Moose turned Tyler loose, he saw movement outside in the

brush. "Now who's the fool? A sheriff's posse has followed you. There're men out there ready to take us out." Tyler took two giant steps to the window and he saw Juan crawling on the ground to hide behind the water trough. He remembered allowing his horse to roam loose in the front of the cabin. "Damn!" he shouted. He went to the next window and saw his horse in the stall with Moose's big bay.

"We're getting out of here. Come here brat. You're riding with me."

Sammy hurried behind Moose's tall legs trying to escape Tyler's reach. Moose reached his big hand behind his back and patted the boy. "Now Tyler, you go on and leave us be. That will give you a head start to the border. All they want is the boy back."

"No! That brat is my meal ticket for the future. He is going with us—me! You can stay behind and let them stretch your neck but he is leaving with me." Tyler reached behind Moose, snatched Sammy's right arm, and pulled him in front of his body. Moose stepped toward Tyler but before he knew what had happened, Tyler pointed his 45-revolver right between his eyes. "Back off big guy!"

"I can't let you take the boy. You will never have a moment of peace as long as you have him. His folks will track you to the end of the earth. I know I would if he was mine."

"So old man, you finally fell in love. That is a good one. In love with a snot nose brat who whines for his mama's tit. Well, you are going to experience a broken heart, because this boy is running away with me. Now move over to the bed and sit down!"

Moose eased over to the bed, lowered his big frame on the mattress, and watched Tyler's every move. Sammy was wiggling and reaching his hand out toward Moose. "Please," he whined as he tried to make Tyler release him.

"Stand still brat before I slap you silly."

"Do as he tells you Sammy. He won't hurt you if you do as he says," Moose said, as he waited for an opportunity to jump Tyler.

"You better listen to your new grandpa, or else, you will regret it." Tyler laughed as he pushed Sammy to the front door. "We are going to run to the stall and you better not fall. Got that?"

Sammy looked back at Moose and shook his head up and down. He let Tyler push him out the door in front of him. "You out there. I see you! If you want this boy alive, you better back off and let me ride out of here. I will drop him off on the trail after I feel safe. You hear me?"

Matt looked toward Juan who lay behind the water trough. "Yes, we hear you loud and clear. But if you hurt that child, you'll regret it 'til the day I find you and shoot your ass."

"That's tough talk for someone who doesn't have the upper hand."

Tyler pulled his horse out into the open part of the stall. The poor animal had not been unsaddled, fed or watered. He had moved close to Moose's big bay and helped himself to some hay. Tyler leaped upon the saddle and lifted Sammy up in front of him. All of a sudden, Moose came from the back of the stall and grabbed Tyler from behind. Tyler turned and pointed his gun at Moose. When he did, Sammy, shivering from fear, took the opportunity to bite down on Tyler's hand that held the reins of his horse. Ty screamed and shook his hand away from Sammy and fired his gun at Moose. The big man fell backwards as Sammy bucked his little body backward into Tyler's neck connecting with his Adam's apple. He turned Sammy loose as he grabbed his throat. Sammy took the opportunity to slip off the horse and went under the belly of the animal. In a fraction of a second, he raced out the back of the stall. Tyler knew he would never catch the boy, so he plunged his big spurs into his horse's flank and yelled like an Apache Indian. His horse flew out of the stall as Tyler laid his body down over the animal's neck. When Juan realized that Sammy was not a shield, he fired his gun several times. Tyler was out of sight in a flash.

Matt rushed into the stall and saw the big man lying on the dirty floor. He was moving his legs and attempting to sit up as blood oozed from his back. He gently turned the big man over so he could see his face. Moose groaned and tried to pull himself up on his knees. Gritting his teeth together he asked, "Did he--did he take the boy?"

"No! Here I am Moose!" Sammy yelled as he flew into Matt's arms and cried. "Oh Mr. Matt, oh Mr. Matt. I'm so happy to see you."

"You're all right son. Everything is all right. Let's get this big man into the shack and see how bad he is hurt."

Juan came hurrying into the stall and when Sammy saw him, he leaped into his arms. "You came after me too! I knew you would find me."

"Of course, I would have tracked you to Mexico. I could not work those cow ponies without your help." He rubbed his palm over Sammy's hair and pulled him into his side for a hug. "Besides, Mama said I couldn't come home until I found you."

Sammy laid his head on Juan's shoulder and wiped away his tears. He was a big boy and he did not want them to see his tears.

Matt helped Moose up off the floor of the stall as he weaved and swayed, determined to stay on his feet. The bullet had hit the old bearded man high on his left shoulder. Matt could see blood on the man's hands as he grabbed his shoulder and fell sideways as he attempted to walk toward the cabin. Sammy hurried to Moose and offered to help hold him as he walked.

Once Matt settled Moose on the bunk, he removed his bloody shirt. "I am going to make a quick bandage and leave you here with Juan. I think you should stay the night and make sure the bleeding has stopped. If I don't have a good trail to follow, I'll return before daylight tomorrow."

Matt went into the bushes, got his horse, and rode away after the monster that had kidnapped Sammy. Tyler had left a wide-open trail because he was in such a hurry to get away. After an hour, Matt was sure that he was close behind Tyler. Using his spyglass, he watched Tyler riding ahead of him in an open field and finally disappearing in the thicket of pines. A briar slapped Matt on the cheek and blood trailed down his chin. *Damn,* thought Matt. *That hurt like fire.* He pulled his horse to a stop and stood in the stirrups trying to get a better look. He continued through the heavy underbrush and stopped occasionally to listen. The crickets and bats were out. The bullfrogs croaked and he heard an owl hoot. His horse stepped carefully and very slowly as he made his way through the tall brush and low bushes. Out in the open the small cactuses were a hazard if a horse walked into one. Matt decided that he best stop and camp for the night. He was sure he was pretty close to Tyler so he did not think a fire would be a good idea. A cup of hot coffee would taste good about now, but the smell of the smoke would warn his prey that he was near. Matt pulled his horse to a stop and looked around. Moments went by as he tried to decide if he should continue with the chase all the way to Mexico or allow the bastard to get away. Matt looked around for a good campsite and got down off his tired animal. He loosened the cinch on his saddle and tied the horse to a tree. He used the same tree to kick some mud off his boot spurs. There wasn't a place on his body that did not have a scratch or mud. Trailing that man through thickets of bushes and low marshy ground was hard on man and beast.

Matt tossed his bedroll on the ground at the base of the same tree where he had tied his horse. If anyone came too close, his horse would warn him—almost as good as a trained dog. He placed his left leg on a fallen log and rubbed his old wound. His leg was throbbing.

He relaxed for the first time since Sammy had been kidnapped. He exhaled and took a deep breath. He had learned to love that little rascal and if anything had happened, he just did not know what he would have done. He had never killed a man or really ever harmed anyone. However, he hated to think what he would have done to that hombre if Sammy had been hurt. Clutching his bedroll up around his neck, he whispered a silent prayer to the good Lord above. Moments dragged by as he tried to drift off to sleep. His last thought was of Kathleen, his Katy, waiting at home for his return with Sammy.

An old owl hooted several times waking Matt out of a deep sleep. The sun had not come up yet, but it was daylight enough to see his surroundings. He walked into the brush and relieved himself. He decided to walk his horse to see if he was still on Tyler's trail. After walking a couple hundred yards, he knew that he had lost the tracks. Tyler was probably near the border by now. "Well," said Matt to his horse as he rubbed his cold nose and gave him several good pats. "We have Sammy back and that is all that matters. Let's head back to the shack and gather everyone and head back home." His horse neighed several times as if he understood Matt's words.

After a few hours had passed, the sun was light enough and the stars had disappeared. The air was cold on his face as he wrapped a scarf across his face and neck. His breathe was like steam coming from behind it. After a few hours, the temperature increased in warmth and he packed the scarf away. After what seemed like forever, he rode back to the cabin where he left Juan, Sammy and Moose. Matt finally stopped his horse in front of the falling down stall. Before Matt could get down off his mount, he noticed three other mounts. While he was looking at the horses, Kathleen raced out of the shack.

When Matt saw Kathleen, he leaped off his horse and pulled her into his arms. His lips covered hers as he pressed his hard body into hers. Kathleen folded her arms around his muscular chest and felt her whole body melting from the heat between them. His large frame covered her body and demanded more from her. She was drifting away from reality when she heard a cough from someone near. When they broke away from their powerful kiss, they both were gasping for breath. The desire that they had for each other was almost uncontrollable. A wedding date was going to have to be set.

Matt stared at her with so much warmth that tears formed in her eyes. "We have Sammy and I still have my money. That is all that matters. Bless you, Matthew Moore, my dear man."

"Yes, the good Lord has blessed us all on this journey. Juan helped me watch over Sammy and Moose," he said laughing, "as I chased that bastard almost to the Mexican border. I hope we have seen the last of him."

# Chapter 24

The long ride home was very uncomfortable, as the weather had turned to nearly freezing. Kathleen allowed Sammy to ride double with her so they could share their body warmth. Matt smiled at the two as they cuddled close while wishing he were the one holding Kathleen. After a long day of travel, they made camp for the night. The wind had died down making the cold weather bearable. Kathleen, along with the help of Carlos, cooked beans with long links of smoked sausages and hot coffee.

Matt watched Kathleen as she sat on a log near the fire. The long day of riding had left her muscles aching all over her body. She pulled her heavy jacket together and gathered her long riding skirt around her ankles. After a few minutes, Matt unrolled her bedroll and spread it out near the fire. He carried her saddle over and laid it down near the top of the bedroll.

"Come, Katy," Matt held out his hand to help her up from the log. "You have had a long day; time to hit the hay." With a sigh, Kathleen allowed Matt to help her stand and watched her lay down. Once she was comfortable, he spread an extra blanket over her tired body. "Pedro will take the first watch. Come Sammy, you can sleep next to me."

"I want to sleep with Moose. He's really warm." Sammy said as he walked toward the big man. "Not tonight, buddy. You might roll over on Moose's shoulder." Moose smiled at Matt and gave him a nod.

"Carlos will check your wound before turning in. Come on Sammy; let's take a trip into the bushes so we can turn in."

After returning home, Dr. Squires patched Moose's shoulder and said there wasn't any chance of him dying. The sheriff shoved him toward the cell. "He won't be kidnapping no one else's young'un. The judge will put him away for a long time; if he decides not to string him up first," declared the sheriff as he threw the keys back in his desk drawer.

Sammy watched the sheriff push Moose into the jail cell and lock the door. "Please, Mr. Matt," cried Sammy as he pulled on Matt's sleeve, "don't let him put Moose in that old jail cell. Moose took care of me! Please Mr. Matt. I love Moose." Sammy lowered his face down to his chest and tears rolled down his cheeks. "That old Tyler would have hurt me, but Moose pro'texted me! Moose is good and I want him to go home with us. Please!" Sammy buried his face between Matt's legs and cried.

Moose had done wrong but he was very sorry for his part in the kidnapping. He had met Tyler Chambers a few months back in Abilene. They had worked a few jobs together on a couple of ranches. Tyler helped him out some and they became friends, but he had begun to see that Tyler was not a very nice man.

On the trip back to Sweetwater, Moose never tried to escape and he was very respectful to Kathleen. The sheriff looked from Sammy back to Matt. Kathleen stood quietly as Sammy pleaded Moose's case to the sheriff and Matt.

Matt asked the sheriff if he could be responsible for Moose until the Judge arrived back to town. The sheriff was not too happy about allowing a known kidnapper to roam free. "Kidnapping is bad," said the sheriff, "right there next to being a horse thief. But, I reckon if you want to take on the responsibility of having him appear before the judge, then I won't have to feed him."

Matt told Moose that he had to stay on the ranch and would have chores like the other ranch hands. Lucy was not sure about having a bad man on the ranch. Matt assured her that Moose would be a big help to her while he was recuperating from his shotgun wound. Lucy still was not convinced, so she planned to sleep with a knife under her pillow.

Matt took Moose out to his bunkhouse and introduced him to his men. He did not try to cover up what Moose was doing on his ranch. "All of you know that Sammy was kidnapped by two men. Well, this here is one of the men that did it. Moose did a stupid thing by being in cahoots with his partner. If not for this man, Sammy may not be with us tonight. The sheriff is allowing me to be responsible for him until the judge arrives in town after the holidays. I want everyone to treat Moose as if he is one of you. I do not think you will have to worry about your personal effects. He is no thief. As for working, he will not be able to do many chores while his shoulder is mending but he will be helping Lucy with some of her chores and with the cooking."

Matt looked around at the three men and pointed at a bunk in the corner of the room. "You can take that bunk," he said to Moose. As Matt turned to leave, he stopped. "Oh by the way, you can all go home tomorrow for Christmas. I have a small bonus, Christmas gift, whatever you want to call it, for you in the morning. Use it wisely."

********

Glory was still very sick. Rosa was sure that she was not going to be alive the next daybreak. However, everyone was happy to learn that the sheriff had placed a five hundred dollar reward for Tyler Chambers. "I hope the reward will keep him from coming back here," mumbled Glory.

Glory was still sitting up in bed, coughing up blood and struggling to breath. Sammy was a good helper. After school, he would sit on the side of Glory's bed and tell her everything that he learned in school. He served her dinner and practiced his reading lesson while she laid listening to him.

With Christmas only a week away, everyone was silently sneaking around preparing special gifts for each other. Kathleen had been making a western vest with a fleece lining just like the one that Matt wore for Sammy. Carlos was trimming down a small western belt to fit his tiny waist. Matt was Sammy's idol and he wanted to be like him in every way. Kathleen was busy making warm ponchos for the boys and Carlos.

Carlos and Pedro had tagged the perfect tree to chop down to bring to the house the day before Christmas Eve. They would stand it in the barn to dry out and later place it in a big bucket of water. Kathleen and Rosa had decorated the fireplace in the parlor with evergreen branches and woven red ribbon and bows all through it. The place was beginning to look very festive.

With the planning for the Christmas holiday, Kathleen had only a few days to prepare for her wedding. Kathleen decided to go into town and stop by Dolly's Dress Shop to check on some lovely fabric and ribbons for her wedding dress. Dolly was very excited to see Kathleen but Lillian hurriedly made her excuses and left the front room. "Don't pay her no mind, Kathleen. She's still upset over losing Matt to you."

"I understood that she and Al are a couple now," said Kathleen very quietly.

"Well, to tell you the truth, there is a man in her life, but it isn't that big burly Al," she said as she moved stacks of white cloth around on a table. "There is talk around town that some tall man who rides a big black bay horse comes to her backdoor regularly. At the post office this morning, I heard her man must have left town because he has not called on her in at least three nights."

Kathleen stood very still and tried hard not to display any of the emotions that were running through her mine. *Matt rides a big black bay and he had been out of town several nights; but he was looking for Sammy,* thought Kathleen. *No, no, this cannot be,* thought Kathleen. As in a trance, Kathleen walked out the door of the shop.

"Look at this lovely piece of white satin, Kathleen," said Dolly, as she watched Kathleen exit her shop without a fare thee well. Dolly rushed over to the door and called to Kathleen, "Kathleen, where you going?" Dolly watched Kathleen climb into her carriage and head out of town. She never even looked back at Dolly.

Lillian walked up behind Dolly wearing a smirk on her face. "Can you beat that?" Dolly said as she stared hard at Lillian. "Kathleen and I were talking and she just rushed out the door."

"Well, I can't blame her for leaving. I heard you telling her about my nightly visitor. I am afraid you let the cat out of the bag."

"What are you talking about?" Dolly was still very confused over Kathleen's departure and Lillian's statement.

"I am afraid there will not be a wedding between Kathleen and Matt. You see, Matt is going to marry me."

"What?" Dolly screamed as she backed herself into a chair and flopped down.

A light snow began to drizzle as Kathleen drove the small black carriage as fast as she dared toward home. As she drove closer to Matt's ranch, she decided that she was going to confront him with the gossip floating around town. She was not the type of person to let something go.  She wanted to hear what Matt had to say about this rumor.  Nearing Matt's yard, she  drove near the front of his house, climbed out of the carriage, and tied her horse's rein on the hitching post.  Walking to the front door, Lucy opened it before she could knock.

"Kathleen, come in.  What are you doing out in this nasty weather?" asked Lucy.

"I need to see Matt.  Please tell him I am here. Now."

"He's not here.  He went out in the pasture to check on new calves and bring them closer to the barn."

"I see," said Kathleen softly.

"Let me get you some hot coffee. Come, get out of that snowy, wet coat," Lucy said as she started toward the kitchen.

Kathleen turned and walked out of the house without saying a word to Lucy. "Kathleen, what's wrong?" Lucy called.

Kathleen gave no answer as she untied her horse, climbed into the small carriage and drove out of the yard without a backward glance at Lucy.

"Oh my," said Lucy to herself. "Something is very bad."

Kathleen went into the ranch house and went directly to her room.  She undressed and slipped on her long flannel white night gown over her head. She felt damp and cold all the way through. She pulled back the covers and curled up under the quilts. Rosa knocked softly on Kathleen's bedroom door.  When she received no answer she called, "Kathleen, I am coming in."  Rosa opened the bedroom door and immediately sat down on the edge of Kathleen's bed.

"What's wrong Bebe'? Are you sick?"

"Please just let me be. I cannot talk about it now," she whimpered.

"Now, you know me better.  My girl is hurting and I must know what is wrong." Rosa snuggled closer and pulled the covers down from her face. "Tell me."

"Oh, Rosa, I found out in town that Matt is cheating on me. Cheating, sneaking, and lying to me. I can't believe that I have been a fool . . . again."

Rosa could not believe what she was hearing about the wonderful man that she knew. Matthew Moore was an outstanding man who loved Kathleen very much. She would not believe what

Kathleen was saying.

"No! That is not true. You are no fool for loving Matt. He is good man. I lay my life down. He loves you. Why do you say these things?"

"He has been with that woman—Lillian, every night behind my back. Everyone in town has been talking about them for weeks and laughing behind my back, for not knowing. Here we are planning this big wedding. Why would he let me plan a wedding when he's going to marry somebody else? Not me!" Kathleen hid her face in her pillow and cried until she had the hiccups.

"No, none of what you say is true. Lies! All lies. We know Matt and he has not been with that woman." Rosa stood and placed both of her hands on her round hips. She made a swirl around the room picking up of some of Kathleen's wet clothes. "Why do you say these things about Mr. Matt?"

"His horse has been seen in the alleyway behind the dress shop for weeks. He has not been there for several days because he was out of town trying to find Sammy," cried Kathleen.

"I'm sure there are many horses like his," Rosa said as she placed the discarded clothes away.

"I wish I could trust him the way you do. Men, men are alike. I do not want to see him and I do not want him in this house again."

"Now, Bebe', you have to hear Matt's side of this ugly rumor," Rosa said, trying to calm Kathleen.

"Carlos can take the Christmas gifts that we have for all of them over to his ranch. I do not want Sammy hanging around with him anymore, either. You hear me Rosa. I do not want that man on my ranch," she said as she sat straight up in the bed, pounding her fists on the mattress.

"There's another thing . . . I can't believe that he would give up ownership of my ranch for that two timing –woman!" She screamed, as she pulled the cover over her head, muffling the sound of her words.

Rosa could not believe what she was hearing. Everyone had been working hard on Christmas gifts, candies, cookies and surprises for each other. Matt and Lucy were like family, and they were going to spend Christmas Day with them. Everyone was counting the days until Christmas Eve.

"Now Kathleen, I know you are hurt. Something is wrong. I

do not believe all those lies that you have heard about Matt. That woman yes, but not Matt. We are going to have Christmas as we have planned."

"Never," mumbled Kathleen from under the quilts.

Rosa stood and looked down on Kathleen. She shook her head and made the sign of the cross over her chest. She turned the lantern down and walked out of the bedroom. Carlos was sitting at the kitchen table drinking a cup of coffee and talking softly to Sammy. Glory was having a bad evening. Her coughing seemed to be worse.

While in Kathleen's room, Rosa could hear coughing coming from Glory's room in between Kathleen's hissy fits. Rosa walked to the cabinet and took down some medicine. Carlos had dipped a fresh cup of water for her and he followed Rosa into Glory's bedroom. Carlos and Rosa saw all the bloody rags on the nightstand. "When trouble comes, it pours." Rosa mumbled under her breath.

"You mean when it rains it pours," replied Carlos.

"You mean what you want old man. We have trouble—lots of trouble."

"What's wrong? Is Kathleen sick? I know she went straight to her room and I could hear loud voices." Carlos stood as he looked at his wife's worried expression. "Can I do something for her?"

"We talk when we are alone," she said as she nodded her head toward Sammy. Glory laid her head down on the pillow and held Sammy's hand. "Go and finish your supper baby. Mama wants to go to sleep. I am better. See, I am not coughing like before."

Sammy slipped off her bed and kissed her on the forehead. "Night Mama. I love you," he said very quietly. Carlos followed Sammy back into the kitchen, poured him a big glass of milk, and dipped him a small bowl of apple cobbler.

After Sammy had completed his dessert, he asked if he could go and see Kathleen. "She hasn't come and eaten supper. I wanted to talk to her about Matt's Christmas present."

"You can't talk to her tonight. She isn't feeling well." Juan and Pedro looked back and forth at each other. They knew that Kathleen had been in town. While in town, they had heard the rumor that the wedding was going to have a different bride. Of course, both of them were in disbelief. They had heard the rumor that Al Thornbees was so angry that he had practically torn his livery apart and made threats that he would do the same to Matt.

Once Sammy was in bed and the two girls were fast asleep, Rosa came to the table and sat her weary body down. She placed her sad face into her old tired hands and shook her head back and forth.

"Out with it Rosa." Carlos looked at his wife of nearly fifty years and knew that something was very wrong. He looked at the faces of his two sons and knew that they were already aware of the problem.

"That woman, the snake in the grass that followed Matt to Sweetwater, is telling lies. Kathleen went into town to look at some things for her wedding dress and she was told some of the vicious lies."

Carlos did not make a comment. He waited patiently for her to continue. "His ex-fiancée is telling everyone that Matt is going to marry *her* and not Kathleen."

"Did you boys hear these rumors, too?" Carlos looked to Juan and then over to Pedro. Both of the young men gave him a nod.

"Si Papa, at the livery stable from some of the men. They were joking around and one man said that Mr. Thornbees plans to bust Matt up pretty badly. You know, Papa, he is twice as big as Mr. Matt. He could hurt him."

"What has the livery stable man got to do with this woman and Matt?" Carlos looked from one son to the other.

"Oh Papa! Everybody in town knows that Thornbees and that woman have been sneaking around at night for months. He calls on her in her little apartment in the dress shop. How she can say that Matt has been with her, I don't know," said Juan.

"We need to go to Matt's tonight and have a talk with him," said Carlos as he put on his heavy coat and big sombrero, he headed out the front door.

\*\*\*\*\*

After Matt had gotten Moose settled in the bunkhouse with the men, he asked if any of them had anything to say before he turned in for the evening.

"Who is going to care for the animals while we are all gone home for Christmas?" Timmy asked.

"I believe Moose and I can care for the animals for a few days. Lucy and I will be spending Christmas Day at Kathleen's home."

"You're kidding about that, aren't you?" asked Joseph, the older of the ranch hands.

"Why do you ask that? Kathleen and I are getting married Saturday following Christmas Day. Where else would I be?"

"Well, it's none of our business, but we were told," hesitating he looked around at the other ranch hands, "that the wedding was called off; with Miss Parker anyway." Joseph rubbed his boot over the bunkhouse floor while looking down as he answered Matt.

"What in the Sam hell are you talking about? Who told you that?" Matt looked at Joseph with disbelieve in his eyes.

"Look Mr. Matt, I don't want to rile you, but we overheard men talking in town to Mr. Thornbees about you and that woman getting married. Boy was he mad."

"Why would he be mad that I am marrying Kathleen? He has known our plans for a while."

"No, not Miss Parker; that other woman named Lily—no Lillian. That's her name!"

"What the hell! You all know that I am marrying Kathleen. I would not marry that woman if she were the last woman on earth. I wonder who started that lie."

"Someone's coming, Mr. Matt." Timmy looked out of the bunkhouse window and saw Carlos and his two sons. "It's Miss Parker's foreman and two sons."

Matt jerked open the door and stormed out in the snowy night. He met Carlos, Juan and Pedro at the hitching post in front of the barn.

"Hi fellows," Matt said, as he greeted them while trying to hold back his temper. "What has brought you out in this bad weather?"

"Matt, we have to talk. Kathleen heard rumors about you two not getting married. Rosa and I do not believe such lies. We need to hear what you got to say about all of this."

"How is Kathleen doing?" Matt asked softly.

"Not good. She took to her bed and will not talk about it."

"Damn it, I guess Katy believes this rumor, too. Hear me out, Carlos. I just heard about this damn lie from my men. I am going to get my jacket, ride into town, and have a talk with Ms. Lillian. I have a feeling she started this trouble. If she has, I am going to break her lily white neck."

"Give us a minute of your time before you hurry off. Please." Carlos led his horse into the barn with Juan and Pedro trailing him.

# Chapter 25

Matt had ridden his horse as fast as he could in the starless dark night. The snow was peppering down like hard raindrops making riding slower than he wanted to travel into town. He was anxious about confronting Lillian. He was sure that she had started the rumors about them getting married. Carlos had said that Kathleen was mad and hurting from the ugly lies. Once he talked to Lillian and made her understand that he was not going to marry her, maybe he would get her to admit to spreading the lies. Hopefully, he could make Kathleen believe the truth.

The front of Dolly's Dress Shop was dark but Matt knew that Lillian had a big room in the back. The last thing he wanted to do was to be seen going to Lillian's back door, but he had no choice. Swearing under his breath, he rode his horse around to the back of the shop. Several lanterns glowed from her apartment windows. He tossed his horse's reins across a barrel and stepped onto the back porch. He knocked hard several times and just as Lillian opened the door, a loud booming voice called to Matt from the front of the alley.

"Hey you! What are you doing at my woman's back door?"

Matt stepped off Lillian's porch, adjusted his jacket up around his neck, and answered the big bear of a man, Al Thornbees.

"I've come to talk to 'your woman' about some lies that have been spread about a wedding that is not going to take place. I want her to admit that she is the one telling these false rumors. I am not marrying her and she knows that. Besides, everyone in town knows that she is your woman."

"Lies, that's a lie," screamed someone from the other side of the apartment door. "We are going to be married and you know it. Al, well Al is just a friend!" Lillian motioned to Al while holding the backdoor open.

"A friend. I'm just a damn friend you say!" Al's face distorted with anger as he charged up the porch with balled fists toward Lillian. Matt stepped in front of him and stopped him from harming the woman he claimed to love. Before Matt knew what had happened, Al hit him square on the jaw, and then he hit him again. But the second punch doubled him over, expelling the air from his stomach. Matt went down to the soggy, wet ground on his knees.

Lillian screamed and wanted to run outside, but she felt danger all around her. Al was watching her as he yelled for Matt to get up on his feet. Lillian backed up into her apartment, locked the door, and raced out the front of the shop to get some men to come and break up the fight. In her heart, she knew that Matt was no match for big Al.

"Get up –you sneak! I am going to beat the hell out of you for sneaking around with my woman."

After a second, Matt had recovered his breath and came up. With the flat of his hand, he aimed for Al's nose and connected. Al jumped backward, grabbed his face as he realized that his nose was broken. Blood spattered on the clean white snow.

"Gaud all mighty! You broke my nose," he grunted as he looked at the blood on his hand. "Now, I am really going to bust you up."

Lillian came back into the alley with two men, hoping that they could stop the fight. Deep down she was thrilled to see them fighting over her. She knew that the fight had to end soon, because Al was so much bigger and stronger than Matt was. He might do some permanent damage to Matt's body. The two men looked from Matt to Al and decided to be spectators.

Al stood back, face to face with Matt, confused and dumbfounded. He never thought that Matt could handle himself so well in a fight. After spitting out a mouth full of blood, he suddenly lunged toward Matt as he drove his fists into Matt's ribs. Matt winced. The pain quivered across his chest. Al grabbed Matt's body and using his palm pushed Matt's head back as far as it would go. Matt felt as if he was going to break his neck. Slowly, Matt jabbed his fist into Al's throat causing him to release his hold and reel backwards. When Matt finally straightened up, he could feel Al's eyes on him; blood thirsty and concentrating on the kill.

Matt was still trying to get a good breath when Al drove his fist into Matt's face. Matt's head flew upward as his eyes locked on the dark, snowy sky. His left foot slipped on the wet ground. His right hand covered his nose squeezing his eyes shut. As Matt recovered from the blow, he turned sideways while lying on the freezing ground. Al started toward him. Matt lifted his leg and slammed his big western boot into the big man's leg below his kneecap causing a solid crunch sound.

Al bellowed like a sick calf as he fell to the soft snowy ground. The snow was coming down harder making it almost impossible to see. Using the round trash barrel in the alley, Al slowly pulled himself up. Wiping the frosty snow from his eyes, he attempted to move forward and teach this man a lesson he would remember the rest of his life. *'No man messed with my woman,'* he thought to himself. Al felt himself slipping downward as the pain in his leg was too much to stand on. Darkness over took him as he fought to stand and tumbled forward to the ground.

A large crowd of men from the saloon had gathered and some of the men were taking side bets as to whom the winner would be. Juan pushed through the crowd and bent down beside Matt on the cold, wet ground. "Mr. Matt, place your arm around my neck and let me get you up and take you to the doctor's office."

"Boy, where did you come from?" Matt grunted as his mouth and jaws hurt so bad he could hardly speak.

"I told papa that I was going to follow you to town. I was afraid for you because that livery man much bigger than you," Juan grinned.

"Maybe so, but look who's still standing," Matt replied with a silly smile as he sat on the cold ground. "I think I broke his leg."

Lillian rushed over to Matt. She lowered herself to the ground and spoke softly to him. "I'm sorry Matt. I hope Al didn't hurt you too bad?"

Matt grabbed Lillian around the neck and pulled her down on one knee. Looking her directly in the eyes he said, "Listen to me you damn little liar. That is a good man lying over there. A damn rich man to boot. You could do much worse. You get my meaning woman?"

Lillian looked over at Al as two men were attempting to load him onto a stretcher. "Rich, you say?" whispering she asked as she stood. "How do you know he has a lot of money?"

"You ever see him spending any of his money? Besides, my banker told me. Now go care for him and leave me and Kathleen alone before I have to break your lovely neck," he said through clenched teeth.

Moving between Matt and Lillian Juan said, "Come on Mr. Matt. Let's go to the doctor."

"No, boy, help me to my horse. My fists hurt like hell," he grunted as he looked at the blood and broken skin on his knuckles. I need a lift up. Get me home. Lucy will care for me."

As Juan was helping Matt on his horse, he heard Lillian giving orders to the men to take extra good care of Big Al. "Take him to the doctor's office as fast as you can before he wakes up."

Later that evening, Juan and Timmy helped Lucy undress Matt and put him in his bed. After Lucy mixed a strong drink for Matt, he seemed to relax and allowed her to examine his face, neck, ribs and hands. She requested that Timmy go outside and bring her a bucket of clean snow. Matt's face had taken a beating from Al's fists and his eyes were nearly swollen shut. His lips were twice as big as they should be. Lucy placed an old pillowcase filled with snow on Matt's face. She patted it so it would lay smoothly over his eyes and mouth. She placed one of his hands into the remaining snow in the bucket.

"Are you trying to freeze me to death old woman? Damn, I am liable to die of frostbite." Matt commented as he tried to use his unwrapped hand to pull the cover up around his neck.

"I know you cold but I will get you more quilts. You need to have the cold compress on your face for a little while. You would scare Sammy to death if he saw you now."

Lucy walked out of Matt's room to get more bedding and led Timmy to the front door. "You go on to bed. I will care for Mr. Matt. He will be in a lot of pain for a few days, but I will make him comfortable. You boys know how to run this ranch. Do your job and leave him in peace."

Tim shook his head and said for her to call and he would come running.

All during the night, Matt was in pain as he tried to get comfortable. His ribs and stomach were already black and blue.

His body had taken a real beating and he was feeling the effects. Several times Lucy lifted Matt's head and forced him to drink some strong whiskey. She did not have any other pain medicine but she would send for some come daylight.

\*\*\*\*\*\*\*\*

Late in the afternoon, Rosa sat beside Kathleen's bed. Kathleen lay with her eyes shut while pretending to be asleep. "Kathleen, I have known you all your life. I know when you are trying to pull the wool over my eyes. Sit up and talk to me."

"Please, let me lie here. I am not ready to face the world."

"Face the world, or Matt? I have let you sleep the day away because I felt you needed the rest. I think you need to know what happened in town last night. Are you listening to me? Juan said that Matt and that Thornbees fellow were fighting with their fists last night. Matt is hurt but the liveryman is worst. Matt broke his leg."

Kathleen quickly sat up in bed. "What were they fighting about?"

"Juan said that Matt was going to make that woman tell the truth about all the rumors she was spreading about you, her and him. Mr. Thornbees came along and fight starts."

"Help me get dressed. I have to go to Matt. I know that he must be hurt." Kathleen slipped out of bed and started pulling her white gown over her head.

"Juan says that he took him home. He didn't want the doctor," Rosa said.

"More the reason for me to go to him; I can help Lucy care for him."

"So, now that he is hurt, you believe his story that you have not heard?" Rosa said.

"I may have jumped to the wrong conclusion about him. He will tell me the truth when he is better, but he needs me and I need him." Kathleen rushed over to give Rosa a hug.

As Kathleen dressed in a long sleeved flannel shirt and her old denim jeans, she asked about Glory. "How is she doing this morning?"

"She is one of God's miracles; one-day bad, the next fine. This morning she eats well and she and Sammy are playing checkers. The snow came down heavy last night. There will be no school."

"I don't want anything to eat. I must hurry and get over to Matt's place. Please tell one of the boys to saddle my horse. I can travel the road better on horseback than with the wagon."

"Lucy will feed you. Take some pain medicine for Matt. Juan said that Matt took a bad beating from that man."

"Good, this medicine will help him. I'm sure Lucy is taking excellent care of him but he is my man, or will be soon, I hope."

After agreeing with Kathleen, Rosa walked into the kitchen with a very hopeful grin on her face.

Kathleen found riding over to Matt's ranch very difficult. The snowdrifts in the road were deep and the frigid wind was blowing hard. It was difficult to travel. She walked her horse slowly as not to step in a hole and cause him to stumble. Once she made it to Matt's home, Timmy hurried out of the bunkhouse and took her horse in the barn.

"I'll take care of your horse, Madam. Go on in the house!" He yelled as the wind was blowing briskly, making it hard to communicate.

"Thank you," she smiled and yelled back.

Kathleen hurried to the front porch and wiped her boots to remove the wet snow she had walked in getting to the door. She knocked as Lucy opened the door.

"Come in, hurry. That wind is freezing cold," Lucy said.

Kathleen removed her hat and scarf from her head, and then took off her big jacket. She slipped out of her boots and rushed over to the fireplace in the big front room. "Lucy, how is Matt? Juan said that Al hurt him."

"He is asleep now but he is better. His face swollen last night but after many cold compresses on it, he better. His hands are busted up bad, too."

"Oh Lucy, I am afraid I hurt Matt—I came to help you care for him. May I see him?"

"Kathleen, he is your man. See him all you want."

"Bless you. I will not wake him. I know he needs rest." Kathleen gave Lucy a hug as she walked quietly into Matt's room.

Kathleen opened Matt's door very slowly. She peeked at him, as he lay covered in the center of his big bed. She walked to his side and gasped as she looked down on his black and blue face. His lips were swollen twice the size they should be. Both his hands were wrapped in soft white cloths.

As Kathleen covered her mouth trying not to make a sound, Matt tried to speak. "If you think I look bad, you should see the other guy."

Kathleen leaned into the mattress and placed her hand on Matt's forehead. "Oh Matt," she uttered.

"What are you doing here?" Matt tried to speak but it hurt his face to move his lips.

"I came to take care of you."

"I don't want you here. Go home. We are not getting married. Remember?" He slurred the words.

"Oh Matt. I'm so sorry. I was in shock, in disbelief, angry when I heard the rumors about you and Lillian. I didn't know what to believe."

"I know. You chose to believe the worst—lies. Go home. You have never trusted me. I told you before that I would never hurt you. However, you would rather believe someone else. Now, get out. Go home."

Matt turned away from Kathleen and called "*Lucy!*" It hurt him all over to yell.

Kathleen turned and hurried out of the room. "Lucy, Matt wants you. I brought over some pain medicine that Rosa sent for you to give him." Handing the bottle to Lucy, Kathleen stood in the foyer and placed her boots, jacket and hat back on.

"Kathleen, don't leave. Stay and make him listen to you. He is upset because you listened to that *woman*'s lies. He loves you." Tears flowed down Kathleen's cheeks as she dressed for the trip home in the cold weather. "Thank you, dear friend," she said as she headed to the barn to get her horse.

# Chapter 26

Lillian sat next to Al Thornbees' bed doing needlepoint when he moaned, opened his eyes to look around and attempted to raise his head. She quickly laid the needlepoint pillow aside and stood over him. Placing her hand on Al's shoulder, she pleaded with him to lie still. "Please darling, you must not move. The doctor doesn't want you to move your leg."

Al looked at the golden hair beauty and was very surprised to see her at his side. "What the hell are you doing here? Get out." He said as he touched the large bandage across his nose. "I don't want you near me."

"Now Al," cooed Lillian as she straightened his quilt closer to his shoulders. "You know that I don't want to be anywhere else. You need me and I want to take good care of my man."

"You want that Moore fellow, not me. You want to marry him, not me."

"You must have got hit harder on the head than I thought. I only want you," smiled Lillian.

"You are a lying two timing witch. Why are you here? Oh!" Al felt pain on his bottom lip. When Matt knocked his tooth out, it had cut his lip.

"Listen to me Al. I'm sorry I told those lies—but I had a good reason." Lillian tried her hardest to squeeze out a tear but none would come.

"What reason could that be?"

"I wanted to make you jealous. I wanted you to come to me and propose marriage. You were coming every night to see me, but you never had marriage on your mind. I have wanted to marry you for a long time."

"That's a laugh! Why do you want to marry me all of a

sudden?"

Lillian slowly reached for Al's right hand, pulled it over, and placed it on her stomach. "Because, because our child needs his papa."

Al lay looking from his right hand to Lillian's beautiful face. He was speechless. Finally, Lillian broke the silence. "What have you got to say?"

"Lillian—you wouldn't play me for a fool, would you?" Al was not sure whether Lillian was telling him the truth. He had always wanted babies but he wanted his own, not some other man's leftovers.

"No Al. You have to know that I have not been with anyone since I arrived here, but you. Matt has not so much as touched me, I promise. He loves Kathleen—not me."

"Do you love me?" Al asked Lillian as he laid watching her facial expressions, searching for the truth.

"Yes, I do. We can be very happy together, all three of us."

"Maybe four or five—of us?" Al said with a grin on his face.

"Don't push it big boy. Only time will tell." Lillian laughed at her own joke.

As Lillian leaned over to kiss Al, the doctor came into the room. "What's going on in this room so early in the morning?"

"Nothing to concern yourself over, Doc. Lillian and I are going to be married as soon as I can get up off this bed," replied Al.

"Well, that is going to be a spell. Your leg is broken in two places and you are going to have to stay off it for at least four to six weeks. We are going to have to move you home and you will have to get someone to care for you around the clock. Miss Larson cannot take care of you that is for sure. Her name will be mud in this town if she stays at your place after dark."

"Well, Doctor, you better go get the Parson because we are going to have a wedding this morning. This is my man and I am going to be the one caring for him." Lillian smiled sweetly at Al and he grinned back at her; after he closed his mouth.

\*\*\*\*\*\*

As the daylight faded into the dark cold night, stars came out and sparkled down on the clean banks of white snow. Any other time Kathleen would have enjoyed the lovely winter evening.

Tonight she was heartbroken and weary. She had hurt the one and only man that she really loved. She had not trusted him. Matt sent her away because her actions showed him that she believed all the ugly rumors about him and Lillian. Way down deep in her soul, she had not wanted to believe that Matt would have cheated on her. He had been a good man and a wonderful friend. However, she did believe the rumors at first. She had been hurt as a young girl. All those hurtful memories of seeing her young man take money from her papa and ride out of her life forever were still raw. Matt was the only man she had given her heart to and trusted to love her since that had happened twelve years ago. Now she had hurt him; just the way she had been hurt.

Kathleen rode her horse into her barn. She moved slow as she unsaddled the animal and filled the feed-bin with an extra helping of oats. She took a large rag and wiped the horses' back until it was dry. She walked over to her milk cow that she had raised and wrapped her arms around the cow's neck.

"Oh Betsy, I have messed up this time," she said as she slipped down on a stack of clean hay and lay looking up at the rafters. Betsy mooed, nudged Kathleen's shoulder, shook her head as she folded her front legs under her big belly, and stooped down next to Kathleen as if she were a dog. Kathleen rubbed the cow's nose and ears as tears flowed down her wind chapped cheeks.

Early the next morning, Carlos dressed warm and went out to the barn to begin his morning chores while his wife Rosa cooked breakfast. He entered the barn and found Kathleen lying cuddled next to Betsy, her faithful old milk cow. Katherine was shivering and murmuring words that sounded like *marry me* and *please*. Carlos stooped down and looked at the beautiful young girl who had grown into a lovely woman. Finding her like this reminded him of a time when she was about fifteen. Betsy gave birth to a calf and the poor little creature died. Kathleen slept with Betsy for two nights and vowed that she would not put her pet cow through that again.

Carlos touched Kathleen on the shoulder and she did not stir except to cry out words that sounded like *please Matt*. He placed his cold rough hand on her forehead and found her to be burning up with a fever. He looked around for a blanket and not seeing one, he realized she had slept in this barn without any covers or heat. As he moved around her, she cried out more words that were unrecognizable. Hurrying outside to the corral, he waved Pedro over and asked him to help carry Kathleen into the house.

"She slept out in this freezing barn last night and now she has a fever. Please help me get her inside the house."

"We thought she was over at Matt's house. Good gracious, she could have frozen out here as cold as it was last night. Mercy." Pedro just stood looking at Kathleen and shaking his head. "That's true but we have got to carry her inside. Now, stop chattering and help me," Carlos said.

Rosa could not believe that Kathleen had slept out in the freezing barn. She fluttered around Kathleen, giving orders to poor Carlos, who was as upset over Kathleen as she was. "Put hot water on the stove and warm some of those bricks to go at the foot of her bed."

"Pedro, hold this quilt in front of the fireplace and get it warm. Then get on your horse and ride into town for old Doc Squires. Tell him to hurry out here. Kathleen is burning with fever." Rosa gave orders like a general in the Army.

Rosa bathed Kathleen with a cold damp cloth. She wet the rag and ran it all over Kathleen's body as she kept her covered. Glory heard all the commotion and eased out of bed using the wall to steady her frail body. She managed to get to Kathleen's doorway before Rosa noticed her.

"Go back to bed, Miss Glory. I have my hands full with my baby girl. I don't need to have to stop and pick you up off the floor this morning."

"Please Rosa, I can help give her a cold bath for the fever," she said as a coughing spell took over her body. As she wiped her mouth, she eased down in a chair near Kathleen's bed.

"All right, if you are determined to help. Watch her while I go and warm some coffee. She needs to be warm inside and out."

"I'll watch her good. I promise." Glory pulled her housecoat closer to her body and leaned over on the bed. She rubbed Kathleen's hair back away from her face and dipped the cloth in the pan of cool water. Kathleen felt something cool and wet moving slowing all over her body. Glory turned her over to expose her back to the cool air and applied gentle caresses.

Rosa hurried in the kitchen and placed the blue granite coffee pot on the burner while watching Carlos bring in more firewood. "Man, it is cold out there. Is Sammy still asleep?"

"Si," said Rosa. "School is out until the first of the year. I am happy too. It is much too cold for children to have to ride into town." Rosa poured some coffee in a cup and pushed it toward Carlos. "I will finish breakfast after I care for Kathleen. She needs warm coffee inside her cold body too."

"Mama, here is the warm quilt. I will ride into town and get Doc Squires," said Pedro.

"Be careful son, and dress warm. It is very cold this morning."

# Chapter 27

After a long restless night, Matt finally fell into a sound sleep. The medicine that Kathleen gave Lucy to help with the pain had finally taken effect. The cold snow compresses on his face had helped reduce the swelling. Matt was lucky that Big Al's fist did not break his nose or jaw. His lips were nearly twice the normal size but the snow pillow had taken some of the swelling out of them. He did not have any broken ribs but his stomach, rib cage and back were black and blue from the hard blows he had taken to his body. It hurt him to move or breathe deeply. In Lucy's opinion, Matt would be spending many days in bed recuperating. She had sent Timmy into town to get white man's medicine man to come and look at Matt. Timmy rode toward town with a grin on his face remembering what Lucy called old Doc Squires.

After lunch, the old rickety black carriage pulled up in front of Matt's house. Old Doc Squires climbed down, gathered his doctor's bag off the seat while trying to hold his worn brown hat on his head. The wind was brisk with frozen crystals of water in the air. He pulled his big overcoat close to his body as he limped to the front porch. Lucy had heard him arrive so she hurried to open the door to allow him to enter.

Lucy reached to help him remove his big wet coat, hat and scarf. He stomped around in the hallway with his dirty, muddy boots. Lucy made no comment to the man as he asked what room Matt was in.

"Come," said Lucy. "He not want to see you."

"Hell woman, why did that boy come after me if I'm not wanted? I am ready to get home, get a shot of whiskey, and sit in front of my fire. These old bones are nearly frozen."

"I give you whiskey after you look at Mr. Matt. Mr. Big

Britches nearly killed him."

The doctor stopped in the hallway and howled with laughter. "Woman, I have heard big Al called a lot of names but never big britches! I can't wait to tell the fellows in town his new name."

"Matt is asleep or was until you make loud joke. I gave him pain medicine a few minutes ago. Come, he is in here."

Doc Squires walked into Matt's bedroom. The room was large with a nice roaring fire in the corner fireplace. It was very inviting to his cold old bones but he walked over to the bed. He looked down at Matt's face and snickered.

"Land sakes man! Big Al did a job on your face. How are you feeling?" he asked as he touched the side of Matt's face.

"Somewhat better," Matt grunted as he tried to turn his face away from the doctor's hand. He did not like the doctor and he hated the way he touched him. "Have you seen him?"

"Shore. I set his left leg. His nose was broken, too and he is missing a bottom tooth. He is strong as an ox. He is going to be fine now that he has a new wife to care for him. I witnessed Big Al and your old fiancée being hitched yesterday. He may have lost the fight, but he shore enough got the prize."

"Listen to me, you old fool. We were not fighting over Lillian. I got—or had a good woman. I went to town to stop her from telling a bunch more lies." Matt sighed and rubbed his hand over his lips. "Damn, it hurts to even talk."

"Let me feel your ribs and check you over good. I would not want you to have a broken rib that could puncture one of your lungs. Old woman, help me pull back all these covers and let's get this exam over quickly."

In a few minutes, the old Doc declared that Matt was in fair condition from the beating he took. "You will be sore for a few days. I will leave some pain medicine but with all that brandy, you may not need any. In a couple of days, you may feel like getting up and moving around. It would be good for you to sit up and walk slowly around the house. Now, man, use common sense. If it hurts, don't do it." He took his bag, snapped it shut as he walked over to the fireplace, and backed his behind up to the roaring warmth.

"Old woman, where is that whiskey you said you would give me?"

Lucy continued to smooth the covers back over Matt's body. She looked at Matt a second longer, turned, and left the room. Once Matt was sure Lucy could not hear him, he said, "Listen old man. I want you to show more respect to my housekeeper. She may be an old Indian, but she is a nice old woman, and she works for me. You understand?"

Lucy walked back into the bedroom with a tray that held a large glass of dark whiskey and two round sugar cookies. She walked over to Doctor Squires and placed the tray down on the table near the fire.

He looked at the tray containing the whiskey and the sweet cookies. "Thank you, madam," he said with a sweet smile. Lucy was so surprised by his response that all she could do was give him a nod, as she walked over and sat in a chair by Matt.

The doctor quickly swallowed the whiskey. "I had best get on back to my office where I am sure I have patients waiting. I have been over at the Parker's ranch all morning."

"You were checking on Glory," asked Matt.

"No, but I wish I could do something for that poor girl. Rosa sent for me early this morning to help with Kathleen. Carlos said he found her out in their barn this morning lying in the hay. Fool woman slept in the barn last night and nearly froze to death. I am afraid she has a bad cold that could turn into pneumonia. I have done all I can do, but she is safe with Rosa. I will be back out tomorrow to check on you and Kathleen."

"Matt don't need you anymore. Spend all your time caring for Kathleen." Lucy helped him with his overcoat and handed him his scarf. "Thank you for coming," she said as she closed the door behind him.

Lucy walked back into Matt's bedroom, started grunting, and shaking her head. Matt was attempting to pull himself up on the side of the bed. "No, you cannot get up." Lucy straightened his pillow as she slowly pushed Matt down into the bed. "You cannot do anything for Kathleen right now. You must get better."

"I'm not going to Kathleen. She doesn't want a liar and cheat," Matt said just above a whisper, "but it is my fault she was out in the cold. I sent her away last night and I know-- I hurt her. She must have-- gone home and just stayed in the barn. I'm sorry about hurting her Lucy, but damn she has a problem with trust, and that hurts me." Matt sat up on the side of the bed. "Lucy, I need to get to the water closet. Help me."

"I get you a bed pan. Now lay back. When you are better, you both can talk and forgive each other. Big misunderstanding!"

"Katy has got to trust me." His words slurred together as the pain medicine was finally taking effect. Matt could not form words or keep his eyes open. He faded off to dreamland where he had nightmares of Katy drifting away from him.

*********

Rosa sat all night beside Kathleen's bed, watching, and listening to her breathing. When she was not bathing her body to keep down the fever, she was down on her knees praying for her recovery. Several times Carlos came into Kathleen's room to encourage Rosa to go and get some rest while he sat with her. She would only wipe her tears and shake her head. There was no way that she would leave her baby's side. Kathleen struggled and pushed away the quilts. The heat was unbearable as she shivered with chills .She was delirious and frantic with worry about Matt. She was cold. She felt weighted down with something heavy on her chest. She had to get up and get away from this inferno. Matt needed her. She cried out for him and begged him for forgiveness.

Rosa held her in her arms tight against her bosom, rocking back and forth. She remembered that Mrs. Parker, Kathleen's mama, had a long, hard labor and the doctor was sure that the child would be stillborn. The old doctor insisted that she just lie still and let nature take its course. The babe would come when it was ready, was his only answer. Rosa remembered telling that old man to get out of her way and she and Mr. Parker lifted his wife up off her bed and began walking up and down the room. Crying and whimpering she walked. After an hour of dragging her across the room, back and forth, the baby decided it was ready to come into the world. Rosa still remembered the blood curdling screams coming from Mrs. Parker as her baby made its entrance into her waiting hands. Once Kathleen's mama laid eyes on her beautiful black-haired baby girl, all the pain and suffering was like it never happened.

Early in the morning, as the old rooster crowed announcing another freezing day, Kathleen's fever had broken and she had fallen into a deep sound sleep. Carlos walked into the kitchen and put on the coffee. Rosa staggered into the warm room and sat down at the table watching Carlos as he took two cups off the shelf.

"You know, Carlos. I like Mr. Matt but there are times, like yesterday and tonight, I wish he had stayed in Abilene. Kathleen loves that fool of a man and all they do is hurt each other."

Carlos murmured an agreement and said he had better get outside and milk the cow. "You know that darn cow was lying down on the hay next to Kathleen, just like a dog. I believe Betsy actually kept her warm most of the night. Funniest thing I ever seen," he said laughing as he dressed to go out in the freezing cold weather.

"Hurry back. After breakfast, I have to get busy cooking for tomorrow night, Christmas Eve. We have a child in the house again, and I want to make it the best holiday ever for him and Glory," Rosa said with a sigh. Carlos walked over to his lovely wife and took her in his arms.

"Yes, we'll do everything we can to make this a very special Christmas for them and our two boys, too. They are still very young at heart," he said as he kissed her on the forehead and hurried out the door.

Sammy woke up and raced into the kitchen. "Morning, Mrs. Rosa!" said Sammy. "Mama told me to be as quiet as a mouse this morning because Miss Kathleen is sick. Golly, do you think she will be well by tomorrow night?"

"No baby boy. She may be awake but she will not be strong enough to get out of bed. I have plenty of cooking to do today and you can help me."

"What you going to be cooking? I ain't never done much in the kitchen except sweep."

"I am going to make some cookies and I will need help in getting them out of the pan. I will be mixing up and rolling out pie dough, too. You can do that, I'm sure."

"This is going to be a great day! When do you think Mr. Matt and Lucy will be coming over? I shore like playing checkers with him. He don't let me win like Carlos does."

"Sammy, you know Mr. Matt has been hurt. He and that livery stable man got into a tussle and Mr. Matt is hurt. He might not be able to come over tomorrow."

"He's got to come!" cried Sammy. "I got a present for him and he said he had me something special too. I ain't never had anything special."

"Well, please try to understand if he doesn't come. You want to make your mama happy today. If you are sad, then she will be too."

"I'll try," Sammy said as he sat down at the table to wait for his breakfast. "Maybe Christmas morning Mr. Matt will be better," he said as he laid his head down on his arm, determined not to show his disappointment.

Carlos hurried into the house with Pedro and Juan following close behind. After removing their jackets and boots, Juan rubbed Sammy on the head. "Hey scout, how would you like to go with me and Pedro to cut down our Christmas tree after breakfast?"

"Really? You will let me use the axe and chop the tree?" he asked very excited.

"Well," Rosa began when she saw Carlos raise his hand to silence her.

"Of course. How are we going to get the tree down if you do not do some of the chopping?" replied Juan.

"I've got to go tell my mama," he said as he scooted out of his chair and raced down the hall into Glory's room.

"I guess that means he's going with us," said Juan as the men all laughed.

# Chapter 28

Lucy was busy from morning to evening cooking chicken soup and caring for Matt. His face was so much better since all the swelling had gone down but his mood had not improved. He was angry that he could not ride his horse. Hell, he could not even sit up in bed without excruciating pain shooting all through his body. He had refused the pain medication because it made him sleepy.

Lucy was preparing the big turkey that Timmy had purchased from the mercantile. She had a big pot of boiling water on the stove making the small kitchen hot as Hades. Her long braids were soaked from sweat as she pushed the big bird down into the steaming water. Once the bird was cool, she would pluck all the feathers off. Normally, this was a job done outdoors but with the freezing wind and snow continuing to fall; it made it impossible to work outside.

She had already peeled onions, boiled eggs, scrubbed yams, and cleaned several bunches of collards. In between scurrying around the house caring for Matt, she had accomplished many small chores and prepared several of the dishes for Christmas dinner. The original plan for Christmas Day was to take most of the dishes over to Kathleen's home to celebrate the day together. Now, Lucy would only have Moose, Timmy and Matt to eat all of her Christmas dishes.

Matt was in a foul mood. He did not want to eat, sleep or talk. He was determined to get up so he could go out into the barn. He wanted to make sure the pony that he had picked out for Sammy was groomed and saddled. He wanted Moose to take it to Kathleen's ranch and put it in the barn. Carlos could present it to him Christmas morning, something that he had planned to do. Plans had changed and he was not going over to spend Christmas with Kathleen's family. He knew Lucy was disappointed but he and Kathleen were not going to get married so it was better for all of them to make this separation as easy as possible. She didn't trust him and most likely never would. Relationships are built on trust and she didn't trust him. Her actions spoke loud and clear to him that she didn't love him like he loved her.

He wondered how he was going to be able to exist without her in his life. She lit up a room when she entered. She delighted him. He loved their spirited conversations and the debates they had over all the changes in the country. He could not see a future without her in it.

Nevertheless, he had hurt her. He had not gotten over the look on her face when he demanded that she leave. He knew that she had believed the lies told by Lillian and he wanted to punish her for not trusting him.

He took a deep breath, gritted his teeth and moved his legs off the bed. He was sitting on the side of the mattress, with one foot touching the floor while the other dangled free. The pains in his sides were as if a big bear was squeezing all the air out of him. He bit down on his bruised lip and quickly stood before he lost his nerve.

He turned and held on to the edge of the bed as sweat formed on his top lip and across his forehead. He had to endure the pain and go out to the barn. He bellowed for Lucy to come and help him. Lucy entered his bedroom. She was not surprised to see him standing beside the bed in his long white underwear and bare feet. Lucy swore under her breath and walked over to him.

"Foolish man," she said as she walked over to the peg on the wall and retrieved a pair of pants for him. She took down a warm flannel shirt and helped him loop his belt threw his pants. After completely dressing him, she said that she would get Timmy to come in and help him out to the barn.

"You are not to touch that pony. Moose and Timmy will do whatever needs to be done, you foolish man," said Lucy. She gave that order and did not expect a refusal or argument from Matt.

Timmy dressed as warm as possible in his old worn out jacket. He came into the house to help Matt outside.

Lucy had helped Matt into his big coat and boots. The wind was fierce and the sun had gone behind dark clouds making it appear to be later than it actually was. Timmy helped Matt out to the barn and once they got inside out of the wind Matt asked, "Why are you still here? Why didn't you go home with Joseph and Gabe? Moose is here to help care for the animals."

"Shucks, Mr. Matt. I do not have a place I can call home like the others. I was living with them, but it was time for me to move on. When you hired us, I figured this was as good as a place as any to call home. Besides, Moose's shoulder ain't as well as it should be. It is hard for him to pick up heavy sacks and some of the critters, even though he would never admit that. I hope you don't mine that I'm staying here over Christmas."

"Of course I don't care. Does Lucy know that you are staying behind with Moose?"

"Yes sir, she knows. That is one sweet old woman. She takes good care of Moose and me. She even brought us several more blankets to make sure we were warm enough in the bunkhouse. I ain't never had anyone looking out for me before. I have been on my own since I was about ten. My ma died and my old man stayed drunk. The sheriff was going to put me in an orphanage but I wasn't having no part of that, so I just up and started wandering from town to town."

Matt shook his head in a sad gesture. He was happy that young Timmy had found his way to his ranch. This young man would have a place to live as long as he wanted, if he had any say in it. He was going to have to speak to Lucy about having a present or two for him under the tree.

After returning inside the house, Matt asked Lucy if she might have something in her gift basket that she hid every time he walked into the room for Timmy. He knew that she had made a scarf for Timmy, Gage, and Joseph but he wanted Timmy to have something else under the tree.

Lucy did not answer him but left the room and came back carrying a new-fleeced lined jacket and several pairs of long wool socks. "Where in the blazes did you get those?"

"Out of the trunk you have in your room. These are your things. The jacket is too small for you and the socks are new, too. Do you care if St. Nick brings them to the boy?" she asked with a grin on her face.

Matt took the jacket out of her hands and looked it over. "I remember this jacket. I bought a few pieces of extra clothes to have on my trail drives for some men who might need something. Fortunately, for Timmy, no one did and you found them. Anything else in that trunk I might could use?" he asked laughing.

She smiled and said, "Timmy good Brave."

# Chapter 29

**At Kathleen's ranch**, all the preparations were ready for Christmas Eve. Juan, Pedro and Sammy had gone out the day before and chopped the tree down. They placed it in the barn to dry out as they built a stand. Later the men carried the tree into the parlor to be decorated. Kathleen, still very weak from her sickness, sat down at the table and helped Rosa bake gingerbread men and showed Sammy how to decorate them.

Kathleen held a star made from thin branches. Her papa had made the ornament when she was only a small child. Each Christmas, she opened the box and unwrapped the delicate ornament that was brittle from old age and she held it close to her heart. Her papa would lift her up high so she could place it on top of the tree. Her eyes had become misty as she remembered the very first Christmas Eve that her beloved papa had made it especially for her.

Once the tree was decorated, Kathleen still very weak, passed the star to Pedro to place the treasured Christmas star on the very top. Carlos and Rosa joined hands and smiled at each other. They remembered that very special Christmas Eve, too.

After a long quiet evening, Sammy and Glory went off to bed. Sammy was so excited Glory did not think that he would settle down. It was not long before his sweet snoring sounded in her ears as she lay thinking that this would be her last Christmas with her precious little boy. It was getting very hard for her to breathe and she did not have much of an appetite at all. She had to force herself to eat. The doctor had left medicine for her to take to help her rest, but she was trying not to take it. It was important to stay awake and spend as much time with her son as possible. She wanted Sammy to remember his last Christmas with her to be a good one. She prayed she would not pass away during the holidays because she wanted Sammy to love Christmas and not have a sad remembrance of Christmas each year.

Glory laid in her bed listening to the sounds of the house. Rosa was in the kitchen humming as she washed the dishes and Kathleen was rocking in her rocker in front of the fireplace. The boys were coming back in to the house after checking on the animals before turning in for the night. They were laughing and joking about what they were expecting from that fat old man who flew around in the sky every Christmas Eve. Glory laughed to herself thinking that you never get too old to expect something under the tree as she rubbed her little one's hair.

She looked out the window at the bright stars in the sky. The landscape was lovely with a lot of snow covering the ground and a luminous glow shining down from the big orange moon. She stared out the window for what seemed like hours. She wished she could see St. Nick flying across the sky into the moonlight as she drifted off into a light sleep.

Early Christmas morning before the old rooster announced the new day, Sammy woke up and looked out the window. It was light enough to run into the parlor and see if St. Nick had come to see him. He slid out of bed quietly as not to wake his mama. He was down on his hands and knees peeking under the tree when Rosa surprised him with a big smile and a cup of hot coffee with extra sugar and milk in it. "Oh, Rosa, you scared me!" He whispered.

"Come into the kitchen and have some coffee while we wait for the others to wake up. I will put on some bacon and eggs and that will get their attention," she laughed.

"You ain't never given me any coffee before."

"Well, you haven't been awake this early and the house is still cold. Coffee will warm your insides." Sammy crawled up to the table and sighed. "Rosa, do you think that St. Nick came to see me. There are presents under the tree but I ain't sure any of them are for me."

"I think that you will be very happy today. That is all I am going to say," she said as she looked up and saw Carlos and Kathleen standing together in the doorway of the kitchen.

"Merry Christmas everyone!" Kathleen walked over to Sammy and grinned. "Coffee?"

"Yes madam. Rosa thinks that I am big enough to drink coffee now."

"Sammy that is not the reason I gave you the coffee." Rosa continued to fry the bacon as she laughed at the child's remarks.

"Sammy, go wake those lazy head sons of mine and tell them that breakfast is ready and to get in here." Carlos pulled down two cups and poured coffee for him and Kathleen.

Kathleen glanced up from sipping her coffee when she saw Glory walking down the hall. She jumped up from her chair and went to help her into a kitchen chair.

"Oh, Glory, it is so good that you could join us this morning. Are you all right?"

Glory wiped her mouth and smiled. "Yes, I am better this morning."

After a big breakfast, they followed Kathleen into the parlor. "Well, look at all the presents under the tree," Kathleen said. "Juan and Pedro, will you both pass out the gifts. I am still too weak to stand very long."

"Wait, Katy," said Sammy using Matt's pet name for her. "We have to wait for Matt and Lucy."

"I'm afraid that Matt will not be coming over today," said Rosa. "Let's get those presents passed out."

"Is that right, Carlos? Mr. Matt won't be bringing me a surprise after all?"

"I'm sure you will get your surprise from Mr. Matt very soon—maybe not today."

Sammy snuggled up to his mama's side and poked out his bottom lip.

**********

Early Christmas morning at Matt's ranch, Lucy cooked a big breakfast of flapjacks, bacon and slices of ham. Timmy's favorite foods; strawberry jam, fresh butter and milk sat on the table. The men came into the kitchen and smelled the wonderful breakfast. Timmy walked over and hugged Lucy as he lifted her off the floor. She pushed on his shoulders making him put her down. Moose stood in the doorway and watched all the commotion. Matt patted Timmy on the back and told Moose to come and take a seat.

"Lucy has prepared a nice Christmas breakfast for us. Afterward, we will see if that old, fat man stopped here last night

232

and left anything under our tree."

"Don't count on it," said Timmy. "I ain't had a Christmas present since I was a little fellow. One time a neighbor left a pair of oversized boots on our porch for me. I needed them something fierce. My old shoes had newspaper in the bottom for soles."

"Sit down and eat," Lucy said with a sizeable lump in her throat. She looked at Matt and both of them were thankful that their tree had presents under it for this young man.

After breakfast, the men walked into the parlor and Lucy sat in a straight chair as Matt made a big deal out of searching under the tree. He had eased down on his knees, moving as slow as possible. He passed Moose a big brown bag with a red ribbon tied across the top. "Look here! I believe this one is for someone –I cannot make out the name. Lucy? No, it says Timmy." He looked directly at Timmy and tried to hand it to him. Timmy just sat and stared at Matt. "For me? That big present is for me?"

"I think you are the only Timmy here in this room."

Matt pushed the package toward Timmy. It had a green ribbon wrapped around it several time to hold it together. "Go ahead, both of you and open your gifts."

"Where are your gifts?" Moose asked still holding his present.

"We will open them later." Matt sat down on the sofa and watched the two men. Neither of the men were in any hurry to open their gifts. They both seemed to be enjoying the moment before they destroyed the lovely wrappings. Moose looked at Timmy and they both smiled at each other. Moose immediately tore into his package and pulled out a long, navy blue scarf. He stood and wrapped it around his neck, running his big hands over the soft knitted threads. Timmy untied the ribbon and tore away the brown paper. He pulled out the blue fleece denim jacket and looked at it in wonder. As he stood to try on the jacket, he saw several pair of new socks.

"Holy cow! Look! New socks." Before anyone could say anything, Timmy raced into the kitchen. Moose made a motion to Matt with his fingers, telling him that Timmy was crying.

Matt walked into the kitchen, turned Timmy toward him, and pulled him in his arms. "It's all right son. Lucy and I are happy that we were able to celebrate Christmas with you. We are pleased to have you here with us. We want you to stay on here as long as you like."

"I didn't mean to act like a baby. Sorry."

"You are happy and that makes us happy. I still cry, occasionally, so don't think nothing of it." Matt wanted to cry out as Timmy gave him a bear hug, but he was trying his best to pretend his body was on the mend.

"Oh, shucks, Mr. Matt. You are just saying that to make me feel better," he said wiping his tears on his sleeve.

"Well, did it work?" He said they walked back to the parlor. "I have another gift for you—from me." Matt walked over to the tree, took down two white envelopes, and handed one to each of them.

"Open them!" Matt said as he looked at them. Both men immediately tore into the envelopes and they were astonished at the green bills that were inside.

"This is a Christmas bonus. I gave the other men theirs the day before they went home. All I ask is that you use it wisely. No whiskey or gaming tables for you Timmy, and no gaming in the bunkhouse with the other boys either when they return."

"Moose, once the judge comes to town and hears your case, if you get probation, you can do whatever you want. Until then, you are to stay on the ranch."

"Yes Sir. I hope I get probation. I want to stay here, that is, if you let me. I like it here with you and Lucy. You know I am sorry about getting involved with Tyler."

"I know we have all made foolish mistakes. Just learn from them." Matt said and he motioned for the two men to come with him. "I need you two fellows to go out to the barn and bring in the box from the tack room. I want to bring Lucy's Christmas present inside while she is busy.

In just a few minutes, Matt was calling for Lucy to come into the parlor. "Mr. Matt, I busy. Them pies won't bake themselves," she said as she wiped flour off her hands.

"Merry Christmas!" All three men chimed together, making her jump.

Lucy looked down at the box that had something whimpering in it. She stomped down and lifted the lid. "Oh my," she said very softly. "Oh my, is this mine?"

Standing up on his four little legs was the cutest brown and white spotted puppy in the world. He looked all around and his little tail started wagging when Lucy picked him up.

"He has big paws. Going to be a big dog. I like him," she said as she placed him up under her chin for a tight squeeze. She looked to Matt and smiled.

"Yes, *she* is all yours. You can train her to stay in the house if you like." Matt said as he rubbed the puppy behind the ears. Lucy snuggled the pup up to her face and kissed her.

"What you gonna call her Miss Lucy?" Timmy asked.

"Got to ponder on her name, must be strong, fierce name." The men laughed because the puppy looked sweet and not a bit like something fierce.

"I need for you two to deliver Sammy's Christmas present now. I want the boy to have the pony with the new saddle this morning so please dress warm and lead it over for me."

The two guys looked at each other and shook their heads. "We'll do it right now."

"So, Mr. Matt, we aren't going to Kathleen's today? You are not going to try to fix problem between you?"

"Lucy, Kathleen does not trust me. She cannot really love me the way I want her to if she does not trust me. There must be trust between two people who are going to spend the rest of their lives together. You can go to Kathleen's and visit with them anytime you want. You work for me. I do not control what you do or where you go."

Matt went out to the barn and looked the pony over once more. He was a nice pinto pony like Juan's and the saddle was perfect for a boy Sammy's size. He would like to see the surprised look on his face but that was not to be.

He watched Moose and Timmy lead the new pony out of the barn and down the road. Sammy was a good boy and he deserved happiness in his young life. His mama had done her best but she too had fallen under the charming spell of Tyler Chambers, a once handsome but cruel man.

Timmy jumped down off his horse and knocked on Kathleen's front door. Carlos came to the door and immediately invited him inside.

"Can't come in this morning Sir. I got a delivery for a very special little boy—Sammy!" Timmy said loudly, hoping Sammy would hear him.

Kathleen came to the door and looked at Timmy and Moose. She looked at the pony and looked beyond both of the men and the pony. "No one else came with you to bring this very nice gift?"

"No madam. Just us, I'm sorry to say this morning," replied Moose.

"Sammy," Kathleen called. "There is something very special for you outside."

"Mr. Matt, Mr. Matt," called Sammy. "I knew he would be coming this morning."

Sammy raced pass Kathleen. He leaped off the porch directly in front of the new pony. He looked at Timmy and Moose and finally asked, "Where's Mr. Matt?"

"Sorry Sammy. Mr. Matt is still hurt and he could not come over today but he wanted you to have this special gift."

His squeal could have been heard a country mile when he got a glance at the new brown pony. "Is he really mine, all mine?"

"He sure is, son. all yours to ride and care for." Moose got off his big horse and walked over to Sammy. You want me to lift you on his back?"

"Sammy, you got to have your jacket on," cried Rosa as she handed the coat to Kathleen.

"Look at me Carlos, Juan and Pedro! I have my own pony now and a new saddle. Now I can help with the cattle and horses. Oh Kathleen, can I ride over to see Matt and thank him. Oh, Kathleen, please let me go over there," he pleaded.

"I will ride with him," Juan said softly for Kathleen's ears only.

"Of course, after you come inside and put on some warmer clothes. You are still in your pajamas. And you can take Matt and Lucy's gifts to them." Kathleen laughed but her smile did not reach her eyes.

# Chapter 30

For several weeks, freezing north winds had kept everyone close to home and inside. On Monday, after a long miserable cold weekend with no church services, the good Lord had showered down warm sunshine. "Hurry, Sammy, if you want to ride into town with me this morning. I have a long list of items to get for Rosa and I want to get some new seeds for our spring garden. *If spring every gets here,* she said under her breath. It was so wonderful to wake up to a beautiful day. She had been so miserable the last several weeks shut in and not being able to get outside or have visitors. She was thinking of Matt and Lucy. Not that Matt would visit her but Lucy had not come over either.

Because of her sickness before Christmas, the men would not allow her to ride over the range and view the cattle or baby calves. They had assured her that everything was all right and she needed to get her strength back. The men did not realize that most of her health problem was a broken heart. She had caused this problem and she did not know how to fix it. Matt had stayed very far away from her ranch and she had heard very little about what he was doing. She missed him so much and wanted to be able to talk to him. She wanted him to accept her apology for her misunderstanding.

Sammy walked out of the house carrying a long thin box that contained a lovely scarf for the table in the vestibule of the church. Rosa had made the scarf and embroidered gold crosses on each end. Kathleen took it from him and placed it on the high bench seat. He raced back into the house to give his mama one more kiss and make sure that he had her list of personal items she needed.

"Everything I need is written on the note, Sammy. Are you warm enough?"

"Yes, madam, Rosa said I could play with Mikey, the postmaster's son, while the women clean the inside of the church."

"Well, that's just fine." Glory was in her bedroom resting in her rocking chair near the front window. She was watching Kathleen and Sammy load up into the wagon.

She sat rocking and smiling at her young son who walked and acted like a big boy. He offered his hand to help Kathleen on to the wagon seat. He hurried to the other side and climbed up on the seat, taking the package that held the precious scarf onto his lap. Just as Kathleen was turning the wagon in the yard, a tall man dressed in all black tied his horse to the back of her wagon. He crawled low onto the wagon bed. He scooted his way up to the front seat, and whispered something to Kathleen as the wagon came to a standstill.

"Oh no," screamed Glory. She recognized the man to be Tyler Chambers, her old boyfriend, the mean cuss who had kidnapped Sammy.

"Rosa!" She yelled from the top of her lungs, nearly causing herself to faint from the exertion. Hearing no answer, she called again, this time for Carlos. She realized that everyone must be outside leaving her alone in the house. Someone had to help Kathleen and her baby boy.

She reached for her heavy coat with a wool scarf wrapped around the collar and put it on. With a raging flow of adrenaline throbbing through her body, she staggered out of her bedroom door, shouting for help as she made her way down the hallway to the front entrance. Jerking open the front door, she yelled again for help. Receiving no answer, she knew she was their only chance. Looking down, she saw a pair of big heavy outdoor boots. She slipped them on her dainty feet. Her eye caught a glimpse of Carlos's holster with his pistol tucked in it. She pulled the gun out of the holster and placed it in the deep pocket of her coat. She opened the door and immediately thanked the good Lord for the beautiful sunny day. The air was freezing cold but the sun felt good on her face. She walked her fragile body out on to the porch. She held on for dear life to the hitching post and used a shovel leaning up against it as a crutch. Finally, she was in the barn holding onto the big red door. She yelled again for help but the barn was empty except for several workhorses in their stalls.

Looking around in the barn, she saw a bridle hanging on the wall. She pulled on it until it was down around her feet. She walked over to the stalls and chose the smallest horse. The small animal was wary of the stranger so he began to move around trying to distance himself from her.

"Whoa boy," she whispered in almost a silent breathe. After getting a scent of the young woman, he settled down. He stood still while she slipped the bit of the bridle into his mouth.

"Good boy," she said to the animal as she adjusted the reins around his neck. She laid her face up against the horse's neck and tried to take slow even breaths. Her legs felt like they might fold under her any minute. She walked the horse over to a stack of hay bales. She pushed one bale off the stack with her big boot. Managing to lift one foot off the floor, she held her hand against the wall for balance so she could stand straight and tall. She held the reins and placed her body head first over the back of the horse. She had never ridden bareback before, but she would have never been able to lift a saddle on to the horse's back. The animal stood very still.

Glory prayed. "Please God, give me strength, what little I have left in my body, to get on this horse. I have to do everything I can to save my son from that monster." After she caught her breath, she slid her legs over the horse's back and straddled him. Blood was trailing out of her mouth and nose and down onto her chin. The animal got a whiff of the blood and he started twisting and turning. "Whoa fellow. Let's go to town," she said to the small horse hoping to calm him. "Please God, please help me to remain on this animal's back. Guide this poor horse to town," she prayed.

As Glory rode the animal outside, the horse stepped on the long box that held the white scarf. The animal led Glory down the slushy muddy road to town.

********

Kathleen drove the big wagon down the muddy road at an uncomfortable fast pace. The horse's hoofs tossed snowy slush up on her and Sammy as the wind blew sporadically from the north. Kathleen was not thinking about the condition of the road because Tyler Chambers had his colt .45 pointed directly at the back of Sammy's head.

"Make one wrong move and I will blow his head off. I am not nice like Moose and this little fellow knows that. Right sonny?"

Sammy only looked up at Kathleen and showed her his empty hands. He was signaling to her that he had dropped the long box with the white scarf with hopes that someone would find it.

"What do you want, Tyler?" Kathleen spoke with a deep strong voice, trying her best not to show any fear. "Glory is very sick and she cannot go with you. So if you didn't come back for her, what do you want?"

"I want the same thing that I came for before, money!" A sudden jolt rocked them and Kathleen reached for Sammy to keep him from falling off the wagon. The wagon slid to one side nearly causing Tyler to topple overboard.

"You better be more careful woman. I would hate to have to shoot this youngster before I get some of your money." The deep lines in his face made him look older and mean.

"How do you plan on getting my money?"

"Easy, Sweetheart," Tyler answered sweetly. "You are going to give me some of the money you got for selling off your herd. I want twenty-five thousand dollars today. I figure that is as much as this small bank has on hand."

"You sound like you know a good bit about banks. This must not be your first bank robbery."

"Hold on honey! This here is not a bank robbery. You are going to be giving me the money out of the goodness of your heart. Can't no one say I robbed your bank." He tossed back his head and laughed heartily.

Kathleen slowed the horses down as she entered the main street into town. Several people called to her from the boardwalk and she and Sammy smiled and waved back.

"That's nice. Just keep up the act and no one will be the wiser or get hurt," Tyler said as he lowered the pistol so the people on the street could not see it. "Pull up in front of the bank."

"We aren't allowed to park on the street in front of any of the businesses. We are supposed to go to the end of town or to the livery. That's a new law."

"Do as I say. Pull up and put the brake on the wagon. We're going into the bank here."

Kathleen did as Tyler instructed her. He jumped down off the wagon onto the boardwalk directly in front of the bank door. He offered his hand to Kathleen and then he lifted Sammy down while still holding onto the collar of his jacket. Sammy wiggled to free himself but Tyler jerked him off his feet. "Boy, walk straight ahead next to Kathleen or you will be sorry."

"Please Sammy. Do as the fool says. I am going to give him some money and then he will ride away out of our lives for good. Isn't that right, Mr. Chambers?"

"Whatever you say, woman, but move; the bank will be closing for lunch soon!"

Kathleen, Sammy and Tyler walked into the bank and saw two customers standing in line at the first teller's window. "I'll be right with you Miss Kathleen," said Mr. Ellis.

"Is Mr. Underwood in his office this morning? I have some important business that I need to discuss with him."

Mr. Underwood came out of his office about the same time Kathleen asked for him. "Good morning, Miss Parker. Come right this way. Whom do you have with you this fine day? Sammy? Is that right, son?"

Once Mr. Underwood closed his office door, Tyler put his gun to his neck. "Now, Mr. President, I need for you to open the safe and place twenty five thousand dollars in a nice brown bag. Kathleen is giving me part of her money so I don't want you to mistake this as a bank robbery," he said laughing as if he did not have good sense. Kathleen reached for Sammy and slowly pushed him behind her long heavy coat. Mr. Underwood, stalling, asked Kathleen if this was true. "Are you giving this man twenty-five thousand dollars?"

"Yes. Please do as he asked. I want him to have the money and he said that he will leave and never come back."

"Now ain't you just the sweetest little filly. You were always so nice and sweet to me when we were together. I should have stayed and married up with you when I had the chance." Kathleen could not believe her young love had turned into this vicious, ugly man standing in front of her.

Mr. Underwood was not sure when or how Kathleen knew this desperado, but he was certain that he was holding Kathleen under duress. She was doing her best to convince him that she wanted this despicable man to have her money.

"Well, Kathleen. I would gladly give him the money, as you have requested, but I do not have that much money on hand. The stagecoach took a large shipment of our money to Abilene yesterday. I am sorry."

Tyler reached and jerked the banker's right arm up behind his back, slamming his head down on to his desk. Placing the gun on the banker's neck, he asked. "How much money you got here old man. If you want to live, you will go into the vault, fill up a bag with money, and bring it out to me. I am giving you five minutes to get what I want, or I will kill the boy."

"Surely, you jest. He's just a wee lad."

"Don't make me show you that I mean business."

"Please, for goodness sakes, Mr. Underwood. Give him some money!" Kathleen cried, while trying to shove Sammy under the desk while Tyler was not looking.

Mr. Ellis walked into the office and stopped dead in his tracks. "What's going on in here?"

Tyler turned and faced the bank teller. "Is everyone out of the bank?"

"Yes," he replied with a huge knot in his throat. He knew that he had walked into a bad situation.

"Lock the front door and get your ass back here, or I will shoot you on the spot."

******

At the mercantile, Matt and Timmy were inside ordering supplies for the new house that he had planned to build for Kathleen as a wedding present. During the past few weeks, Matt had hired four men who contracted, designed and built houses. The men were living at Matt's ranch and working every day with a crew of men to prepare the land for the foundation. It was a lovely piece of property on a hillside located between his property and on the boarder of Kathleen's land. It had several water oak trees surrounding the lay out of the house. Some of the townspeople were happy to have some extra work during the long winter months.

Moose was helping Lucy with the cooking and cleaning of the house with four extra men to care for on a daily basis. Matt had hired the Heavenly Hash Café to make and deliver sandwiches and hot coffee every day for the crew of fifteen men.

As Matt and Timmy were loading items into the back of his wagon, he noticed Kathleen's big flatbed wagon parked in front of the bank. He would love to get a glimpse of her. As he went back into the store, he wondered why she had parked on the street in front of the bank. She knew that it was against the law for wagons and carriages to park in front of a business unless it was being loaded or unloaded.

Mr. Ellis hurried to the door and locked it while pulling down the shade on the glass door. He walked back into the office and when he did, Tyler knocked him out cold with the butt of his pistol. The small man fell down on the floor blocking the doorway of the banker's office. Tyler reached down, grabbed the teller by the back of the neck, and dragged him further into the office.

"Now, get a move on it Mr. President so I can be on my way."

Outside Glory was holding on to the horse for dear life. She had laid her head down on the horse's neck and let him carry her into town. She was surprised that she had not met anyone traveling to or from town that could have helped her. She entered town and the horse stopped at the first water trough he came upon. Glory slid off the animals back and laid sprawled out on the muddy ground. A man and woman walking down the boardwalk rushed to her aid. She was coughing so bad she could not speak. "Get the doctor," yelled the man as he held Glory up on his knees while his wife wiped her mouth and chin.

"I must get help for Kathleen," she mumbled through her coughing fit. "Help me to stand, please."

The man and woman lifted her up so she could stand. She swayed but she was determined to stand. "I'm fine now," she said as she attempted a smile. "Which way to the Sheriff's office?"

"Someone has gone to get Dr. Squires. You need to let him check you over," said the woman as she still held tight to Glory.

"Thank you, but he cannot help me. Please, I must hurry." Glory swayed and stumbled toward the sheriff's office. As she was making her way on the boardwalk, she saw Kathleen's big wagon parked in front of the bank. This is what Tyler was up to, she thought. He'd come back to force Kathleen to give him money.

Glory stood looking at the wagon and back to the bank's door.

The shade was lowered but it was well past the time for the bank to be open .Well, Mr. Tyler Chambers' has bit off more than he can handle now, she said to herself. He had taken all he was going to steal from good people as long as she had breath in her body. These people had treated her like family, nursed and cared for her and loved her son. She was not going to allow this piece of scum to harm them in anyway. Leaning on the wall of the bank, she reached down in her coat pocket, pulled out Carlos's big pistol, and checked it for bullets. She shook as she cocked the trigger back and staggered toward the door of the bank.

Before she could enter, Tyler rushed out of the bank holding Sammy's hand, practically dragging him. He untied his horse from the back of the wagon and tossed Sammy up on the saddle. Sammy screamed for help, as several old men playing checkers on the boardwalk just watched. "Shut up boy!" Tyler shouted. "I'll hit you over the head with this pistol if you open your mouth again."

"Stop Tyler," Glory spoke a little above a whisper. Blood was seeping out the corners of her mouth but she did not seem to take notice. "Put my boy down."

"Mama," cried Sammy, reaching his small arms toward her.

Tyler was surprised to see Glory. He knew that she was very ill but he almost did not recognize her. She was pitiful thin and frail. Her complexion was as pale as death and she was bleeding from the mouth and nose. He did not even know how she was standing, much less holding that big gun she had pointed at him.

"Put that gun down before you hurt yourself or someone else," he said as he stuffed the bag of money into his saddlebag. "When I am close to the border, I will leave your boy with some people who will care for him. Now get back out of the way!"

"You're not leaving here with my baby," she said as he was attempting to get on the horse. A small crowd had gathered but no one was trying to help in any way. They were not sure what was taking place.

Glory raised the pistol higher and pointed it directly at Tyler. "I am going to shoot if you don't put Sammy down on the ground now." Her hands were shaking and she looked like she was going to fall over any second. Tyler was not afraid of her in the least, but the bystanders were. They scattered when they saw this young girl's hands shaking as she attempted to point the pistol at the stranger.

Tyler's next attempt to get on his horse was successful. He kicked the horse in his flanks and rode away from Glory. She pointed high and pulled the trigger hitting Tyler in the center of his back. He screamed and fell sideways off the horse. He plunged to the ground with Sammy wrapped in his arms. Tyler died instantly.

Sammy hit the ground hard but he pushed Tyler's body away from him as he stood. Blood had spattered on him, but he did not notice. He watched the big black horse run down the street. He turned and raced to his mama as he saw her fall on the boardwalk. He called to his mama, repeatedly, as he ran to her. Kathleen had rushed to Glory and lifted her head into her arms. Sammy came running and fell over Kathleen onto his mama's frail body and wept. Tears flowed down Kathleen's cheeks as she held both Glory and her child.

The Sheriff arrived and asked Mr. Underwood what in the devil was going on. In a hushed voiced he gave the Sheriff all the sordid details about what had taken place. "Mr. Ellis woke up from the blow on his head and untied him and Miss. Parker," he said. "We come out of the bank just as that young lady shot the man that robbed the bank. Miss Parker rushed over to help the little woman but I'm afraid it might be too late." The Sheriff eased over to Kathleen where she sat on the edge of the boardwalk.

"Kathleen," said the Sheriff. "Let's get this young woman over to the doctor's office." Kathleen stood slowly as she lowered Glory onto the boardwalk. She pulled Sammy up off his mama's bloody body, holding him as close as she could. "It's too late for the doctor." Kathleen looked down at Sammy as she fought back tears. "I want to take her home," she said to the Sheriff. Stooping down on one knee, she brushed Sammy's hair back out of his eyes. "We'll take care of your mama." The little fellow wiped his nose on his sleeve and nodded his head.

Matt and Timmy had heard the explosion of gunfire out in the street. They hurried out of the store and saw a man lying in the street. Sammy was racing back down toward the bank. Both men jumped down off the boardwalk and walked swiftly toward Kathleen's wagon. Matt saw Sammy sobbing into Kathleen's skirt as she talked to the Sheriff. Two men were lifting a body into Kathleen's wagon.

Matt stepped toward Kathleen. Sammy rushed over to Matt and he stooped down and lifted the boy into his loving arms. "My mama is dead," he cried.

Kathleen stood frozen in place as she looked into Matt's questionable eyes. When Matt did not speak, she reached for Sammy and turned away from him.

Dolly and Lillian had walked through the crowd and watched the men place Glory's body in the back of Kathleen's wagon. The men had spread a large piece of canvas and a quilt in the wagon. One of the men picked up Glory's body allowing her lovely hair to drag on the muddy boardwalk. A man jumped up in the wagon, took Glory's body and laid her down while another man wrapped the cover over her.

"Kathleen, I am so sorry but happy that you and the little tyke aren't hurt. This isn't much but I have a white gown and robe that will look lovely on Glory. I will send it out to your ranch in a while," Dolly said, as she wiped her eyes.

Kathleen patted Sammy on his back as she tried to console him. "Thank you, ladies."

Back at the ranch, Rosa and Carlos were frantic when they came into the house and found Glory missing. Rosa had been in the root cellar choosing yams for tomorrow's dinner while Carlos was rounding up some of the young calves. The first sign of trouble was when Juan found Kathleen's white scarf for the vestibule lying in the road and a different set of horse tracks following the wagon.

"I am going to track Kathleen's wagon and see who is with her," he said as he saddled his horse.

"Hurry son. Maybe you can catch up with them," said Carlos with much concern in his voice because he did not know how long she had been gone from the ranch.

Juan found Kathleen's wagon sitting in front of the bank with a small group of men standing around and talking. He jumped down off his horse, and walked over to the wagon. The wagon was empty and there wasn't any sign of Kathleen or Sammy.

A long piece of brown canvas laid rolled in the back. The men watched Juan without saying a word or giving him any idea what was in the canvas. After a few minutes, he saw Kathleen, Sammy and the Sheriff walking toward the wagon.

"Miss Kathleen, we have all been so worried. What is going on?" Juan looked at Kathleen and down at Sammy's red, tearful face. "Where's Miss Glory?"

"Juan, my Mama is dead," he cried as he wrapped his arms around Juan's old leather chaps and hid his face. "Mama shot mean old 'chamber pot' man!"

"May God have mercy on her soul," he said as he made the sign of the cross. "When, how?" He was full of questions but Kathleen appeared to be in a trance. Her face was stark white and her eyes looked out into space without seeing anything.

"Come, Miss Kathleen," he said. "I will drive you home." Juan hurried and tied his pinto onto the back of the wagon as he stopped to look at the long brown canvas again. Now he knew what was inside. As Juan helped Kathleen up on the wagon, he saw Matt and Timmy standing on the other side of the wagon. He looked from Matt to Kathleen; both looked forlorn. He gave Matt a nod with his head and lifted Sammy up to Kathleen.

After settling Kathleen and Sammy on the wagon, the sheriff said that he would be out to talk to Rosa and Carlos.

"Si, that will be helpful. You will be welcome at our dinner table." The Sheriff gave a salute as Juan drove the sad members of his family home.

# Chapter 31

**Carlos and Pedro** built the burial box. They chose a smooth piece of soft pinewood to use. Sammy stood off to one side of the barn watching the men work on his mama's box. Carlos encouraged Sammy to help smooth out the inside. Carlos felt that it was important for him to help, if he wanted to be a part of making it nice for his mama.

Rosa lined the inside of the coffin with a white sheet and placed some of the left over satin that was from Kathleen's wedding dress around the sides. She took her time gathering the material around the top edges so it looked extra special for this lovely young Mama. Rosa dressed Glory in the lovely white gown and robe that Dolly had donated. She had loosened her hair and pulled it forward. A soft pink ribbon tied into a small bow framed her lily-white face. She looked just like an angel.

Even though it was January and freezing cold, several men came out to help Carlos and the boys dig the grave. It was not long before the yard was full of carriages and wagons. The dining table was covered with fried chicken, pot roast, cornbread and all kinds of vegetables and desserts that the neighbors had prepared and brought to have after the service.

With the grave completed, six of the townsmen carried the coffin out to the gravesite. Lillian and Al Thornbees were among the mourners. Lillian was dressed in her finest silk black dress and matching cloak. She stood beside a chair that Big Al sat in. He could not walk on his bad leg, but he wrapped his arm around Lillian's round belly, letting everyone know that he was going to be a proud papa in a few months. Mr. and Mrs. Crocker gathered their three children in a tight semicircle to keep as warm as possible. Mrs. Washington, the owner of the boarding house, and

Dr. Squires bowed their heads as they whispered to each other. Kathleen walked over to the gravesite with Sammy. She was pleased that the people of Sweetwater had come to pay their last respects to a young woman they hardly knew.

Several of the women from town even managed to shed a tear or two as the Reverend read the short eulogy. Poor Glory, she was so young and nothing good had happened in her life except giving birth to a beautiful baby boy. Reverend Mills had spoken with Rosa before the funeral about Glory's life. He had never met her and he was embarrassed that he had not visited her while she was ill.

At the graveside, Kathleen stood close to Carlos and wept silently while the mourners sang "Shall We Gather at the River." She wiped her face and looked straight into Matt eyes. He looked tired, sad and older. He lifted his chin and she saw pride reflected in those dark blue eyes. She had seen this characteristic in him before. He was a man's man and he would not bow down to anyone who had wronged him. She had hurt him. His eyes showed his disappointment in her.

Kathleen could feel his eyes on her. He thought she was intriguing. He had never thought that about another woman. He enjoyed observing her as she held Sammy's hand tightly. She looked very young and vulnerable with her midnight hair braided, hanging down onto her crisp white blouse tucked so neatly in her long pleaded black skirt. He could tell that she was fighting back tears that were on the brink of spilling over onto her pale cheeks. He wanted to stand beside her and give her assurance that everything was going to be all right, but his pride prevented him from taking a step toward her.

As the men lowered the coffin into the hard, cold ground, Sammy held Kathleen's hand and tried not to cry. He stood straight with his little chin pointed toward the clouds as his bottom lip quivered. Once the coffin was in the ground and the men pulled up three long ropes, the mourners sang Glory's favorite Christian hymn, "In the Garden." Kathleen could visualize her sitting in the rocker at the bedroom window while softly singing the words:

*"I come to the garden alone while the dew is still on the roses .*
. .

*He walks with me and He talks with me . . ."*

Kathleen could not hold back her tears any longer as she remembered the coughing spells and the sight of blood coming from Glory's nose and mouth. Hearing those words and knowing that this young mother knew she was dying was too much for her to bear. She took Sammy's hand and led him away from the fenced cemetery. As they walked to the wagon, they saw several men pick up a shovel and began tossing dirt into the hole.

Many of the townspeople filed by Carlos and Rosa; they shook their hands and thanked them for coming. They invited each one to come to the ranch house for lunch. It was almost dark before the last of the guests had left. Sammy had fallen asleep in Kathleen's lap and Pedro had taken him to his room; the room that he had shared with his mama. Now it would be his room—all alone.

Kathleen, weary and bone tired stood at the door and looked toward the small fenced cemetery. *Matt, oh Matt, how I need you,* she thought, wiping away the tears. At least Sammy could place flowers on his mama's grave whenever he wanted. Kathleen felt comfort whenever she visited her folks. Maybe he would, too.

A few weeks had passed as Kathleen stood at her kitchen window staring out at the barn. Pedro was in the corral using his new rope on a pony that Juan had given him for Christmas. She watched the pony circle the corral. Her life was going around and around just like that pony. One day, she wanted to go to Matt and beg him for forgiveness; the next, she felt it would not do any good. She was heartbroken. She missed him so much. Her mistrust of Matt had caused everyone on the ranch to be sad. With Glory's death and Matt's absence, there was very little laughter. Carlos and Rosa missed Matt, and Sammy was miserable. Juan and Pedro missed him, too.

The snow was beginning to melt and she wondered what Matt was doing today. Was he working with his new calves or getting ready to plant his wheat fields? She missed talking to him about his daily routine and his plans for the future. She missed watching him play with Sammy and how he enjoyed teasing her. He had brought life back into her world and now she was lonelier than before. She wanted to go over to his house and tell him again that she loved him and she would never again doubt his word or his actions. She believed that he loved her and he would never betray her with another woman. She was truly sorry for allowing her mistrust of men from her younger days affect her love and trust for Matt today. Maybe in time Matt would miss her as much as she missed him.

The next morning the cold wind had died down and Matt's construction crew were back working on the new house. Lumber and bricks were coming in on the train today and he needed to hire some wagons to haul the supplies out to the property. As he rode pass the telegraph office he heard someone calling his name.

"Mr. Moore, Mr. Moore," yelled a young man who was preparing to get on his bay horse. "Man, am I happy to see you. I was on my way out to your ranch. A telegram came for you a while ago and I was bringing' it out to you."

Matt reached for the telegram and inquired about who sent it. "Now, Mr. Moore, you know we ain't supposed to discuss the privacy of a telegram. I could get fired," he said as he looked back at the Telegraph Office. He leaned close to Matt and said, "It's from some woman in Abilene."

"Gracious, I don't know any woman in Abilene," he murmured mostly to himself.

"Like I said, that is what I overheard Mr. Toomey say."

"Thanks son," Matt said as he reached into his vest pocket and tossed the young man a coin. "Gee thanks Mr. Moore," said the young boy as he untied his horse's reins from the hitching post.

Matt continued to the livery stable. Once he arrived and hired four large wagons with big strong mules, he walked over and sat down on a big closed barrel that held oats. He flipped up the top page of the telegram and read it over several times. It was from his sister whom he had not seen since he left home about ten years ago. Home was Independence, Missouri. His sister was just a young girl with gangly long legs and golden pigtails. She must be in her early twenties now. His sister needed him to come to Abilene. She sounded desperate and needed help with her child. *She must be in trouble*, he thought. In all the years since he left home, he had never heard from her. *He wondered how she got so far from home. Maybe she had traveled with her husband,* he thought.

"Oh, Theodore, I am going to need to hire some men to drive

my wagons out to my new construction. Do you think you can do that for me before the afternoon train gets to town?" Theodore was a tall, slim, black man who Big Al had hired to take charge of the livery stable while he was laid up. "My foreman will be there to show the men where to unload."

"I can do that Mr. Moore. Shore can do that for you. I will have the men drive down to the tracks and be there when the train arrives. They can help load your supplies and drive them on out to your place. Shore can do that for you."

"Here's some money. If that is not enough, please put it on my tab and I will pay it when I get back from Abilene. I have to catch the noon stage today so I have to hurry. Is that alright with you?"

"You have a safe trip and don't worry about your supplies, the men or wagons. I will take care of everything for you," said Theodore with a big smile.

Matt stuffed the telegram into his jacket and mounted his horse. He headed back to his ranch to pack a small carpetbag and give Lucy and Gabe some orders to follow while he was gone. He really was not sure how long he would be away but he hoped it would be only a few days. He would send Carlos and Juan a message to ask them to check on his place while he was gone. He trusted Moose, Timmy and his other two men, but he would feel better if Carlos would stop by and keep an eye on everything.

Once Matt arrived at his ranch, he told Lucy about the telegram. "I may be bringing my sister and her child back with me. I have no idea what is going on but as soon as I know, I will send you a telegram. You will be safe here with Moose and Timmy. Do you want Moose to sleep in the house with you?"

"I have your shotgun, my dog, and the men are just a little ways from the house. I am not afraid," she said giving him a small grin. "Be careful."

"Carlos or Juan will be over every day to check on the place. Visit Rosa and Kathleen if you like. Just because Kathleen and I are having 'differences' doesn't mean that you can't continue your friendship with them. They love you and I know you care for them."

Matt pulled Lucy into his hard body and gave her a bear hug. Over the months that she had come to live with him, he had learned to love her like a mama. She was a very caring little woman and he felt blessed to have her in his home. He reached for his carpetbag and walked out of the door heading toward the barn. Timmy was driving him into town to catch the noon stage.

The stagecoach driver stopped late in a small town called Pine Hill. It had a small inn and a changing station for the animals. He had changed his horses twice over the narrow roads and in the morning he would have a fresh set. The Innkeeper served a hot meal to all the passengers. The men slept in the barn on a clean bale of hay while the women folk were furnished a clean cot inside the Inn. The next morning, the stagecoach driver set his sights on his established route and schedule. Matt was sure that he hit every bump and pot hole on the dusty, dirt road. Once the coach pulled into the busy streets of Abilene, Matt was dirty and tired. His body was still sore from the beating he took from Big Al and the rough ride did not help. He walked over to the boarding house, where he had always stayed while in Abilene. He wanted to have a good hot bath and some food before he located his sister.

The next morning Juan stopped at Matt's ranch to talk to him about working on his big house. Things were slow at Kathleen's ranch and he had the time to earn himself extra pay. He had been courting a little senorita in town on Saturday evening and he wanted to build himself a nice bank account just in case things got serious between them.

Moose came out of the barn and met him. "Howdy, Juan. Good to see you?"

"I stopped by to talk with Matt about working on his new house. Is he around?"

"No, he had to go to Abilene yesterday. He caught the noon stage. Timmy took him into town." Moose said.

"What was so important that he had to leave in such a hurry? He is just now able to get around good," Juan said as he pushed his sombrero off his head and allowed it to hang down his back. He knew that Matt was still in pain whenever he did anything strenuous.

"Shucks, I don't rightly know for sure. It was something about meeting some woman with a baby."

Juan stared at Moose without asking any more questions. *Maybe all the mistrust Kathleen felt about Matt might be true*, he thought. No, he sighed quickly. He would never believe that Matt was cheating on Kathleen. He had witnessed the love between them. Matt was an honorable man and he knew there had to be another reason he left on that hasty trip.

Once Juan had arrived home, he discovered that Kathleen had already heard that Matt had gone to Abilene to see another woman. He did not know now who the bearer of the bad news had been.

He could hear her raised voice coming from the kitchen. He stood in the hall and listened to her voice her unladylike opinion of Matt Moore to his mama and papa. It was probably a good thing Matt was miles away. From what he heard, Kathleen had gone to her room and cried for hours. Now, she was finished crying and she had built up a head of angry steam. In all the years that he had known her, she had never raised her voice to another soul.

As Kathleen lay crying in bed over the news that she had heard at the post office she was feeling like a fool. "Matt Moore had gone to Abilene to get his woman and their child. He had a family in Abilene and he was going to bring them back here to Sweetwater." Everyone was talking about this rumor; true or false. It was too good of a story not to repeat. While lying in bed, she was trying to wrap her head around this awful gossip. "Was this only gossip or was it true?" she thought. He had left town on the stage headed to Abilene. That much was true. Well, she thought to herself, "I am going to Abilene and find out why he had to rush out of town."

"I will show him!" She screeched from the top of her voice. "When I get to Abilene, he is going to be one surprised man. He is going to wish that he had never heard the name Kathleen Parker! I told myself that I would never let a man into my heart again. Every man who has called on me only wanted my land. I thought Matt was different but our properties combined would make an empire. I should have listened and had Carlos haul his carcass back over to his place. Did I listen to myself? No! I had to allow that two-timing fool into my life and now I am paying for it. I can assure you he will pay dearly for playing around with my feelings –sprouting lies about being in love with me. How he wanted me to be his wife. Lies! Rosa, do you hear me? All lies!"

Rosa shook her head side to side. "No, you are wrong Kathleen. You are wrong this time. I cannot and will not believe that Mr. Matt has done what you say."

"Listen, Rosa. He could not cheat on me once—no! He had to do it not once, but twice!"

"Kathleen, please wait for Mr. Matt to come home and talk to him. He is a good man and loves you dearly. I see it with my own eyes. Please do not go chasing after him with a wild temper and unladylike ways. Tell her Carlos! Make her stay home," she pleaded as she looked at her husband.

"Rosa is right," said Carlos. "Over the years, I have tried to let you have your way. I have always sat back and let you do what you wanted, but you have to know I think you are wrong this time. Matt will be home in a few days. He will not stay away from his ranch and the construction of his new ranch house. You cannot ride to Abilene and accuse him of these things that are not true," said Carlos.

"I can't believe that both of you still want to believe that he hasn't done anything to me," she said as she shook her head back and forth. "He sneaked around with Lillian while pretending to love me and now he has raced off to be with another woman in Abilene. Wait until he brings her back here. Then you will learn the truth." Kathleen walked over to the window in the kitchen and looked outside. She was so angry and sad. Her tall slim body shook from frustration... In her heart she knew that she and Matt belonged together. They would never be happy living apart. Matt had to love her; no man could pretend to love her the way he did. She needed to confront him and made him admit the truth; did he love her or was he playing her for a fool all along?

"You do not know for sure what is true," Carlos said, pleading with Kathleen to stay home.

"I wanted to trust Matt." She said softly as she walked around the room. "Well, I trusted him with my heart and what has he done with it. He has crushed me!" Kathleen sighed and then anger rose up inside her again. "Well, I may shoot him right between his lying eyes. I am going to leave at first light. I am going to take Juan with me. He is a good guide and we can travel faster on horseback. We will both take an extra horse along with a pack mule. We can be there in a day and half."

"Si, Missy. You have your mind made up. I will help you get ready for this wild trip. I will pray that Matt will prove to you that you have made a big mistake. I know this man and I am sure you believe lies that are not true about him. You will have to learn the truth for yourself."

Juan turned around in the hall and nearly knocked Sammy over. "Hey, I'm sorry. What are you doing standing here listening. You should not be listening to grownups."

"But Juan, she was screening like a wild animal. I couldn't help but hear her. She is awful mad at Mr. Matt. What did he do to make her want to shoot him?"

"Sammy, listen to me. She is not going to shoot anyone. She's angry but she will be fine after she talks to him. Understand?"

"Why did he run away? I miss him so much," he said as he wiped away tears.

"Hey Bud. Matt did not run away. He would never leave you or Lucy. Now, you know that, don't you?"

"I guess," he said as he twisted his boot on the floor.

"Come with me out to the barn. I've got to ride over to Matt's new house. You want to go with me?"

"Sure, if Rosa says I can go."

"Let's go ask her."

# Chapter 32

Matt felt so much better after a hot bath and a good meal. He headed to see his good friend, Walt Williams, Abilene's Sheriff. If anyone knew where to find his sister, he would surely know. He walked down the boardwalk and recognized a few of the citizens. He nodded and said softly, "Good morning" as he opened the door to the Sheriff's office.

Sheriff Walt looked up from reading the day old newspaper and said, "Hot damn! Look whose back. What's happening son? Ain't you happy in Sweetwater?" The Sheriff jumped up from his desk and held out his right hand to Matt.

"Good to see you too, old man. What has happened to your long mustache?"

Walt howled with laughter as he rubbed his bare upper lip. "Well, you know how these women folks can be. Mary, the woman at the café, well, she and I are seeing each other and oh, hell Matt; I don't have to explain myself to you!"

Matt laughed and sat down on the corner of the sheriff's big wooden oak desk. With a grin still on his face, he told Walt that he needed some information. "I got a telegram from my sister. She said she was in trouble and I needed to come here and help her. Have you seen a stranger? Young woman, maybe with some children?"

"There was a new family that moved into a cabin outside of town. I heard over at the general store that her man left her. I intended to go out and check on her but I have been kinda busy. This girl could be your sister. Come on and I will take you out to see her."

"Appreciate it," Matt replied.

As the two men rode out of town and came near the cabin,

blood curdling screams came from inside. Matt leaped off his rented horse and nearly fainted when his feet hit the hard ground. He had forgotten his own injuries as he raced to help the person who was afraid or in severe pain.

Matt pushed on the old planks that were nailed together to form a door. He looked around in the dark room. From a window, the morning sunshine cast down on the young woman's face as she lay on a small bed. "Help me," she murmured. "My baby has already come."

"Oh Lord, Walt. Go get the doctor and hurry please. Are you Julie?" Matt asked as he stooped down beside her bed. She was sweating but her lips were parched dry. He reached into his vest pocket and pulled out a clean handkerchief. He dipped it into a bowl of water that was sitting on a chair beside the bed. He immediately wiped her face and rubbed it over her dry, bloody lips. She had bit down on her bottom lip until it bled.

"Please check on my baby," she pleaded as she tried to lift the quilt off her thin body.

Matt stood and slowly lifted the quilt and peeked down between her legs. He almost fainted. A tiny, precious baby lay as lifeless as death. The cord still attached as it lay in a puddle of bloody mucus. He had never seen such a bloody mess.

"Please give me my baby," she said with a numb expression on her pale face. Matt looked around for some rags, towels, or old sheets. He looked at the chair beside the bed and saw a new pink baby blanket. Suddenly from out of the corner of the room, a beautiful small child with gold ringlets hanging down her back handed him the blanket. Matt had never noticed that a child was in the room with him.

"Thanks," he said to the little girl. Before he lifted the covers, he took the little girl's hand and led her to the door. "Stand here and watch for the doctor. Will you do that?"

She looked at her mama and finally nodded her head yes. Matt watched her as he walked back to the bed. No small child should see any of this. He took the blanket and laid it at the side of the bed. Talking his handkerchief in one hand, he lifted the small girl child from his sister's thighs and wiped the mucus off the perfectly formed face. He swaddled her in the pink blanket and laid her on Julie's stomach.

He looked around the room and found a clean sheet. He lifted Julie and placed the sheet under her to absorb some of the bloody mess and wrap her private parts until the doctor arrived.

"I failed her," Julie mumbled. "I didn't protect her. Now, I will never see her smile, laugh, or even feel the flutter of her tiny heart." Julie was so weak and exhausted that she could hardly speak. She knew that her baby had died because the infant never made a sound.

"Try to rest. The doctor will be here soon," he said as he took her wrist and tried to feel for a strong pulse. He moved his hand up and down her wrist but couldn't feel any sign of life. Every breath she took seemed to be an effort for her.

"Matt," she said so softly he had to lean over her mouth to hear her. "I knew you would come. Thank you, big brother. Take Junie home with you. She is everything to me. She deserves a good home. Please tell me that you will take—care—her." Before Matt could give her an answer, she passed from this world.

As Matt stood, Sheriff Walt and the town's young doctor rushed into the cabin. Matt thanked the doctor for coming but indicated that it was too late for mother and child. He led the Sheriff and the little girl outside while the doctor examined his sister and her baby.

The little girl pulled on his leg to get Matt's attention. "Are you my uncle? Mama said my uncle was coming to get us."

"Yes, sweetheart, I am your Uncle Matt. I will take you home with me and I will take good care of you. Would you like that?"

"Will Mama and the new baby come too?"

Matt swallowed hard and said as truthfully as he could. "No Junie. Your mama and the baby have gone to Heaven."

"She has gone to live with Jesus? I want to go with Mama," she cried. Junie knew about God and Jesus because her mama had told taught her all about them as she read her Bible.

Matt could not answer so he just hugged her close and patted her back. He looked at his friend and asked if he knew of someone he could leave Junie with while he took care of the funeral arrangements.

"Sure. Mary will care for her while you take care of business," he said, proud that he could do something to help.

"Do you think that she would do some shopping for her? I feel that she is going to need something warmer to wear on our trip home. I'm sure she needs some necessities, too. I can get more items for her once I get back to Sweetwater." Matt could tell without going back inside the cabin that there wasn't much to retrieve."

After two days the funeral service was over. Matt had spent many hours consoling his niece. The service was quiet with only Walt, Mary, Matt and Junie in attendance. Junie cried for her mama almost constantly.

Matt went to the stage line and purchased two tickets back to Sweetwater. He had been so busy that he had not had time to grieve his sister's death. Listening to Junie cry nearly broke his heart. He felt bad that he had not taken time to go back home and visit Julie and his parents. Julie was a small child when he left and he had not seen her but once since he left home at the age of seventeen. His home was in Texas and his work kept him from visiting.

Two days earlier, Kathleen and Juan had traveled toward Abilene as fast as their horses would carry them. They spent the night about forty miles from Abilene and rode into the city about mid-day. The more miles Kathleen rode, the madder she got. Juan was hoping that her temper would cool down some before they arrived in Abilene. He tried to defend Matt as much as possible but his words only made her angrier.

Kathleen was wearing her blue denims pants with a heavy jacket. She had her hair pulled back in a tight rope under her hat. She was dirty and tired. A good bath and a hot meal would make her feel human again, she thought as she tied her horse to the hitching post in front of the Sheriff's office.

Matt and Junie were walking toward the café to get some lunch when he saw the two riders stopping in front of the Sheriff's office. He was sure the young man was Juan. He continued to hold Junie's hand but he stood as still as a statue. As Juan wrapped his reins on the hitching rail, he looked up and down the street. He saw Matt immediately.

"Matt," called Juan.

Kathleen stepped around her horse and looked in the direction that Juan was waving. She stood still, not moving a muscle in her tired body. Her breath caught in her throat and she could not speak.

She looked at Matt and she had a flash of memory of him and Lillian together. She thought only a wicked woman would lay with a man without marriage. Well, she knew one thing about his choice of a woman. She was a bitch! At least, she was married now. Wonder what the other woman is like. He came here to be with her, she thought.

Juan and Matt shook hands and said some words that she could not hear. Her heart swelled as she looked at Matt. She wanted to run to him and throw her arms around his neck but she wouldn't dare. She would never do that to a man who was despicable and a liar—a sneaking cur who was only a woman chaser.

Matt stood in the street looking from Juan to Kathleen. He pondered the strange situation. "We need to talk; get off the street with so many gawkers," Matt said, as he felt Junie's little body move closer to his right leg. She tugged on his vest and he looked down at her.

Katherine had not noticed the lovely child until the moment that Matt stooped down to the child's level.

"Uncle Matt, is that lady my new mama, I mean your woman?" she whispered.

Matt rubbed Junie's back and said without taking his eyes off his Katy. "We'll have to wait and see."

Matt stood, cleared his throat and said that he was taking the child to lunch. "I know you are ready for something to eat after your long trip, so follow me." He passed the café and continued down to the restaurant. It was warm and spacious. The floor to ceiling windows allowed the bright sunlight to give the room a cozy feeling.

If Kathleen's emotions had not been so confused, she wouldn't have gone to lunch with him. She felt out of place in her dirty jeans and wrinkled shirt. She was tired and needed a bath. She was so surprised to see Matt on Main Street. She wasn't ready to talk with him. She had wanted to clean up and fix her hair before meeting him.

They followed a woman to a table with a white tablecloth and a large candle in the center. Junie's eyes were open wide as she looked up at the beautiful chandelier hanging from the ceiling.

During the meal, Kathleen just looked at Matt and the little girl he called Junie. She was a lovely child but Kathleen did not see any resemblance between her and Matt. She wanted to scream at Matt and ask him how he could be so calm while it was hard for her eat. She kept looking down at the table, praying for this meal to be a quick one so she could be alone with him. She desperately needed him to explain what had happened.

Once the meal was over, the four of them stood outside the restaurant on the boardwalk. "Juan, would you take Junie for a short walk and let her choose some penny candy for herself. She would enjoy some on our trip to Sweetwater," said Matt.

Matt and Kathleen watched Junie reach and take Juan's hand. "I'm too little to walk on the boardwalk by myself Mr. J---." Reaching down Juan took Junie's small hand in a tight grip and smiled down at her. "Call me Juan."

Watching the two walk away, Kathleen had pulled herself together and the anger that had festered inside her came out. She led Matt to the nearest alleyway. She whirled on him so fast he did not know how to react at first.

Rage swooped over her as she swung her hand and slapped his cheek so hard his head turned. "You lying sneaking cur!"

Matt was stunned at her instant reaction. He thought that they were going to have a quiet, sensible conversation where she would beg for his forgiveness. Instead, Kathleen had turned into a shrew of the worst kind. She raised her hand again to render another slap as Matt caught her small wrist. "Slap me once, but not twice Katy or I may have to retaliate."

"You wouldn't dare strike me!"

"Don't try me, sweetheart," he said through a tight smile. He tossed her hand away and she looked away fighting tears back.

After a second, she spoke again in a calmer voice. "Listen to me. I came here to find out who you were with this time." She skewered him with her eyes and waited for a response.

"The hell with you woman, why do you care who I am with? You will not believe me. You can't trust me or for that matter— any man."

Matt turned to leave her standing in the alley but she was faster. She moved her shaking body into his pathway.

"You're despicable, you know that!" She cried, tears flowing down her rosy cheeks. "Why Matt, why wasn't I woman enough for you? I gave you my heart and you played me for a fool!"

Feeling light-headed, she would have fallen to the ground if Matt had not caught her.

He took her arm, but she shook it loose. "Why Matt, why? I have been waiting and hoping that you would find it in your heart to forgive me . . . for not trusting you. I have struggled with myself to remain at home and not go running to you again. I wanted to beg for your forgiveness. All this time, I have been praying that you would come to see me and let me explain but *no*, here you are in Abilene seeking out another woman and your child."

He pulled her close to his chest and kissed the side of her face. "Katy, I'm sorry." Matt looked up and saw a crowd of people who had heard the racket standing at the entrance of the alleyway. "We can't talk here."

"We can't talk anywhere," she said as she tried to slap his hands.

"Behave yourself Katy," Matt growled. "I have been through hell the last couple of days. My patience is wearing thin and I am tired of you jumping to the wrong conclusion." Matt dragged Kathleen behind him. At the boarding house, he entered and marched her up the stairs ahead of him.

"I can't go to your room, alone, with you. What will your landlady say?"

"She will not say anything if you keep your voice down," Matt commented as he closed and locked the door. He pulled Kathleen over to a comfortable wing back chair and pushed her none too gently in it. "Sit still and keep your mouth shut, while I explain to you why I had to take the stagecoach and travel here." Matt tossed his hat over onto the bed and ran his hand through his hair. He noticed his carpetbag and a new one filled with Junie's new clothes and other items sitting next to the door.

"I doubt you can tell me anything I don't already know," Kathleen sneered as she spoke.

"One more word out of that sassy mouth of yours and you will not be able to sit comfortably on the way home. Understand?" Matt pointed his finger in her face, took a deep breath and turned away. Kathleen settled back in the soft chair and observed Matt's sad expression.

Matt walked over to the window and pulled back the floral

curtain looking out over the busy street. "I got a telegram from Julie, my sister. She needed help and sounded desperate for me to come. I was surprised to hear from her because I have not seen her in years. She was just a small child when I left home. I have no idea how she knew I once lived in Abilene. After she arrived here, her husband left. I am not sure why. The Sheriff said he heard that her husband left her all alone with no plans of returning. If I saw him today, I would break his sorry neck."

Sighing, Matt turned the desk chair around and sat facing Kathleen. "When I arrived, she had just had the baby. She delivered the child all alone. The poor thing was born dead. The doctor called it stillborn." Matt placed his fingers over his eyes, trying to rub the sight of the baby out of his mind. "Julie pleaded with me, as she was dying to take Junie and give her a good home. I buried my sister and the baby together, poor little mite. She was perfect in every way. Junie knows about Heaven so she understands that her mama is gone but she is terribly sad. It breaks my heart to hear her cry for her mama."

Kathleen slipped out of the chair and sat on the floor in front of Matt. It was all she could do not to burst out crying. Matt had been through so much grief; while she thought he was here with another woman. She laid her head in his lap and mumbled she was sorry. "I am so embarrassed that I mistrusted you. Please—I would like to go home and you and I begin again. Please forgive me."

Matt stood and pulled her up on her feet into his arms. She shook nervously as he caressed her hair, nuzzled her rosy cheeks and kissed the side of her neck. She nested in his strong arms and began groaning from a strange pleasure that she had never felt before. His hands moved over her slim back and pulled her limbs closer to his. The passion mounted between them until he could not contain himself any longer. Pushing her away, he picked her up and walked over to the big chair beside the window. She snuggled in his lap while laying her head onto his shoulder.

"Katy, I want us to be together forever, but you have to trust me. Do you think that it is possible that you will be able to trust again? Tyler Chambers is dead, Lillian is married and there never was another woman here in Abilene."

# Chapter 33

**Matt purchased a** large black carriage with two lanterns on the front and it was pulled by four big black horses. On the doors were gold painted lettering 'JUDGE WILLIAM HATHAWAY, JUDGE OF THE 12th MISSOURI CIRCUIT COURT. When Junie saw it, she said it looked just like a carriage in her storybook, except it was white. "Can we paint it white?" she asked Uncle Matt.

Kathleen and Juan tied their horses to the rear of the carriage. Matt sat inside the carriage with the two girls. After traveling with short breaks, they decided to make their own camp for the night instead of spending the night in a flea infected country inn. After a hot meal of sausage and beans with store bought bread, Junie was very inquisitive about Matt's home and Kathleen.

"Are you going to live with me and him?" she asked Kathleen as she pointed at her uncle.

"Not right away. Your uncle has a nice house and a wonderful housekeeper who is going to love you very much. Later, your uncle and I are going to talk about getting married. Then I will be your aunt."

"What will I call you?" she asked as she twirled her hair and placed her thumb in her mouth. Her big brown eyes were drooping as she sat on a log looking into the campfire.

Kathleen eased over to the child and placed her in her lap. She snuggled her close and kissed her on the forehead. "Sweetheart, you may call me whatever you like."

"Okay," she said as she dropped her head forward in a dead sleep. Matt and Juan watched the interaction between Kathleen and Junie. They were a natural together already; mother and child. Juan walked over and took Junie out of Kathleen's arms and both of them walked over to the carriage. Kathleen climbed inside, took Junie out of Juan's arms, placed the sleeping child on the big firm carriage seat, and covered her with a blanket. She looked just like an angel.

Juan helped Kathleen back out of the carriage and went to check on the animals before he turned in to his bedroll under the carriage.

Kathleen walked over to the campfire and sat close to Matt on a log. "You know who is going to love little Junie?" Kathleen asked Matt as she tossed a few sticks in the fire.

"Yep, besides Lucy, you mean?" Matt grinned. "Sammy is going to be over the moon with a playmate. I am sure the two of them will grow to love each other like brother and sister."

Matt pulled Kathleen real close and whispered, "I want us to give them a brother and sister real soon."

"We have to get married first and then--." She said but stopped talking as Matt held his hand over her mouth. Both smiled into each other's eyes.

Carlos and Rosa were thrilled to see Matt and Kathleen getting out of the big black carriage together. They hurried to the front porch and hugged both of them. "Oh, my goodness; who is this precious angel?" Rosa said leaning down close to Junie.

"Rosa, this is my niece, Junie. She is going to be living with us," said Matt. Junie looked at Rosa and slid behind Matt's legs. Matt reached down, picked up the child, and gave her a hug so she would know that she was welcome here.

"Oh, how wonderful. I love little girls and I know that Lucy will too."

Rosa moved to Matt and placed her arms around his waist. "I am so happy that you and Kathleen have made up. We care for you like one of our sons. Always be good to her and you will stay in my good graces, Si?" she inquired.

"Si," Matt replied. "I have never given her a reason to mistrust me and I don't intend to hurt her. I love her with all my heart."

"Carlos and I have never doubted you. Now we must plan a wedding!"

At sunrise the next morning, Carlos and Rosa planned a big celebration in honor of Kathleen and Matt's marriage. By afternoon, everyone in town and the surrounding areas had been invited to the celebration. "What happened to our small wedding?" Matt whispered to Katy, his pet name for his love.

"As far as Rosa is concerned, this is small. She has accepted that we were not willing to wait so she planned this small get together as she called it. Just go along with her plans and we will all be happier when it is over," Katy laughed as she reached up and kissed Matt.

"Good night love. See you at the church." Kathleen hurried into the house with a huge smile on her face. She felt twenty years old again.

Sammy was sitting at the kitchen table watching Rosa as she placed the final touches on the big wedding cake. The reception was going to be at Kathleen's ranch.

"Why don't you go outside and help Carlos with the beef that he is cooking over the pit?" Rosa asked Sammy as he lifted his head off the table.

"I have been pondering something," he said with a sigh. "I want to ask Katy a question."

"You know she doesn't like you to call her Katy." Rosa spoke very sternly to him.

"I don't know why not," he said excited. "Mr. Matt calls her that and I like the name."

Someone was knocking on the front door. Rosa waved her hand at Sammy to go and let them in. "Bring them back to the kitchen." He jumped up from the table, opened the front door, and threw his arms around Lucy's waist.

"Hi, my little brave, you happy about the wedding today," Lucy asked?

"I guess. I am happy that you and Mr. Matt will be living with us." Lucy raised her eyebrows at Sammy but did not make any comment about the living arrangements.

"I'll see you later, Miss Lucy. I am going to talk to Kathleen." He walked down the hall and knocked softly on the bedroom door.

"Come in!" she called. "Good morning Sammy. Are you ready for the wedding? I do not want you to get dirty because you had a good bath last night. Rosa is going to help you dress in your new dark suit and brand new black shoes. You will look just like Matt."

"I won't get dirt on me. I want to ask you something

important," he said as he walked closer to her. "You know, Junie?" He looked into Kathleen's eyes as he asked the question.

"Of course, I know her. Why do you ask?"

"Well Rosa said that Mr. Matt and Lucy will be bringing her to live with us. Lucy said that she will be my sister?"

"Well, you know she is Matt's niece and she will be my niece after we are married."

"What am I? I mean, what will I be to you and Mr. Matt? The Sheriff wanted to place me in an orang'ist and you would not let him take me away. So who am I going to be?"

"Matt and I are going to adopt you and that will make you our son. Our own little boy, if that is all right with you. You will live here with us."

He threw his arms around Kathleen and tried to hold back his tears of joy. "But what will Junie be to me?"

"Well, I think cousins might be a good answer. You could be 'kissing cousins," laughed Kathleen as she picked him up and placed him on her lap.

"No way! She's a girl and I ain't going to be kissing her. I'll just tell everybody she is my little sister!"

"Well, we will all live together and be happy," said Kathleen as she kissed him while tickling his ribs until he was laughing and the problem about Junie was forgotten.

A few hours later with family and friends gathered together inside the small church, Matt stood at the altar with Juan as his best man. Over the year, Juan and Matt had grown as close as any father and son, and there was no one who Matt had rather be standing up for him. Matt looked out over the congregation and on the second pew he saw Lillian with Big Al Thornbees. They were expecting a baby and seemed to be very happy. Sitting directly behind big Al, Mr. and Mrs. Crocker was glowing with happiness as their three children surrounded them. The banker, Mr. Wilbur Underwood and his wife sat next to the bank teller, Mr. Ellis. Standing in the corner of the sanctuary, Sheriff Walt Williams stood along with Sweetwater's own sheriff. All of his ranch hands except Moose were on the back pew dressed in their best shirts with string ties. Matt was sure that the whole town turned out for this special celebration.

As Mrs. Wingate, the church's organist played the first note,

Sammy and Junie stood in the vestibule waiting to begin their march to the front of the church.

"Give me your hand," demanded Sammy.

"No, I ain't gonna hold your sticky hand," she replied because she had seen him eating candy earlier. She felt like a fairy princess dressed in her long soft pink gown. She was not going to let that dirty boy get her all sticky.

"Give me your hand, now. Rosa said we had to hold hands," he whispered.

"No, I don't wanna." Junie held her hands up and away from Sammy.

"Give me your hand you brat."

"I ain't no brat. You can't boss me! You are only one year older."

Sammy reached and grabbed her right hand and held it tightly as she tried to wretch it away from him. Pedro stepped behind them and said. "Hey! Behave yourselves. Walk, with hands together, you two monkeys."

Both glared at each other with fire in their eyes. Once the two beautiful children made it to the front, everyone was watching their every move. Sammy whispered to Junie, "Stand still or I will pinch you."

Junie turned to him and gave him a sickly sweet smile, which made several of the women whisper loudly, "Oh, aren't they the cutest little things."

Once the wedding march began, Carlos waited for Kathleen to appear and placed her arm through his. He had watched this young girl grow into womanhood and he loved her as his own. He kissed her on both cheeks and held her close as they walked through the door toward Matt Moore, the stranger who had come into her life by moving into the ranch next door.

At the front of the altar, Carlos placed Kathleen's hand into Matt's and took his seat.

Matt and Kathleen turned to face Reverend Mills.

"Dearly beloved . . ."

The reverend offered a small message about what makes a marriage successful and flourish. He spoke of giving of oneself; to be able to be understanding and forgiving. He offered his thoughts on the virtue of staying true and faithful to each other. Last, he mentioned the importance of future children that may be blessed into this union.

"Matt, repeat after me."

"I, Matthew David Moore, take thee Kathleen Elizabeth Parker," his voice deeper than normal as he spoke his vows.

Kathleen thought her heart would overflow with love for this wonderful man that stood beside her. He had come into her life when she least expected. His love had given her a bright future of hope; to become a wife and possibly a mother, something that she had given up on ever having.

". . . 'til death do us part."

The Reverend cleared his throat to draw Kathleen's attention back to him. "Please repeat after me."

"I, Kathleen Elizabeth Parker take thee Matthew David Moore . . . "

Matt held Kathleen's hands as he listened to her soft voice as she fought back tears. He squeezed her fingers trying to give her some of his strength to be able to finish. He was so thankful that she had come into his life.

*Kathleen,* he thought, *I promise you that I will never give you a reason to mistrust me. I will care for you with everything I have in me.*

". . . 'til death do us part."

"The ring, please." Reverend Mills looked at Juan and waited. Juan jumped to attention as he searched his jacket pocket for the ring. A big smile appeared on his face as he felt the sharp diamond. He smiled as he passed it to Matt.

Everyone watched Matt slide the ring onto Kathleen's small finger. He smiled at her as she glanced at the lovely diamond.

"I now pronounce you man and wife."

Matt bent down and kissed Kathleen--his wife now and forever. The couple turned to the congregation and both smiled. The groom and bride walked over to a covered table with two tall candlesticks. The Parker's family Bible lay opened. Kathleen took up the quill pen, dipped it into the black ink and wrote their names on a page that contained other entries and dates. Matt kissed Kathleen again. Reverend Mills announced to the congregation that the wedding reception would be at the Parker's ranch and all were invited.

Once they arrived at the ranch, all the guests wishing them happiness and good wishes separated them. It was an hour before the couple was together again to share a glass of bubbling water called champagne. Kathleen wanted to introduce Matt to many guests she had not seen since summer. The wedding feast was served buffet style and people scattered across the front lawn where makeshift tables were set up for them to eat. Many spread blankets on the grass and sat enjoying the small Mexican band that Juan had hired.

As the day grew longer, the night air turned too cold for many guests to remain. Matt secretly wanted everyone to go home. Carlos and Rosa were gracious hosts and thanked everyone for coming as they departed. Sammy and Junie, had played hard with the other children, but had fallen asleep on the couch—not two feet apart.

After the majority of the food was put away and all the dishes washed, Kathleen insisted that Rosa and Lucy go to bed. Matt planned that his honeymoon night was to be at his own ranch— alone except for his ranch hands.

He whispered for Kathleen to get her carpetbag and tell everyone goodnight. He would bring their small carriage out to the front of the house. After a farewell to Rosa, Carlos and Lucy, Matt told his bride that he wanted to present her with a wedding gift. As they drove, they passed Matt's ranch house and continued up the hillside to his new construction. Kathleen was very curious. "Matt, why are we going to your new house? We can't see much of anything by moonlight."

Once he stopped the horse in front of the big house he said, "Katy, I have been building this house for you. I had planned this before I ever asked you to marry me. It was always for you. Now I want you to have a say in how everything will look inside and around the outside." He reached inside his coat pocket and pulled out a piece of folded paper. "This is the deed to this property and house. If something happens to me or we cannot live together for some reason, this property will be yours. I want you to have this new home—a place that is yours, not your papa's ranch. Your name is the only one on this deed. But, if you don't mind, I would like to live here with you and the children."

"Oh Matt, I don't know what to say. This is a wonderful

house. I have watched the men work on it almost every day. I was so jealous. I cannot believe that this will be mine. Thank you from the bottom of my heart."

"Well, now you will have a lot of planning to do. Of course, I would like to help you," he said smiling.

"Katy, I was thinking that after we move into this new house, we could let Rosa and Carlos live in your parent's ranch house— like always, but better. It would be their home. Juan and Pedro will be marrying in the future and they can live there too with their wives. Lucy, my little hardheaded Indian, wants to stay at my ranch where she can continue to cook and clean for the ranch hands and Moose. She treats those young men as if they belong to her, especially Timmy. When she gets too old to handle all the work, I will hire another woman to come and help her out. What do you think?'

"Oh Matt, you are a wonderful man," she giggled. As she laid her head over on his shoulder, she whispered, "It's our honeymoon night. Let's go home so I can thank you properly."

# Prologue

**"Sammy, you better** put that book down and pay closer attention to that tree limb that you're perched upon," Junie, his nine-year-old sister teased.

"You better stop eating those green apples. You're going to have a stomach ache for sure, and Rosa will give you some of that foul tasting medicine."

"Oh shucks! There you go again trying to ruin my fun. You know how much I love these apples. Why do you have to be so bossy? You're only a year older than me."

Sammy and Junie were not really brother and sister. Sammy was Matt and Katherine Moore's adopted son, and Junie was Matt's niece. They loved each other but were constantly minding each other's business. Junie was Sammy's shadow. To have privacy, he had to hide from her, but she knew all of his hideouts.

Junie tossed her half-eaten apple core to the ground and stood on the same limb that Sammy was reclining on as he read his new science book. Junie bent her knees and gave the tree limb a good bounce. The limb shook up and down. Sammy jerked straight up, losing his balance and tumbled down through the smaller tree branches to the ground. His wire rim glasses went one way and his new book went in a different direction. Sammy's shirtsleeve got caught on a branch and ripped a long tear in it. He hurt his backside as he landed on a pile of green apples that had fallen out of the tree.

"Gosh! Darn you, you stinking brat. Get your tail down here this minute. I am going to beat you over the head when I get my hands on you. I can't find my glasses and just look at my new book! The front cover has broken away from the spine. Now I really am going to beat the snot out of you."

"I ain't done nothing to you. You are just a sissy who can't keep his balance. You fell because you didn't hold on to that branch. You were supposed to ride it like a bronco."

Junie jumped up and down on another tree limb. "I ain't coming down. You best not touch me either or Uncle Matt will wallop you good."

As Sammy was down on his knees in the fall leaves looking for his eye glasses, Junie climbed down the tree and raced across the apple orchard as fast as her nine-year-old legs would carry her.

"Oh no you don't you scalawag. You won't get away from me this time," Sammy said as he raced behind the long legged girl. He could hear her giggling as he chased her into the house, up the staircase to her room. She slammed the door in his face but he opened it and charged right into the room, directly behind her and slammed the door. She jumped on her four-poster bed and bounced away from him. As she bounced, she got too close to his long slim arms and he grabbed her around her tiny waist. "I got you this time and now you are going to be sorry." He pulled her close and turned her upside down while holding her two long legs. He stood her head on the floor as she held her arms down to balance herself. He lifted his arms up and down causing the top of her head to hit the floor. "How does that feel?"

Before Junie could answer, Matt entered the bedroom and saw Sammy holding Junie, his precious, mischievous niece upside down. He immediately wondered what had she done this time, but he would have to make Sammy turn her lose before his anger got the best of him and he actually did harm to her.

"All right break it up you two. Stop that screaming Junie. Katy is rocking Amelia Jane to sleep or she was trying to when you two wild Indians came charging in the house, slamming doors."

Sammy dropped Junie none too gently and walked away from her. Junie rolled over on her head and bounced up on her two feet as if nothing had happened.

"Sammy, you go first; I know Junie does not know anything. She never does," said Matt.

Sammy stood looking at his little sister dressed in her denim pants. She never dressed like a sweet little girl. She was a hellion as far as he was concerned.

"That little brat caused me to fall out of an apple tree. I lost my glasses in the leaves on the ground, my new shirt was torn and my science book looks ten years old now. Of course, she denies that she made me fall." He gave her a glare that said boldly, I am not finished with you yet.

"What do you have to say for yourself little Miss?" asked Matt.

"I can't help it if he's a sissy . . ."

"That will do young lady. Now you get out in that orchard and look for Sammy's glasses. Do not come back to this house until you have found them. Do you understand, or I will do more than stand you on your head." Matt gave her a sharp look as she strolled passed him.

"I'm sorry about your new book, Sammy. I will order you another one. I am sure Kathleen can repair your shirt, too." Matt turned to walk out of the room and looked back at Sammy. "I just don't know what to do with that gal."

As Matt walked down to the parlor, he stopped before he entered. Kathleen sat in the new rocking chair holding their two-month-old baby, Amelia Jane, to her breast. He loved watching Katy nurse their child. Matt had begun to think that the good Lord was not going to bless them with a child of their own after almost four years of marriage. Then came spring and Katy was with child. What a joyful occasion for their family and all the townspeople of Sweetwater.

After their marriage, Matt and Kathleen had worked hard to complete their new home. It was a grand affair; large parlor, dining room, kitchen, several water closets and five bedrooms. A large porch wrapped all around the house like loving arms for protection. It was a very inviting home and Matt and Katy enjoyed having their friends and neighbors over for parties.

The citizens of Sweetwater had approached Matt many times about running for Mayor of their small town but he refused each time. His ranch was too big for him to take time away to tend to other people's business. Carlos managed the Parkers old homestead and Timmy, along with Moose, were overseers at his old place. Lucy still cook and cleaned for her boys, as she called them, but several hours each day, she and Rosa came to visit with Kathleen and Amelia Jane.

Katy had never been happier. She was planning to go to church next Sunday. This would be her first outing with her new baby girl. She had missed Lorraine and even Lillian, who was in the family way again. Kathleen was a little jealous because Big Al and Lillian already had two boys. At least, Amelia Jane would have many playmates.

"Hello darling." Kathleen noticed Matt standing in the doorway watching her. "Come and tell me what Junie has been up to this afternoon. I know she has done something to make Sammy mad," she said chuckling.

"One day, Junie is going to push Sammy too far. He is going to forget that they are supposed to be kissing cousins."

He walked over to the rocker and sat down at Katy's feet watching her nurse their precious child. "Happy love," Matt asked?

"Words cannot describe the joy I have in my heart

since you came into my life.   Happy? Very," she replied with a sweet smile.

## Other books written by
## Linda Sealy Knowles

*Journey to Heaven Knows Where*
*Hannah's Way*
*The Secret*
*Bud's Journey Home*

Made in the USA
Lexington, KY
08 September 2019